Good for You

tammara webber

PENGUIN BOOKS

PENGUIN BOOKS

Published by the Penguin Group
Penguin Books Ltd, 80 Strand, London WC2R ORL, England
Penguin Group (USA) Inc., 375 Hudson Street, New York, New York 10014, USA
Penguin Group (Canada), 90 Eglinton Avenue East, Suite 700, Toronto, Ontario, Canada M4P 2Y3
(a division of Pearson Penguin Canada Inc.)
Penguin Ireland, 25 St Stephen's Green, Dublin 2, Ireland (a division of Penguin Books Ltd)
Penguin Group (Australia), 707 Collins Street, Melbourne, Victoria 3008, Australia
(a division of Pearson Australia Group Pty Ltd)
Penguin Books India Pvt Ltd, 11 Community Centre, Panchsheel Park, New Delhi – 110 017, India
Penguin Group (NZ), 67 Apollo Drive, Rosedale, Auckland 0632, New Zealand
(a division of Pearson New Zealand Ltd)
Penguin Books (South Africa) (Pty) Ltd, Block D, Rosebank Office Park, 181 Jan Smuts Avenue,
Parktown North, Gauteng 2193, South Africa

Penguin Books Ltd, Registered Offices: 80 Strand, London WC2R ORL, England

penguin.com

First published by Tammara Webber, 2011
Published by Penguin Books Ltd, 2013
001

Copyright © Tammara Webber, 2011
All rights reserved

The moral right of the author has been asserted

Set in 10.5/15.5pt Sabon LT Std
Typeset by Palimpsest Book Production Ltd, Falkirk, Stirlingshire
Printed in Great Britain by Clays Ltd, St Ives plc

British Library Cataloguing in Publication Data
A CIP catalogue record for this book is available from the British Library

ISBN: 978-0-141-34750-9

www.greenpenguin.co.uk

Penguin Books is committed to a sustainable
future for our business, our readers and our planet.
This book is made from Forest Stewardship
Council™ certified paper.

ALWAYS LEARNING   **PEARSON**

PENGUIN BOOKS

Good for You

Books by Tammara Webber

EASY

BETWEEN THE LINES

WHERE YOU ARE

GOOD FOR YOU

Dedicated to Tim
I miss you every day

1

REID

My thoughts upon becoming fully conscious: first, *Shit, I'm in the hospital again*, and second, *How bad is the damage to my one-week-old Porsche?*

'I see you're awake.' That would be Dad, stating the obvious – a skill at which he excels.

'Oh, honey, I'm so glad you're okay.' A warm hand grasps mine, and I turn towards Mom's voice out of a natural inclination to ignore my father. Especially to his face.

My satisfaction lurches to a stop when I see Mom's eyes, swollen and red-rimmed, and her mouth, clamped tight in a failed attempt to restrict the trembling of her lower lip. Unfortunately, this isn't an absurd maternal response. If memory serves, I had a little too much to drink and then crashed my car into a *house*. Not one of my more reassuring exploits.

In a futile effort to divert attention from the bodily-harm part of my vehicular mishap, I ask, 'Um, how's the car?'

'How's the *car*? How's the *car*?' Dad's eyebrows almost

meet his receding hairline. 'That's what you choose to enquire about first, after this debacle? Do you have any notion of the destruction of property you've caused, not to mention what you may have done to your career?'

Would it have been that hard to just tell me the damned thing was totalled?

'Mark,' Mom's lower lip quivers, 'he's *alive*. Everything else can be fixed.'

I wonder if she means *fixed*, like the emergency appendectomy that landed me in the hospital last fall right in the middle of filming my last blockbuster, or *fixed*, like when I got busted a year ago at a party where everyone was smoking weed, but I got off for lack of evidence.

'Can it?' Dad shoots back, grabbing his jacket from the chair and heading for the door. 'God*dammit*, Reid, I'm not sure if anything about you can be repaired. You've had a low regard for the needs of everyone else for some time – and now you've extended that carelessness to your own life. I can't imagine what you were thinking.'

I don't answer. I figure he doesn't want to hear that *not thinking* was sort of the point.

Dori

I try to keep my voice encouraging, even though I'm yelling at the top of my lungs. 'Okay, guys, let's take it from the top!'

That thing they say about herding cats? Try herding eighteen five-year-olds into practising a vocal finale for Vacation

Bible School Parents' Night when they're intent on the swimming pool time they've been promised for good behaviour.

'Miss Dori?' I feel a tug on the side of my denim Capris. It's Rosalinda, from whom I hear *Miss Dooooooriiiii?* at least a dozen times a day.

'Yes, Rosa?' I say, and before the words leave my mouth, seventeen five-year-olds are springing out of their seats and shouldering each other aside at the window to stare longingly at the pool shimmering just outside under a brilliant, haze-free June sky.

'I need to *go*.' *Again*? This kid has a bladder the size of a quarter.

'Can you hold it another minute, sweetie? We're almost done –' A squeal sounds from across the room. Jonathan has scissors in one hand and Keisha's braid in the other. 'Jonathan, *drop it*.' I bite my lip at the startled look on his face. Must not laugh. It's not funny. *Not funny*.

He blinks, eyes shifting from scissors to braid. 'Which one?'

I narrow my eyes. 'Let's start with Keisha's hair.' He releases the braid and she runs to her friends, who gather round her while glaring at him. I've never had a group of girlfriends like that – a protective clique, a guardian posse.

'Miss *Dori*,' Rosa whines, tugging harder. I take her hand to keep her from pulling my pants down. I'd *never* restore order if that were to happen.

'Just a minute, Rosa.' I squeeze her hand gently. 'Jonathan,' I say more sternly. 'Bring me those scissors.' Eyes on his untied sneakers, he shuffles over as slowly as is humanly possible. 'Where'd you get them?'

He holds the scissors out with both hands as though presenting a gift to royalty. Not falling for his fake contrition, I arch an eyebrow.

He chances a peek at my face. 'Mrs K's desk,' he mumbles, scowling at his feet again.

Our church secretary, Filomena Kowalczyk, speaks with a heavy Polish accent despite having immigrated to the US about a hundred years ago. She keeps a huge jar of candy on her desk and wears creaky orthopaedic shoes which have the same effect as a bell on a cat's collar. The kids hear her coming down the hall five minutes before she arrives. Judging by the smear of chocolate on Jonathan's mouth, I'd say he sampled a Hershey's Kiss or two before making off with her scissors.

'Do we take Mrs K's things without permission?' I fix a disappointed look on him.

He shakes his head.

'Is taking things that don't belong to you what Pastor Doug means by good behaviour?'

His wide, dark eyes snap up to mine. Bingo, kid. Pool time is in jeopardy.

'But Miss Dori!' he says. 'I didn't *cut* it!'

'We aren't talking about Keisha's braid yet. We're discussing you taking Mrs K's scissors –'

'I'll put them back!' Tears fill his eyes. 'I'm s-s-sorry!'

'You're sorry because you got caught,' I say, and he bursts into tears. Oh, dear Lord.

'Miss Dori!' Rosa wails, cupping herself, one leg raised and pressing against the other.

I sigh in defeat, giving up on the programme rehearsal for today. 'All right, everyone line up for the bathroom!'

'Me first! Me *first*!' Rosa says, keeping her death grip on my hand. As I walk to the head of the line, she hops lightly behind me on one foot.

'Jonathan, come stand by me.' Rubbing tears away with his fist, he takes my other hand and I leave the classroom with eighteen ducklings trailing behind.

In a few weeks, I'll be on a mission trip to Ecuador. As exotic as that sounds, I'll be doing much the same thing I'm doing now – I'll just be doing it in Spanish.

2

REID

I loosen the tie the second I turn to head out of the courtroom. The next thing to go will be this crap in my hair that makes me look like one of my father's fuckwit subordinates.

'Put that back on,' Dad barks, his shoulders rigid. He's judged me guilty as charged even though the prosecution accepted our plea bargain – sort of.

I contemplate ignoring him for half a second, until my manager's less dictatorial voice urges discretion. 'Reid, there will be press. *School Pride* is out in theatres. This is no time to look like a rebel. We've already lost a couple of endorsements – your image is suffering enough without you giving the impression that you're ungrateful to have gotten off easy for something that would land 99.9 per cent of regular people in jail.'

'You call that *easy*?' I never snap at George, but I can't agree with his assessment. The judge's mandates for my plea bargain are beyond ridiculous.

'Yes – as would anyone with half a brain,' Dad butts in.

Subtlety has never been in my father's nature. 'Put the goddamned tie back on, Reid.'

My jaw works overtime as I refasten the top buttons of the white Armani dress shirt and loop the perfect half-Windsor knot back into the understated Hermès tie. By the time I'm thirty, I'll have worn my teeth down to nubs.

Friends ask why I don't just ditch my dad. I'm nineteen, an adult in every legal sense of the word (except the ability to drink legally, which is annoying as shit). I'm a legitimate Hollywood star, with a manager, an agent, a PR guy, or woman, as the case may be – Dad may have fired Larry when he didn't move fast enough to save those endorsements last week.

That's the thing. My father takes care of *everything*. He's the CEO of my life, and I'm the product. He manages my career, my money, my legal issues . . . I don't have to do jack shit but show up for auditions, movie tapings, premieres and occasional commercial endorsements. I can't stand him any more than he can stand me, but I know he won't screw me over.

My manager was right. The media is camped out on the courthouse steps, ready to take my statement. I had nothing to do with writing it. George handed it to me last night when Dad and my attorney – whose name I can't recall because I couldn't care less which junior kiss-ass partner wannabe Dad selected from his firm to represent me – were reviewing the bargaining strategy for this morning. Time for my Oscar-worthy performance of contrition.

Dad fades behind me as planned while I'm flanked by

George and junior kiss-ass. I fix an appropriately repentant expression on my face. 'I just want to apologize to my fans. I'm so sorry to have let all of you down. I assure you that this incident was a momentary lapse in judgement, and it won't be repeated.'

Someone shoves a mike in my face. 'Will you go into rehab?'

Cue the look of shame layered over remorse. 'The judge didn't believe that would be necessary at this time. But I intend to follow the terms of the court's orders to the letter, and this occurrence will *not* be repeated.'

A guy from one of the local Hispanic stations looks like his bullshit detector is set on high. 'What about the home you destroyed, and the family you displaced?'

Come on, asshat. It was one room of a house, and no one was in it, so no one was hurt. 'The homeowners are being compensated,' I say. 'The details are private, but the reparation has been agreed upon by all parties.'

'Your father's paying them off, you mean.' The hell? This guy is persistent. Maybe he's related to them or something.

'No, sir.' I look him in the eye, all *mano a mano*. 'I was responsible for the accident. *I'm* the one paying.'

'And you feel comfortable calling it an *accident* when you, an under-age boy, chose to drink yourself to more than double the limit for a *legal* adult, and then drive a two-thousand-pound vehicle through a residential area?'

'Well, I –'

'The owner of the property is a real-estate company. What about the family living there, renting the home? They're hardworking people, but uninsured, and now they've lost belongings they can't afford to replace, in *addition* to the fact that they're currently homeless. What about them?'

You've *got* to be kidding me. I want to kick this guy's ass so bad my fist is already knotted.

Junior kiss-ass decides this is the time to step in and earn that partnership. 'Thank you, ladies and gentlemen – as Mr Alexander's legal counsel, I assure you that he takes full responsibility for his actions and intends to repair *all* of the damage done, and then some.'

Isn't that what I just *said*?

And what the hell does he mean by *and then some*?

Dori

While Dad says grace, my mind wanders. I don't mean to be disrespectful, and I always keep my eyes shut, but sometimes I have so much to keep track of that my brain is making lists and checking off details any time it perceives a calm moment to do so.

Parents' Night rehearsals with the kids will have to wait until next week. My Habitat for Humanity project has a more pressing deadline thanks to the self-centred, egocentric moron who drove his stupid sports car into the living room of our future family's rental place. I don't get people like him – people who think of no one, ever, but themselves. They just take up space on the planet, never contributing anything worthwhile.

He's the reverse of someone like my dad – Pastor Doug to the parishioners of our church and the surrounding neighbourhood. Dad would tell me that God wouldn't be pleased about my biases concerning Reid Alexander.

God has a purpose, even for him, Dad would say.

Yeah, right.

Ugh, there I go again.

I'll be spending the next several days straight working on the Habitat house. Luckily, we have much of it done. Unfortunately, that doesn't include the A/C, and it's already hot and hazy. Much of Los Angeles lives without central air; I shouldn't complain. I have a comfortable home, even if it's not chock-full of luxury items like big-screen televisions and rooms of furniture where everything matches. Mom knows her way around with a paintbrush, and she's amazing at using saris bought at the bazaar as colourful window coverings and tablecloths, or plants to cover a stain on the carpet or a crack in the plaster walls.

I've got a few more things to get turned in to UC Berkeley before I start next fall: AP exam results, graduation certificate, housing deposit. Almost everyone who knows me seems puzzled by the fact that I intend to pursue a degree in social work rather than music. I'm often told that I have a beautiful voice, but that would be an impractical career path. I'd rather *do* something.

Dad's the only one who really gets that sentiment. He's also where I get my voice. Mom and Deborah, my older sister, are absolutely tone-deaf, but they have useful natural and applied skills. Mom's an obstetric nurse specializing in low-cost prenatal care, and Deb recently began her hospital residency in Indiana – she's going to be a paediatrician. Dad and I just had to be more creative about finding our ways to contribute.

This summer, like the last several years, I'm working the summer programme our church offers for the poverty-stricken neighbourhoods nearby. The van picks the kids up in the morning, enabling their parents to go to work without worrying about what to do with them. The kids stay all day, which means we have to come up with lots of activities. The swimming pool was Mom's idea. Some members of the church finance committee baulked at installing something so lavish, but Mom convinced them we could use it for Vacation Bible School, family days and monthly baptisms.

Dad says Mom could talk the Devil into baking Christmas cookies.

'. . . Amen,' Dad says, and I open my eyes, banishing thoughts of Satan wearing an apron and icing reindeer.

'Dori, your dad has some news that might interest you.' Mom hands me the bowl of mashed potatoes, and they're both watching me closely. Weird.

Dad clears his throat. 'You got a call just before you got home. I guess Roberta doesn't have your cell number.'

Roberta, my project leader at Habitat, doesn't get that people can be easily reached on the phone they carry around with them. Her cell phone is always in her bag and *off* because she believes the battery will run down if she leaves it on, and then it wouldn't be at the ready in case she gets mugged and needs it. I've never asked her how she plans to hold the bad guy off while her phone boots up.

'There's a new volunteer starting tomorrow, and she wants you to help him acclimatize, show him the ropes.'

My brow furrows. While we appreciate volunteers, this isn't exactly huge or unusual news, plus my parents are being downright odd. 'Okay. No problem.' Waiting for the punchline, I pass the potatoes to Dad. 'Is it someone with electrical experience, I hope?'

'Er, I doubt that.'

When he doesn't elaborate, I finally say, 'Dad, spit it out.'

Dad isn't meeting my eyes, unusually cryptic. 'Well, this volunteer may be someone you know. Not *know*, exactly. But know *of*.'

Good grief, I'm way too tired for this. 'Am I supposed to guess who it is?' I sigh. 'Is it someone from church? Someone from school?'

'It's Reid Alexander,' Mom blurts out, unable to contain herself any longer.

'What?'

Dad tries the logical spin. 'Apparently, working to get the house ready sooner for the Diegos was part of his plea bargain.'

Oh, no. No, no, no. This is not happening. 'Wait. So he's not even actually a volunteer, then – he'll be on-site under court-ordered *coercion*?' They cannot expect me to babysit that self-absorbed, womanizing, probable alcoholic.

'Roberta said that since you're about his age, she was hoping you could . . . er . . .'

'Babysit him.' I scowl. 'Please tell me it's only for a day or two.'

Dad shrugs and starts to eat. 'You'll need to ask Roberta that. I'm just the messenger.'

I close my eyes for a moment, imagining the absurdity of Reid Alexander on-site, the wasted time accumulating hourly. I'd planned to tile the master bathroom shower tomorrow. No way I could trust him to help with that – tiling is pretty much skilled labour, and while I've done it enough to be proficient, he's probably never touched a trowel in his life.

'Why me?' I hear Dad's answer in my head before he says it.

'Don't know, honey. But there's a reason for everything.' Dad pats my hand. 'We'll just have to wait patiently to see what it is.'

As I do every time he says that or something like this, I bite back what I'd say if I could reply honestly. I don't believe there's a reason for everything, and having faith doesn't mean I'm blind. I believe people make poor choices. I believe bad things happen to good people. I believe there's evil in the world that I will never understand, but will never stop fighting.

If I believed for two seconds that there was a reason behind some of the awful things that occur in this life, I wouldn't be able to stand it.

3

REID

'Well, this is promising.' Dad walks across the kitchen, setting his attaché case on the granite-topped buffet.

I don't bother to reply. He's been goading me like this since I was a kid. Took me a while to learn not to take the bait and let him prove how much more intelligent he is. My father gets *paid* to argue – and by the size of this house, the cut of his custom-made silk-blend suit and the cars in the garage, he's brilliant at it.

It must gall the crap out of him that I do what I do and earn more money than he does. Of course, he has no idea how hard I work when I'm filming, but who cares. Let him think I do next to nothing. Just pisses him off more, which is fine with me.

'I even made coffee.' I gesture to the half-full carafe, still warming.

He fills his travel mug and screws the lid on. 'Is your mother up?'

'Haven't seen her.'

'You'll need to call a car to get to *work*,' he reminds me, 'since your licence has been suspended for six months.' He sounds way too satisfied about that.

'I thought you were gonna take me.' I blink my baby blues at him. His mouth opens and no sound comes out as I fight for a straight face. 'I'm *joking*, Dad – I already called the service. They'll be here in ten minutes.'

'Oh.' Scowling, his mouth snaps closed. 'Well, fine then.'

I'm not sure if I should be amused or pissed that he's so surprised.

When I hand the driver the sheet with the charity build-a-house address, he studies it before looking at me with a perplexed expression.

'Yeah, dude, it's correct,' I say, anticipating his question. 'Just take me there, okay?'

He opens the back door to the black Mercedes. 'Yes, sir, Mr Alexander.' As we pull away, it occurs to me that this car will be fucking conspicuous in the neighbourhood where I'll be for the next month. If I took a regular taxi, it would only be marginally better. To blend in, I'd need to hire a gang member in a pimped-out Monte Carlo to drop me off.

On the drive, I read through some of the scripts George and I are considering for upcoming projects, but none of them motivate me to look beyond the first page. A year ago, I'd have been happy enough with several, but now I'm thinking they're all the stupidest shit I've ever read. I attribute this new perception to Emma, my co-star in *School Pride*.

She told me last fall she'd rather do serious films than movies that have immediate blockbuster potential. Why her viewpoint rubbed off on me at all, I have no clue.

Emma is also the only girl I've bothered to pursue but not caught in years, and I screwed up any possible second chance by hooking up with other girls when she didn't cave. I begged her for another shot, but the damage was done. By the time the cast met up for the premiere, she was with Graham, another co-star. My long-time ex, Brooke, wanted *him*. She offered me a devil's bargain: Brooke would seduce Graham, and Emma would fall right into my arms.

Graham didn't go for it, but thanks to Brooke's scheming, Emma thought he had. She was distraught. Fragile. I had her right where I wanted her, but I couldn't do it. One of the few principles I have where girls are concerned: lying to get a girl in bed is cheating. If I cheat to win, I didn't really win.

I got a little overly introspective after that. A short-lived state, luckily. I snapped out of it after my accident, when I had a few compulsory meetings with a court-appointed therapist who suggested that maybe I was *trying* to kill myself. I laughed in his face. I mean, there's a difference between being suicidal and not giving a shit if you live or die. Right?

'Sir?' the driver says. 'We're here . . . if you're sure this is where you want to be dropped . . .'

Outside the dark tinted glass lies a sea of generic bungalows – paint fading, bars on windows and doors, each house separated by a few feet from the next one and surrounded by limp, untended palm trees amidst otherwise sparse vegetation. I stare at the partially-completed house, which is literally steps from the road – just like all the others. A house number sloppily painted on to a piece of bare plywood leaning against the front matches the number on the court info.

'Yeah, this is it. Be here at or before three to pick me up. I don't want to wait, for obvious reasons.' I normally wouldn't be caught dead driving through this neighbourhood, let alone helping to build yet another piece-of-crap house. This sucks ass.

'Yes, sir, I'll be here by 2:45.'

Activity around the house has come to a standstill because everyone is staring at the guy exiting a chauffeured Mercedes in the gang-infested neighbourhood. Man, I seriously should have thought about arriving in some other mode of transportation.

As I walk up the unfinished pathway, a girl comes out to greet me . . . although *greet* is generous. She's glaring as she walks towards me, her brows drawn together in an expression I go to concerted efforts to avoid making, even when I'm pissed.

I have about twenty seconds to sum her up physically. The process takes me ten.

She's wearing an oversized, faded t-shirt bearing the M.A.D.D. logo. Unintentional? Doubt it. I can't tell breast size or shape under that thing, ditto whether or not she has a waist. In my experience, if a girl has either, she's going to dress to at least hint at the fact. Her tent of a t-shirt tells me she's hiding inadequacies, not assets.

Her shorts are so far out of style that I'm not sure they were ever *in* style. Sprinkled with flecks of paint, her construction boots are worn and scuffed. Still, she manages to pull off this part of the manual labourer look because her legs are the only thing remotely hot about her. Her calves are perfectly shaped, strong and muscled. Most of the girls I know – actresses, society girls – want long, thin legs. But legs like hers are what I go for when I'm feeling particular.

She's tan wherever I see skin. Not a Rodeo Drive sunless tan, either – the real thing. I know this because there's a pale strip of skin on one wrist where she usually wears something – a thick-banded watch, maybe. I don't know a single girl who goes outside without a million SPF sunblock.

Hair – generic brown and pulled back from her face into a ponytail. Probably goes well past her shoulders when down. Assuming she ever wears it down.

Face – predictably, no make-up, not even a swipe of blusher or lipgloss. Dark, dark eyes. A light smattering of freckles across her cheeks and the bridge of her nose – the girls I know would have had those burned off or bleached out or whatever they do to remove freckles years ago. Finally, her mouth – another oddity, like her legs – her lips are perfect and full, even set into a harsh line like they are now.

I stuff both hands into the front pockets of my jeans, stop a few feet from the street and wait.

'Mr Alexander, I assume?' she says, still striding forward. I nod, adding something further to the short list of her attractive features: her voice. It makes me want to hear her sing, even though her inflection says she wishes the ground would swallow me.

Legs, lips, voice. If one of these proves too appealing to ignore, a few veiled insults will give her self-esteem enough of a hit to back off, though it seldom chases them off completely. Girls are irrationally attracted to assholes. I don't intend to be cruel, but I'm not hooking up with some tiresome, bleeding-heart do-gooder. I just want to do my time and get the hell out.

Dori

A Mercedes? *Really?* I am so not looking forward to this.

The moment His Highness arrived was easy enough to determine since everyone just flat-out stopped what they were doing to gawk at the big celebrity and his ostentatious car. One minute the house hummed with the sound of people talking, laughing and working side by side, and the next there was silence punctuated by hissed undertones, not a hammer or paintbrush moving. I fail to see how this sort of daily interruption will be beneficial to the project . . . but no one asked *me.*

He's dressed appropriately – jeans, t-shirt, work boots – but I get the feeling those jeans were more expensive than the nicest outfit I own. Possibly ditto the t-shirt, which has some sort of insignia I don't recognize. I'm guessing it isn't a brand found at Target.

When I walked out to meet him, he gave me a careless

once-over – I should have expected as much – and dismissed whatever he saw. Most girls might be offended, or at least displeased, but I'm grateful. I don't want Reid Alexander's interest. If I had my choice, I'd love for him to perform his community service elsewhere, but the judge wanted him to assist in building the home for the family he displaced, and I can't argue with that logic.

Cramming his hands into his pockets, he watched me indifferently, as though he couldn't care less about anything that has happened or will happen. Out of nowhere an absurd feeling of inconsolable grief washed over me. Like nothing could be more tragic than this boy standing in front of me. Ridiculous.

'Mr Alexander, I assume?' I said, and he nodded shortly. I turned before he could see what I was thinking. When it comes to having a poker face – I don't. Usually that's not a problem, since lying is something I strive not to do because I just don't see the point. But with someone like Reid Alexander, it would be unwise to let him sense any vulnerability where he's concerned. I live in Los Angeles, after all, and while I might not run in his circle, or even within the same galaxy as his circle, I know his type: careless, spoiled and heedless of anyone's needs outside his own. Even with that angel's face, he cannot be trusted.

I glance over my shoulder and he hasn't moved. Without slowing, I say, 'Come with me, please,' and hope that he complies – because no one's told me what I'm supposed to do if he doesn't.

Releasing a breath as I hear the crunch of gravel under

his boots, indicating that he's at least following me inside, I tell myself that I can put up with anything for a few weeks. I wanted to scream when Roberta told me that his community service agreement was for a *month*. Meaning he'll be my problem for the entire three and a half weeks before I leave for Ecuador.

As we pass through the small house, my fellow volunteers gape, star-struck. Even grown men stop what they're doing, though the women are worse – straightening their clothes, patting hair into place – holy cow. You'd think they've never seen anything pretty before. That's the first thing I must admit and get past – the sheer fact of how beautiful he is.

I've seen the magazine covers, the posters on girlfriends' bedroom walls, his likeness on backpacks of *nine*-year-olds who attend our church's after-school programme, for Pete's sake. I knew he'd be handsome. The fact of the matter, though, is 'handsome' doesn't do him justice. Mom would term his hair dirty blond, and Dad would say it's a little too long. His eyes are a dark blue I'd always assumed was photoshopped. He's so sensually attractive that I should add every girl on whom he'll turn his attention to my prayer list because they're going to need all the divine intervention they can get to resist him. I'm thankful that he dismissed me so quickly.

'I was going to tile the bathroom shower today . . . but that's a complicated procedure and you'd just end up watching me do it. So we're going to paint the bedrooms instead.' We arrive in the master bedroom, the walls and ceiling of which are unfinished. I texturized and primed last week.

Carpet hasn't been laid, so at least I don't have to worry about him ruining the floor. 'I'll do the ceiling because it's more –'

'Complicated?' he interjects, regarding me with an amused look.

I take a slow, deep breath. It's going to be a long three and a half weeks.

4

REID

'So do you have a name – or do I just call you boss?'

Introductions: Basic Etiquette 101. The tips of her ears turn bright pink, but she otherwise doesn't blush.

'I'm sorry.' She steps towards me, offering her hand. 'I'm Dori.'

I take her hand and give her one firm shake, annoyed that the combination of her pitch-perfect voice and the touch of her hand is like a tiny electric shock. 'Call me Reid. Only my subordinates call me Mr Alexander.'

Comprehending me instantly, she blinks and her ears turn an even darker shade of pink, and I decide that this month may prove more entertaining than I'd thought. Any direct hits will come with a visible signal. I'll bet she wears her hair pulled back every day too.

She clears her throat and indicates the pile of stuff in the middle of the room, clustered round a ladder. 'Okay, then, *Reid*, here's the paint we'll be using, and the rollers, brushes, etcetera. Have you painted before?'

Is she serious? 'Not *rooms*.'

She doesn't miss a beat. 'Then I guess you'll be learning a new skill.' Pulling a small metal instrument from her pocket, she squats next to the paint cans. I'm trying not to focus on the line of muscle flexing from the top of her boot to where it disappears at the hem of her shorts.

'I doubt I'll feel the need to paint the walls at my place any time soon,' I say, scoffing at the notion of wasting my time doing any form of manual labour when I could pay some illegal immigrant almost nothing to do it.

She prises the lid off a paint can, ignoring my comment and smiling at the sky blue inside. Without glancing up, she sets the lid aside. 'What if you accept a film role where you need to act like you can paint, but you don't know how? I can make you look like an expert by the end of the week.'

My estimation of her ability to manipulate goes up several notches. She's downright dangerous.

So she's going to make me an 'expert' at painting? How hard can it be?

I'm rolling paint on the final bit of the last wall, biceps and delts burning (at least I won't have to worry about deteriorating muscle tone while I'm here), while Dori is on the ladder 'cutting in' with a brush – painting the wall space between the ceiling and the spot where the roller can't go without hitting the ceiling. Which I learned the hard way.

The windows are open to save us from being asphyxiated by paint fumes, but there's no breeze to speak of and summer is gearing up to be a bitch. This would be a perfect day to be at the beach. Or pretty much anywhere else.

'It's fucking hot in here.' I set the roller in the tray and examine my hands, which are splattered in blue. There's blue on my nails, under my nails, speckling my forearms and the yellow Prada t-shirt that, luckily, isn't a favourite. Since the shirt's already streaked and spattered with blue paint, a few more smears from my fingers won't matter.

I pull the shirt over my head and toss it next to a pile of dust sheets after mopping my face with it. Dori is on her ladder, motionless and staring at me while a line of paint runs from the upturned brush down the handle and continues along her arm. When I cock an eyebrow at her, she snaps her attention back to the paintbrush in her hand, dropping it into the shallow paint tray hooked to the ladder.

Grabbing a cloth, I climb on to the ladder behind her, take her wrist in my hand and stop the drip of paint with the cloth. This seems to unsettle the shit out of her.

'This ladder is only built to hold *one*,' she says, taking the cloth from me.

Shrugging, I hop down. 'You're welcome.' Her legs, smooth and unblemished, are eye level when my boots hit the ground. I resist the urge to run a finger over the soft spot behind her knee. She'd probably fall off the ladder . . . at which point I'd catch her . . . And then she'd start screaming.

Holy shit, man, cut it out.

'Thank you.' Ears pink, she unhooks the tray and avoids looking at me.

I've been here half a day and I've schooled her in manners

25

twice. That's gotta sting. She's backing down the ladder with the paintbrush and tray when I ask if we're done with this room. Cocking her head to the side like she's trying to figure out if I'm serious, she looks at me. 'No . . . we're just taking a lunch break to give it time to dry so we can apply the second coat.'

'You've *got* to be kidding me,' I say. 'We have to paint this entire room *again*?'

She clenches her jaw, but resettles herself with one breath. 'Yes. You'll see why when we come back after lunch.' Her voice is all patience and fortitude.

I possess neither of those traits. 'Fine. *Whatever*. I've got to be here for a month. Doesn't matter if I paint the same damned wall fifty times.'

Her lips set in a line, she huffs a breath and glances at me and away. 'Could you put your shirt back on, please?'

I have to grin. 'Why? Does it bother you that I'm shirt-less?'

She rolls her eyes in a big exaggerated gesture, and I struggle not to laugh. 'I don't care if you want to strip naked. But we have retired people helping out today . . . and some of them are of the "no-hats-indoors" variety, so I doubt they'd be thrilled to see you at lunch *sans* shirt. But suit yourself.'

I grab the shirt off the floor and pull it on, following her out of the room. 'Strip naked, huh? I don't know about that, Dori. We just met.' She doesn't reply, but her ears go pink. *Score*.

Dori

I can't believe I just invited Reid Alexander to be naked in my presence. As if I didn't know he wouldn't take that sort of remark silently.

I was expecting to find him difficult to motivate and just as difficult to teach, but he listened (though he seemed bored out of his mind), and for the most part he followed my instructions. I had to let him try it his way first because apparently, he's a learn-the-hard-way type. (Shocking.) He didn't trust me about not getting too much paint on the roller. Or rolling in arches instead of straight lines on the first pass. Or not rolling too near the ceiling.

In front of the first wall he painted, there are splotches of paint all over the floor. I had to point out several drippy globs he needed to back up and fix before they dried that way. And of course, he hit the white ceiling in two places and the skirting board in two more, trying to roll all the way to the crease. By the second wall, he'd improved, more so the third and the last was nearly perfect. I was starting to relax until he took off his shirt.

I've managed to remain unaffected by male torsos for eighteen years, but good golly, I've never been confronted with a torso like his. He's like an ad for cologne or beachwear or gym equipment – all perfect skin stretched over flawlessly-toned muscle. Luckily, his arrogance is such a turn-off that I didn't have any problem asking him to put his shirt back on.

Like the walk through the house this morning, conversations break off when Reid and I emerge into what will be the backyard, once we lay sod. Twenty or so people sit on upturned buckets and folding lawn chairs scattered about the concrete patio, paper plates of tamales and tacos on their laps. Some workers will be here every day – notably the crew leaders like Roberta. Others vary day to day – college students, church groups, garden clubs or employees from area companies that support community service projects by giving them time off to volunteer.

I walk to the water tap to wash my hands and Reid does the same, and then splashes water over his face and runs his wet hands through his hair as though everyone out here isn't watching him do it. Following me to the card table where the food is laid out, he acts as though there's nothing odd about a Hollywood celebrity being handed a paper plate and pointed to the plastic utensils and the cooler holding bottled water.

I sit on a step, balancing my plate on my knees, and he sits next to me. Everyone is still staring, though whispered conversations are resuming.

'So why are *you* here?' he asks. 'I'm guessing you haven't been arrested for drunken driving or gotten caught with a joint in your gym locker.'

'Um, *no*,' I say, once I've finished chewing. 'I'm a regular.'

He peers at me, and I can't decide if he's puzzled or amused. 'So you do this all the time. Hmm.'

'What?'

While he's studying the other volunteers, appraising each one without any alteration in expression, I'm gazing at his profile, waiting for him to continue. He has the longest eyelashes I've ever seen on a guy, and his now-damp hair, darker blond when wet, curls at the ends over his ear and at the nape, grazing the neck of his paint-smeared t-shirt.

'Nothing.' He shrugs. 'I just wonder what else you have time to do, if you're doing this all the time,' he adds, biting off half a taco. People like him never understand people like me. It's like we come from different species.

'Well, since I don't make a habit of getting drunk, smoking pot, clubbing and sleeping with everything that moves, I have plenty of time for other activities.' *Oh my gosh*. I did *not* just say that.

He laughs softly, turning to face me as I scowl. His blue eyes are striking, framed by thick, dark lashes. 'Let me guess – Monday is book club, Tuesday is family game night . . . Wednesday is Bible study and Thursday you meet up with the sewing circle to make quilts for the elderly . . . Am I close?'

Without answering, I get up to go back inside. This isn't the first time I've been ridiculed for what I am, but for some reason – maybe because it feels so incompatible with where we are – it's more disheartening.

'Wait,' he says, and for some stupid reason I stop, expecting him to apologize. 'When do you have time for the soup kitchen?'

He's chuckling when I go inside without looking back.

5

REID

Wow, that was a dickhead thing to say. For someone so minimally impressed by celebrity proximity, she's been cool enough. Right up to that laundry list of corrupt activities in which, truth be told, I do engage. Still, Jesus. Superior much?

I stand to go inside when conversations taper off and people go back to whatever they were doing before break. Those still outside are stealing glances at me as I throw the plate and utensils away, finish the bottle of water and toss it into the recycling container.

'Mr Alexander,' someone says – that Roberta woman. 'How's it going so far?'

'Awesome.'

'Oh, good.' She smiles, oblivious to my sarcastic tone. 'Dorcas is one of our best volunteers. We're really proud of her; maybe she'll even teach you some new tricks!'

'Uh-huh,' I answer, smiling at her while my brain processes – *Dorcas*? Who the hell names a kid *Dorcas*? And by the way, lady, the day a little prude named Dorcas teaches me a new trick is the day I'll be finding a nice tall building to leap from.

I go back to the room we were painting to find her with earbuds in her ears, an ancient model iPod clipped to her shorts, the wire threaded under her shirt. She's gathered the equipment she used to paint the ceiling this morning. Pausing the music without removing the earbuds, she says, 'You know what to do in here; I'm going next door to start on the ceiling, unless you need me here to supervise you.'

I bite back half a dozen forward answers. 'I think I can handle it.'

She nods shortly.

As she gets to the door, I add, 'Oh and, *Dorcas*, I'll need you to sign my sheet for the court before I go.'

Her shoulders stiffen, but she continues out of the room, her ears lit like a flare. I clamp my lips together to keep from laughing. Getting on her nerves is just too easy.

By 3:00, I've finished the room. Dori shows up at 3:01 with a pen in her hand. As she glances around, checking my work, I pull the form from my back pocket and hand it to her. Except for a couple of blue swipes on the ceiling above the first wall (turns out she was right about not getting too close with the roller), it looks pretty good. Without commenting, she signs the form – *Dorcas Cantrell* – and hands it back.

I thank her, thinking she'd love nothing more than to turn round and leave without replying, but she doesn't risk it after my earlier chiding. 'I'll see you tomorrow,' she says. Her lyrical voice gives me a small jolt, but she's already leaving the room.

My driver is waiting at the kerb. He starts at the sight of me, sweaty and speckled in blue paint. I'm sure he's imagining what my clothes will do to those leather seats, but he says nothing beyond, 'Good afternoon, Mr Alexander,' as he opens the back door and waits for me to get in.

Thanks to that fucking plea bargain, I have to serve twenty days of community service. I'm expected on location in Vancouver mid-August. There won't be any breaks. So. One day down, nineteen to go.

Dori

Dad picks me up a couple of hours after Reid leaves.

Pulling into traffic, he drums lightly on the steering wheel. The trek home requires some freeway time, and he's got the classical station on to de-stress. Bach's *Concerto for Two Violins* fills the car. I lean my head back and close my eyes, grateful I don't have to drive. I hate driving on LA freeways. Mom says it brings out the devil in me. The way people drive on the 110, I don't think I'm alone.

'So how'd today go?' Dad is so obvious when fishing for information. Just the fact that he waited a few minutes into the drive to ask tells me he's working to sound offhand.

What do I say? That Reid is as spoiled and arrogant as I thought, stubborn but teachable, and more beautiful than any guy has a right to be?

'Fine.' I can't keep the exasperation out of my voice.

'My dear, I've seen you wrangle two dozen munchkins

into a chorus of little angels.' He pats my knee. 'I doubt this will be more difficult than that.'

'The little angels were scared of me, Dad.'

He laughs. 'The kids always love you, Dori.'

'Love and fear, Dad – that's the key to motivation. Love and fear.'

The 110 is a parking lot during rush hour. We're barely moving; I could *walk* faster. Literally. I crack an eye open. The windshield view is the back of a truck, and we're blocked on either side by other, also stationary cars.

'Are you planning on applying that tactic to Mr Alexander?'

I bristle at my dad calling him that. And someone like me will never inspire either love or fear in someone like Reid. 'I can't imagine how I'd be able to get him to do anything he decides he isn't going to do.'

Dad frowns. 'Did he refuse to work today?'

Thinking about the shocked look on Reid's face when I told him the room needed a second coat of paint, I stifle a laugh. 'No, he painted *one* room – with my assistance.'

I set up the bathroom to do the tiling tomorrow. Reid seemed capable of painting without guidance by the end of the day, so maybe he won't need constant monitoring.

'I guess that's something – if he actually *worked*, instead of pulling a prima donna act.'

Eyes closed, I roll my head back and forth to stretch the kinks out of my neck after spending the day painting ceilings. 'I had to sign some sort of court document at the end of the day, verifying he was there and doing actual labour.

I guess he'd be in trouble if he didn't *perform* the community service.'

The concerto swells, and neither of us speaks for several minutes. Music, to both of us, is the purest expression of emotion. When it's inspired, it leaves tears in my eyes, leaves me breathless. For me, there's nothing better than singing and knowing I've affected someone that same way.

'So what's on the agenda tonight – partying till the wee hours? Drag racing on the strip? Hot date?' My father laughs at his little joke. I know he doesn't mean anything by it – to him, I'm an incorrigible good girl. I may be the only girl in the history of California whose father encourages her to stay out later with friends.

'Sure – all of the above. Don't wait up.'

'So are you still seeing –' He snaps his fingers twice. 'Nick?'

'That's the one.'

'We were never really a thing, Dad.'

Nick is a guy from school who's known for his civic-minded volunteer efforts. In other words, he's a male *me*. Everyone's been trying to push us together since he transferred in during junior year. We've been out a few times and still hang out occasionally. He's nice enough, and certainly good-looking enough, but I can go for days without thinking about him. So I do.

'Is he aware of this?'

'Dad, sheesh.' I'm amused by the fact that my father is interested in my love life. Or lack thereof. 'We get along fine. He's nice. Fun. Easy to talk to.' Everything Reid isn't.

Why am I thinking of *him*?

'Ouch,' Dad says, wincing. 'No chemistry, huh?'

'What?'

'Nice, fun, easy to talk to – sounds like you're talking about me!' He glances over his right shoulder to change lanes, winking at me in the process.

'I could do worse than someone like you, Dad,' I laugh.

He pretends to admire himself in the rear-view mirror, waggling his eyebrows. 'True. There's no hurry, though.'

'Definitely not.'

I'm eighteen, so he's right – there's no hurry. I don't tell him how much I *want* that sort of connection – a relationship like he and Mom share. The trust and respect between them is plain to see, but I know that under the surface, their relationship simmers with passion. I don't tell him how much I worry it will never happen for me. I don't tell him how some days, I feel as though everything I do is an attempt to be worthy of being loved like that.

6

REID

Mom meets me at the door with a drink in her hand. 'Reid!' Plucking at the shirt, her eyes widen and her mouth screws up. Dropping the fabric like it's covered in manure instead of paint, she rubs her fingers together.

'It's just paint, Mom. And it's dry.' I pull the shirt over my head and keep walking towards the curving marble staircase.

'Did you get any on the walls?' Clearly, a smart-ass temperament is genetic, and I was dealt a double dose.

'Yeah, I actually did. I'm gonna take a shower – when's dinner?' I call down when I hit the second landing.

'Immaculada should have it on the table by seven.'

'I think I'll nap too. I'm going out later, and I'm dead tired.'

I don't wait for an answer. If Dad isn't going to be home – he usually isn't – I have no idea how she'll spend the evening, besides having another cocktail or three.

*

'I still can't believe you destroyed your 911, man.' John down-shifts his Jaguar XJ to take a curve. 'It sucks ass, seriously.'

My one-week-old Porsche 911 GT2 RS was sweet. I don't even remember getting into it that night. Guess I should be glad I hadn't taken anyone home from that club – the whole right side was crushed in.

Man, *that's* a more sobering thought than I want to be having tonight.

'Gonna replace it?'

'No point right now – my licence is suspended for six months anyway.' Six months. *Damn.* The judge didn't even count the time from the accident to my court date against it – he started the sentence from the court date, leaving five months, two weeks and four days to go.

John frowns, confused. 'So?'

I should know better than to expect my best friend to get why I won't be driving on a suspended licence. He has no concept of consequences. He's the luckiest bastard I hang out with – he never gets caught doing anything. It's bizarre. Not to mention unfair as hell.

'I've gotta lay low for a bit. First getting busted at that party, and now this DUI and community service crap.'

'But they dropped the charges on the weed, right?'

'Yeah. But standing there in front of a judge, you can't help feeling like he knows everything you've ever done.'

'Whoa.' John is one of those guys who frequently comes across as stoned off his ass. He's brighter than he seems – unless he's actually stoned, in which case he's practically brain-dead.

We're heading into the Hills for a party some girl is having. John says she's an heiress who's struggling to make it as an actress in Hollywood. The houses we're passing on the way are as posh as my parents' place. Yeah, she's really struggling.

'So about this party – any decent prospects for hook-ups?' I want nothing more than to get totally wasted, grab some hot, legally-aged, equally wasted girl and find a room. No brown hair, no brown eyes. No supervision, direction or advice. No sarcasm. No *talking*.

'Yeah, man. Ample possibilities.'

'Sweet.' I'm thinking a tall, leggy, blue-eyed blonde with huge tits.

This is LA – I can't throw a rock and *not* hit one of those.

Dori

Day three has *not* gone as I'd envisioned it. Of course, neither did day two.

First, he showed up an hour late and hung-over. He thought he was hiding it (with sunglasses – really?), but just because I'm personally naïve when it comes to getting drunk or doing drugs doesn't mean I don't know it when I see it. The neighbourhoods where I work are rife with the ways and means people use to cope with their disappointing lives – and those coping mechanisms sometimes include substances that don't do any more than mask the real problems and valid issues.

Frankly, his slightly bloodshot eyes and lack of energy – coupled with the tardiness and an even more contrary attitude than the previous day – almost pushed me over the edge. I wanted to bundle him right back into the back seat of his fancy car and send him home. I'm supposed to be above such reactions. Some social worker I'll make, if I can't keep a more even keel. I'll have clients with bigger personality limitations than he's got, as difficult as that is to imagine at the moment.

He was a walking safety liability. There was no way I could leave him alone with a paint roller, not to mention what paint fumes might do to him in his already taxed physical condition. Anything with tools, especially power tools, was out. The only task I could imagine assigning to him was helping to lay sod in the backyard. I thought I was doing him a favour – he could wear the sunglasses and be out in the fresh air (such as it is – this is LA, after all), and he wasn't going to put a nail through his hand.

Of course, depositing him outside meant I had to abandon the tiling I'd planned to do so I could paint because *somebody* had to do it before the carpet arrives. Determined to get back to work, I left him outside with Frank, who's in charge of landscaping.

When I came out to check on him just before lunch, hoping he hadn't given Frank any trouble, he was standing in the middle of the half-sodded yard, shirtless, leaning on a tamping tool and chatting up a cute girl in cut-offs and a pink tank top. Judging by the cooler at her feet, she was supposed to be passing out bottles of water. When she turned, I saw that she was Gabrielle Diego, the daughter of the people who would soon own this house – and into whose rental house Reid had crashed his car.

Her family of five was living in a motel room because of him, and she was smiling up at him like he could crash into her house any old time, no big deal.

When she spotted me standing on the porch slab, she touched his arm and said something that made him turn. Our eyes locked. Without severing that connection, he took a long swallow from the water bottle, leaned close to her and spoke. At the sound of their laughter, my patience snapped. I stomped back inside and finished painting a second coat of pink on Gabrielle's bedroom walls and a coat of primer on the boys' room without stopping for lunch or a break. By the time Dad arrived to pick me up, the muscles in my back were screaming for mercy. Reid must have got Frank to sign his sheet because I hadn't seen him again until this morning.

We finished the master bedroom and bathroom walls today, not speaking beyond obligatory Q & A. He sat with Gabrielle at lunch, which made me uneasy. As I scrawl my name on the line marking the completion of his third day, I say, 'You're not here to socialize, you're here to assist with construction of the Diegos' house, and possibly become more communally aware.'

He gapes before making a remark about my (F-word) humanitarianism and how *he* doesn't need a saviour and if he did, it wouldn't be me.

Instead of biting my tongue, I tell him I wouldn't give

him a glass of water if his hair was on fire, nor does he ever have to worry about me trying to *save* him because I learned years ago that some people aren't worth the effort.

'What – so according to you, someone like me isn't worthy of redemption?' He smirks at such a preposterous notion.

I turn away from his smug expression and begin sweeping arches of plaster on to the shower wall with a trowel. 'I don't believe in wasting my time on hopeless cases.'

He laughs. 'What about me constitutes hopeless?'

I don't bother to look at him. 'What *doesn't* constitute hopeless?' I press a tile into the corner, add a spacer, pick up the next tile and line it up faultlessly level with the first one. 'From your language to your lack of morals to your inability to consider anyone's needs or hardships but your own – honestly, what is there of any value to anyone? Besides to yourself, I mean.'

'I'm *here*, in this shithole gangster barrio, volunteering to do manual labour –'

'Volunteering? Manual labour? Really?' I scoff, ignoring his elitist estimation of the respectable blue-collar neighbourhood. 'First, you're here by court order, and second, you don't do as much by lunch as the rest of us do before you arrive. You're done for the day the exact moment your plea bargain agreement specifies, or before, if you get distracted by something, or some*one*.' He's actually worked harder than I'd expected him to, but his superior attitude just makes my usual unbiased judgement fly out the window.

'Ah, so I noticed an attractive girl. *That's* your problem? Jealous?'

I sputter and shake my head. '*No*, far from it. You disgust me.'

He laughs. 'Disgust? That's a little strong –'

'No. Trust me, it's really not strong enough. If you'll excuse me, I have actual constructive things to do –'

'What in all of your *altruistic* training authorizes you to differentiate between hopeless and salvageable?' he asks, ignoring my attempt to dismiss him. Something about his choice of words and his deadly calm tone makes me look up as he towers over me.

I stand slowly. He's at least eight inches taller and we're not two feet apart in the small space, but this boy doesn't scare me. I see right through his arrogant indignation, so accustomed to getting what he wants that denial is incomprehensible. In all honesty there might be something worthwhile in there, but it doesn't matter because he'll never acknowledge its existence. I'm calm because now I know why I felt such a wave of melancholy when I met him.

'Like you said – you don't want saving, Reid. That makes any effort pointless, assuming I planned to bother trying – which I do *not*.' My voice is as composed as his, but my anger has fallen away while his still radiates from him like heat waves off a pavement.

'Mr Alexander, your car is here,' Roberta says from the doorway.

'Thanks,' he says without turning.

I squat down and dip into the plaster again, smear another glob on the wall and begin to smooth it out. Hyper-aware of the fact that he's still next to me, I refuse to acknowledge him further. He can stand there until his legs collapse for all I care.

'So you only rescue those who fit into your preordained notions of worth? Doesn't seem like much of a victory. Seems discriminatory and hypocritical, in fact.' He turns and walks out, the front door slamming a moment later.

So ends day three. Holy Moses, this is going to be tougher than I thought.

I didn't mean to let it get to this point, I honestly didn't. Like driving in freeway traffic, Reid just brings out the devil in me.

Tomorrow we'll prime the skirting boards, doors and bathroom cabinets. I'd like to finish tiling the master bathroom, but it's foolish to perform tasks that require a steady hand when angry. The tile needs to be perfectly level, not a crooked mess. I take a deep breath, and then another. I have an hour or two until Dad gets here – plenty of time to push Reid from my mind and get a good start on this shower.

Except for a nagging insinuation, one I'm not even sure he's aware of having made. I called him a hopeless case, and he called me a hypocrite for writing him off as someone not worth saving – right after telling me he doesn't *need* saving.

I don't like having to modify my position once I've chosen one, but that doesn't make me incapable of doing so. So I can't help wondering – was he merely set on winning a verbal battle, or did Reid Alexander just tell me he wants to be rescued from himself?

7

REID

You disgust me. This is such an unprecedented statement that I have no idea what to do with it. If she was anyone else, I'd reject it as prejudice because I'm young, famous, rich, entitled – I've heard it all, or thought I had. The only other reason for unreasonable animosity is the random girl who doesn't turn out to be the love of my life after a hot one-nighter – and is somehow surprised by this. *Please.*

Could Dori be resentful that I haven't made an effort to get into her unfashionable shorts? I thought I had her pegged as the sort who wants nothing short of respect, though she can take a fair amount of mockery and come back curiously unperturbed. She may be the most patient person I've ever encountered, besides George. No matter what I do, including showing up an hour late with a massive hangover, she tolerates it. Maybe that's her weird way of showing attraction. Maybe there's a girl under those ginormous t-shirts who just wants attention like the rest of them.

Or maybe I'd add a sexual harassment charge to the drunk-driving conviction.

Three weeks and two days to go. I've worked on movie sets that were way more gruelling, endured co-stars who were ridiculously unprofessional and survived directors whose tyrannical outbursts would send Dori running for cover. Three and a half weeks and I'll be back to my life.

John is about to chew through my last nerve. He and some other guys want to go out tonight. There are no unlame parties, so they've decided to bounce through a few clubs. And since we're all under age, they want me along because I can usually get us all in anywhere, plus VIP treatment.

Most nights, no problem. Happy to oblige. Tonight, I'm dead – and I already had a couple of shots to cool down after that exchange with *Dorcas*. The last thing I need is noise, people and paparazzi. I just want to stay home and flip through the channels until I fall asleep, so I can get up again tomorrow and take a hired car to a pathetic unfinished house that I'm helping to build and landscape ... God, what an out-of-character inclination.

John is having none of it. 'Come on, man, just a couple of hours. Why not?' He's like a whiny toddler. A self-absorbed, fully-grown, nineteen-year-old toddler.

'Because I'm exhausted and sunburned and have to get up at the crack of ass again tomorrow, not that you give a shit.'

'It's summer!'

'So?'

'Time to go out and party, not hibernate!'

'John, we live in Los Angeles. It's never time to hibernate. Whatever. I'm dead. We'll go out Friday.'

'Fine,' he says, dejected. 'If me and the guys are bored to death by then, it's on you.'

I don't bother answering beyond repeating, 'Friday,' and hanging up. I have a back-up of texts all basically wanting the same thing. Parties I'm invited to, parties someone wants entrance to, requests to go out, people bored out of their minds and everyone wanting to score the next high to escape it. After making sure none of the texts or missed calls are from George, I toss the phone on the table next to my bed and turn up the volume on the television before clicking it off again and walking around my room, clinking the ice at the bottom of my glass.

I'm restless, and I *never* get restless. At the first hint of it, I'm usually out the door, not stalking around my room like a prisoner in a cell. What am I staying in for, anyway? So I don't have a hangover tomorrow morning that *Dorcas* will disapprove of? Why would I even give a shit what she sanctions as acceptable behaviour – she's probably at home *knitting* for chrissake.

I grab the phone and call John, who's on his way before I can change my mind.

A couple of nights ago I wanted to find the opposite of Dorcas Cantrell, but that didn't exorcize her from my head. Tonight I'm searching for her twin, as impossible as it will be to find someone so plain in the hang-outs we frequent. Once I find her, I'll be damned if she isn't begging me to screw her up against the bathroom wall before me and the guys take off.

Dori

'Hey, baby girl. When do you leave for Ecuador?' Deb must be exhausted, but she always makes time for me. I guess she could tell in our last few texts that I'm stressed. She can always tell. It's like she's had a wireless connection to me since I was born.

'Twenty days.'

'Got it down to days, huh?' I hear the smile in her voice. 'Are you counting down till you *go* to Quito or till you *leave* LA?'

'Both.'

'So . . . I hear you've got a daily celebrity sighting at Habitat.'

I sigh heavily and moan, lying back on my bed. 'Let's not talk about him.'

Deb laughs. 'Oh, come on. You don't want to talk about him even a little? Hmm.'

'What?'

'I was eight when you were born, Dori; I know you pretty well. If you don't want to talk about him at all, he must be frustrating you in some profound way.'

'Trust me, there's nothing profound about him. He's as superficial and vacuous as you'd assume.' Great. I'm almost sputtering.

'All right, all right, I'm just teasing.' Deb is rarely unkind. She's one aspect of my life that gives me the most joy and the most guilt. I have a loving and supportive family, always enough money for necessities – food, clothing, books – while others have poverty, neglect, illness and the constant hunger of never enough. For some reason this line of thinking makes me think of Reid, which is absurd. He has every advantage and more, with no excuse for forcing his egocentricity on people who have so much less.

Pushing him from my mind, I ask Deb about her residency. After four years of college and another four years of medical school, she's finally Dr Deborah Cantrell. To become the paediatrician she's always wanted to be, she'll be working crazy long hours for the next three years, making barely enough to feed herself and begin paying back her student loans.

'You wouldn't believe how many ER cases are drug seekers.' She sighs, frustrated. 'They're desperate for a fix, so they come in with phony symptoms. The more experienced doctors assume that everyone who gives "pain" as a symptom is a fraud. We keep a list of the repeat offenders.'

I try to imagine my sister in that environment, with her social idealism and her ambition to help people. 'Maybe you're just what those other doctors need – a balance to the pessimism.'

'Well, it's going to be a contentious three years.'

'So . . . met any cute doctors?'

She laughs at my change of subject. 'Yes, actually – one of the attending physicians. But as luck would have it, he's also the most cynical. Last night he almost missed a possible placental abruption because the mother-to-be is a known addict. She claimed severe back pain, and he was about to send her out the door with Tylenol. I convinced him to let me do an ultrasound on her, for practice, and we had to do an emergency C-section. If she'd gone home, the baby would have died and the patient could have bled to death.'

'Wow.' I'm not sure exactly what she's talking about, but it sounds intimidating. 'You saved their lives, Deb.'

'Yeah, well. She swore she hasn't used since she knew she was pregnant, but to him, *once an addict, always an addict.*' She breathes an exasperated sigh.

'We know that's not true.' Our parents have helped dozens of people kick all types of drug addiction through the years. Though a depressing majority start using again, some stay clean. Dad says he has to keep fighting for those few because you never know who's capable of kicking it for good.

'Bradford was brought up in a different environment than we were. He didn't know much about addicts or poverty until he became a doctor. I got him to talk about it a little bit today. He grew up in an upper-middle-class suburb, and the worst thing he encountered was other kids who smoked pot or did a little X. To him, someone who's hooked on cocaine or meth is forever hopeless.'

I think of Reid, and how I told him he was hopeless. How angry he was that I deemed him unworthy of my time or attention. I don't know if he's addicted to any particular substances, though he's certainly addicted to his hedonistic lifestyle. But is he hopeless? Maybe he's right. Maybe my snap judgement concerning him makes me a hypocrite.

'So you're educating Bradford about real life, eh?'

'I'm attempting to, but he's the most opinionated, obstinate man I've dealt with since Dr Horsham in second-year pathology.' Deb almost quit medical school because of Dr Horsham, until Mom convinced her to go back and prove she was made of tougher stuff than that.

After I hang up, I lie on my bed thinking about my sister fighting for an ex-addict. She was right this time, but she won't always be. There will always be addicts who lie to get their fixes, taking hospital resources from those who have actual need. Still, Deb will find the people everyone else has given up on and resolve the most unmanageable problem – assuming there *is* a solution. That's just how she is.

Mom was pulling twelve-hour shifts in the maternity ward when she found out she was pregnant with me. She spent the last two months of her pregnancy on doctor-ordered bed rest, so her plan to fix up the nursery was wrecked.

My sister's old crib, unearthed from the attic, stood pathetically in the centre of the otherwise bare room until Deb and Dad took over nursery decoration. Mom had a lamb-based theme planned, but that idea was tossed. Thanks to the Discovery Channel, Deb was on a marine life kick, infatuated with the Great Barrier Reef. She insisted on decorating my room with fish.

Dad says I lucked out – her next fascination was lizards.

Deb and Dad painted the room turquoise. Twisting up from the floorboards were sections of coral created from orange posterboard, and twenty-two fish were strung from the ceiling, cut in Dad's woodshop from a pattern and all painted the same iridescent blue-green. Mom had suggested that they be multihued, but Deb refused anything that wasn't identical to her *National Geographic* images of damselfish.

The posterboard coral is long gone, and Mom and I repainted the room a lighter blue just before I started high school. The fish, though, remain. Attached to strands of transparent fishing line hooked to the ceiling, they swim in a school from my bedroom door to the window. My earliest memories are of those fish. As I lie with my head at the foot of my bed, they sway fluidly in the A/C-generated breeze, forever passing through.

8

'Supermodel checking you out, two o'clock.'

I glance in one direction and then the other. 'John, dude, that's ten o'clock.'

Aside from his inability to remember how to tell time on the face of an actual clock, my wingman is correct. Actual supermodel. Actually checking me out. And now that I've noticed, she's walking over. Stick-figure thin, she swings non-existent hips, her body and face all planes and angles, a long way from any Dorcas Cantrell doppelgänger.

'Hey there,' John says.

'Hello.' She offers me her hand. 'I'm Dorika.'

Of course she is. And the only reason I'll remember her name tomorrow is because it's ridiculously close to that of a girl she doesn't resemble at all, who I can't stop thinking about for some insane reason.

'I'm Reid.' In her heels, we stand eye to eye. Make-up flawless, dark eyes half-mast and ringed with amethyst, she smiles when I graze her knuckles with my lips.

'Yes, I know. Reid Alexander.' She knows who I am. Better and better.

'And I'm John.'

Her gaze never wavers from my face; John doesn't even register with her, though he's *not* a bad-looking guy. He might be a little short for her, unless she's barefoot – but she's got to be used to that. She's taller than the majority of the guys here.

I motion to the waitress to bring her another drink. 'Where are you from, Dorika?' Her accent is eastern European.

'I am from Budapest.'

'So what brings you to LA?' I couldn't care less about her answer; it's just part of the game.

'The handsome men, of course,' she laughs, tossing waves of dark hair over her shoulder. Her look is calculated, and I chuckle along with her to confirm that I've grasped her insinuation. 'Also I am doing, how do you say it, a *spread* for *Elle* magazine.'

I sense a vulgar comment coming from John and flash him my shut-the-hell-up face. To my amazement, he complies.

The waitress removes the near-empty glass from Dorika's fingers and deftly hands out a fresh drink. 'It is rather loud here,' Dorika says, sipping.

'Well, this *is* a nightclub.'

'I know a quiet bar nearby,' John interjects, but he might as well be mute, for all the attention she's paying him.

'My hotel is a few blocks away. It is more comfortable. Less noisy. You will come with?'

I regard her for a moment longer. There's no reason to say no. No reason at all.

Dori

I pull the stirring stick out of the paint to test the consistency, dribbling a spiral on to the smooth white surface, where the liquid squiggles disappear almost instantly. Perfect. I take a satisfied breath, the chemical aroma something I've never disliked, even while it singes my nostrils.

Identical to the past three days, work slows to a standstill when Reid arrives. Now that he's acquainted with the layout of the house, I'm determined not to go looking for him. When the scent of espresso mingles with the odour of the paint, I know he's found me. I close my eyes for a count of three and a breath of composure before I turn, straightening.

He's holding two Starbucks cups, one of which he extends towards me. 'Truce?'

I take the cup, confused.

He's smirking, having anticipated my reaction. 'It's a double-shot soy latte. If you hate it, my driver can go back and get something else . . .'

Blinking, I wonder what kind of stalking he did to know my favourite coffee drink.

Right. Because a celebrity is going to stalk *me*. 'No, this is . . . fine. Thank you.'

He glances around the small bathroom, takes a sip from his cup. 'Second coat on the cabinets and trim today, right?'

'Um. Yes, that's right.'

'You finished the tiling? How late did you stay?' He looks impressed, his fingers reaching towards the wall and curling back. 'Is it okay to touch it?'

I nod. 'Sure. It's dry.'

Stroking one finger across the glossy white squares, he says, 'They're so even.' His laughter is unlike the derisive chuckle I've become accustomed to over the past few days. 'If I'd done this, it would look like a shitty optical illusion.' His half-grin dares me to disagree.

My mouth pulls up on one side, involuntarily. 'Um, thanks.'

When I finish caulking the master bathroom shower, I check to see if Reid is on task with the cabinets in the second bathroom. I hear Gabrielle's voice before I round the corner, so I hover just outside the door, listening.

'I just want to live my life, you know? I don't care about college. I've been in school long enough.'

From what I remember of a conversation with her mother, Gabrielle spent the past six weeks in summer school after having floundered her way through tenth grade, more interested in boys and partying than keeping up with her assignments.

'Mmm-hmm.' He's non-committal, when I would be trying to discourage such a foolish decision.

'I want to be a model. And then an actress, you know, later. After I'm too old to do, like, swimsuit shoots and stuff.'

'Gabrielle?' They both start at the sound of my voice,

which echoes in the small room. I pretend not to notice their matching reactions. 'I thought you were working outside with Frank today?'

She glares at me, petulant. 'I was just taking a break.'

'Ah,' I say pleasantly, leaning a shoulder on the door jamb and pointedly waiting for her to leave.

She huffs a sigh and rolls her eyes, turning back to Reid. 'See you at lunch?'

'Sure.' His eyes flick to her and straight back to the cabinet, stroking the brush downward with the wood grain, remarkably straight. As he dips the brush into the paint, he looks up at me. 'Need something, boss?'

'She's only sixteen, you know.'

The brush stills and he crooks an eyebrow, eyeing me. 'I'm aware of that.'

'*Are* you?'

'What's it to you?' His voice is pure challenge, his eyes narrowed.

I straighten, running my finger along the groove in the door trim. He should have primed this when he primed the cabinets. Doing all of the priming first is more efficient. 'She's the daughter of the people for whom we're building this house. I feel a responsibility to them where she's concerned.'

'A responsibility to what?'

I glance at him and know he's uber-aware of what he's doing. Making me spell it out. Fine. I can do that. 'A responsibility to make sure the court-ordered "volunteer" understands that he needs to keep his distance from the under-age girl while on this property.'

He stares at me for a moment. 'So if I run into her off property, for instance –'

'*No*. That's not what I mean. I mean . . . just stay away from her, period. Why would you even – I don't get why – don't you ever want to be a better person?'

My breath catches. I can't believe I just said that.

'Okay, *what*?' he says, taken aback.

That was *so* out of line, but before I can backtrack, he slams the brush down, surrounding it with a halo splatter of paint on the plastic sheeting. He stands up and glares down at me. 'What I choose to do or not do is none of your business. *Who* I choose to do or not do is *also* none of your business. *Shit*.'

Shouldering past me, he goes straight out into the back-yard. I should follow him and apologize, but I doubt he wants to hear anything I have to say. Besides, I'm right about Gabrielle. She's young and she's star-struck. In no way are they on an equal playing field. I may think she's a little twerp, but that doesn't stop me from wanting to keep her from ending up emotionally damaged by a guy like Reid Alexander.

So much for that truce.

9

REID

REID

What the hell *is it* with this girl? No matter what I do, I can't catch a break from her non-stop condemnation.

Truth? That Gabrielle chick is hot, so in the interest of not being bored off my nut, I don't mind her flirting with me. I'd also be willing to bet she's no virgin. But virgin or not, she should be hooking up with some guy her own age, if that's what she wants, not some guy who's well past eighteen. And since I'm not a complete *idiot*, I don't need to be told that.

When I said that thing about taking her off the property, I was just pointing out the big fat hole in Dorcas's reasoning. Exhibit A: Gabrielle Diego is jailbait *anywhere*, not just 'on this property'. (Side effect of having a crack attorney for my paternal role model: if you're going to argue a point with me, don't leave gaps in your logic.)

I'm so pissed my hands are shaking. Usually this type of response follows a chat with my dad, after which I retreat to the basement to pound the shit out of a hundred-pound heavy bag. We've got an entire gym set-up down there; my trainer meets me several times a week when I'm not on location. Or performing compulsory community service.

The backyard is thickly populated, and of course, this is where Gabrielle was banished. Judging by the look on her face, she assumes I followed her outside. When she glances at me with a provocative smile, a boredom-exterminating scheme pops into my head. One that will drive Dorcas batshit crazy for the next three weeks.

Community service just got considerably more interesting.

Dori

I'll give him ten minutes to throw his temper tantrum before I bring him back inside. He needs to understand that messing around with Gabrielle is unacceptable. I would march outside and say it just like that, but he's evidently taking anything I say as a dare, which is the last thing I want.

Finally, I settle on apologizing to him for the *better person* comment – I still can't believe I said that – and discussing my anxiety concerning Gabrielle with Roberta, privately. Hopefully she can keep an eye on the situation. Without me involved, he won't feel goaded to do something everyone would regret.

The backyard is teeming with volunteers because we got a shipment of trees and shrubs yesterday, which should be transplanted from containers to ground promptly. It doesn't take long to locate Reid because every woman in the yard and most of the men are watching him. Much as I'd like to,

I can't blame them. The sight of him is simply compelling.

While digging a hole for one of the three thirty-gallon live oaks that will line the back fence and provide shade for the yard, he's stripped off his t-shirt. Hard lines of definition ripple across his back and shoulders as he plunges the shovel into the ground, heaving mounds of earth out and piling it to the side. His jeans ride low on his hips, showing off his enviable movie-star abs. Muscles flexing and contracting, it's clear that what he's doing is strenuous, yet he doesn't slow or tire when other volunteers take wheezing breaks for water.

Looks like I'll be finishing the cabinets myself.

Before I turn to go back inside, I spot Gabrielle standing a few feet from Reid. After tossing one contemptuous look my way, she flips her glossy black hair over her shoulder and turns back to watch him. Though she's only two years younger than me, it feels like a lifetime of difference. Testing her sexuality, she thinks she's caught a beautiful fish, when in reality, she's netted a shark. As soon as she gets too close, he could snap through the fragile filaments and consume her.

I want to trust Reid not to be what I fear he is, but I know better. There's not a trustworthy bone in that impeccably muscled body.

10

REID

I haven't seen Dori since I left her standing in the bathroom with her mouth hanging open. I wanted some privacy to get my shit together after that exchange, but with a yard full of people, solitude wasn't an option. So I did the next best thing – I grabbed a shovel and dug a big fucking hole.

By lunch break, we've planted three trees and half the shrubs. Dori materializes outside, talking with some tool I haven't seen before today. They load their paper plates and she takes the lawn chair next to him, eating her burger while he talks. He seems unfamiliar with a basic principle of conversation: *reciprocal speaking*. Despite this, she seems engrossed in his monologue. Either that or she's too polite to be real with people other than myself.

Gabrielle is literally sitting at my feet in the still-patchy new sod. I don't have to do anything to keep her enthralled outside of an occasional smile. She's jabbering about her modelling and acting aspirations, her loathing of school and her immature classmates, and what kind of car her older ex-boyfriend drove. (A Mustang? Please.) I think this last is an attempt to illustrate her experience with boys. And/or fast cars.

'The car you had was a Porsche, right?' She flutters her lashes as though this isn't a peculiar subject for her to bring up, or for us to discuss.

'Um, yeah. *Had* being the operative word.'

Her eyes widen. 'I guess you're pretty pissed it got wrecked, huh?' As though my car wrecked itself.

'You could say that.'

She lays her hand on my knee. 'Aw, I'm really sorry, Reid.'

I can't help but chuckle. This is the most awkward exchange ever. 'You're sorry . . . that I drove my Porsche into your house?'

'It's not like you did it on purpose.'

I laugh out loud and smile down at her, 'Well, that's true. I wish *you'd* been the judge in my case.' She beams up at me.

I hazard a glance at Dori, who's staring daggers at me. I swear if we were within striking distance and she had a *plastic fork* in her hand, I'd be concerned. Instead of returning her heated expression, I keep the grin affixed to my face and add a sardonic air to it – one eyebrow arched, indifferent eyes. This look has been refined to perfection over many years with Dad. Sends him through the goddamned roof. Does it work on Dorcas?

Oh, yes. Yes, it does.

I can hear the guy next to her saying, 'Uh, Dori? Did you hear what I –' just before she leaps up and charges inside without answering him. From the look on his face, this is uncharacteristic behaviour for her.

I think I'll spend the last couple of hours planting shrubs, and get Frank to sign my sheet. No sense in pushing her too far this afternoon. I have two and a half weeks to harass her to the edge of insanity.

Dori

'I understand your concern, Dori, but I don't think he'll actually *do* anything . . .' Roberta's sentence trails off indecisively.

It's up to me to convince her. 'I'd be less concerned if Gabrielle was assigned to work with someone who'll keep a better eye on her, that's all.' I feel like I'm tattling. Having just told the project director that I suspect an adult volunteer of socializing too warmly with a juvenile volunteer, I guess I *am* tattling. 'Just to be safe,' I add.

She taps her pen on her clipboard, gnawing her lower lip. 'Well, the least confrontational thing might be to reassign Gabrielle to *you*, and reassign Reid to Frank.'

A puzzling sense of disappointment settles over me, but I shake it off. 'That works for me.'

'Gabrielle doesn't come in on Fridays, so I'll leave Reid with you tomorrow, and I'll talk to him about moving to Frank's crew next week before he leaves for the day. We'll get Gabrielle situated on Monday.'

'Thanks, Roberta.'

'Yes, well, better safe than sorry, I suppose.' She bustles off as I clean up for the day and prepare for tomorrow. Reid is going to be furious at the interference, and Gabrielle will probably have a meltdown when she isn't allowed to hang around him. There's no way for her to see that we're trying to protect her; the separation will look like pure malice from her point of view.

My last day to supervise Reid has been almost stress-free. He showed up on time and made no comments or snide remarks (other than calling me Dorcas all day, and what can I say to that since it *is* my name). He was a model volunteer. He even kept his shirt on.

My iPod fried itself last night, so I brought a radio this morning and had it tuned to a pop station when he came in. I told him he could change it to whatever he wanted, but he hasn't moved the station. As we're wrapping up for the day, the DJ plays a new duet. Without realizing it, I hum along. At the end chorus, Reid turns to me and sings into his paintbrush, 'Where were you, baby, where were you? When I was all alone, with no one of my own?'

I sing back, 'Where were you, baby, where were you? When I needed you there, when nobody else cared?'

'I was here, I was right here, looking for you, yeah . . .' we both sing, and then we laugh at our own goofiness.

'You have a great voice,' he says, but not like he's surprised.

I lower my glance and mumble, 'Thanks,' oddly pleased. Coming from him, the words feel different, as though I haven't heard that exact expression of praise a hundred times before.

From the doorway, Roberta says, 'Mr Alexander, could you see me before you leave? I'll be in the kitchen, checking the sink hook-ups.'

'No problem.' Sliding his eyes back to me when she disappears, his head tilts a fraction to the side and he asks, 'What's that about?'

Uh-oh. With Gabrielle gone all day, I almost forgot about her and the supervisor swap occurring on Monday. 'Um, something about work assignments. Probably.'

'Work assignments? I thought you were the boss of me.' His smile is tentative, like he's teasing me, but also testing to see if there's something I'm not telling him.

Coward that I am, I shrug and begin cleaning the paintbrushes, and Reid is silent for a moment before he hammers the lid on to a five-gallon bucket of paint and then places his folded timesheet on the floor next to me. 'I'll swing by to pick this up after I talk to Roberta.'

When he returns five minutes later, I brace myself for an offensive comment or another quarrel over my unwelcome judgements or interference, but neither occurs. He snatches the paper I've signed without a word and leaves. As he storms out, I cringe, guilt-ridden after the illusory camaraderie in which we spent the day. At the inevitable slam of the front door, someone in the hall exclaims, 'Jesus!' and a moment later, I remember to breathe.

Monday is going to be a nightmare.

Nick is coming over tonight. After he showed up at the Diego house yesterday – a breath of fresh air in his non-designer jeans and thrift store t-shirt – I couldn't say no when he asked if we could hang out.

I hear his voice downstairs, his courteous, 'Good evening, Reverend Cantrell,' though Dad has urged him countless times to call him Doug.

As I leave my room, I glance at the clock on my wall. He's exactly on time, the minute hand clicking on to the twelve as my father intones, 'Good evening, Nicholas.'

Nick fails to hear the playful nature I immediately recognize behind Dad's words. 'It's actually just Nick, sir.' He spares a quick look in my direction as I reach the last step.

'And it's just Doug, Nick.' My father slaps his shoulder lightly.

'Do you want to go out?' Nick asks after Dad disappears back into his study. 'I think that movie starring your new associate is still out . . . *School Pride*, right? I heard it was . . . cute.'

Nick isn't into cute, and generally speaking, neither am I. I'd not even considered seeing *School Pride*, but now that Nick's mentioned it, I'm curious. I know Reid Alexander from his fame, but I know nothing of his so-called talent. I've never seen a single one of his movies – like Nick, I don't really term them *films*. A film is something socially consequential or historically evocative. A movie is hollow entertainment.

Oh my gosh. *I'm a film snob.*

Despite my sudden compulsion to see Reid's movie, there's no way I'm sitting through it with Nick. 'Let's order Chinese and watch something here. Dad just got a new batch of DVDs.' Nick smiles his agreement. Pulling the takeout menu from our menu drawer and grabbing the phone, I determine not to think of Reid again tonight. 'I'm getting sesame chicken. Anything with chicken is pretty good. Their beef dishes, not so much.'

When the food arrives, Dad materializes momentarily.

'Would you like to watch the movie with us, Rever– uh, Doug?' Nick asks.

Dad sighs and shakes his head. 'This week's sermon is being a *butt*. I'm determined to wrestle a few inspiring concepts down.' Grabbing a diet soda, his carton of fried rice and a pair of chopsticks, he adds, 'I won't be leaving the study until your mother comes home.' Then he winks at me, as though Nick and I plan to canoodle on the sofa (a Dad term more fitting for his parents' generation than his own). Mom's shift ends at midnight.

I'm never sure if Dad just has absolute confidence that I'd never do anything wicked, or if he actually thinks I should loosen up. I hope it's not the latter because if I'm the girl whose pastor father thinks she's too uptight, that would be pretty darned depressing.

Nick takes the centre of the sofa while I nestle into the corner, legs pretzelled. His elbow rests lightly on my bent knee in between bites. Everyone in my family tends to comment throughout anything we watch, but Nick never talks during films. It's a sure bet I'll end up biting my tongue figuratively or literally at least half a dozen times. Finally, the credits roll.

'That was less clever than the reviews promised,' he observes, clicking the remote. His hand rests lightly on my knee, a non-insistent pressure not easily read. The world has gone dark outside, the room dim in the solitary lamplight without the glow of the screen. 'Your house is always so quiet. Mine is the exact opposite – thinly contained chaos.'

Nick is an only child, but his parents take in special needs foster children and train service dogs, and his house is in an almost constant uproar. I've wondered but never had the nerve to ask if he ever yearned for the individual attention he would have been due as an only child, or if he felt neglected by his parents' dedicated care of other people's children.

My eyes find our elderly dog, curled on her pillowed bed across the room. 'That's true, Esther and I don't produce a lot of commotion.' Her ears perk at the sound of her name, black eyes blinking as she waits to see if I require her attention. Her whitened muzzle rests on her equally whitened paws.

Nick leans into my line of vision, pushing thoughts of Esther from my mind as he inclines his head and kisses me. His lips are warm and his kiss careful and gentle. I kiss him back, wishing he would deepen the kiss, that his hand would stroke my leg, or stray to my waist to pull me closer. None of these things occur. This is not our first kiss, but each one we've shared has been the same: *pleasant*.

He pulls away, smiling. I smile back, and tell myself I'm not disappointed.

Neither am I in danger of losing control. Which is good. Safe. And exactly what I need.

Esther huffs a soft doggie sigh from her pallet and closes her eyes. Nick, even with the multiple dog and people scents attached to him, is no risk to me.

11

REID

Dori doesn't trust me. I've got that much figured out. She clearly has no idea of what a guy in my position is offered on a daily basis. I could sleep with a different girl, or several, every night. There's always another one, ready to go. I've had offers – which I absolutely do not accept – from girls so young it makes me want to track down their parents and tell them they should be arrested for raising baby whores. Even when it comes to the ones who are borderline old enough, I won't do some chick who thinks she's all grown-up just because she's experienced.

I underestimated Dori's determination to keep the Diego girl away from me. Not only did she manage to get me moved outside with Frank permanently, she's now super-vising Gabrielle herself. I'm not sure what was expected from this arrangement, but I bet it wasn't the shit-fit that went down this morning when Gabrielle found out about it.

Allegedly, she picked up a hammer and *threw it*. Not at a person, but supposedly it narrowly missed a window and lodged itself in the drywall of the dining nook. I didn't witness this meltdown, but thanks to Frank being a gossip addict, everyone outside stays fully informed of every rumour inside or out. It's not unlike a mini movie set.

'Roberta threatened to call her mother and send her home if she didn't calm down, but Gabrielle still owes at least thirty hours.' Frank looks at me and shrugs. 'I had no idea that girl would miss working with me so much.'

'In your dreams, old man,' quips his wife, Darlene, who's loading bedding plants into a wheelbarrow. Her hair is entirely silver and longer than I've ever seen on a woman her age. It hangs in a fat braid down her back. 'Come on, kid, let's get these pansies in the ground.'

I realize she's talking to *me* when no one else moves.

By lunch I've learned how to plant pansies ('Not too deep! Not so close together!'), and the fact that Frank and Darlene retired five years ago, declared themselves bored stupid six months later and decided to design landscaping for Habitat homes instead of going on cruises and taking up crafts.

'What did Frank mean, about Gabrielle owing thirty hours?' I'm staring at my hands, which are filthy. I couldn't plant flowers with gloves on (earning, 'Noob,' from Darlene), so there are solid black lines of dirt under all ten fingernails. My manicurist is going to kill me.

'The families approved to get a house have to put in a few hundred hours of "sweat equity". Gabrielle's parents both work two jobs, and her brothers are too young to put in time.' She gives me a weird look. 'Up until last week, Gabrielle was totally uninterested in helping out.'

I follow her to the tap where she rinses off the hand tools we just used. When she doesn't elaborate, I roll my hand. 'And . . .'

'And then *you* became a . . . volunteer.'

Ah. 'So you think my presence, er, motivated her to participate.'

She nods, giving me that squinty, old-lady, I-see-through-you look. *Christ*. Has Dorcas alerted *everyone* that I'm preying on the under-age girl?

'Look, I'm *not* interested in Gabrielle. She's a *child*. I want nothing to do with her, okay?'

Several things happen at once. Darlene blinks, eyebrows rising, as she stares over my shoulder. In the same moment, I hear a strangled whimper and rapidly retreating footsteps.

Well, shit.

Dori

I knew Friday that I was in for it today with Gabrielle. I spent the whole weekend dreading it. Even so, I misjudged the level her outrage would reach at being separated from Reid. I should have known.

The *thunk* of the hammer hitting the wall was, oddly enough, the catalyst for calming her. I think it stunned her that she could do something so destructive and potentially deadly. Thank God no one was in the path of that airborne tool; the claw *imbedded* itself into the drywall. Roberta, Gabrielle and I stood there in shock for a full minute before

Roberta cleared her throat and asked, 'Maybe you're too upset to work today?'

Gabrielle's answer was a whisper delivered towards her feet. 'No.'

Roberta and I exchanged a look and I gave her a faint nod. 'All right, then. Follow Dori, and I'll see you at lunch break.'

Gabrielle and I spent the morning patching the damaged kitchenette drywall, followed by measuring, marking and drilling holes in every cabinet door in the whole house for the hardware we'll install this afternoon. My ears were ringing from the constant high whine of the drill in confined spaces.

Gabrielle hadn't uttered a single word during the entire three hours. 'Two more and then it's time for lunch,' I said, turning to find she wasn't in the room. I had no idea how long she'd been gone, but I had a good idea where I could find her.

'Rats,' I muttered, stalking towards the back door.

I forgot to take off the goggles or leave the battery-powered drill behind. Thank the stars I was carrying the darned thing business end down, because as I yanked the back door open, Gabrielle bulleted through it. I jumped back as she lurched past me, crying.

'Gabrielle?' The sound of my voice only speeded her up.

She shoved the front door open, throwing, 'Leave me *alone*!' over her shoulder. The engine on her twenty-year-old clunker thundered to life out front a few seconds later.

Reid.

As I stride on to the back patio, he turns from where he stands with Darlene at the faucet. 'What did you do to her?' I step closer and lower my voice when I notice the audience of people pretending not to listen. I don't care about embarrassing *him*, but Gabrielle's distress is no one else's business. 'What did you say to her?' I hiss.

His eyes travel the length of me, just as he did last week when we met, except today his gaze lingers on my legs, the drill clutched in my hand and the safety goggles still on my face. His answer is all lazy insolence. 'I don't know what you're talking about.'

Shoving the goggles on to my head, I raise my chin. 'I'm talking about Gabrielle, who just stormed through the house, very upset. Stop acting like you're oblivious, when we both know you're the one who caused it.'

He steps closer and looks down at me. 'I didn't do or say a damned thing to her.' He gestures towards Darlene without breaking our eye contact. 'And I have a rock-solid alibi, *Dorcas*.'

Darlene steps closer. 'Dori, calm down, hon. Gabrielle came outside and overheard something she misunderstood, that's all. She'll get over it.'

I am stunned speechless. I cannot *believe* this. He's managed to win over *Darlene*! Is there a woman in this *world*, besides me, who's immune to him? I turn and stomp back into the house without replying, which is incredibly rude of me and I'll have to apologize to her later.

I would dearly like to take a hammer to the drywall myself. It's too bad there's no demolition on this job because

75

I'd be a whirling dervish of destruction today. Gabrielle and I could team up and take down a house this size like twin tornadoes.

After lunch (during which Reid and I sit on opposite sides of the yard), I grab the ratchet screwdriver set, gather the handles, knobs and screws, and head for the master bathroom. I've resigned myself to working alone for the rest of the day, which is fine with me, but it's boring with no music. I forgot to bring the radio today, and my iPod, tragically, is unfixable. If I want music, I'll have to provide it for myself.

Starting with the under-sink cabinets, I line up the screws with a chrome hinge while balancing the door on my foot, and fit the ratchet to a screw and crank it, *click-click-click*. By the time I'm adding the chrome handle, I've got a slow, steady beat going and I'm singing a soft song called 'Gravity' by Alison Krauss. It's about a girl who leaves home and kind of never looks back because once she's gone, she realizes that life isn't as straightforward as she'd once thought.

When I stand up to grab another hinge and set of screws for the next door, Reid is standing in the doorway, his hands shoved into his pockets. My voice falters, but I finish the last line before going silent. I don't know how long he's been there. For a moment he doesn't say anything, and then his eyes shift to the cabinet doors stacked against the wall. 'Roberta sent me to help with the cabinets.'

I grab a door without replying and position it as I did the last one. Since the hinges will be placed on the opposite side from the last one, it won't be as easy to attach, but I know what I'm doing, and it's not an impossible job to do alone.

Aside from the fact that I'd rather do it without him standing there staring at me.

When he doesn't take the unspoken hint, I say, 'I don't need help.'

I expect him to turn and go, but he doesn't. Bracing his shoulder against the door jamb, he crosses his arms over his chest and watches me. I ignore him, balance the door, line up the hinge with the pre-drilled holes and attempt to twist the screws in partway by hand.

The first screw doesn't catch, pops out of the hinge and flies across the ceramic tile floor, stopping when it bumps against his boot. Without missing a beat, I grab another screw and repeat the process, with an identical result. 'Holy Moses,' I mutter, which earns a rude laugh from Reid as he leans to pick up the screws at his feet. He jingles them in his hand like Dad does with loose change.

'Any time you want me to hold something, or screw something, just let me know.'

Wonderful. A patented Reid Alexander double entendre.

Finally, the screws catch, and I offer up a silent prayer of thanks while wondering how much trouble I'd be in if I stood up and kicked him in the shin with my steel-toed boot. *Hard.*

12

REID

I think she seriously wants to strangle me right now. I haven't decided if that's how I want her to feel or not.

I watch her attach the third cabinet door – the one with the hinges on the right. She's left-handed, so it's easy enough for her. The last thing she wants is my assistance. I'm weighing the desire to keep her irritation level as high as possible against the suspicion that the longer I loiter in the doorway, the higher the likelihood she'll refuse to sign my timesheet at 3:00.

She sighs before lining up the hinges with the last door, and I imagine the words threading through her head as she pleads with the hardware to cooperate. The first time it begins to angle off course, I step up and take it from her, our fingers brushing. She jumps like my hand is fire, recovers quickly and begins twisting the screws in by hand. When they're in as far as they can go without the screwdriver's assistance, she picks up the tool and drives them in the rest of the way as I brace the door. She doesn't speak, and neither do I.

I hate that watching her handle that screwdriver is turning me on.

I hate that I'm waiting for an excuse to touch her again.

I hate that I narrowly resisted begging her to continue singing.

Following her to the next bathroom, I'm staring at the curved lines of her calves and the not-quite imperceptible sway of her hips (hidden under another oversized t-shirt – this one says D.A.R.E.). I get this sudden impression that she's psychic because I swear to God – her ears are darkening like she can read my mind. So I concentrate harder.

When she sets the tool on the counter, I pick it up. 'I'll do the next one,' I say when she turns and sees me holding it. 'You're supposed to be teaching me, right?' Her mouth snaps closed and she spins back round to select the door. There are only two doors to install in this microscopic bathroom that all three Diego kids will share. The entire *room* would fit inside my shower.

Two minutes later: I admit that I thought this whole working-with-tools thing would be easier than it is. Getting the damned screw to stay connected with the driver bit is a bitch. One interesting note, though – despite some of my more colourful curses, it's obvious Dori is enjoying the fact that I don't have the innate ability to wield a ratchet screwdriver with ease. Her smile is a little too smug for my liking.

'I guess I'm not a natural at *this* type of screwing,' I say, and my God, her face. I've just discovered the secret to spreading the blush *everywhere*.

*

'Okay, I don't get it. So . . . she's hot, or not?' John asks. We're hanging out on the terrace of his twenty-second-floor apartment on Olympic, lounging on Adirondack chairs, a cold six-pack on the glazed concrete between us. Downtown is alive and beckoning, but I've persuaded him, for the time being, to take a break for one night.

'It's hard to say,' I answer, and he shoots me a confused look, tipping back the bottle in his hand as I stare out over the cityscape. For some reason, I mentioned something about Dori, and now I'd rather drop it.

'Tell me more about the apartment,' I say. For the past couple of weeks, John's been trying to convince me to rent the penthouse suite that's opening up a few floors above him. I told him I'd think about it, though I'm not sure I want to be that near John 24/7. He starts rattling off square footage and view and party possibilities while I'm trying not to answer his question in my head.

Dori Cantrell: hot or not?

She's nothing like my usual fare. Nothing at all.

But that doesn't exactly answer the question, does it?

Dori

'I miss you.' I try not to sound like I'm pouting, but I feel Deb's absence more than I ever have. 'You're so far away now.' Technically, she's been gone for eight years, but she did her pre-med undergrad and med school close to home. Now she's in a different time zone, and the hours she keeps are impossible to figure out. Working a mind-numbing eighty hours a week at the hospital, she has no consistent schedule. Texting or calling me whenever she has five minutes has become the norm, if she isn't spending that five minutes eating or sleeping.

'I know, baby girl.' She sounds exhausted and I feel contrite for sulking. 'I miss you too.'

'How's, um, Bradford?'

She's quiet for a moment, and I read the silence between us. 'Dori, can you keep a secret?'

'Psshh,' I say. 'You know I'm the ultimate secret-keeper.'

I savour the sound of her warm chuckle in my ear. 'True. Well . . . we had sort of a date Sunday night. I mean, it wasn't a date, really . . . he just shared his takeout with me when I had ten minutes for dinner.'

'Isn't he sort of one of your bosses?'

'He's not evaluating me – the one time we interacted was because he was stepping in for someone else . . .' The way her words trail off, she's either falling asleep on me, or she's thinking about what she isn't telling me. 'So, um, how's the Habitat place going?'

'I'm counting the days until I'm gone.' I'm thinking to myself *Deb and Bradford, sittin' in a tree* . . . but I resolve to let her tell me about him at her own pace. We've never hidden anything from each other indefinitely.

'Reid Alexander still being a jackhole?'

'Yeah, you could say that.'

'You'll be in Ecuador soon. By the time you return, his community service will be over, and you'll never have to see or work with him again.'

'Yeah.' I'm not disappointed at the thought of his absence. I'm not. He does nothing, says nothing unless it's calculated to make me uncomfortable.

'Hmm,' Deb says, a subtle challenge before I change the subject to college concerns like dorm life and how to dodge the freshmen fifteen.

13

REID

I was wondering when an uninvited film crew was going to show up. I'm actually surprised it took them this long.

Paparazzi, as careless as they appear, know better than to trespass on personal property. But the Habitat property is tiny, and telescopic lenses are standard for these guys. Camped out in adjacent yards, the shrewd ones undoubtedly paid the neighbours off to get closer. This is the sort of thing George would term 'free positive PR' – an occurrence that I, apparently, can't get too much of. The only hitch is the fact that I have to be here the rest of this week plus two more; this situation could morph into insanity central if it isn't managed.

Stripping the heavy work gloves off as I go, I wander inside to find Roberta. She's talking to the general contractor about what grade of insulation to use in the attic. I could fall asleep from extreme disinterest any minute. Luckily, they finish up in a minute or so and she turns to me warily. 'Yes, um, Reid?'

'I just wanted to let you know that there are photogs out there – paparazzi – not *on* the property, but as close as they can legally get. With me outside, it's gonna be a zoo. Thought I should warn you.'

'Oh.' She's immediately flustered; obviously this is something new for her. She moves to a rear window. 'They're out there now?'

'Yeah.'

Peering out, she narrows her eyes, scanning, and then gasps softly. 'What in the world? There's someone balancing on top of a swing set . . . and on the *roof* next door!'

I shrug.

'What should we do? I guess I should have considered this probability . . .'

'They're not going anywhere, now that they know where I am. I already called my manager. He's sending bodyguards to make sure they keep their distance from me, and he's alerting the police to make sure they respect property boundaries.'

'The police? Oh, dear.'

Roberta continues to stare at the guy on the roof next door while I push off from the counter and head back outside, pulling the work gloves on. Frank says we're demolishing an old fence at the back of the property – so termite-ridden that one good kick could turn it into a cloud of splinters. Painting walls was tedious. Tearing shit down? Not.

Predictably, the photogs wake up when I exit the back door. Some of them try calling to me, like I'm walking the red carpet or something, which pisses me off.

I'm *working*. Can't they see that?

Dori

As I fell asleep last night, I considered telling Roberta to finish this job without me. I miss my Vacation Bible School kids and their joyful, artless voices practising the choral arrangements. I miss singing along with them. I miss baby-sitting people who are immature because they're *five*, not because they're arrogant buttheads. Most of all, I miss being unacquainted with Reid Alexander.

Just when I think to myself *what next*, it turns out I shouldn't have wondered. Of *course* the paparazzi would show up. There's an A-list celebrity on the premises.

Pressed against the living room wall like a ninja assassin, I peek out the window. Reid continues to work, paying no attention to the photographers, who are simply *everywhere*. They remind me of a nature special about army ants that I watched in a state of unmoving horror when I was six. Devouring everything in their collective path, ants swarmed across the landscape in a bold undulating line of black. I couldn't sleep for a week, until Deb convinced me that African army ants weren't generally known to raid urban California.

Exhausted after a night of tossing and turning, I consider whether or not I'm hungry enough to risk appearing in even the outer fringes of those photos. This is ridiculous. Several hours stand between me and my next meal. I shouldn't feel the need to skulk around inside because of some silly photographers. Besides, they aren't interested in *me*.

The Plan: go out, grab something to eat, dash back inside.

Minutes later, I'm skirting the crowd with a bowl of fruit

and an iced tea when one of our corporate volunteers veers directly towards me, ogling the photographers gathered on the neighbour's roof. Realizing too late that she doesn't see me, I scoot as close to the patio edge as possible. As she passes, our sleeves grazing, I exhale in relief. And then she whips round and accidentally elbows me right off the patio's four-foot no-railing-installed-yet drop.

Everything is slow-motion. Eyes widening, mouth rounding into a shocked 'O', she grabs for me as I lurch over the edge, backwards. She catches nothing but air, and neither do I. The bowl flies up, chunks of fruit tossed in every direction. The tea levitates from the cup in an arc above me. And though I know I've generated a squeak of surprise, I can't hear anything – it's as though the world has been muted.

If you've never fallen and been caught by someone before, I am here to tell you that the landing is not as smooth and effortless as Hollywood portrays it to be. In reality, parts land where they land, and though hitting a human body is probably less painful than hitting the ground, it's not like landing on a sofa or a trampoline or anything that *gives*.

My limbs still flailing uselessly, my head slams against a shoulder and I knee myself in the chin as the body I've tumbled on to goes down under me. 'Oof,' he says as he hits the ground, my elbow jabbing into his abdomen as he absorbs my entire body weight.

I don't have to see his face – I know the voice – but I can't help looking. With a yard full of people looking on, plus several yards full of photographers, I'm lying halfway on top of Reid, who is sprawled on the ground, holding me tightly, blinking as the blue sky rains fruit on top of us.

Camera shutters whir and snap in the distance. And to think I feared being in the peripheral background of a photo taken of him.

I scramble to roll off him, and he releases me slowly enough that I'm pulling against his hold for a couple of seconds, until he realizes we're not actually falling any more. My iced tea has splashed a swathe across both of our white t-shirts, and pieces of pineapple, cantaloupe and various berries tumble from our clothes and hair as we move to sit upright.

People who a moment ago were all frozen, agog, are rushing towards us, asking if we're okay, helping us to our feet.

Mortified, I stare down at my soggy, fruit-laden outfit. My legs are wet too – rivulets of iced tea dripping from my shorts and snaking down my bare skin. I can't look directly at Reid. 'I'm so sorry,' I say in his general direction before mumbling, 'I need to go clean up,' in answer to offers of assistance from half a dozen people.

Grabbing a stack of napkins, I walk inside, fighting the urge to run. The bathroom plumbing has been hooked up, thank God, though mirrors haven't been hung yet. After mopping the tea from my legs, I press a damp napkin into the shirt where the tea has stained it, though it's a hopeless gesture. Running my fingers over my head, I pluck out bits of fruit, struggling not to picture what might get into the gossip rags or, oh golly, on the *internet* tomorrow:

Unbalanced Fan Tackles Heart-throb, see page 2.
Clumsy Girl Falls for Reid Alexander – Click Here for Photos!

Good grief.

'You missed some cantaloupe.' Reid stops me from turning, one hand on my shoulder, his fingers in my hair, plucking a thin slice of orange melon from my ponytail. 'It could be worse, you know.'

'Oh?' I'm sure he's correct, but at the moment, I can't imagine how.

'Sure. Spaghetti and meatballs would be worse. Chocolate milk. Sangria. That stuff stains anything, trust me.' He dislodges a blueberry from my shoulder and it lands in the sink, rolling, leaving a purple trail. I make a mental note to get some bleach-containing cleaner from Roberta to scour the sink so it won't discolour the white porcelain.

Picturing myself covered in spaghetti, I turn and face him without even a hint of a smile. 'We don't usually serve pasta. Or sangria.'

'I guess you're safe from tomato sauce and red wine stains, then.' His expression is serious, but his eyes dance.

'Yes.'

'Hey, make sure I don't have any stray fruit in my hair, will you?' He angles the top of his head towards me. 'I ran my hands over it, but I think I missed some.'

'I don't see anything . . . oh, wait. There are a few strawberry bits.' I try to remove the squishy stuff without actually touching his head, which proves impossible. Strawberry seeds are tangled along a strand a few inches over, and I give up and comb my fingers across his scalp, checking for concealed fruit.

'Mmm,' he says, as though he likes my hands in his hair,

which is softer than I would have imagined. The bathroom suddenly feels very small.

I drop the berries and seeds next to the one he flicked into the sink. 'I don't see any more . . .'

He lifts his head, his eyes still playful, and I have no idea what he's doing until he does it. At first I think he's spied another piece of fruit in my hair, so I don't react right away when he lifts his hand. The wall is only a foot or so behind me, and it takes little effort for him to push me to it, one hand cradling the back of my head and the other skimming my hip as he leans down. Something in my brain sparks awake and I jerk my face to the side as his mouth grazes the outer edge of my jaw. My hands come up to his chest and shove him. 'Reid, *no*.'

He backs up immediately, hands up and out. Smirking, one corner of his mouth turns up and he shrugs. 'Sorry. Won't happen again. Just, you know, curious.'

'About *what*?' My voice is somehow steady, when I'm anything but. He almost kissed me. *He almost kissed me*.

He shrugs a second time, which makes me want to punch him. He's so *whatever*. 'I didn't mean anything. Seriously. Won't happen again.'

There's no responsibility to accept because everything just *happens* around him, as though he's at the eye of a storm he has nothing to do with causing or sustaining. I shove past him, my heart hammering. He barely touched me, and he stopped the second I protested. He said it wouldn't happen again. Twice, in fact.

People glance up as I pass, ask if I'm okay, and I fix a fake smile on my face, tell them I'm fine, even while I feel like I might hyperventilate. *Why?* Because he's a rich celebrity? Hardly. Because he's beautiful? Because of his casual arrogance – that intangible thing he exudes that some women find so irresistible? No, and *no*.

Okay. Then *why?*

Because everything I wanted to feel when Nick kissed me last Friday, I felt in the near-miss that just occurred.

14

REID

Shit. Well, *that* was stupid.

On the other hand, what the hell? I haven't been shoved away that decidedly in a while. If ever. I'm getting, like, Stockholm syndrome or something, and Dorcas is my jailer. That's why I tried to kiss her, obviously. I need out of this situation as soon as possible.

Maybe I should have let her hit the ground, but when I saw that woman knock her off the patio, I just reacted. It wasn't the most graceful fall or the most adept catch in the history of accidental dismounts. The consequences: my shoulder is bruised and one elbow is scraped raw, my abdominal muscles narrowly managed to withstand rupture and I discovered – inadvertently, I swear – that Dorcas Cantrell is concealing some noteworthy curves under her collection of enormous, altruistic t-shirts.

Once I'm in the car, I call George – again. 'Reid?' He's surprised to hear from me within hours of the previous call.

'Yeah, just an FYI on some photos that are probably being

uploaded as we speak – a girl at the house sorta fell off the patio, and I sorta caught her.'

'*Fell* off the patio?'

'Someone ran into her. Knocked her right off.'

'Jesus.'

'No, some inattentive middle-aged woman.'

He ignores my quip. 'So this girl you sorta caught – she's not under age, married, an illegal alien, a meth dealer . . .?'

I laugh. 'Eighteen, single and straight as the road to hell.'

'Um-hmm. Anything else I should know?' He hangs the question out there as he always does, no leading statements, no fishing for details. One of the many things I love about George. I trust him more than pretty much anyone and he knows it. He knows, too, that I'll be upfront with him, even if I seldom follow his good advice.

'Nothing anyone would be privy to. She's not interested in me, man.'

Outside the car window, East LA flies by, everything worn out, decrepit – the buildings, the sidewalks, even some of the light poles leaning – weary of the dismal setting. A guy with massive tattooed biceps steers his wheelchair round a fire hydrant that might or might not work if needed to put out a fire. Inches from the kerb, he whips round the hydrant like it's part of some serpentine course for wheelchair racing. If he misses a hairpin turn, he'll be in the street and run over. Extreme sports, disability-style.

'Oh?'

I'm flattered by George's disbelief. 'Yeah, she's a genuine do-gooder.'

'Ah, I heard we had one of those in LA.' George is a funny guy. 'I guess it would be too much to ask that you leave her as you found her.'

Minutes ago I was impatient to be finished with this Habitat gig – and Dori. Telling myself that this too shall pass. George's allusion to the end of my association with Dorcas Cantrell, or rather my reaction to his allusion, tells me I wasn't fully connecting those two things. I'm surprised to find that I'm not ready for this to be over.

George sighs. 'Oh, well, the suggestion was worth a shot.'

I tell him what I always tell him – and it's the truth, for what it's worth. 'Thanks for the advice, man. I'll consider it.'

'Mm-hmm.'

Dori

I'm. Such. A. *Chicken*.

I woke up at 3 a.m. last night, dreaming about him. In the dream, I didn't turn my head away. His mouth landed on mine rather than grazing my jaw. My hands pulled him closer rather than pushing him away. And instead of backing away with a mocking grin, he moved closer, pressing me to the wall in a kiss that went on and on until I woke with a start, breathless.

Esther raised her head from the end of my bed as I sat up, her ears lifting in a canine question and her head angling when I pounded the bed with one fist and whispered, 'Son. Of. A. *Biscuit*.' I touched my lips, half expecting them to be swollen because they were tingling, and then threw the covers off and stomped to the kitchen to make a cup of chamomile tea. Esther jumped down and followed out of either curiosity or solidarity.

I called Roberta early this morning and told her they needed me at VBS and I couldn't report for Habitat duty the rest of the week. It wasn't exactly a lie. It wasn't exactly the truth, either, so I find myself clinging to the uncomfortable grey zone in the centre. She was great – all *no problem* and *of course those kids miss you*, and I felt ashamed until I thought about Reid and that almost-kiss. I need a break from this temptation because that's all it is for me. Temptation. For him, it's nothing more than gaining the upper hand, and I'm not about to let him do it.

I'm supervising pool time and thinking about what we have left to do at the Diego house when I catch myself daydreaming about him again, as though all thought patterns eventually lead to Reid. The earthy smell of him in that enclosed space. The contradiction of him shoving me to the wall with one firm hand while cradling the back of my head with the other. The deep blue of his eyes right before he dipped his head closer. Right before I pushed him away.

With effort, I force my thoughts to the kids and their impending performance, Deb and the challenges of residency, my college checklist, Nick. Dad's waterproof watch on my wrist will beep when it's time to go inside. If I could get it to zap me when my thoughts wander to Reid, I'd be golden.

Forcing him from my mind isn't working so well. I think I need an exorcism.

When I'm finished for the day, I scroll through my texts. A couple are from Aimee and Kayla, friends from school I've only seen twice since graduation. The two of them have been BFFs since junior high. They allowed me within the circle of their friendship during the first month of tenth grade. I've never been as close to either of them as they are to each other, but that's okay. Neither of them has a sister like Deb.

> **Aimee:** So when were you gonna tell us about REID ALEXANDER???
> **Kayla:** Srsly, there are pics all over the internet of you two at that habitat place and you are full frontal ON TOP OF HIM

I call Aimee, knowing there's a ninety-nine per cent chance she's with Kayla after their coordinated texts. At school, everyone called them the twins because they did *everything* together. They took the same classes, joined the same groups, dated boys who were friends – or brothers. In a few weeks, they're starting at UCLA. Rooming together, of course.

'Dori!' Kayla answers Aimee's phone. 'Are you *friends* with Reid Alexander? Are you *more* than friends? Ohmigod, the parties we could get into . . . you *will* take me and Aimee, *right*?'

'We aren't actually friends, and we're certainly not more than friends.'

'But that picture! You're stretched across him like he's *wearing* you!'

Ugh, I can't believe she just said that. Can the photos be *that* bad?

The phone jostles and Aimee's hyper no-punctuation voice takes over. 'Dori I know you don't really trust guys and Reid Alexander is the last guy on the planet to trust but honestly this is not a trust or not trust sort of moment this is a once in a lifetime sort of moment!'

I don't trust guys? What?

I sigh, knowing they would strangle me with their bare, perfectly manicured hands if they knew what happened in private a few minutes *after* I landed on top of Reid yesterday. 'You guys know how the press manipulates things to look a certain way . . .'

'Dori need I repeat myself you were *on top of him*! Unless you are suggesting *superb* photoshopping that was not press manipulation.'

Wow. This is not good. 'I fell. He caught me. That's all that happened.'

She sighs, as though I've just confirmed a passionate affair. 'That's what the stories are saying – that you tripped off the edge of the patio – freaking *brilliant* by the way! And then he caught you. So romantic . . .'

My head still feels bruised, my knee is abraded and I'm pretty sure I got felt up when we were going down, even if Reid wasn't aware of doing it . . . not exactly my idea of romantic.

'Dori.' Kayla has taken the phone back. 'You honestly aren't friends with him?'

'No, I'm really not.'

'Well, crap.' I hear Aimee saying something in the background, and then Kayla's voice returns. 'Could you *make* friends with him?'

I can't help laughing. Aimee and I grew up with Hollywood down the street, and Kayla moved here when she was a kid. We should all be a little less easily star-struck. 'I'm not even going to be there again until next week, and I leave for Ecuador the week after that. Besides, he's a big-headed celebrity. He's not interested in ordinary girls.'

'Humph.' Her tone is sullen. 'I guess we'll just have to look forward to regular college boys, then.'

This is particularly funny, considering the fact that I've listened to the two of them wax poetic about college guys for the past three years solid.

15

REID

The paparazzi swarm has ballooned. George is fielding hourly calls from journalists proposing in-depth, exclusive, one-on-one reporting of my rehabilitation. We both know they're far more interested in digging up juicy info about my possible hook-up with a member of the peasantry.

I wasn't shocked when Dori didn't show up yesterday, between our little interface in the bathroom and the fact that my fansites were going crazy over photos of the two of us looking like we're making out in the backyard. I'm accustomed to groundless rumours and misinterpreted photos. You have to laugh that shit off or you could end up in handcuffs after decking some asshole photographer or stalker weirdo . . . or turn into a recluse, hiding from public scrutiny.

Still, I was sure Dori would bounce in today, sporting a t-shirt proclaiming her loathing of some vice I've revelled in at one time or another, if not on a regular basis. But Roberta just told me she won't be back until next week.

'Was she that shaken up by all the photos online . . .?' I gesture vaguely to the surrounding yards full of photographers after grabbing a bottle of water from the cooler. What I don't say: *Or was it the attempted kiss that freaked her the hell out?*

'Oh, I don't think so.' Roberta frowns, uncertain. 'She's working with her church's VBS programme, and they needed her this week.'

'VBS?'

Roberta looks at me like I'm an alien because I don't recognize the acronym. 'Vacation Bible School?' she prompts.

No help. Those three words don't go together in any way in my experience. 'So what's she doing there that's so important?' I twist the cap off the bottle and drink as we move towards the line for lunch.

'Actually, she co-wrote the musical portion of the Parents' Night performance with the music director, and she's in charge of the kindergarten performance.' Roberta's obviously proud of this accomplishment, but it's out of my sphere. Church musical performances are the lowest form of community theatre imaginable. Directing a religious musical performance for five-year-olds? Kill me first.

'Wow. That's awesome.' (Seriously. Kill me first.)

'Hi, Reid.'

Ah, Gabrielle. Just the distraction I need. 'Sitting with me today?' I say, smiling down at her. She must have forgiven me for that comment about wanting nothing to do with her.

Gabrielle tosses a look of defiance at Roberta before

smiling and poking me in the chest. 'Duh, that's why I came over here.'

Roberta purses her lips, wracking her brain to come up with a reason why the two of us can't fraternize at lunch. When she comes up blank, I pretend not to notice.

Dori

Three days with no Reid, and I am so *not* conquering that temptation. I've alternated between wondering if he caused any trouble in my absence and wondering if he was disappointed that I wasn't there – if he noticed at all.

Tonight, in the privacy of my room, and in opposition to any good judgement I've ever thought I had, I google Reid Alexander. First up: the silly photos of the two of us, with me sprawled atop him like a linebacker sacking a quarterback. There's rampant speculation online about who I am, and whether or not I'm something more than just an uncoordinated girl from his volunteer site (I grit my teeth – *volunteer*, my eye). His fans are also debating what we're *doing* in the photo, but we had more than enough eyewitnesses, so really, the worst anyone could say is that I stupidly fell on him. Or, as Kayla and Aimee think, brilliantly fell on him.

The majority view is that I'm a plain, unattractive nobody – stated more harshly in most cases. I shrug it off because on one hand, I *am* a plain, unattractive nobody, and on the other hand, none of these people know me personally. They all base their verdicts on the same thing: what I look like in

relation to him. Their assessments are superficial and excessive. Pretty similar to their appraisals of him, actually – based
on little more than circumstantial evidence. (In his case,
circumstantially *appealing*.)

I ignore further editorials and fan comments and go
straight for the images link because image is what Reid
Alexander is all about. His beautiful face. His lean, muscular body. The blatant sex appeal that wells up from that
inner confidence and projects itself to the camera. I click on
a cache of photos from a year-old *GQ* spread. He graces
the cover shot and several out-takes in a dark pinstripe suit
which was, I'm sure, precisely tailored for him and insanely
expensive. He wears nothing but jeans in several shots, low
enough to show off his chiselled abs. His chest and arms are
defined and flawless without the aid of computer graphics,
as I know from multiple close-range shirtless encounters.

I click the arrow and the next photo appears – a mesmer-
izing close-up. My stomach drops and I exhale a dazed, 'Oh.'
Wearing a black tank top, he grasps a tree branch angled
just overhead. In the other shots, his expression is expertly
arrogant – identical to his standard, now familiar veneer.
But this one is the opposite. Open. Affectionate. Sensitive.

I snap my laptop closed.

Googling him was a very bad idea.

16

REID

I'm supposed to start filming in less than two months. Since I locked up the lead role by convincing the production team and the director that I could beef up *and* do the stunts, I can't just be in decent shape. I have to be in prime form. My personal trainer commences the torture sessions tomorrow morning, so tonight ends early.

Which sucks because I'm out with my friend Tadd, a co-star from *School Pride*, and he's going back home to Chicago tomorrow. We meet for dinner and end up at the bar in his hotel after.

'Seen anyone since May?' he asks once the waitress, who's trying her damnedest to act like she doesn't know who the two of us are, leaves our drinks.

'Partied with Quinton once, and ran into Jenna at an awards show last month. She's looking pretty hot.'

Tadd pauses, his dirty Martini halfway to his lips. 'Dude, Jenna's like sixteen.'

'God, what the hell is it with everyone and the under-age

girl alert? I'm *aware*, okay?' I sigh, running a hand through my hair and reining in my temper. In light of the whole Gabrielle–Dori issue, I may be overreacting a bit.

'Chill, dude – I'm not accusing you of anything.' Tadd leans forward, elbows on the table. 'I know you're smarter than that.' He smirks. 'As much of an asstard as you are in other matters.'

I laugh and shake my head. 'Emma, right?'

'I was referring to the fact that you wrecked your car and almost killed yourself . . . but yeah, man, you screwed up your love life too.'

We're silent for a minute, and I know he's waiting for me to ask what he knows I'm going to ask. 'Have you seen her?'

He leans back, gives me a once-over like he's gauging how much I can take. 'We got together a couple of weeks ago in New York. She's starting NYU in a few weeks, but she moved there last month. She and Graham, uh, didn't want to be apart all summer.'

I imagine the two of them together, waiting to feel wounded, but it's not really there. 'So that whole thing is working out, I guess.'

'So far, yeah.' Tadd takes a sip of the Martini, checking my reaction through the pale fringe of hair hanging perpetually over his right eye. 'I met up with both of them, actually. They seem comfortable – like they *fit*, you know? I can shut up now.'

I shrug and shake my head. 'No. I'm glad she's happy.' Surprisingly, I realize I mean it. 'So what about you, lover boy? Getting any from a regular source, or still breaking hearts and balls all over the country?'

Tadd leans forward again, his face earnest. 'Dude, I met someone a month ago, and I'm so in love it's not even funny. I'm like head over heels, first time ever. It's *sick*.'

'All right, Thaddeus.' I put up my fist and he bumps it with his, beaming. 'So who is he?' I lean forward. 'Are you about to out somebody? 'Cause if so, you know you can trust me.'

'Nah, he's an architect. So damned smart it blows my mind. Creative, gorgeous, funny, sexy . . .' He's lost in his own thoughts for a couple of seconds.

'Okay, okay, stop or I'm gonna have to consider going gay, man,' I say, and he laughs.

'Dude – it's all we can do to keep our hands off each other in public. It's always felt a little daring – all the covert stuff.' He shrugs. 'I've never felt like this before. I want to hold his hand when we're walking, or brush the hair out of his eyes when he's got coffee in one hand and the dog's leash in the other.' His mouth quirks up on one side again as he stares into his drink. 'It's different when you're in love.'

I think of all the things I take for granted. I could grab a stranger, kiss her in public and the worst anyone will think or say is *get a room*. Tadd's in love, but they can't hold hands in most public places without worrying what someone might do or say.

'Sucks to be you, man,' I say, and he makes like he's gonna punch me in the arm. I flinch and spill part of my drink on the table. 'Dude!'

We're both laughing when he says, 'So what about you? Anybody new?'

I shake my head. 'You don't even want to know.'

'Oh?' Both eyebrows angle up as he leans closer. 'Oh, yes I do. I *so* do. Lay it on me, man. Is it that girl from the Habitat place?'

Damned paparazzi. 'That was just a clumsy girl falling off a patio.'

Out of nowhere I remember the fruit falling from the sky, so surreal. The feel of her in my arms as I caught her. Her face flaming as she struggled to move off me. I almost made a smart-ass comment about her lack of grace, but she was already so humiliated that I couldn't do it. I followed her inside instead.

I don't know what I expected. I sure didn't expect to try to kiss her – that was completely spontaneous. When she ran her fingers across my scalp to search for stray bits of fruit, I had a sharp, three-second vision of her lying under me in my bed, her hands thrusting into my hair as I lean down to kiss her . . .

'Earth to Reid.' Tadd's voice is pure cynicism. I blink and look up and he shakes his head slowly. 'Oh, yeah. There's nothing going on *there*. Not at all.'

Busted. 'Yeah, well, she's not the slightest bit into me. I tried to kiss her and she objected in a *resounding* no-means-no sort of way. And then disappeared for the rest of the week.'

Tadd smiles and holds his drink aloft towards me. 'Here's to challenges, dude.'

My friend may have a point. Maybe Dori's just playing hard to get better than any girl I've ever met, and I've just got lazy.

Dori, one. Reid, zero.

But not for long.

Dori

Nick and I were planning to hang out tonight, but he'd forgotten his promise to watch his foster brothers while his parents take his foster sister to San Diego for a supervised visit with her birth mother. I assured him several times that I understood completely and was fine with the late cancellation.

Mom and Dad are out with friends. 'Well, Esther, it's just you and me tonight,' I tell her, scratching gently behind her floppy spaniel ears, which are the only spaniel components in her. The rest of her is a curious mix of – as far as we can tell – golden retriever, shepherd and possibly dachshund. She's a true mutt. 'Let's make sandwiches.' I pull ingredients out of the fridge and pantry, and roll slices of deli turkey for her. Her tail tick-tocks gently side to side as I set the plate in front of her. 'Need a pickle with that? No?' I ask as she gingerly lifts each roll and gobbles it down.

She lies next to me on the sofa (an Esther no-no she gets away with when we're alone) while I eat my pita sandwich and scroll through network TV options. Nothing looks interesting, so I browse the pay-per-view selections. I'm in the mood for something cute. No slashers, no thrillers, no buddy flicks. No historical drama or redemption-through-pain-and-or-suffering films. Especially nothing that says *profoundly moving* or *grab a hankie!* in the description.

'Here we go, Esther: "Trey begins his senior year at a new school with girls swooning for him, and jocks as friends. Things get complicated when he falls for quiet, bookish Amanda, who becomes a social pariah after she rats out the football players' cheating ring, half the first string fails English and the team loses the big championship game."'

Esther turns on her side and lays her head on my leg. 'I think we have a winner.' I click *buy*, press the play button and grab a handful of popcorn, thinking that I should be sad that Nick had to bail on me. That I didn't have time to make plans with anyone else. That I'm spending my Saturday night alone. But I'm fine. I'm more than fine.

The movie is everything I hoped for. Until about ten minutes in . . . when one of the random jocks turns out to be Reid. I gasp, and Esther raises her head sharply and looks at me, and then swivels around, looking for the unknown menace.

I should have looked up his filmography on IMDb last night. All I really know of him are his last two, more major roles. This movie is almost three years old.

His role is minor, and he spends most of his onscreen time in the background, but once I recognize him, I'm either watching him or waiting for him to show up again. The movie is an hour and fifty-seven minutes long, but it takes me nearly twice that to get all the way through it because I'm rewinding and replaying every moment he's onscreen.

In one party scene, several couples are in various states of making out. I spot Reid on the left side of the screen, sitting in a chair, kissing one of the cheerleader characters, who's straddling him. Their mouths are fused, but I watch his hands – gripping her arms, sliding down to the small of her back, holding her like he held me when I fell on him. I rewind the scene and watch it a third time.

'Oh, fudge,' I whisper, and Esther looks at me and sighs.

17

REID

Olaf is a beast.

I don't think my trainer expected me to still be in decent shape, though I told him I'd been working construction for Habitat. Not a fan of bodybuilding through natural means, he employs weights, pulleys, rubber bands and medicine balls to shape his clients. As far as Olaf is concerned, exercise is not painting, digging fence posts or swinging a sledgehammer to break up a 200-pound boulder. Exercise is done indoors, while a guy who could break you in two over his rock-hard quadriceps provides motivation like, 'What do you want to be when you grow up? A *girl*?'

I think I pissed him off, flaunting my organically maintained muscle tone. I should have feigned weakness. Once he saw that I was primed for what he had planned, he stepped up the pain factor by several notches in what I can only assume was an attempt to kill me, so he could resuscitate me and kill me again.

I went out with John last night – *not* the best idea after

a session with Olaf – and crashed on his sofa around 2 a.m. I hear him snoring from the bedroom, the sound on exhale a cross between the horn on a truck and a walrus's mating call. I have no idea what time it is, but judging by the light, it's not quite noon. Every muscle in my body is aching, my head is throbbing and I have no one to blame but myself. And possibly John because I can.

I shuffle into his kitchen to make coffee . . . but there isn't any. Awesome. There's also nothing in the fridge but beer, a mostly empty tub of margarine and questionable takeout boxes of sweet and sour chicken and beef with cashews. No milk. No juice. The pantry boasts a box of stale cereal and an equally stale bag of corn chips. The kitchen in this place is state-of-the-art, and this is all the food it has to offer? Sad.

Starving, I have no choice but to shower and go out in search of food. John and I are close enough to the same size that I can borrow a t-shirt and shorts, though ten to one there's something of mine in his closet that I can just reclaim.

There's a bagel place a few doors down from John's building. I want bagels and cream cheese, but Olaf is determined to pump up the muscle I've got and reduce me to near-zero per cent body fat. A compromise is in order – bagels and lox. Lox has protein, right?

Going out without a bodyguard or a car is always tricky. Fans in LA or NYC are much less likely to mob celebrities, but it's far from unheard of, and the paparazzi are always on the lookout. I grab my sunglasses and a hat (Lakers – pretty sure it's mine). Pulling the brim low, I take John's apartment key off the counter and head out.

Dori

I'm assisting with the coffee and doughnut distribution after Sunday school, waiting for the caffeine to kick in from the cup of coffee I gulped while setting up. The coffee isn't very good – but Mrs K gets it in bulk from a discount warehouse, along with powdered creamer, one-ply napkins and flimsy paper plates. High expectations would be unrealistic.

'No chocolate with chocolate sprinkles?' Mr Goody, the most ancient parishioner in the church, frowns at me over the bar where I stand, completely zoned out. His gaze swings over the several open boxes of various doughnuts.

'Um, no – what's out is what we've got. There are a couple of chocolate with nuts –'

'Nuts! Goodness, no!' He grabs a plain glazed, and glares at me like I suggested a pastry covered in slime.

'Humph.' Mrs Perez glares at his retreating back. 'Who doesn't like nuts?'

'Maybe he's allergic,' I offer.

'Allergic to *manners*.' She straightens the stack of tissue-thin napkins as I check my cell. My message light is blinking.

> **Kayla:** Me n aimee r goin to see school pride again. Wanna join? Come on, u know u wanna.

School Pride, Reid's latest blockbuster hit. My pulse stutters, stop-start-stop-start. After a five-day hiatus from Reid, my foolish little infatuation is *worse*. How is this possible?

I should definitely say no. The last thing I need to see is a movie in which Reid *stars*.

Me: Sure, come get me, i'll be home by 1

I sometimes think Dad can read my mind. In first grade, I was a *huge* Hello Kitty fan. One day Annabelle Hayes came to school with a tiny package of HK coloured pencils. During recess, I swiped it from her desk. That Sunday, Dad preached on two thou-shalt-nots: coveting and stealing. When I started bawling in the pew, Mom ushered me to the bathroom, thinking I was sick. Turned out I was a six-year-old with an easily assessed guilt complex.

Dad's sermon this morning – *temptation*. When his eyes meet mine, I imagine he knows every errant thought in my head concerning Reid. There's no way Dad could know, but there he stands, detailing how to identify temptation and how to resist it. Meaning to pay strict attention and take notes, I click my pen and open the small notebook I keep in my bag.

And then I can't stop thinking about Reid's hands in my hair and splayed at my waist, propelling me to the wall, his lips brushing over my cheek as I turned my face away.

There is no logical reason for my inability to stop

thinking about that almost-kiss. No reason at all. *Especially in the middle of church*.

The page in my notebook is still blank at the end of the sermon.

18

REID

Dori seemed surprised but appreciative the day I brought her a soy latte (after having heard her tell someone on the phone the previous afternoon that she was craving one), so I add it to my morning coffee run. Just to throw her off balance, I bring Gabrielle the same thing.

When I get there, the two of them are in Gabrielle's future bedroom, which we've painted a stomach-turning shade of pink. Ceiling fan parts are spread in an organized manner on the floor – nuts, bolts and fan blades in neat piles. Dori reads over the instructions while Gabrielle stands with her arms crossed, looking annoyed – until she sees me. 'Reid!' she beams.

For a split second, I wish Dori was that enthusiastic about my presence . . . but no, her unwavering pretence of indifference is a major aspect of the challenge of her. She doesn't look up, but she's so aware of me – hands gripping the instruction packet tightly enough to crumple the edges, ears almost matching the walls.

Taking my caramel macchiato from the tray, I choke back

a laugh at Dori's apprehensive expression and focus on Gabrielle, who makes a face when I mention the soy. 'Is there syrup in it?' she asks hopefully.

'In the latte? Uh, no . . .'

'I'm sure Roberta has some sugar packets,' Dori interjects. Her eyes flick to mine and skitter away. Gabrielle gives me an enthusiastic hug (Dori purses her lips, but makes no comment) and goes in search of sugar.

'C'mon, Dori – the first hit is always free.'

She reluctantly accepts the cup I hand her and says, 'Thanks,' like it takes a Herculean effort to speak the word to me.

She studies the instructions and sips the latte while I regard her silently. She's sporting the faded red M.A.D.D. shirt again, but today her hairband matches her shirt, and she's wearing thin silver hoop earrings. And is that *lipgloss* on her mouth? Interesting and atypical Dori behaviour.

On the day I started work here, I stupidly assumed that getting into Dori's pants would be effortless, and in the same thought I concluded that I couldn't be bothered to hook up with her. Had she sensed that vain mental verdict and decided to make me pay for it?

'This isn't the first . . . *hit* . . . for me, you know.' She's obviously hesitant to use addict jargon, even in jest.

'Hmm. I guess you'll owe me, then.'

She doesn't respond, just sets her cup on a window sill and takes one last glance at the instructions. Armed with a screwdriver, she picks up the bulky mechanical component and climbs the ladder directly beneath the hole cut into the centre of the ceiling. I gather from watching her that she has to get the wiring hooked up before she can attach the motor to the electrical box in the ceiling. She balances the bulky thing in her right hand while she twists the wires together with her left, pulling safety caps out of her pocket and affixing them to the connected wires.

Halfway through, she fumbles the motor, almost dropping it and exclaiming, 'Popsicles!'

I climb up behind her and take the weight of the motor in my hand, but there is no goddamned way I can keep from laughing. What does *popsicles* even correspond to? I've heard her say *fudge* – a way more obvious substitute. I'm beginning to think she just tosses out whatever food item she thinks of first.

Without a word, she hooks up the wiring.

If I wasn't aware of her proximity before, I am now. The light press of her body against mine and the unanticipated sweet scent of her make me abruptly, fully conscious of it. Standing on the rung below her places my mouth level with her ear. 'You smell good. What are you wearing?'

Her breathing goes shallow, from either threat or desire. 'Deodorant.'

I laugh softly, inhaling carefully. 'Mmm, no, something more than that, I think.'

'I . . . I don't know. Lotion? Some store brand, I think.'

She doesn't know? My mother and every girl I've ever dated, Emma included, coordinated lotions, powders and colognes. If asked, any of them could have said what scent they were wearing without thinking.

'No . . . it's more like . . . cake, or something else . . . edible.' I'm staring at the fine hairs on the nape of her neck, her small left earlobe, the silver hoop threaded through it, her dark lashes in profile. She's shut her eyes, as though she's light-headed.

'Um . . . okay . . .' She opens her eyes, turns slightly towards me. 'Reid, I . . . I want to get down now.'

I hop from the rung to the floor, reach up and swing her lightly to the ground, my hands lingering at her waist. She grips my upper arms, not letting go once her feet are on the ground. We look as though we were dancing and someone hit the pause button. Common sense tells me not to try to kiss her again. She's not ready yet. So we stand there, staring at each other, silent and unmoving.

She's conceding ground already; it's in her eyes. I suppress a smile at the conflict I sense in her because she's scrutinizing every nuance of emotion on my face, looking for anything that might betray my intentions.

'Hey.' Gabrielle's voice startles both of us – perfect timing.

I drop my hands as Dori jumps away. Turning to snatch my cup from where I set it on the stack of fan blades, I say, 'Later,' giving Dori a surreptitious wink and bumping fists with a confused Gabrielle on the way out the door.

Dori

If I can just get through one more week, I'll never have to see him again.

The fan motor was heavy and unwieldy, and I should have waited for Gabrielle's help to hook it up. But I could feel his eyes on me from the moment he walked into the room, and I couldn't pretend to look at those instructions another minute.

Then my heart was slamming from nearly dropping the stupid motor, and in the next moment he was behind me, laughing at me for my choice of swear-word-that-isn't while taking the motor and holding it aloft like it weighed nothing. I would have chastised him for breaking the one-person-on-the-ladder rule, but I couldn't speak.

His chest pressed against my back while his arm reached round, his bicep hard against my ribcage, just grazing my breast. I stretched up, my arms burning, and worked to get the wiring hooked up as quickly as possible. Once the part was snug against the ceiling, I thought he'd step back down. Instead, he remained where he was, our bodies connected, however slightly, in several key spots. Then he told me I smelled good.

Trapped on that ladder, all I could do was close my eyes and concentrate. *Breathe. Breathe. Breathe.* Until his hands were at my waist, lifting me down like I weigh nothing.

I've never been so pleased to see Gabrielle.

Once Reid disappears, I tell her to take the fan boxes to her brothers' and parents' rooms and get them unpacked so we can install them before lunch. That should give me enough time to attach the fan blades . . . and recover from what he just did to me.

19

REID

Javier, one of the new volunteers, is a member of a frat group that'll be here for the week – Pi Kappa something. I think he's decided we're BFFs for the duration. We're the same age, but for the most part, I feel like I'm talking to a kid.

During lunch break, I entertain him with celebrity anecdotes – the websites, the starlets, the parties, the fan mail – while he's rubbernecking at all the photographers hovering in neighbouring yards. 'So there might be pictures of *me* on celebrity gossip sites? Like, tomorrow?'

I can't help laughing – celebrities go miles out of their way to dodge being harassed by the paparazzi, but Javier is ecstatic over the prospect. 'They'll probably be up by this afternoon, if not in half an hour,' I tell him.

He pulls his phone from his pocket, starts typing a text. 'Seriously? *Awesome.*' Ten to one he's texting a friend to check websites to see if he's made it into any shots yet. Ultimate photobombing. 'So, like, what do you do with all those pictures girls send you? Do you ever, you know, call up one of the hot ones and hook up?'

I shake my head. 'No way. The more, er, *stimulating* photos don't make it to me – my mail and email is prescreened. I get the fully-clothed shots. And the *You're a god* and *I think you should have won an Oscar* mail, not the *You suck* and *I wish you'd curl up and die* shit. My manager shreds or deletes anything inappropriate.' We each take a paper plate and head for the food.

'Even hot naked girls? *Why?*' Javier is aghast.

'Because photos of naked fifteen-year-olds are *not* something you want to keep, even if they *say* they're eighteen.'

'Yeah, I guess not.' He grimaces, but doesn't look convinced.

'Hi, Reid.' Speak of the under-age devil.

'Hey, Gabrielle. This is Javier.'

Javier's eyes widen slightly, taking her in. She smiles and chirps, 'Hi.' While he checks her out, she turns back to me. 'So Dori's *boyfriend* showed up again. God, he's so *boring*.'

Boyfriend? 'What?'

She blinks innocently. 'Her boyfriend, Nick – he was here like a week or so ago? I'm going to kill myself if I have to work with the two of them *all freaking afternoon*.' She glances towards the back door. 'God, there they are.'

I'm staring when Dori locks eyes with me. *Nick* is the guy Dori sat next to at lunch during the first week. The one with the poor conversation skills. She breaks eye contact with me and turns to direct him to the line, her hand on his arm as he drones on about something. *This* guy is her boyfriend? You've got to be shitting me. He looks like he just stepped out of a nerd sitcom, where he plays the character who constantly manages to destroy his chances to hook up with *anyone*.

And then I wonder if nerds are what floats Dori's boat because I've heard that some girls are like that.

Javier invites another frat guy to join us. We all sit on the edge of the patio to eat, and Gabrielle is flushed and talkative, relishing the male-to-female ratio. Javier and his friend Kyle are more than happy to accommodate her, and while I appear to do the same, I'm watching Dori and *Nick*.

Her smiles seem real and her body language is relaxed; when their knees brush or he leans forward to say something, she doesn't pull back or shy away. He's not hot, but not repulsive. But there's no observable chemistry between them, not even guarded touches . . . and she's sneaking looks in my direction every few minutes while I appear to be engrossed in whatever Gabrielle is babbling about.

Lunch is almost over when Dori glances over once more, and this time I stare back. Her eyes widen almost imperceptibly, and while she returns my gaze, I count five long seconds. As a slow smile steals across my face, she snaps her attention back to her boyfriend – if that's what he is – and doesn't look my way again.

Dori

Minutes after Reid left the room this morning, Nick showed up, determined to make up for cancelling our plans on

Saturday and spoiling my night. When I assured him again that he did no such thing, he ducked his head shyly and admitted that he just wanted an excuse to see me, and if a little manual labour was all it took, he was up for it. He's so sincere and sweet that I wish for the hundredth time that I felt more for him than an intense admiration of his character and a mild attraction to his person.

Gabrielle was her usual crabby self all morning, but with Nick helping out, I found her tormented sighs humorous. I had to bite my lip to keep from laughing out loud during the first interaction between the two of them.

While I attached outlet covers, Nick was on the ladder, connecting the heating and A/C vent. 'Hey, Gabby – can you hand me that set of driver bits, please?'

'The. Name. Is. *Gabrielle*.' She glared at him, her hands clenched into fists at her sides.

Nick blinked at her vehement tone, then smiled. 'Oh, sorry. *Gabrielle*, please hand me that set of driver bits?'

She spun round, grabbing the package from the floor and slapping it into his open hand. '*God*,' she said under her breath.

'Thanks, Gabrielle.' He smiled again, which seemed to infuriate her further.

Nick's presence helps keep me focused on work, but doesn't inhibit the scenes from Reid's movie that have been on a constant loop in my head since yesterday afternoon. I didn't know anything about *School Pride* before we went, while Aimee and Kayla had parts of it memorized. The premise was a bit silly – a present-day adaptation of *Pride and*

Prejudice, set in a high school – but casting Reid as an arrogant Will Darcy was genius. His natural self-assurance was easy to see in the heated scenes between Reid and his co-star, Emma Pierce. And when he kissed her, I swear I felt it. *Ugh*.

When we went outside for lunch, my attention was drawn to him repeatedly, sitting with Gabrielle and two of our fraternity volunteers from UCLA.

Nick was talking about a mission trip he did earlier this summer to Honduras. '. . . because fifty per cent of the population is under the poverty line – can you imagine?'

'Uh, wow, that's appalling.' My eyes drifted to the other side of the patio. The first half dozen times I looked, Reid didn't notice. That last time, though, his dark blue eyes locked with mine. My pulse galloped. And then his mouth kicked up on one side and I had no choice but to rip my gaze from his.

I stared into Nick's eyes, thankful for his comforting voice, his gentle smile. And I fought the magnetic pull of the boy sitting across the yard who is everything I do not need and should not want.

I'm up late, compiling a list of stuff to pack for my mission trip when Deb calls. As soon as I say hello, she says, 'Dori, he kissed me,' sounding like the giddy girl she never was, rather than the capable, independent woman who earned the title of doctor two months ago.

'Who – old Doc Bradford?' I can't help teasing her.

'He's thirty-one!'

'Hmm, thirty-one is reasonable, I suppose.' I know she can hear the smile in my voice. 'So when did this romantic encounter occur? I thought you were working twenty-four seven.'

'He picked me up last night for my dinner break, around ten thirty. We only had about twenty minutes, so he brought burgers and we parked at the back of the hospital lot and talked.'

'Talked, eh?' I leave the list on my desk and lie back on my bed. My ceiling fish are all stationary, waiting for the A/C to cycle on.

'He told me he wants to make sure I know how he feels about me, since we can't show it in front of anyone in the hospital. Any gossip could get ugly, even though he's not directly supervising me.'

'And how does Doc Bradford feel about you?'

My logical, analytical sister *giggles*, and I cover my mouth and wait for her answer. It's been so long since she's been this interested in anyone. 'He likes me. A lot, he said.'

'What if someone finds out? Or if it gets serious? I mean, you can't pretend like you don't know each other for your whole residency . . .'

'I asked him about someone finding out. He said it's happened before. As long as there's no supervisory relation-ship, the worst that could happen is we'd get a stern talking to.' She doesn't answer the second question.

'My big sister, skulking around kissing boys in parking lots. I'm shocked! Details, please.'

'I had to get back inside, so I said I could just walk back

up, and he said no way, he didn't want to waste his last two minutes with me. And then he reached over and touched the side of my face, and we moved towards each other like magnets, and, well . . .'

'Don't leave me hanging! How was it? Hasn't it been like ten years since you've kissed a boy?'

'Ha. Ha. Very funny. I guess it has been a while, but kissing Brad was just . . . perfect.'

The air comes on overhead and my fish begin to sway. 'Please tell me you were a *little* late getting back in.'

'A little.' She sighs, and I know she's reliving the whole thing. 'I have to get back on the floor. I just had to tell you.'

'I love that you did. And I'll say a prayer that you don't get caught.' We laugh and say goodnight, and I lie there, smiling, for another few minutes. Until my thoughts cycle back to Reid, and the blocked kiss. Maybe I should have let him do it, before pushing him away.

But if I'd let him kiss me, I might not have been able to push him away at all.

20

REID

Just before I left yesterday, Darlene told me that I've been assigned to Dori for the next couple of days to help finish off the closets and pantry.

'I assume that means Gabrielle is off Tuesday and Wednesday?'

Her answer was her best squinty stare, while Frank, sauntering up behind us to wash his hands, wasn't as restrained. 'Son, you should take some lessons in when to keep your thoughts to yourself. See, women are always saying that they want honesty and communication, but that's just because they don't know all the jackass stuff we guys think about on a regular basis. A more intelligent fella, like myself, knows to keep the mystery alive by knowing when to shut up.'

'Humph,' Darlene said, smirking.

Dori is removing six-foot-long boards from the supply storage unit when I arrive with her latte. Though less surprised than she was yesterday, she's still guarded. I drag the tips of my fingers over hers as I hand it to her. She glances at me as I feign interest in the trellis Frank is installing on the opposite side of the yard.

'So . . . these boards need to be painted before we put in the shelving, right?' When I look at her, she sets her cup on a stack of jagged shale stones and turns back to unloading the boards.

'Um, yeah.'

This morning, she's wearing a white t-shirt that would fit a linebacker, the back of which is emblazoned with what I assume is the name of her church and the VBS theme: *In His Hands*. On the front is a child's drawing of the globe covered in blue and green splotches. On the illogically green Arctic Circle are stick-figure kids of every colour (including purple). The earth levitates just above two huge hands.

I hand her my coffee. 'Hold this, and let me do that.' I grab a stack of boards. 'Where are we going with these?'

'First, we have to trim them down to size. I already did the measurements.' She pulls a slip of paper from her back pocket, grabs her latte and leads me to the circular saw.

As I carry the remainder of the boards over, she measures and marks them, flips the switch on the saw and begins cutting. The process looks simple enough, and after a few minutes, I'm not content to stand and watch, so I ask her to show me how to do it.

We cut the first two boards together. The sensation of her palms on the back of my hands, guiding them firmly, is like a pulsing current. I feel almost high, standing close enough to inhale her subtle, familiar scent, coupled with running boards through a whirring saw that could lop off my hand in a split second of inattention. The adrenalin junkie in me is fired up.

While I cut the last few boards alone, my ears adjusting to the shrill whine as the blade chews through the wood, she sands the rough edges on the finished products. A portion of the ground and the fence has been tarped where we're doing the painting. She takes several of the smaller boards and I follow with the larger ones. 'Lean them there; we're spray-painting them.'

'Sounds fun.' She glances at me, unsure if I'm being sarcastic. I turn back to get the rest, letting her guess. Keeping the mystery alive, as Frank would say.

Dori takes up the paint sprayer and quickly coats the first board with even strokes, leaving a smooth white surface. She hands me the sprayer. 'Start towards the top and go slowly, side to side.' I aim it at the board and press the trigger just as she's saying, 'Back up first!'

I basically blast it with paint all in one spot, so it looks like shit and bonus – since I'm holding it too near the flat surface – Dori and I end up with a rebound spatter of paint everywhere except where the goggles and particle masks cover our eyes and mouths. She blinks at me behind paint-misted goggles. There's paint in her hair, on her shirt and misted over every inch of visible skin.

'Oops.' My voice is muffled by the mask. I'm expecting anger or at least irritation, but she looks at my face and bursts out laughing and then so do I and soon we've caught the attention of everyone, including the photogs in the surrounding yards.

Shaking her head, she pulls her particle mask down and it hangs around her neck. 'You have to learn everything the hard way, don't you?'

I shrug. 'I prefer to call it learning by experience.'

She laughs again and rolls her eyes. 'Ooooh, well, in that case, far be it from me to interrupt your learning processes. Next time, please warn me to wear head-to-toe plastic sheeting while you're learning.' She uses air quotes around *learning*.

'Yes, boss.' I take a giant step back and so does she as I raise the sprayer. And then she takes another, pulling on her mask while I mumble, 'Funny girl,' through mine.

When I'm done, we stand surveying the boards, sipping our coffee drinks, masks around our necks, goggles pushed to our foreheads. She looks at me and smirks at my hair, which is sticking straight up behind the goggles. I push them back so they sit more like sunglasses on top of my head and point at her shirt. 'So what's the story with this VBS gig? Roberta said you were in charge of some musical performance, and that's why you disappeared last week.'

She watches me over the lid of her cup. 'It's just a few songs for the kindergarten class. For Parents' Night.'

'You're directing them?' At her nod, I say, 'I know nothing about kids that age, except that I was one. Or so I hear.' She smiles, and I become aware of the freckles that were protected from paint mist by her mask and goggles. Scattered across the bridge of her nose, they're actually kind of cute.

'You go to this church regularly? I've never really been; my parents aren't big on religion.'

Her smile weakens and her gaze skitters away and back. 'Yeah, I do.' She swallows another sip. 'My dad's the pastor.'

Whoa. I didn't expect that. 'Ah. So how much of that VBS job is you volunteering and how much is you *being* volunteered?'

She doesn't hesitate. 'Oh, I love teaching the kids to sing. It's the most rewarding thing I do.' Her eyes slide away again.

'I thought attempting to rehabilitate *me* was your favourite thing.' I hadn't expected to make her blush, but her ears colour under the paint.

Dori

I can't respond to that comment, of course – a comment made more awkward by our previous argument about whether or not he needed or wanted rehabilitating, and whether or not I'd consider him worthy of the task. He's either forgiven me for those heated words, or he's forgotten them.

I think he seldom forgets anything.

We finish painting the first coat on the boards, and at lunch Reid's frat boy groupies join us. There are four of them clustered round him today. I consider sitting with Roberta, Darlene and Frank, but they're huddled together discussing grandchildren and real-estate taxes and for some reason, I just want to feel eighteen today.

'So what's it like, being *you* at some party? I bet you score all the chicks,' a guy named Javier is asking Reid, who makes room for me on the edge of the patio.

'I can't complain,' he answers, his eyes hitting mine for a split second.

Javier leans closer. 'Do any of them ever put up any fight? Turn you down?'

Reid laughs. 'Yeah, sure.'

'But not, like, often,' another guy, Kyle, says.

Reid shrugs. 'I guess not.'

I'm rethinking my desire to be an eighteen-year-old girl *and* my decision to sit with this particular group of boys when the one on my other side offers his hand, 'Hi, I'm Trevor.'

I shake his hand. 'Dori.'

He leans forward, speaking in a low voice. 'Ignore them – they're a bunch of morons with *no* manners.'

I take a bite of my sandwich rather than reply, curious about whatever inappropriate thing Kyle is asking Reid. (I swear I just heard the word *boobs*.)

Trevor clears his throat, blocking out whatever Kyle is saying. 'So are you a celebrity too?'

'Uh, *no*.'

'Oh, okay. I just noticed you seem . . . acquainted . . .' He inclines his head towards Reid.

'Oh. No.' I wave a dismissive hand. 'We've just been working together since he's been here. So what are you studying? UCLA, right?'

'Yeah. Applied mathematics.' He removes his glasses and rubs a smear from a lens with his shirt tail. 'What about you?'

'I'll be starting at Berkeley in the fall. Social work.'

His eyebrows rise. 'Berkeley? Cool.' He chuckles a little. 'Social work, eh?' I bristle, having endured appalled reactions about my chosen major from everyone from my maternal grandparents to classmates. He puts the glasses on and says, 'I didn't mean that how it sounded. I was just thinking how everyone is always horrified at my major, like it's so difficult and all, but I hear "social work" and think *that* sounds hard.'

I nod. 'My sister just finished her medical degree, so pretty much everything pales in comparison to that.'

He puffs his cheeks and blows air out. 'Oh, man, yeah. My room-mate's pre-dental, and he studies non-stop – some nights I go to bed and he's studying and I get up and he's studying. So does your sister practise nearby?'

'She just started her residency. In Indiana.'

'Cool.'

Javier and another groupie high-five each other, and Javier says, '*Dude, yes*,' to Reid. 'I want to be you *so bad*.' I glance at Reid, who's smiling and shaking his head. Whatever he's just admitted to, I'm sure I don't want to know.

'So why social work?' Trevor gestures to the house. 'I take it you're one of the regulars here, so you must know what a challenging field you're going into.'

I nod. 'I'm not starry-eyed about it. My dad's a pastor and my mom is an obstetrical nurse working with mostly low-income women, so I guess I have some built-in feelings of obligation to do what I can for my community. Lots of people who plan to go into social work talk about all the people they're going to help . . . but more often you save one person while losing nine. It could be a really discouraging field if you're not realistic about the odds.'

He nods. 'Sounds like you've considered every angle. I think the world needs more people like you.'

I turn to grab my drink and hide my self-conscious smile. 'Thanks. So why applied mathematics?'

He smiles, a small dimple appearing in his right cheek. 'Well, I'm *really* good at math.'

The remainder of lunch ticks away while we discuss college courses, dorm life and going Greek, which I'm certain is *not* for me, though he insists I'd be perfect for a sorority leadership spot. 'Scholarly types are needed too. Trust me – I *am* one of those.'

As we get up to throw our trash away and get back to work, he says, 'It was nice to meet you, Dori. Good luck at Berkeley, and, you know, saving ten per cent of the world.' He winks at me before signalling to his frat brothers to follow him inside.

I'm seldom so blatantly flirted with. Except for Reid, when he's entertaining himself by torturing me. Which doesn't count.

21

REID

I learned more about Dori in fifteen minutes of eavesdropping on her conversation with the math geek than I've found out about her the whole time we've been working together. Not only is her father a pastor, but her sister is a *doctor*, her mother is a *nurse* working with low-income pregnant women and Dori intends to become a *social worker*. She must have been bred to this service-to-society mentality from birth. She's like the reverse of me. For about two seconds I want to go home and hug my parents.

Then Dori's ears did their pink transformation. Up to that point, I'd just been observing that Trevor guy flirting with her. It was humorous until her ears started glowing. Shit. Now I'm territorial over making her *ears* change colour? What the hell.

After tossing my trash, I scan the yard for Dori and spot her walking in a tight circle, talking on her cell. I grab a couple of water bottles and head over to the shelving boards, which need a second coat of paint.

'No, I mean, of course I still want to see you.' Her voice carries the few feet between us. 'Can we not do this now?' She stops her circular pacing. 'No, there's nothing you're doing wrong.'

She's silent for another couple of minutes, restarting her pacing after glancing at me. I busy myself setting up the paint sprayer, pretending I can't hear her.

'Nick, I don't know if I'm even capable . . .' Eyes tightly closed, she makes a fist and bumps herself in the forehead three times. 'I don't know why. There's obviously something wrong with me. Something missing.' Opening her eyes, she swipes the back of her hand across her cheek. She's breaking up with the guy? It's like a gruesome collision. I can't look away.

'We're going to different colleges, and you'll find someone who'll be everything you want and deserve. I'm just . . . not that girl. I never have been.' She searches her empty pockets, looking for a tissue, I think. She turns to go into the house, and I can't follow without being *really* damned obvious.

When she comes back out, I'm painting the boards. Her eyes are red, but not repulsively so. 'Oh,' she says, smiling, though barely. 'You got started already. Thanks.'

I shrug one shoulder. 'No problem.' I turn the motor off on the sprayer and examine her for a couple of seconds. 'Wanna talk about it?' I ask. She shakes her head, and I nod, hand her the water bottle. 'What's next, boss?'

She swallows half the bottle of water, and then says, 'Did you know that "boss" is what guys in jail call the guards and deputies?'

As a matter of fact, I do know that, but I raise my eyebrows in mock surprise. 'You don't say.'

She rolls her eyes, sighing, her smile growing wider. 'Why don't you finish painting, you reprobate, and I'll go inside and start getting the closets ready to be shelved.'

I turn the sprayer back on. 'I've been called worse, you know.'

She laughs, which is incongruous with her tear-stained face, but somehow attractive at the same time. 'You don't say,' she mocks, and I have to laugh.

Dori

'I have a question,' he says, just before we leave for the day.

We're moving the painted boards inside so we can start installing the shelves in the morning. I know him well enough by now to know he'll insist on using the drill tomorrow – something I understand. The first time Dad agreed to let me wield a power tool, I jumped up and down. Reid's not as enthusiastic as that . . . but he's close.

'Yeah?'

'Why social work and not music?'

This is far afield from the subject of power tools, so my brain has to redirect. 'What?'

'You told Trevor you're going to Berkeley, right?' he asks, and I nod. 'So why, with your voice, are you studying social work instead of music?'

While I thought he was doing nothing more than regaling

the others with corrupt Hollywood tales, he was listening to my conversation with Trevor. Before I can compose an answer, he adds, 'Seems like a waste of time.'

What? 'Is that how you feel about this project, after three weeks of working here? Can't you see that these families *need* what we do for them?'

He holds his hands up. 'Yeah, sure. But you seem to feel some guilt complex for being born smarter, or having a better life. And you're planning to spend your life beating your head against a wall trying to help people who don't bother to help themselves.'

I do feel accountable for my blessings – but he seems to feel nothing but entitlement. 'These people didn't do anything to *deserve* being born into poverty, any more than I *deserved* to be born into a family that can afford to give me food, decent health care or an education.'

He stacks the final board against the others. 'Why does it have to be about deserving something? So it's luck of the draw, and granted, their hand sucks. I mean, sure, there are things you can do – and here you are, doing them. But there's only so much. Why live your life feeling guilty?'

'It isn't guilt – it's a social conscience.' I try to suppress my defensiveness. 'I can't just stand by and do *nothing*. Because my life *is* easy in comparison, and that isn't fair.'

'Don't, you know, fly off the handle or anything – but doesn't the fact that you think it isn't fair make you distrustful of the idea of a "higher power" orchestrating everything?'

'No.' His eyebrows rise at my quick reply, and I can't let him know how close to my doubts he's come. 'Because people like my dad exist. Because faith is part of who I am, and a measure of faith is being willing to do what's needed. I just want to make a difference. I have to believe I have a purpose. Maybe you don't understand that, but that's how I feel.'

He's quiet for a minute, and I'm thinking I've wasted my breath and got worked up for nothing. 'You're right, I don't understand,' he says. He tilts his head like Esther does when I talk to her and I use words outside of her canine experience. 'Your principles seem real, though. Usually there's something deceptive about people who throw words like *faith* around. Like they're using it to mask ulterior motives or baser desires . . .' He smiles a wicked little smile and my heart flips over. 'The sorts of values I *do* understand.'

22

REID

The camaraderie lasted all morning. We ate lunch separately – she sat with Roberta, and I sat with Frank, Darlene and Gabrielle – but I don't think that's what changed her mood. She was on the phone again after lunch, and though she was standing too far away for me to hear anything specific, her tone was on edge. She's been bitchy since she hung up.

She's installing brackets in the closets, and I'm adding the shelves and bolting them in. Since we're working on the same closets at the same time, we're almost on top of each other. The third time she criticizes something I'm not doing perfectly and then takes over and does it herself, I can't take any more of this shit.

'Look, just because you had a grisly break-up yesterday doesn't mean you can take it out on *me* today. I wasn't responsible for it.'

She glares at me. 'What. Are. You. Talking about?'

'The phone call yesterday? The crying?'

Her mouth drops open and snaps closed. 'Were you *listening* to me?'

We're standing inside a closet having this conversation, and the harsh resonance of our voices ricochets around and through us, unable to fully escape the confines of the space. 'You were outside, in public, talking on your phone. It's not like I fucking *wiretapped* you.'

Her jaw sets. 'First, you shouldn't have been listening to what was clearly a private conversation. And second, there was nothing to *break up*. We just agreed to never actually start . . . whatever we might . . . flippin' *flapjacks*. It's none of your darned business.'

Once I start laughing, I can't stop. 'Flipping *what*?' Where the hell does she get these things?

'If you were capable of doing *any* of this without assistance, it would be a joy to leave you to it,' she says, glaring.

'Oh, please. This isn't rocket science. It's screwing a bunch of boards to a wall. Big fucking deal.' Side note: I love how much it bothers her when I say *fuck*. She winces every time, like she's being jabbed with a needle.

'You don't even know how to use the stud finder to find the studs first.'

'Pardon me?'

She sighs exaggeratedly and fixes me with a stare. 'You have to locate the studs first –'

'*Stud finder?*'

'You use it to find the framework? Inside the wall?' Her sarcastic pitch is hitting a boiling point inside *me* because frankly it's a little too reminiscent of Dad, which I can't handle from more than one person in my life. 'The skeleton to which we attach stuff that needs to be anchored – like, I don't know, *shelves*?'

I stopped listening before she resumed talking. 'You finish in here,' I say. 'I'll do Gabrielle's closet.'

In answer, she hands me a small gadget containing a miniature spirit level and a red arrow-looking thing. This must be the wondrous stud finder. I have zero idea what to do with it, so I slip it into my pocket as I leave the room.

Dori

'I'm an idiot,' he says.

'No argument,' I say.

He's installed the hanging rod and an entire row of shelves without finding the anchoring studs first. The weight of the brackets alone probably seemed fine, but when the shelves were added, the weight began pulling the brackets out from the wall, screws and all. If Gabrielle adds so much as a pair of boots to a shelf or a couple of hangers to the rod, the whole mess is coming down.

Without speaking, we begin to angle the shelves to remove them from their unstable brackets. The boards scrape the walls on both sides, wringing simultaneous exclamations – *fucking hell* from him and *gosh almighty* from me – which makes him laugh. 'It's not funny,' I mutter. And then I glance at him and he grins and for no reason it *is* funny and we're both laughing.

Once the boards are removed, we survey the damage. He sighs deeply, arms crossed over his chest. 'Man. That looks like shit.'

I can't dispute his opinion, but something about his defensive pose and his dejected inflection reminds me of five-year-old Jonathan from my VBS class. Slumping against one of the ruined walls, I calculate that the repair and repainting will add a couple of hours to finishing off the closets. I was hoping to leave at three, which is not going to happen.

'What now?'

I straighten from the wall. 'Now we repair the damage . . . and reinstall the shelving.'

He pulls his phone from his pocket, checks the time. 'I assume you have a painstakingly calculated timetable . . . and the closets have to be done today.'

'Yep.' I grab a couple of the boards and haul them from the closet, and he follows with the brackets and the drill.

'Which means you'll have to stay later.'

I answer with a small shrug and a nod.

'I guess I'll stay later too, then.'

This is unprecedented. 'Oh?'

'Well, it's my fault we have to redo the whole closet, so yeah.' Hitting a speed-dial number, he watches me carry the remaining boards from inside the closet and lean them carefully against the pink wall. 'Hey, George, can you reschedule that interview? And also let the driver know to be here at five instead of three today.'

Avoiding his eyes, I listen as he and his manager rearrange

his after-hours agenda. Before now, I hadn't considered that Reid had anything else to do between filming movies, aside from goofing off.

The typical schedule everyone keeps is 8 a.m. to 3 p.m., and I'm used to him leaving with the rest of the transient volunteers. Those of us making up the regular crew come in earlier sometimes, and hang around a bit later sometimes, finishing up projects or readying things for the next day while the house grows gradually quieter, the sounds of an entire crew of workers fading to nothing.

Since we have to repaint the closet in Gabrielle's room, her shelves are the last thing to be done. When Reid volunteers to install them alone (again) while I finish up the linen closet shelving, I take a breath and ignore the threatening sense of déjà vu. Instead, I simply hand him the drill and the stud finder (his lips twist, and I know he's repressing a wisecrack) after showing him how to use it.

While finishing off the linen closet, I stifle the desire to check on him at least a dozen times. Finally, I head back to Gabrielle's room, bracing myself for whatever catastrophe awaits.

Reid's back is to me as he attaches the last shelf, the hard muscles of his shoulders and arms flexed and defined through his white t-shirt as he presses the drill, driving the screw through the bracket and into the wall. When finished, he leaves the drill on the shelf and steps back, every line of his body radiating pride, unaware that I'm watching. He's not wearing the safety goggles (he never does unless I make him put them on), but I won't chide him for it.

'It looks good,' I say, and he moves to the side as I step in next to him. I tug on the shelves, testing them. They don't budge. I could probably climb on them if I had to. They're more than secure enough to hold Gabrielle's shoes and storage boxes.

Relaxing against the door jamb of the closet, folding his arms loosely over his chest, he glances towards the bedroom door. 'It's really quiet in the house now. So weird.'

I nod. 'Everyone's gone except Roberta and Gene, and they're doing paperwork in the office.' His body fills the closet doorway, and he'll have to move for me to exit. Which is an odd thought to have, and makes me very aware of the enclosed space. 'Being in here is sort of like burrowing into a piece of bubblegum,' I say nervously, glancing at the closet's pink walls.

He doesn't answer, staring at me like he's analysing a complex riddle. Uncrossing his arms, he hooks one hand in his front pocket while the other lifts, his fingers catching a strand of hair too short to stretch to the elastic pulling the rest of my hair back. He slides it behind my ear, grazing the tip with his finger, and suddenly there's no sound but the pounding of my heart. This is where I should put my hands up between us like I did before. This is where I should say *excuse me* and get out of here.

His hand drops to his side and he stares down at me, making no movement towards me or away. I suck my lower lip into my mouth, a nervous habit left over from childhood, and his gaze drops there, sticks. A minute passes before he braces a hand on the wall just over my shoulder and leans closer, his eyes flashing to mine. 'Tell me what to do next because I'm not sure what you want.' His voice has gone rusty and low, like he hasn't used it in weeks.

I know what he's asking, despite the words threading across this scene: *This is not happening.* I shake my head, barely moving. Thoughts tumble through my mind, blurred, flashing in and out, opposites: kiss me, don't touch me, come closer, move away.

'All I'm asking,' his knuckles brush along my jaw, 'is that you tell me, Dori, what . . . you . . . want.'

When he straightens and begins to back away, I almost protest, biting my lip to keep from doing so. This movement betrays me, though, because again, he stares at my mouth a long moment before his gaze shifts to my eyes.

'Or maybe, just tell me if I do something you don't want,' he says quietly. And then his palms are skimming down my arms, and his mouth is on mine and he's kissing me, sliding his arms round me and pulling me up against his chest, hands pressing my lower back. Gently, his lips play over mine, teasing and testing and it feels so incredible, but somewhere in my mind is the tiniest nagging disappointment that he's kissing me like Nick did, the few times he'd kissed me – *safely* – the last thing I expect from Reid.

23

REID

The last thing I expect is for her to open her mouth, almost imperceptibly, so subtly that if I wasn't paying attention I might miss it. I'm all about paying attention. Even so, her response is such a shock that I almost pause, but instinctively I know that if I give her a fraction of a second to think, this is over.

Carefully, I run the tip of my tongue across her lower lip and she gasps, opening wider, receptive. Permission to enter granted, and God knows she doesn't have to indicate *that* twice. Sweeping my tongue across hers, I pull her in tight and hard when she responds perfectly and in kind. I suck her lower lip into my mouth and she mimics this the moment I release it, adding the slightest graze of her teeth. Her hands are on my back, kneading and stroking while I'm doing the same to her. And then she makes this sound – a cross between a sigh and a moan, like a soft, subtle, wordless *yes* – and it's all I can do not to come undone.

I can't say if this is the best kiss ever. I've kissed a *lot* of girls. But I can say that I don't remember another girl or another kiss in this moment. I can't remember my own name in this moment. And I don't want to stop kissing her. Ever. And then my hands shift under her shirt at her waist, fingers brushing over the soft, warm skin of her lower back, and she tears her mouth from mine. *Shit*. Too far, too fast. The warning hits my brain too late.

'Stop, stop,' she says, gasping. Her eyes are glazed over and I can't hear anything beyond our mingled, panting breaths and her muted words. 'Oh my gosh.'

I'm waiting for her to shove me away, but her eyes are closed now and she's still holding on to me so I'm not moving. I want to kiss her again and I'm exerting every ounce of self-control to stand here, unmoving, and watch her come back to earth. Shit, she is going to be so pissed off in about three seconds.

Make that one second.

Her hands fall from my sides abruptly, like she's just realized where they were. I loosen my hold on her gradually, as though I can keep her from remembering where my hands were and what they were doing if I move slowly enough. I shouldn't have put my hands under her shirt. I had no intention of going anywhere with that, I just wanted my hands on her skin, a tactile connection, like grounding wires, while our mouths fed the current between us.

Now her eyes are wide open and she's staring at me, but I can't read her expression. This is something new, something more than alarm or anger or exasperation. I don't know what she's thinking, and I don't dare ask. She's shutting down, like shades lowering, and then she's ducking under my arm and I can't do anything but lean against the wall, pound it once, *hard*, with my fist. '*Fuck*.'

She whirls round. 'Why do you have to use that word?'

Ah, the almighty F-word. 'It's just a word, Dori.'

'Well, I don't want to hear it.'

I turn to face her, the judgement in her tone, which I can't even begin to reconcile with the girl who was just kissing me like she was drowning in me. Like she *wanted* to. 'So when I say *fuck*, it really bothers you.'

I'm not even saying it *at* her, but I swear to God, she flinches before she nods.

'Why? It's just a word.'

Refusing to meet my eyes, she bites her lower lip (which only makes me want to kiss her again) while I stand here watching her, equally silent. When she speaks, her voice is barely audible. 'Because it takes something sacred and makes it into something ugly and insignificant. That's what bothers me.'

'So you consider fu– sex as something *sacred*?' I can't wrap my head round this. 'Sex isn't sacred – not under usual circumstances and probably not ever, between mentally balanced people. It's just a physical need, like eating or breathing.'

She looks up at me, her eyes bright, though she's not crying, thank God. 'I understand that it's physical, something we're biologically driven to.' (Now *there's* an unanticipated and annoyingly hot viewpoint for her to have.) 'But when people love each other, it's different. It's like – like eating for pleasure, not just gorging yourself on whatever c-crap comes along.'

She can't even say 'crap' without stumbling over it, and her argument is absurd. *Eating for pleasure* – Jesus, I could make all kinds of comebacks to that. She turns and runs from the room, the front door opening and closing quietly behind her a moment later. Because, of course, she isn't going to make a scene leaving the house.

Dori

I'm driving home shaking. I'm angry, yes. At myself. But I'm not shaking from anger. I'm shaking from something else altogether. Something that somehow, inexplicably, generates a similar physical response. And yet not.

Reid thinks he knows who I am because he's made the same assumptions everyone else makes about me. That I'm a proper, strait-laced *good girl*. That I always have been. But you know what they say about assumptions.

I met Colin Dyer during my first week of high school.

His family attended our sister church – the one with the architecturally impressive sanctuary located in a better neighbourhood, with parishioners to whom *giving back* only ever means opening a wallet. Our church is their charity project, their contributions providing enough additional funds to pay for building repairs and help support our neigh-bourhood programmes.

Colin's mother was my school counsellor, and I was her

office aide during fourth period. Getting an aide job as a freshman was unheard of, unless you had connections, and thanks to Dad, I did. Being selected as Dr Dyer's aide was a highly coveted privilege. She was easy-going, and her office was quiet and comfortable. Her aides had first-hand know-ledge of which students were troubled or *in* trouble, so not just anyone could work the front desk. She needed someone trustworthy and caring. I was both.

I worked the class period after lunch. By the end of that first week, I'd covertly inspected the family photos in her office while making copies or clearing her fax machine of junk faxes, so when Colin stopped by, I recognized him immediately. A senior and on the swim team, he was tall and slim, but muscular. His dark hair was cut very short, making his hazel, almond-shaped eyes even more striking in his olive-toned face. He walked and swam with equal grace, and possessed a confidence I craved and admired.

'Well, hello,' he said, his brows raised slightly, his gaze warm and focused. 'You're new.'

I frowned slightly, confused. It was only the first week of school, so anyone in my position would technically be new.

'I haven't seen you around at school before, so you're either a new transfer . . . or a freshman. Or, in upper-class-speak, fresh meat.' He smiled, his teeth perfect and white, small dimples denting adorably at the sides of his mouth. I felt my face heat. I had no idea how to respond, and though I knew I should be offended, I wasn't.

'Colin,' his mother said, coming in with a stack of folders and a bag from Wendy's, the aroma of French fries filling the office. 'You'll need to pick up those goggles yourself. I couldn't make it by today. I had to stop by the orthodontist to get Tara's new retainer.' Tara was Colin's seventh grade sister.

'Didn't you just get her a new retainer?'

She smirked. 'Yes. That one lasted a month before she "misplaced" it.' She walked into her office to prepare for the afternoon's onslaught of distressed teenagers and/or their parents, her voice trailing off. 'If only they put little strings on those things like they have for bifocals and children's mittens . . .'

He laughed, and I tingled, head to toe. I'd never felt so attracted to a boy before. As he turned back to me, I turned away to switch on the oscillating fan behind my desk.

'So, fresh meat, what's your name?'

My face warmed again. 'Dori.'

'I'll be seeing you, then, Dori.' He quirked an eyebrow and was out the door.

I watched him in the hallways between classes – senior and junior girls constantly orbiting him like planets caught in his gravitational pull, freshman and sophomore girls sighing as he walked by, other guys high-fiving him or throwing out plans for the weekend as they passed. He was extrovert, popular. I was all but invisible.

Whenever he noticed me, he'd smile broadly. 'Hey, fresh meat,' he'd say, anyone within earshot tittering. I was embarrassed and thrilled. Once or twice a week, he'd show up in the counselling office to talk to his mother, but he always stayed after, leaning a hip on my desk and talking to me in teasing tones.

One day, he walked in carrying a dark pink rose. Dr Dyer was in a staff meeting, and I was alone. 'Hey, Dori.' His eyes roamed over me. 'You look hot today.' I stared at the desk, never sure how serious his compliments were. He smiled, moved closer, held the rose to my ear. 'Yep, I was right. The exact same shade.'

He squatted down next to my chair, which he'd never done. 'I have something to ask you.' Viewing him from this new perspective, I stared at his long, dark eyelashes and his full lips. He drew the rose down the side of my face, the petals soft against my cheek, and I felt a stirring to my core. 'Do you have a date for homecoming?'

I shook my head slowly, disbelieving. It made no sense for someone as popular as Colin to notice me, let alone ask me out.

'Would you like to go with me?' His gaze locked on mine as he slowly dragged the rose across my lips, the fragrance of it sweet and overpowering. I nodded, and he smiled. He pulled his phone from his pocket, pushed a few buttons, handed it to me. 'Put your number in. I'll call you tonight and we'll talk logistics.' As I tapped my number, he glanced towards the door and back to me. 'Can I have a kiss, to seal the deal?'

I nodded again, and then his lips were on mine, briefly.

He took his phone, laid the rose on my desk and walked into the hall, whistling. I'd been asked to homecoming, had accepted the invitation and his kiss, never speaking a word.

That was my first kiss with Colin. My first kiss with anyone.

Four months later, it was Valentine's Day. His parents had driven to San Francisco for an extended romantic weekend, and his little sister was staying overnight at a friend's house. He took me to dinner, and then we rented a movie. We had the house to ourselves. As we made out on the sofa, he whispered that he loved me. When he took my hand and pulled me to his room and into his bed, I followed.

We snuck home to his empty house during lunch breaks and got a hotel room on my fifteenth birthday, where we made love in the shower, on the worn love seat and on the floor, laughing at the rug burns we sustained on our knees and backsides from the coarse carpet. I woke up in his arms, hoping Mom hadn't called the friend with whom I was supposedly spending the night, but certain I'd not trade that waking moment for anything, no matter the consequences.

When spring break came around and he took off for San Diego with friends, I didn't protest; I wasn't one of those clingy girlfriends. When he came back home Sunday night – his eighteenth birthday – and didn't call or return my texts, I was concerned. When he didn't show at lunch or stop by the office on Monday, I didn't understand. Not until I saw him in the hallway just before last period, his arm slung round the waist of a senior girl. Not until his eyes passed over and then returned to me.

'Hey, fresh meat,' he said, and kept walking.

That was when I knew it was over.

24

REID

On one hand, that could have gone better . . . and on the other, it couldn't have. Once again, I gave in to the impulse to kiss her, though truth be told I've wanted to kiss her since the moment she fell into my arms and the sky rained fruit on to our heads.

She didn't shove me away this time. At least not until after I kissed her, and she kissed me back. God*damn*, did she kiss me back. And then the conversation about sex – something I *never* thought I'd be discussing with Dorcas Cantrell – and my foul language. I'm not a Neanderthal; I'm capable of curbing it when necessary. I just generally don't see the point. It's who I am. *Deal*. Dori makes it sound like saying the F-word is on a par with burning flags or drowning bunnies.

My phone buzzes while I'm staring into the bubblegum closet, ignoring, for now, the part of the story where Dori ran away. *Again*. My driver is out front, and I forgot to get her signature before she took off. She said Roberta and

Gene were still here; hopefully one of them will sign.

Seven more working days of my sentence to go.

'Reid?' Roberta's eyebrows fly up when I come round the corner and her eyes blink behind glasses that lend her face an owlish appearance. She glances at the watch on her wrist and then blinks at me again. 'You're still here?'

I pull the sheet out of my back pocket as I walk into her makeshift office – a rickety table, a folding chair and a laptop set up in the middle of the master bedroom. Baskets labelled *in* and *out* teeter on the edge of the table, stacked with assorted forms and files. 'Dori needed some help fixing something that I, uh, screwed up. So I stayed a little late.'

She takes the form, gives it a cursory glance and scrawls her signature at the bottom, smiling. 'How lovely of you. I'm sure Dori appreciated that.'

Right. I'm sure *appreciation* was way up there on her list of feelings as she raced out of here. 'When's her last day, anyway?' I ask, as offhandedly as possible.

'Tuesday, I believe.'

By the end of the day on Tuesday, I'll only have three more days remaining of this sentence. I should be looking forward to this ending. Instead, I'm craving some way to slow down time so I can figure out what the hell I want, and get it. 'How long is her trip?'

Roberta's eyes narrow, suspicious of my sudden interest in Dori's plans. 'Three weeks, I think,' she answers. 'Why?'

I shrug and turn to leave. 'Just curious.'

I have to be on location in Vancouver for my next film in less than a month. Little to no time in between her return and my departure. I don't know what I want from this girl. Tadd labelled her a challenge, and God, yes, she's that. But today. That kiss. And now I have a matter of days to figure out how far she's willing to take this. Assuming she plays fair and shows up instead of skipping out like she did before.

Ignoring the paparazzi, bodyguards and fans, I leave the house and walk towards the driver, who stands stoically next to the open back door of the car. A flash of insight nearly stops me in the middle of the newly paved sidewalk. The last time I tried to kiss her, she ducked away and then disappeared for several days. This time, she surrendered – and the way she kissed me wasn't the feel of a girl submitting to something unwanted. She wasn't giving in to *me*, she was giving in to *herself*. She'd contemplated kissing me, at least subconsciously.

She didn't disappear last time and run away this time because I did something she didn't want. She disappeared and ran away because she *wanted* me to kiss her.

The challenge is reading her. She doesn't let her guard down often. To get her to let it slip, only two things have worked – getting her really pissed off or really turned on, neither of which is sustained for long. She protects herself, like a turtle yanking its head back into its shell.

Why does the fact that plain-faced philanthropist and future social worker Dorcas Cantrell *wants me* make me feel high?

Dori

I shoved Reid away and took a five-day breather when he tried to kiss me the first time, right after the Fruit Bowl Incident.

A normal boy would have dismissed me with a shrug of his shoulders and a rude nickname, at least in his own head. But Reid is no normal boy, and my attempts to hide my attraction to him are clearly a big *fail*. Then again, maybe he just thinks every girl on the planet wants him, so a refusal seems like my quirky way of asking him to try again. As infuriating as that thought is, that line of reasoning absolutely worked. *Barnacles*.

'Hello?' Deb's voice is groggy when she answers, and I'm immediately sorry for waking her, but it doesn't stop me from needing her. 'Dori? What's up, baby?'

I take a deep breath. 'I kissed him.'

The swoosh of sliding fabric in the background increases my guilt. She was probably power-napping before another overnight-through-afternoon shift, and here I am bothering her with this silliness. 'You kissed who?' She yawns lightly, affirming my concern.

'Reid.' There's a moment of silence. 'Deb?'

'You kissed Reid Alexander?' Her tone is incredulous, which is understandable, given the circumstances. 'The superficial and – I believe this was stated emphatically – *unprofound* Reid Alexander?'

I'm staring at my closed bedroom door. Scarves, a couple of hats and an umbrella hang from the over-the-door hooks, neat and colour-coordinated one side to the other. On my blue wall is a large magnetic whiteboard with a list of everything I need to do before Quito on one side and everything for Berkeley on the other. Most of each list is checked off. My life is so utterly structured and planned out. 'Yeah.'

'Oh, boy.'

'*Yeah*.'

'Um, may I ask how this took place?'

Recalling the hungry look he wore as he leaned closer triggers unwelcome tremors of longing. 'Well, he was feeling really proud of himself after fixing some shelves he'd messed up earlier in the day . . .' If that isn't the strangest excuse ever given for kissing someone, I don't know what is.

'Okay, wait. Has Habitat instituted some new sort of rewards system? Because kissing seems excessive, even for truly *outstanding* shelf construction.'

My laugh dwindles and fades to a moan. 'What should I do? I told Roberta I'd be there until Tuesday. That's four more days of him, smug and arrogant every time he looks at me.'

'And this differs from his usual demeanour how, exactly?'

'Good point.' The chirp of an alarm sounds on her end. 'Oh, Deb – I'm sorry for waking you up.'

'Meh.' She yawns again. 'It was almost time to get up anyway.'

I picture her cramped but comfortable efficiency apartment and its tiny, south-facing balcony, planters of all sorts and sizes lining the railing and hanging from the roofline. The eight by ten foot space is overrun with greenery and flowers, and from the parking lot her patio looks like a miniature rainforest on the top floor, contrasting with neighbouring porches of bicycles, plastic furniture and bored dogs. 'When do you have to be at the hospital?'

'Well, I'm already here, actually. The hospital has a lovely, windowless room of foul-smelling lockers and uncomfortable bunks for the doctors to crash in, especially the interns, since we basically live here.' Great, now I feel even worse. 'So,' she says in her fully alert, logical, down-to-business voice. 'Work separately if you can. If you *have* to work together, make sure the two of you are never alone. And pretend that kiss never happened. Do that for four days, and that will be the end of the unprofound Reid Alexander.'

I fight the urge to defend Reid's unprofoundness in at least one realm: kissing. If anyone ever kisses me better than that, it could alter the time/space continuum. Yet here I am, getting advice on how to make sure it never happens again.

'Thanks, Deb.'

'You're welcome, baby girl. Any time.'

25

REID

Mom is passed out on my bed and drooling on to the silk duvet when I get home. She seldom comes into my side of the house any more. I can't even remember the last time I came home and found her in my room.

Courtesy of our live-in domestic help, there aren't any remnants of today's bender – no bottles or glasses to tell me what she ingested to find oblivion this time. Not that her poison of choice matters. The house stays clean thanks to our housekeeper, Maya. She and Immaculada have disappeared into staff quarters, but there are always meals in the fridge if I'm hungry. I imagine for a moment what it might be like to have an alcoholic mother at less than our level of opulence. I'd come home to a filthy house, bottles strewn end to end, nothing to eat. She'd be passed out on the sofa, on the floor, in the yard.

Finding the positive in this situation feels pointless, but I do it.

If I hadn't come home early tonight, I might not have

caught her here at all. It's only eleven. Dad must not be home yet, or she'd be in their room or one of the guest rooms. She's not dressed for bed, either, though her mismatched outfit, unkempt hair and make-up-less face tell me she hasn't left the house today. This is an unspoken agreement between my parents – Mom doesn't go out in public when she's been drinking. A quiet, depressive drunk, she's always allowed herself to be coaxed into compliance with this edict. She never drives, either – the car service is on permanent call, so no chance for a DUI. Each member of the staff has Dad on speed-dial. My family has enabling down to an art.

An hour ago, I was at a party with John, staring at the familiar crowd of fashionably-clad, undulating bodies and the smoke curling towards the ceiling, trying and failing to ignore my boredom as the typical laughter rose occasionally over the typical music. While the socialite sitting next to me droned on about her last trip to Amsterdam and the mind-altering experiences she had there, I found myself thinking about *shelves*.

'. . . and then I felt so, you know, at peace with everything and everybody, like I was part of the *universe*, you know?' she said, and I nodded, contemplating the stud finder, which is a clever-as-hell device. I'd attached those brackets with three-inch screws, driving them into the frame, daring them to ever come loose. If the house was demolished by an act of God, those damned brackets would probably remain affixed to the planks of wood inside the wall. When Dori pulled on the shelves to test them, they hadn't moved a millimetre.

My thoughts shifted fully to Dori. Was her kiss a reward for doing something right? And if so, what was I willing to do to earn it again? Not be hung-over tomorrow?

The girl next to me paused in the middle of relaying her substance-triggered existential experiences. 'Wanna find a room?' she asked, mistaking my silence for interest, I guess.

I focused on her for the first time since she'd begun talking. She was exceptionally hot, despite her buzzed, slow-blinking expression. Smiling, she took my hand. Her fingers were dainty, linked with mine – even her hand was pretty, her nails perfectly manicured, French tips folding over the top of my hand. She stood and headed towards a hallway. I stood and started to follow. And then I pulled her to a stop and she turned back, confused.

I leaned closer to be heard over the music. 'Not tonight. Maybe some other time.'

She blinked, nonplussed. I untangled my hand from hers and scanned the room for John. As usual, he was relatively easy to find. I just looked for really tall girls.

I told him I thought I had food poisoning and was ditching for tonight, and he followed me to the door, looking worried. 'Hey, man, you need me to drive you home?'

'Nah, I'm good,' I told him. 'Called a taxi already.'

I waited outside in the heat, the effects of the party slowly falling away. I'd only had one drink, hadn't smoked anything or swallowed any pills. It felt good to be in the open air. A little warm, but nothing like digging holes for trees or tamping down sod in full summer sun. I had to laugh. Reid Alexander, landscaping a yard. Man. No wonder the paparazzi were having seizures over it.

Unsure what to do with Mom now, I leave her on my bed and go shower. When I come back, she hasn't moved. I scoop her up, wishing I'd done so before showering, because her breath is sour, and even her perspiration exudes a noxious odour. As I carry her to her room, I'm sucked into a memory – a day prior to her earliest round of rehab.

I was ten or so, and must have just come home from school because I was wearing the uniform of the most elite private elementary school in the state. Mom was in her sitting room with her wedding album on her lap. 'Reid!' she said when I peeked round the corner. 'Come look with me.'

My parents' wedding had been a social event, organized with a precision usually reserved for royalty, the whole wedding party arrayed like beings from a fairy tale hosted by exclusive designers, courtesy of old money. I don't remember the photos themselves, just my impression of them, except for one snapshot of the two of them emerging from the church, thick wooden doors braced open behind them. My mother – petite, blonde and beautiful in her ivory gown – stood with her arm tucked through Dad's, his opposite hand covering hers. My father, in his early thirties, was tall and good-looking. Impressive. No different from his present-day look and demeanour – except in these photos, he was beaming. And he had more hair, not as closely shorn as the present salt-and-pepper version.

My mother's fingers hovered over the photograph, one frosted pink nail tracing her own torso in the stunning ivory gown. 'My gown had seed pearls sewn into the bodice,' she told me. 'I felt like a princess. And your father was so handsome.' They made a striking pair.

'Reid,' she said then, her fingers shaking, suspended over the princess in the photo, 'Mommy's going to be gone for a little while.'

I frowned at her. 'Gone where?'

She swallowed, and it seemed like she was trying to breathe normally. Maybe she was trying not to cry. I stared at her, concerned, and she smiled through watery eyes. 'Well, it seems that you are going to have a little brother or sister, and I need to go away for a little bit, to make sure I don't . . . make sure I don't . . .' She stared at her shaking hand and the photograph underneath it.

'Don't what?' I asked, reeling with the news of a sibling. I remember feeling happy initially, but something was upsetting my mother, so I pushed the joy aside until I had time to understand what I should feel.

'To make sure I don't hurt the baby.'

I had no idea what she meant. I was sure my mother could never hurt anything or anyone. She couldn't even stand to punish me when I was bad – and I was bad pretty often. There was no way she'd hurt a *baby*. I said as much to her, and she started to cry in earnest, the opposite of the effect I was going for. 'This will all work out; everything will be wonderful,' she said, taking my face in her hands. 'And I hope he or she is just like you.'

She'd gone to rehab, lost the baby anyway, came home and started drinking again.

I lay her on her bed now, turning the lamp on low and folding the comforter over her. There's probably more I should do, but I have no idea what. She's getting worse. I know the pattern, know what comes next. We're almost to her rock bottom, a slow drifting downward until we all slam into the ground. Sometimes, she jerks up momentarily only to crash again. I realize I haven't seen her sober in days. I've told myself this is only because I'm not around much, but that's a lie. Every time she stops drinking, I forget how bad it can be until we get here again.

She flops on to her back, starts to snore damned heavily for such a small person. I roll her less than gently back on to her side, not that she notices, and prop pillows behind her. I don't want her to puke while she's on her back. She'd most likely wake up rather than breathe it into her lungs . . . but I can't take that chance.

I sit on the settee facing her bed, my fingers tracing the patterns in the carved teak frame. This is my mother. I would do anything to help her, but there's nothing. She must hate her life to need this escape so badly. I understand that desire, at least. Just make it numb. Make the failures vanish, from the loss of the baby to her mother's disappointment to her husband's withdrawal. And my own disappearing act, from the moment I could pull it off. I don't know if the misery begets the drinking or the drinking begets the misery. I don't have a clue where it all started. All I know is there is no end.

I wake to my father shaking me. 'Reid,' he says. 'You can go now.' His mouth is a tight line as he glances at her and back at me. He's failed her. I've failed her. She's failed herself.

No end.

Dori

When Deb told me to pretend that kiss didn't happen, it sounded so simple.

Sometimes I forget my own aversion to lying, and how lying involves pretending not to feel things that I actually feel. Thinking about Colin reminded me of the sensation of having my heart smashed to smithereens, and then trying to pretend that I wasn't a walking ghost. When he dumped me, it was such an unanticipated end that I moved through my life in a state of shock for days afterwards, waiting to wake up. When I finally realized that it wasn't a nightmare, that it was *real*, it hurt so much I didn't think I could survive.

But I did. And to do so, I had to pretend not to feel it, at least in front of him. In front of my friends and classmates. In front of my parents. And in front of his mother, who for all of her genuine concern and her experience in counselling troubled teens, was clueless to what her own son had done to one of the students right under her nose.

The key to lying skilfully is never lie to *yourself*. And the best way to keep yourself honest internally is to have one person, someone you trust above everyone else, who holds and protects that secret true thing for you. The thing you have to hide from everyone else. Deb has always been that person for me.

When I told her about Colin, she nearly came unglued. Submerged in her studies as a first-year med student, she'd known I was dating someone, but hadn't been as available during the time of my brief sexual relationship with him. The entire story, from the magical beginning to the devastating end, was relayed in one conversation.

My sister has always known how to hold my heart, and her anger at Colin quickly yielded to my need for the empathy only she could provide. 'Oh, baby girl,' she said, her voice breaking. 'You need a pint of java chip and a funny movie. I'll come home the weekend after mid-terms, and we'll do an official exorcism. Gather a stack of photos and anything else you'd like to set fire to because we're going to burn that worthless boy right out of your memory. It won't hurt like this forever. I promise.'

She was right, of course. Three years later, I can't remember how it felt to love Colin. I recall the loss of him as though it had happened to someone else – some naïve, reckless girl I'll never be again.

I hear Reid's voice just before he comes round the corner, upbeat and friendly as he replies to hellos. He's here uncharacteristically early too, so I haven't had time to go over the steps in my head that Deb and I discussed, like a last-minute cramming session before an exam.

One – act like the kiss didn't happen.

Two – if he alludes to the kiss, shrug it off.

Three – arrange to work in a separate area.

Four – don't get caught alone with him.

'Hey,' he says, this greeting preceded by the usual coffee aroma that announces his arrival. My addicted caffeine sensors perk up immediately in expectation of the soy latte I know he's holding, along with a bounce in my heart rate at the sound of his voice.

My own body is a *traitor*.

I turn, smile, take the latte, thank him. Ignore his fingertips brushing over mine. Ignore his beautiful eyes, the dark blue of them intensified by the snug navy t-shirt he's wearing.

'What are we doing today, boss?'

Ignore his now-familiar husky morning voice.

We're in the master bathroom, in blatant non-compliance of Rule Four. I hear other people in the hallway, but we're definitely alone. 'Um, I think you're working with Frank today.' My eyes slide away from his.

'Mmm. Okay. See you at lunch, then?' He leaves the room, sipping his coffee, not waiting for an answer.

If I didn't know him, I'd think he's following Rule One.

What if he *is* following Rule One? That makes everything easier for me, right?

In theory, if Reid pretends we never kissed, it's easier for me *to pretend we never kissed*.

This is what people mean when they use the term *in theory*.

26

REID

I'm not surprised that Dori's strategy is to act like nothing happened between us yesterday. Avoidance is a clever method for getting past any type of emotional eruption. John and I would never have sustained a friendship this long without turning the occasional blind eye to each other's assholian outbursts. Dori responded to that kiss with uninhibited abandon, after which the logical part of her brain began screaming for a do-over back to the moment she could have kept it from occurring at all.

That is not going to happen.

She wants to pretend I never kissed her. I want a repeat performance. Those goals stand on starkly opposite ends of the spectrum. The first step to pulling her to my way of thinking is to meet in the middle. I just have to figure out where the hell the middle is.

The Habitat project is winding to a close. The house is almost finished, and no one is immune to the building anticipation of that completion, which won't occur until after Dori has departed for Ecuador and I've served out my sentence. I have to admit, I sort of want to see it done, see them get the keys. Gabrielle's parents have been working some hours here and there, so I've seen them around, though we haven't crossed paths while working – I'm sure Roberta made sure of that. So I'm kind of stunned when Mrs Diego appears next to me before lunch, as I'm emptying a bag of mulch into the shrub and flower borders across the backyard.

'Mr Alexander,' she says, her accent thick, *Meester Alisander*.

Since no one was injured when my car ploughed through the front of their house, and since the house was a rental and therefore not their property, it wasn't necessary for the Diegos to be present at court. Regardless, I recognize her immediately from the news reports that surrounded my accident. She's petite, more so than she looked on TV, standing next to her husband as they were interviewed by multiple news stations, gesturing to the gaping hole in the house behind them and praising God and a shitload of saints that none of their children were injured.

Her rounded face is weathered, lined more heavily than Mom's, though I suspect she's years younger than my mother. This is a woman who's worked hard all of her adult life, and probably long before that. Her caramel eyes are warm and spirited, though.

I nod, tossing the empty mulch bag with the others. 'Mrs Diego.'

She glances over the flower beds, the pile of mulch I've

yet to spread around the new plants. 'You are doing a good job. Thank you for helping to build our new home.'

For a split second, I'm struck with a sense of self-satisfaction I have no right to feel. But I'm legally obligated to be here, which of course she knows, so I'm not certain how to respond. 'You're welcome,' is all I can think to say. She inclines her head, accepting this trivial reply, allowing the two of us to pretend that I'm another philanthropic, Dori-like person, volunteering my hands and muscles to assist in providing a house for a deserving family.

Lowering myself to the concrete ledge where Dori balances her lunch on her lap and unscrews the lid on a bottle of water, I say quietly, 'So about that kiss . . .'

Inhaling sharply, she turns to me, eyes wide, hands frozen mid-air with the bottle in one hand and the cap in the other.

So much for meeting in the middle.

I wait while she glances around the yard to make sure we can't be overheard. 'That was a momentary lapse of . . . of *reason*,' she hisses. I smile and she glances around again. If anyone is paying attention, the look on her face would convince them we were plotting a break-in at Fort Knox. Luckily, Dori and I sitting next to each other talking isn't news, and the back of my head is blocking any head-on paparazzi shots of her expression before she pulls it under control.

'Last time I checked, kissing wasn't found on the *reason* scale,' I say.

Her lips compress into a hard line, which is a damned

shame. I try not to stare at them. Or think about how they felt when I kissed her, which makes me *want* to stare at them. I concentrate on the faint dusting of freckles across her cheekbones and nose instead, but strangely this only magnifies my craving to kiss her.

'Look.' Her jaw clenches. 'That shouldn't have happened. We need to pretend that never happened.'

I can't help grinning. 'You mean *you* need to pretend it never happened.' My gaze slips to her lips, back to her eyes. 'I, however, want to try it again.'

'Well, I *don't*.' The words are snapped off like she's flicking them at me. She's got the aloof demeanour down pat – eyes narrowed and chin elevated, but the quick pulse beating visibly at the base of her throat gives her away.

'I think you do.'

'Dori?' Our heads snap up simultaneously, guiltily, as though we've been discovered making out in the middle of lunch. Roberta stands over us, her gaze shifting back and forth between us.

Dori scrambles up. 'Yes?' I want to grab her hand, tell her to take a breath and chill, but that would probably have the opposite effect. I can't hear what Roberta asks, and Dori doesn't look back as they move towards the back door. I'm non-existent, or forgotten.

But no. I know where to look to see if she's affected. Her ears don't lie, even if the rest of her is trying its damnedest to.

Dori

'Are you all right?' Roberta peers at me through her owl glasses once we're inside, but her question doesn't make me uneasy because I'm so relieved to escape Reid's assertion. I wish I could say it was utterly false, but it isn't: *I think you do*. My chest goes tight with the accuracy of it.

'Sure. What do you mean?' My objective is to sound casual, which works right up until *mean* comes out as more of a squeak than a word. I clear my throat and repeat, 'Uh, what do you mean?'

A mosquito buzzes in front of her face and she swats at it while I try to compose myself. 'Nothing –' She swats again. 'It just seemed –' swatting with both hands – 'like the two of you were having a disagreement.'

The mosquito buzzes towards me and I clap my hands together, catching it dead centre and then running my palms down my denim shorts. *Eww, eww, eww.* 'Is that why you called me inside?' I hedge, turning to grab a disinfecting wipe and scrubbing my hands with it.

'Er, no.' She walks towards the bedroom serving as her office, tossing back, 'I just wanted to double-check which day next week is your last. Someone asked me yesterday and I said Tuesday, but it occurred to me that I'm not exactly sure.'

Could Reid have posed that enquiry? 'Tuesday is the plan. I leave early Thursday morning, and I thought I should have a day to pack and make sure I've got everything in order.'

'Well,' she smiles, 'everyone will certainly miss you.'

Everyone?

At 2:45, I volunteer to go with Gene, who has to make a run to the garden centre where we get trees and shrubs. Reid will be gone by the time we return. Not that this fact has anything to do with my offer to tag along.

Coward, my body says.

One day down, three to go, my brain says.

27

REID

'So you're out of here after Tuesday, right?'

Dori straightens from rows of plantation blind parts spread across the recently carpeted floor of the living room – slats, cords, hardware and tools separated and organized. 'Correct,' she answers, hesitant. She takes her latte from my hand with both of hers, one over the top, one under the bottom, making sure we don't touch, heedless of what she's revealing. If she was unaffected when I touch her, she wouldn't need to avoid the physical contact. I stuff my free hand in my pocket because that wayward little strand of hair hangs over one of her dark eyes, taunting me with what I did the last time it fell there.

I decided after her disappearing act yesterday afternoon that I might as well pull out the big guns because God knows I've got nothing to lose. Four days from now will be the last I see of her; I can't imagine our paths ever intersecting again. 'Since you'll be busy then with packing and last-minute stuff, let me take you to dinner tonight instead. To thank you for being such a patient overseer.'

Dori is one of the smartest girls I've ever met, so I know she'll see through the fact that I'm acting as if we've already got a date for next week and I'm just repositioning it to be more convenient. She's not going to fall for it, but I'm not sure if she'll call me on it.

She hides behind her hand momentarily, closing her eyes to draw that too-short strand of hair off her face and tuck it behind her ear. She takes a soft breath before speaking. 'I can't go to dinner with you.' Ah – the simple, no-explanation approach.

Nope. She's not getting off that easily.

'Why not?'

'My VBS kids have a rehearsal tonight.'

'Tomorrow, then.'

She fidgets with her cup lid. 'The programme is tomorrow night.'

I take a sip of coffee, stalling. These are legitimate excuses. Does she expect me to continue asking? I never ask twice, let alone three times.

'Sunday night?'

'Church.'

Strike three. I can't help it – I start laughing and she purses her lips and frowns stonily. I tap my chin. 'Let me guess. Monday night your friends are seeing you off, and Tuesday your family has something planned.'

She scrapes the cup lid, not meeting my amused gaze. Which is just as well because I'm feeling as frustrated as I am amused, and I'm not sure how well my blasé guise is holding up. 'Wednesday,' she says, glancing up. 'The family thing is on Wednesday.'

Some teasing comment is on the tip of my tongue, but that's not what emerges. 'So you're free Tuesday.'

She sucks a little air through parted lips. Probably expecting the teasing comment. 'Theoretically.'

'Is that a yes?'

Her chest is rising and falling shallowly because she's allowed me to work her right into a corner and we both know it. She's going to bolt anyway. I see it in her eyes as her brain casts around for a way out of it.

'Dori,' my voice is low, calming, 'it's just dinner, and then you're off to your life and I'm soon off to mine. Unless you want me to believe that teaching me to paint walls and install shelves was oh-so-easy on you.' I smile my most disarming, innocuous smile. 'I've been a splinter in your pinky for three weeks. C'mon. Make me pay for it.' I want to touch her, my fingers curling inside the pocket of my jeans, but I don't dare.

When she nods, it takes every ounce of self-control I have not to pump a fist in the air and say, *Hell, yeah*. 'Okay,' she says, eyeing me. 'Just dinner.'

'Dinner. Tuesday. Good.' I pull my phone from my pocket and get her number and address before she changes her mind, and then I tap the lid of my cup against hers before I go outside. 'Later, boss.'

Dori

What. Have. I. Done.

28

REID

In the interest of giving Dori less opportunity to back out on tonight, I've kept my distance for the past few days. I ate lunch with Frank on Friday and Gabrielle yesterday, while continuing the morning latte delivery, timed for when Dori was occupied with something or someone that distracted her from speaking to me alone.

Now it's Tuesday morning, and it's clear she's confused. This is a perfect execution of my usual game plan: a shifting pattern of advance and retreat, sidestepping any resistance until I get what I want. That's the problem, though – I still don't know what I want beyond a repeat of that kiss, and I seriously doubt any more than that would be possible.

Maybe Tadd was right, and the mere challenge of her is the thing that's messing with my head. There's something uncontaminated about her, and I don't even mean sexually or whatever. I mean the way she *is*, at her core. Like when you wake up and the world has been blanketed by snow overnight, and not a single footstep or tyre track has spoiled the untouched perfection of it.

Do I want to be that bastard kid who clomps all over the yard, just because?

When I arrive, I find Dori easily by her familiar very-patient voice as she demonstrates to Gabrielle how to apply stencilled patterns to her pink wall. 'Once you have the stencil secure, dab this domed brush into the paint, and then on to the wall. But make sure you don't get too much, or it'll drip.'

'Like this?' Gabrielle asks, and Dori nods, watching her. 'Perfect.'

I haven't spoken or made a sound, but Dori turns slowly, as though I whispered her name. A small crease appears between her brows as she watches me cross the room.

Gabrielle turns then too, skipping up to meet me halfway and bouncing as she pulls up in front of me, hands clasped. 'Oooh, is the one with whipped cream for me?'

'Of course. Maybe all that sugar will make you sweeter.'

She rolls her eyes and giggles, forever unoffended by anything I say to her.

Dori seems so reserved in contrast, and I smile down at her as she murmurs her thanks and takes her cup. She forgets to avoid the slide of my fingers against hers . . . or she chooses not to avoid it. 'You're welcome,' I say in return.

I'm halfway down the hall when I hear Dori say my name. As I turn, I'm scrambling for a rational argument for why she can't cancel on me.

'Are we still –?' she begins, stopping mid-sentence when I face her.

'Yeah. Of course.' The tone of my voice says I'd maybe forgotten the whole thing, when in actuality I'm relieved and switching gears. 'Seven okay?' I step closer, look down into her upturned face. The day outside is overcast, darkening the hallway, so I can barely distinguish her pupils from the deep brown of her irises. She glances at the cup in her hand, and I note the thickness of her lashes, long and straight as they feather across the tops of her cheeks, framing her eyes as she looks back up at me.

'Seven's good. How . . . should I dress?'

I consider her experience with church and school functions, the strict views of proper and inappropriate, dressing up or dressing down. With the exceptions of filming and my recent court appearance, I wear whatever I want because I just don't give a shit. Respect should be reserved for the person, not the outfit.

For my last photo shoot, they put me on a float in a chlorinated pool wearing a Gucci suit, reclining, one pant leg dangling in the water. The suit, worth thousands, was thoroughly ruined by the half-hour soak in pool chemicals. Contrast this with the fact that I regularly walk into jacket-and-tie-only restaurants wearing jeans and a t-shirt. No one ever says anything other than, *Right this way, Mr Alexander*. I suspect this is one aspect of celebrity Dori would appreciate.

'Dress however you want,' I tell her. 'Just be comfortable.'

Dori

Dress however I want? What does that *mean*?

I've never been too caught up in fashion beyond following whatever social constraints were in place – a modest dress or skirt at church, modest jeans and t-shirts for school. *Modest* is the adjective most likely to describe any piece of clothing I own, unless *blah* can be used as an adjective. Not that I want to wear anything provocative to go to dinner with Reid. But I don't particularly want to look like a street person, either. Photographers follow him everywhere. I shouldn't care, but I do, a little. So on Sunday night, when I surveyed the garments hanging in my closet and stuffed into the armoire I inherited from my grandmother, I felt genuine fear. If I knew his phone number, I'd have texted him right then and cancelled.

Now he's telling me to dress comfortably – however I want. And I seriously have no idea what he means by that. What was I thinking, agreeing to this? When I told Deb, she sighed heavily. 'Be careful, baby girl. Forget comfortable – wear something with a padlock. And leave the key at home.'

I laughed half-heartedly. No one could see through me like Deb, even from hundreds of miles away. 'Yeah. I know.'

I could call Aimee and Kayla, but they would hyperventilate at the thought of Reid Alexander taking me to dinner. They would also insist on performing an emergency head-to-toe makeover, and that is *not* happening. This is not a date. This is just dinner.

Just. Dinner.

*

I'm staring into my closet again, and predictably, nothing has magically appeared since I looked two nights ago. I'm obsessing and I know it. I tell myself to choose something already and put it on. He doesn't care what I wear.

I yank a dress off a hanger and pull it over my head, and then search through unlabelled shoeboxes for the heeled sandals I wore to graduation. I usually wear flats with dresses because if I'm wearing a dress, there's a ninety-nine per cent chance I'm at church, and if I'm at church, I'm helping with anything from nursery duty to passing out Sunday service bulletins. Plus heels aren't the most comfortable footwear ever invented. After my interminable graduation ceremony, I whined to Mom that enduring a few hours in those things gave me newfound sympathy for those unfortunate Chinese girls with the bound feet. She laughed, said, 'Welcome to womanhood,' and gave me a foot massage. I haven't worn them since, which means they're still new and are going to pinch the fudge out of my toes.

I move to the mirror and check my reflection. Unsurprisingly, the plain black sleeveless sheath hasn't turned me into a hottie, even with the strappy black heels. The most praise I could give myself is that this is an improvement over my usual grungy construction worker look. I hope.

I stuff my cell, lipgloss and my licence into the tiny designer knock-off wallet-on-a-strap that Aimee and Kayla brought me from their trip to New York last summer. I usually carry an enormous canvas bag that holds every-thing from ibuprofen to a small pack of crayons, and if necessary, a change of clothes. Dad calls it my Mary Poppins satchel and amuses himself by asking me if I happen to have a hat rack handy. A guy at school once told people I kept a sleeping bag in there, which is idiotic and I can't fathom why anyone believed him, but a few people actually did.

I haven't told Mom and Dad what I'm doing tonight yet. I'm not sure *why* I haven't told them. I'm not afraid they'll forbid me from going – as far as they know, there are no irresponsible deeds in my past, so why would there be any in my future? Not that going to dinner with Reid is irresponsible. Odd, maybe. I look in the mirror one last time before I go downstairs. This is far from the partying outfit some starlet or society girl would wear out, but it's equally far from anything *I'd* typically wear.

When my heels strike the worn wood floor at the foot of the stairs, Esther trots round the corner and stops feet from me, ears pricked up, head tilted. Great. My outfit confuses my *dog*. This doesn't bode well for my parents' reaction.

I walk into the kitchen where they're making dinner, and Dad pauses in his account of a parishioner whose eleven-year-old son was caught selling amphetamines at school. 'Not having dinner with us tonight, pumpkin?' he asks, probably noticing no more about my attire than the fact that I'm wearing shoes.

Mom isn't as clueless. Her eyes go a little wide when she turns round. 'Dori in a dress? And *heels*? What's happened? Doug, quick, check the window. Are pigs flying by?' She laughs at her own joke and I roll my eyes at her. 'Seeing Nick tonight?' she asks slyly.

I purse my lips. I should have expected that assumption. 'Er, no, actually. I'm just, uh, going to dinner with Reid.'

They both blink, puzzled.

'Reid? As in Reid Alexander, the movie star?' Mom recovers first.

'That's the one.' My voice is overly bright. I shrug. 'He sort of wanted to apologize – well, you know, as much as he ever apologizes – for being such a pain the past few weeks.'

Her left eyebrow crooks up. 'Reid Alexander, the spoiled movie star, is taking you to dinner to apologize for acting like a spoiled movie star,' she reiterates.

I nod.

'And there's no *other* reason he wants to take you on a date . . .'

'It's not a date,' I say, too quickly, and her right eyebrow rises to the level of the left one, her eyes scanning me head to toe. 'Mom, honestly, this outfit is so . . . so . . .'

'So unlike something my daughter, Dori, normally wears?'

My cheeks warm, and I hope the light is low enough to mask it. Dad's eyes dart between us. He's trying to determine whether or not he should be alarmed.

'I just don't want to embarrass myself in front of the spoiled movie star, that's all.'

Mom looks at Dad pointedly and he clears his throat. 'Um, I don't think your mother is questioning your motives, pumpkin, just *his*.'

Oh my *gosh*. 'We aren't exactly celebrity watchers, but you guys must know the type of girl Reid would be interested in – in *that way* – and I'm so *not* like that. It would be humiliating if I even *wanted* him to feel that way. Trust me, I *don't* and he *doesn't*. He's just being . . . nice.' I struggle not to think of that kiss, certain it will show on my face.

'Humph,' Mom says.

'I don't know, Dori,' Dad says.

Their belief that I could be some sort of celebrity-tempting siren is almost humorous. But since I just twisted the truth claiming I've never wanted Reid to want me – even if that desire only existed for a few seconds – this line of questioning is anything but funny. 'Trust me.'

'We do!' they chorus, just as the doorbell rings, Esther barks, and I jump, one-two-three.

'Okay, well, I'm sure I won't be very late.' As I head for the front door, Mom shoves Dad in my direction.

'I'll, er, get the door and meet the young man before you go. Just in case.'

I don't ask what *just in case* means.

Esther is on full alert, barking like someone is taking an axe to the door. 'Esther, *quiet. Sit.*' Instantly silent, she sits. 'Good girl.' Esther obeys Dad and Deb every time, and Mom and me when she's in the mood. She knows who she can manipulate to bend the rules a little. Like me and the no-dogs-on-the-sofa rule. Mom and the no-dogs-on-the-bed rule. Both of us and the no-people-food rule.

Dad opens the door with his best Dad Smile – the expression that says: *I'm smiling, but if you hurt my daughter, I know a place where no one will ever think to dig.* 'Mr Alexander, I presume.'

29

REID

'Your parents are nice,' I say as she settles into the back seat next to me, pulling the seat belt across her chest and fastening it with a snap. 'Not that I expected anything else.'

She smirks. 'Yes, I come from a long line of nice people.' Her fingertips drift absently over the smooth leather of the car seat. 'Those with a sarcastic edge, like me for example, are expected to marry someone super-agreeable, so our descendants don't become totally unlikeable.'

My first thought is that this removes me from the running immediately and without question. The hell? I don't want to marry Dori. I don't want to marry anyone. *Ever*. I can't imagine why I'm bothered to be eliminated from the running for something I don't want.

'That's too bad.'

Her hand stills on the edge of the seat. 'Oh?'

I can't seem to stop myself. I've switched to autopilot. 'I think you'd be bored to death with someone too agreeable.'

'So you think agreeableness is boring?' She arches a brow, as though I've just called *her* boring.

I shrug. 'It's fine, in moderation. But in a relationship, a little fire is a good thing.' *What the hell is wrong with me?*

'Like you would know,' she says, and then slaps her hand over her mouth, eyes wide.

'Touché,' I laugh.

Through her hands, she says, 'I'm sorry. That was a hateful thing to say.' But she's trying not to laugh at the same time.

Insulting my capacity to maintain a relationship, hateful? Please. That's probably the least insulting slur she's thrown at me. 'Not unwarranted, though,' I say, still smiling.

Her hair is down, drifting over her shoulders – no practical ponytail tonight. The highlights and lowlights I noticed when she walked up behind her dad must be natural because I can't imagine her bothering to add them.

Speaking of practical – her little black dress and the classic-not-trendy heels.

I've never actually *seen* her upper arms before, since the sleeves of her t-shirts hang to her elbows. Her delts and biceps are curved and defined, strong but still feminine. The classic square neckline exposes the lines of her collarbone and the flutter of a pulse at the base of her throat, but isn't low enough to show any cleavage. The waist nips in just under her ribcage, somewhat fitted. I'm familiar with her legs, of course, though her work shorts actually show more of them. Not that this says much.

'This is the best I could do.' She breaks into my reverie,

gesturing to her dress. 'I hope we aren't going anywhere too fancy.' Her hands twist in her lap, and I realize I've been staring at her. No one in the history of my dating life has dressed so sensibly and riveted my attention so entirely while doing so.

'First, we look pretty damned coordinated.' I indicate my grey slacks and black shirt. 'Second, I'm used to seeing you in construction boots and a noble t-shirt *du jour*, most of which are pointedly anti-everything-I-stand-for. Your little black dress is a charming substitute.' She sucks her lip into her mouth and I strive to ignore that token of her uncharacteristic anxiety and the memory it evokes. 'I think you'll like where we're going. No worries, okay?'

She nods, the corners of her mouth turning up, just barely, in a tiny indication of trust.

The restaurant is hole-in-the-wall and below street level, situated just off a standard strip mall. It's mom-and-pop Italian, unfrequented by celebrities, so no one is ever expecting to see one. Even if I'm recognized, I can almost hear the *No, that can't be him* thought that follows. I've never brought a date here because it's my secret and I don't want it spoiled.

The driver drops us at the door, and two minutes later, we're shown to a booth in the corner. This is the best part – the booths around the perimeter are enclosed in their own wooden cubicles. The panelled walls separating each booth extend to the low ceiling and have hinged doors that can be pulled shut, concealing the interior from other patrons. Inside, the ancient panelling is coated in graffiti, Sharpied or carved into the wood: *M+L always & forever, Katie loves Antonio, Stephanie & Lauren BFFs 4ever!*

Dori sits across from me, her gaze drifting over every detail. A trio of flickering low-wattage 'candle' bulbs inside a bevelled-glass hanging lamp casts a soft glow over us both. The waiter steps up to the table with a basket of bread and two glasses of water. He extends the wine list and I take it, asking Dori, 'Do you have a preference?'

I'm not surprised when she answers, 'Oh, I'm fine with water,' but it does make me wonder if she ever drinks at all. The very proper eighteen-year-old daughter of a pastor. I'm guessing *no*.

I hand the list back to the waiter. 'Nothing tonight.' I can go without for one evening.

'Very good, sir,' he replies, offering menus and rattling off the specials before asking if we'd like the doors shut while we decide.

'Sure,' I say. 'And no rush.' He swings the doors shut and we're treated to additional graffiti – more declarations of love forever, plus a few artistic doodles and an Oscar Wilde quote. 'What do you think? You look apprehensive. Do you want the doors left open?'

She smiles, and relief washes over me. 'No, leave them closed. It's cosy. I had no idea this place was here. How did you find it?'

'My parents and I used to come often, when I was young.' The owners remember my parents by name, and ask me about them whenever they're here. Their son runs the place now, so luckily that coincidence is rare.

'You don't ever go out with them now? Do they still live in LA?' Dori asks, as though she's reading my mind. Damn.

'They do. But my father is a workaholic and my mother's an alcoholic, so we don't really do the family outings any more.' I take a deep breath after this disclosure, incredulous to have just divulged that level of familial defect.

Her eyes don't leave mine, her brow creased, compassion all over her face. This is the sort of expression that usually infuriates me – and yes, I know who I'm actually furious *with*, but that fact doesn't stop me from lashing out at whatever unfortunate person sits there, daring to think they know how I feel. 'I'm so sorry,' she says. For some reason, I believe her.

'Yeah, it sucks.' I have to redirect this conversation *now*. 'I take it you and your very nice parents still do family dinners, etcetera.'

She nods. 'We're pretty nerdy.' Leaning forward, she gets a mischievous look in her eyes and stage-whispers, 'We even have Scrabble night. You almost nailed that one, when you listed the stuff I do with my evenings. Except it's on Fridays, not Tuesdays.'

Oh, God. 'Wow. I'm such an asshole.'

'Hmm,' she says non-committally. 'I have a confession.' Her expression is unwavering, and I instinctively brace myself. 'I didn't expect you to work so hard over the past month. Or to be so unpretentious and respectful. With, you know, everyone but me.'

I laugh. 'I was respectful to you! Sort of.' The memory of coaxing her mouth open with my tongue almost knocks the amused expression from my face, and I fight to keep it there. 'But I wasn't, at first. I was a complete dick, and I'm sorry about that. I pegged you as sanctimonious and self-righteous, and I was wrong.'

She's still smiling – a good sign. 'Well, I *am* a little sanctimonious.'

I smile back. 'No. You assumed that I'm self-centred. Used to getting my way. Dismissive of personal responsibility. And you were right – I am all of those things.'

Her expression transforms from humour to something pensive and serious. 'If that's not who you want to be, all you have to do is choose not to be those things.'

'That simple, huh? All "*Be the change you want to see in the world*"?' I feel an undeserved sense of pride when she seems pleased.

'I think people assume Gandhi wanted everyone to adopt his quest for world peace, and they use that quote with that assumption in mind, rather than the doable urging it was.' Her dark eyes are animated. 'Few of us can actually change the world. We can only change ourselves. But if enough people took that to heart, the world *would* change.'

A tap sounds on one of the doors, and the waiter leans in, asking, 'Are we ready to order?'

Dori opens her menu, contrite. 'I'm sorry, I haven't even looked yet.'

'Give us a few more minutes,' I say, and he disappears with a nod.

As Dori reads over the menu I memorized years ago, I pretend to do the same, my mind humming. She believes I have the potential to be someone I've never been. Someone I've never wanted to be, or thought possible to be.

That's not exactly true. I *have* wanted it. Last spring, I thought I could be a different guy if I was with Emma. And then she told me she didn't want someone who needed *her* in order to be a better guy. She wanted someone who was better by himself, with or without her.

For the first time, I see her point.

I've known for a very long time that I can't change anyone else. But I've always looked at self-transformation as means to an end, so any change I made was temporary.

I'm afraid of becoming my workaholic father, but the only thing I'm ever serious about is work. I'm afraid of becoming my alcoholic mother, but the type of drinking I did the night I crashed into the Diego house wasn't an isolated incident. Only hitting a damned *house* was isolated. All the other times, when I managed to get myself home without destroying property or killing anyone on the way – that was luck.

'How's the ziti here?' Dori asks, glancing up from her menu.

'Hmm? The ziti? It's good.' I resolve to contemplate this shit later. I only have a couple of hours with this girl, and I don't want to waste them soul-searching or self-flagellating. Plenty of time for that after she leaves town.

We pull up to the kerb and she glances at her house, then back at me. The porch lamp is on, shedding a spotlight over the front door, pooling on the concrete space in front of it and spilling over the cracked steps, the illumination tapering off once it hits the edge of faded lawn.

This is the sort of pivotal scene I've filmed a dozen times – a typical boy delivering a typical girl home just under the curfew wire. It generally plays out in one of two ways. Either the boy lets the girl out of the car with an *okay, see ya*, or he follows her to the door and tries to kiss her goodnight – the success or failure of which depends on the script.

Dori's dark eyes are impossible to read in the dim interior of the car, but her hands, clasped in her lap, are not. As this thought crosses my mind, she loosens them, offering one to me. 'Thank you for dinner. It was fun and . . . enlightening?' She laughs amiably and I take her small hand in mine. The moment we touch, her laugh evaporates.

'Everything around you is enlightening,' I say cryptically, not even sure what the hell I mean beyond the fact that knowing her has revealed parts of myself to me that I didn't know existed. If that isn't enlightening, I don't know what is.

Clearing her throat, she squeezes my hand once before slipping hers from my grasp. She turns towards the door, fingers on the handle. 'Well.' She looks over her shoulder with a wry smile and I'm frozen in place. I've thoroughly enjoyed tonight, and it feels like it's lasted half an hour. 'Goodbye, Reid. Be good.' Before she can open her door, the driver is there, opening it for her. 'Oh!' she says, laughing again. 'I think it would take me a *long* time to get used to this.'

Her laugh snaps me out of my stupor, and while she's exiting her side, I'm exiting mine, coming round to meet her on the sidewalk. 'It wouldn't take as long as you might think,' I say, extending the crook of my elbow. She swallows visibly, looping her hand through my arm, her fingers cool against my forearm.

We walk towards the door, and I pull her to a slow stop just outside the edge of illumination. She allows me to tug her closer, regarding me silently. Even in her heels, she's a head shorter than me. 'When you tell me to be good, it makes me want to be good,' I say, hearing the undisguised desire in my voice. I run my fingers through the hair at her temples, taking her face between my palms, and she doesn't move. 'It also makes me want to be very, very bad.' And then I kiss her.

Dori

When he kisses me, I forget everything – where I am, where we've been and what we've said. I forget the fact that I'll never see him again unless I buy a ticket or rent a movie to do so. As I climb the stairs moments later, that truth spills out from my subconscious in a rush – *I will never see him again*. It's all I can do to remove the key from my bag with shaking fingers, unlock the door and drift through, turning to watch from the darkened entryway as the car pulls away and is gone.

My head is still swimming, my face burning at the edges where he touched me with his warm hands as his mouth moved over mine. This time there was no negotiation, and he wasted no effort with restraint or testing my boundaries. Pulling my body up against his, one arm encircled me as he leaned down. He kissed me gently but deeply, drawing a response that was all hunger and instinct. My hands clutched his shirt, holding on for dear life until he stopped and opened his eyes, his forehead against mine, his breaths echoing mine – ragged and wanting more.

'Goodbye, Dori,' he whispered, and my own farewell hung in my throat as his lips grazed my cheek, and then he was walking to the car, never looking back.

I fear that I'll compare this kiss with every other kiss I will receive for the rest of my life, an unattainable standard by which to measure future faceless men. Maybe I'm being melodramatic, and the memory of this kiss will begin to fade tomorrow, or next week, or some day. But tonight I'm on fire, walking quietly up the staircase to my room, as though my lips are the conductors of every possible significant feeling, and every neurological receptor in my body is flooded with heat.

Mom and Dad are asleep, the slit of space beneath their bedroom door dark. My bedside lamp is on. The curtains are drawn. Clothes I left in the dryer are now folded and stacked on my dresser; various toiletries cover the top of my desk. Esther waits on my bed, her tail thumping the mattress slowly, like a drum. I run my hand over her silky head and she nuzzles into it, her tongue lolling out one side of her mouth. She looks like she's smiling, this beloved expression of hers one that usually brings an answering smile to my face.

Tonight my lips feel numb. No, not numb. Bereft.

When he asked me to dinner, he said, *You'll be off to your life and I'll soon be off to mine.* No false promises, no option or threat of postponing the oh-so-inevitable end. The dinner, the conversation, the kiss – these were all part of a pleasant but no less certain goodbye. Since the moment I met him, I've looked forward to the end of our frustrating association.

Now it's over, he's gone and I feel a hollow place inside, like he's taken a slice of me with him as a souvenir.

30

REID

'So, think you'll do more volunteering after this?' Frank asks as we lay out a recent donation of decorative pavers from the patio to the back gate.

'After my court-ordered penalty is complete, you mean?' The flagstone slabs vary in size. Making a pathway of them consists of what Frank terms puzzle-piecing and I call guess-work. Frank is usually easy-going, but when it comes to stone placement, he'd give Dori a run for her perfectionism money. *Dammit, I don't want to think about her.* I glare at the cloudless blue sky, removing one glove and using the bottom of my t-shirt to wipe the sweat from my face. LA is enjoying another summer heatwave, and since the saplings we've planted amount to tall sticks with very little foliage, there's zero shade in this yard.

'Dori's not here, you know,' Frank says.

My eyes snap to his. 'What?'

He takes a generous few gulps from his water bottle. 'You may be here under court order, but you could have been a bastard about it, could've given a lot less effort than you have. As far as I'm concerned, you're volunteer enough to go by the title. I'd be happy to have you back.'

This echoes what Dori said the night before last. And clearly, *I can't stop thinking of her*. 'Thanks, Frank. That means a lot coming from you.'

'Yep.'

Frank dislikes compliments, no matter how vague. Last week Dori whispered, 'Watch this,' after making me promise not to react, and then she told Frank that he looked *very* handsome in teal. He glanced down at his teal linen shirt and blushed, mumbling something resembling, 'Mmmph,' before bulleting to the other side of the patio. Dori turned back to me with the naughtiest look ever on her face. With effort, we suppressed our laughter as I fought to disregard the desire to pull her on to my lap and kiss her.

Shit. Stop *thinking about her* already. I'm almost out of here. This day and one more.

'Volunteering for real – I don't know. It's possible,' I tell him, recalling my conversation with Larry a few weeks ago about doing manual labour charity work, when I retorted something along the lines of, *No way in hell*. Wow. I'm a grade-A dick.

Tomorrow is my last day at the Diego house, and George called last night to let me know that production has moved the dates up on my Vancouver project. I'll be on location in three weeks – the day before Dori returns from Ecuador. I have less than a month to beef up and pack on the last five pounds of the twenty I promised to add in order to land the role. George warned me that the director and some of the production team were against hiring me because they wanted the character to be older and bigger, but the guys financing the film wanted my name in the credits. Money talks, but if I screw this up, I could depreciate my future value and seriously lessen the chances of anyone giving me another shot at a film like this one.

To that end, Olaf has promised to kill me starting this weekend. Awesome. If nothing else, maybe I'll be able to get some sleep after he shreds me every day. I tossed and turned so much last night that I found myself up at 4 a.m. Googling Vancouver's weather, popular attractions and hot nightspots . . . and then Quito's weather, topography, possible safety issues and time zone (two hours ahead of LA and Vancouver, which are the same).

I've got to get this girl out of my head. I need time and distance, and I'm about to get both. Despite how she responded to me physically, despite this insistent pull towards her that I'm trying (and failing) to brush aside, she knows and I know that we would never work. Everything about us is different – every damned thing. I've never given a shit about that before. I've never *thought* about that before. When you're hooking up with a girl, all that matters is what she looks like and how fast and hard she'll put out.

Who cares about her past, her beliefs, her aspirations?

Who cares if she has kind eyes or endless patience or the ability to put the needs of everyone on the goddamned *planet* ahead of her own?

*

We're not a mile away from the house when we pass Gabrielle on the side of the road, standing in front of her piece of crap Cutlass – smoke pouring from under the hood and hazards flashing. Some guy in a truck has pulled over in front of her car. He looks about twenty-five and I don't recognize him. 'Hey, Luis, pull a U-turn, man. I know that girl back there.'

Gabrielle's eyes widen when she sees the Mercedes pull up behind her car. As I exit, the guy standing next to her glares at me with undisguised loathing. He's dressed and tattooed like a gang member, which doesn't preclude him from knowing her, but I suspect he's a complete stranger who only stopped to help a hot girl into his car. 'Car trouble?' I say, ignoring him.

'Yeah. It does this every month or so, no biggie.' She shrugs, noticeably embarrassed. This car isn't just a late model, it's *ancient*. Unlike one of my dad's cars – a pristine 1968 Mercedes 280S – this Oldsmobile Cutlass, at least a decade younger, hasn't been well cared for. There are rust spots in the doors and sides, the roof lining is hanging down like curtain swags and the tyres are too bald to be remotely safe. The fact that it's not running isn't much of a shock.

'So . . . is your mom or dad coming to get you? Or a friend?' I ask. Her would-be rescuer stands there regarding me icily, and I'm all kinds of glad Luis is in the car behind us.

'They aren't answering their phones. They don't always get reception at work . . .' She shrugs.

'C'mon, then. I'll give you a ride home.'

She grins ear to ear, but then her smile falters. 'Um, I

promised my little brothers I'd pick them up early from daycare and take them for ice cream. I guess . . . they can just stay till Mama or Papa picks them up . . .'

'Ice cream sounds good after today. If you guys don't mind being stuck in the car with me. I'm sweaty as hell.'

'You know this *pendejo*?' Ah, so her roadside companion speaks – if only to call me an asshole.

One hand on her hip, Gabrielle answers him in Spanish, which I understand *just* well enough to know I'd better steer her to the car before she gets bitch-slapped. 'Thanks for stopping, man,' I tell him while taking Gabrielle by the arm and quickly directing her into the back seat.

An hour later, her car's been towed and we've got the twins in the car. Since they're nine, they're way more impressed that they can make faces through the dark-tinted windows that other drivers can't see than the fact that I'm a movie star. They're also awed by the fact that I've got a guy to drive me around wherever I want to go; their sister better comprehends the way I miss my own wheels.

Gabrielle directs Luis to an ice-cream shop in her old neighbourhood and the boys go into raptures when I tell them to get whatever they want. I don't think the words *get whatever you want* have ever been uttered to them before. It takes them a full ten minutes of discussion to decide what to get, and since we're the only customers, the woman behind the counter takes the break to watch entertainment news on a tiny television by the register. One of the commentators says my name and I feign inattentiveness as the clerk glances between me and my image on the tiny screen. Finally, she stares at me, mouth slightly ajar and eyebrows elevated to the level of her pink visor, and I smile at her. When we leave, she's grabbing up her cell and taking photos of our retreating backsides.

Luis raises an eyebrow when we exit, the boys with what look like quart-sized cartons each, and Gabrielle and I each holding an overloaded cone. 'Dinner is officially *spoiled*,' I tell her as one of her brothers calls shotgun and the other squeezes between us in the back seat. 'Your mother is going to kill me.'

Gabrielle smiles prettily. 'No, she won't. Mama likes you.'

'Oh?' I'm taken by surprise, even though Mrs Diego thanked me for working on the house just a couple of days ago. I mean, Jesus, I ran into her house with my car. 'Must be my infamous charm and good looks.'

She laughs and shakes her head. 'She says you're a hard worker. That's the *only* thing that ever impresses Mama.'

Dori

I was in line for airport security at 7 a.m. for the flight to Miami, and from there, I caught my connection to Quito. I've made this trip twice before – each of the past two summers – but having experience in LA-to-Quito travel doesn't make the thirteen-hour trip feel any shorter. It's almost midnight by the time I get settled into the women's dormitory, and I'll probably be lucky to get five hours of sleep before it's time to get up.

There's always a lot to be done. Children in Quito are sent into the city in droves to beg or shine shoes to help support their families. My first year here, we refurbished a school and organized learning activities with children whose parents spared them from a few days of work. I asked one group of little boys whether they attended school during the regular school year. All of them said no, but some had siblings who did. When I asked why some of their siblings were allowed to go and they weren't, one replied, 'My sister is smart, so she goes to school and we work.' It broke my heart. These kids were exceedingly bright but they were all resigned to the impression that they weren't.

In some ways, returning last year was even more depressing. We'd made an impact that first year I volunteered, and returning a year later to find nothing improved made me want to scream with frustration. I'd never fully understood my parents and Deb when they talked about social progress in terms of two steps up, one step back – sometimes two. Deflated, I called Deb in San Diego, where she was doing a summer research internship before her last year of med school.

'Dori, small gains are still gains. Sweeping changes occur over time. They're hardly noticeable while they're occurring. Think about the difference thirty, forty or a *hundred* years have made in things like race relations, animal testing or recognition of addiction as a disease.'

Her rational words calmed me, but couldn't stop the whine that seeped into my voice. 'It's not fair.'

She chuckled softly. 'I know, sweetie. But the world

doesn't operate on fairness. You know that as well as I do.' Talking to Deb can be like having your hand held while you swallow nasty-tasting medicine or get a shot. She can't make the bad stuff go away, but she makes it easier to take. 'If you want to make a difference eventually, you just keep on.'

I heeded her advice then and over the past year, and here I am in Ecuador for a third time, more prepared for the conditions I'll find and ready to tackle them.

Using this time to overcome the reckless feelings I've developed for Reid is something else I have to do. I vow to return to LA in a more rational frame of mind because over the past forty-eight hours I've done little but recall abstracts of him like a series of film clips: his disdain the morning I met him. His sarcasm and charm, and the unsettling way they combined to make him impossible to ignore. The pride on his face when he finished the shelves. The surprise in his eyes when he blurted out the truth about his parents over dinner. The gentleness of his kiss.

Once I get through customs, I'm met by Ana Diaz, a missionary who resides here year-round, trying to reach and educate as many Ecuadorian kids as possible. 'Welcome back, Dori,' she says, hugging me.

By 1 a.m., I'm staring at the bottom of the bunk above me, restless and awake, surrounded by the soft, slumbering breaths of the women I'll meet tomorrow. I could blame my sleeplessness on the cold – the night-time temps in Quito are around fifty degrees year-round – but I'm not dense enough to think a bit of a chill would keep me from sleeping after this exhausting day.

The truth is I'm sufficiently warm, recalling Reid's fingers playing through my hair, holding my face and trailing down my bare arms, his mouth on mine. The sensations that warm me are the same delicious sensations responsible for my insomnia, but my mind refuses to meditate on something else, anything else. For tonight I surrender, my hands restless under blankets softened and worn from use. Tomorrow will be soon enough to begin erasing him.

31

REID

'You're certain about this?' I can't recall Dad ever looking at me with such an incredulous expression, and believe me, I've witnessed incredulity on his face a million times.

'Yes, I'm sure.'

Saturday mornings, my father is in his home office, catching up on whatever work he didn't vanquish in his sixty-hour work week. The idea that Mom or I would disturb him before noon is inconceivable, since we're usually asleep. So when I knocked on his door at 9 a.m., he seemed disconcerted by my appearance. Then I told him I had a financial matter to discuss, apart from our monthly consultations over my expenditure and investments. He regained his composure quickly, obviously expecting me to request additional cash because I'd run through my allotted spending money ahead of schedule.

Instead, I told him I wanted three cars purchased and delivered to the Diegos, anonymously, on the day they get the keys to their house.

'But the anonymity . . .' he says, brows drawn together. 'No PR? No tax break? It's a significant financial output for no personal advantage.'

His tone says he'll do what I want, even if he's baffled by the uncharacteristic request. It's *my* money, after all; he just manages it for me, since I've never taken much interest in anything beyond spending it. 'It has to be anonymous. And you just described most of my expenditure, when it comes down to it.'

He chuckles in spite of himself. 'Point taken.' He frowns one final time. 'And this has nothing to do with the girl.'

I smirk. 'Dad, what exactly are you suggesting?'

He huffs a breath through his nose and scowls, his gaze never leaving my face, ever the legal eagle. 'I think you know damned well what I'm suggesting, Reid. I usually overlook your . . . indiscretions . . . but the Diego girl is under age.'

Deep breath, in and out, through my teeth. 'Yes, I got the idea after seeing first-hand the unreliable piece of crap she's driving around LA.' I hold up a hand to silence him. 'But I don't want any of them to know about my connection to this, so it can hardly be used as bait. As out of character as this may seem to you, it's something I want to do. Reparation for the harm I caused. Humour me.'

He's silent for a moment, after which he shrugs. 'I don't know what's gotten into you, but all right. These are the vehicles you want?' He points to his monitor, where he's pulled up the links I sent last night.

'Yeah. John and I built them online to confirm which

features were available, so those are the exact specs. They're all reliable, but not flashy.'

He nods. 'Flashy wouldn't do them any favours in their part of town. I'll request all available security components as well, to discourage theft.'

'Thanks, Dad.' I stand up to leave, but turn back. 'Needless to say, don't tell Larry. Don't even tell George, just in case. I think he'd play along, but . . . better to keep this between you and me, I think.'

He's looking at me with that same incredulous expression. 'All right.'

I turn and leave his office, wondering why it took me so long to discover this sort of high. The month with Habitat affected me more than I thought.

Dori

'You're as difficult to get hold of as I am these days,' Deb laughs. Hers is the first phone call I've had since Mom and Dad called me last weekend. We've been playing phone tag for the past twenty-four hours, and I'd almost given up having an actual conversation with her. Quito and Indianapolis are only an hour off, but she works all night and I work all day, our times overlapping at both ends. 'How's it going?'

Perfect timing. I'm sitting on my bunk, sifting through sheet music for this afternoon. 'Really well. I've got an enthusiastic group this year – I'm teaching them songs that help them learn math concepts. They're all so smart! But here's the coolest thing – I've been tutoring a couple of girls close to my age in English and math.' It's impossible to keep the excitement out of my voice. 'When I met them two weeks ago, they both assumed they'd drop out of school soon to get married or start working full-time. Now one is determined to at least finish high school, and the other is talking about going to *college*.'

'That's awesome, Dori.'

'I feel like I'm making a tangible difference this time.' My bunkmate comes in then, climbs the ladder to the top bunk and collapses with a moan. She's Mom's age and arrived in Ecuador the night before last with a group of women from her church in Oklahoma. 'Everything okay, Gina?' I call up.

'Aaaaugh . . . this altitude is *killing* me.' She leans over, peering at me from her upside-down position. 'Are you talking to your sister? Did you ask if she has any recommendations for me?'

'She would tell you the same thing I told you yesterday. No overexertion and lots of fluids.' Deb chuckles in my ear. People – from friends and family to complete strangers – have been asking her for medical advice since she began med school. 'You'll feel fine in a day or so.'

Gina flops back on to her bed. 'God, I hope so. This is not cool.'

'You sure you don't want to study medicine?' Deb asks, still chuckling.

'I'm *positive*,' I whisper, hoping Gina will go to sleep instead of butting in on what will probably be my only conversation with my sister while I'm in Ecuador. 'Now let's talk about *you*. Have you and Bradford progressed from making out in parking lots yet?'

The smile in her voice remains when she answers. 'Oh, maybe . . .'

'Deborah Cantrell,' I say, struggling to keep my voice low. 'What are you hinting at? You sound absolutely guilt-ridden.'

'I'm telling you first, and then Mom and Dad, and then Sylvie . . .' Sylvie is Deb's best friend from college. She married her college boyfriend, has a two-year-old and another on the way, and has been setting Deb up with every eligible friend of her husband's for years. None of them have worked out, and a couple of them are only summoned to be witty anecdotes when she and her female med school friends discuss relationship-hunting fails.

'Well, this sounds promising . . . *wait*. Deb. *Tell me*.'

'He proposed last night.'

I forget to whisper. '*What?*'

Gina hangs down. 'What? What is it?'

'He *proposed*? But you've only known him a few weeks!' I say, and Gina's eyes go round as she makes an excited *eeeeeeeee* sound. I want to knock her on the forehead so I can share this moment with my sister, *alone*, but of course I don't.

Deb's reply is calm, unperturbed after my outburst. Expecting it, probably. 'Dori, I know what you're worried about – whether or not I'm sure. I *am*. I've never been so sure of anything in my life.'

'Oh my gosh.' My eyes tear up, but I'm smiling, and Gina is grinning ecstatically, still upside-down. A tear snakes down my cheek and I wipe it away. Gina disappears momentarily and reappears with a tissue. 'Have you worked it out with hospital administration? When do I get to meet him?'

Deb sighs. 'We aren't sure how to reveal it or what it might mean once we do. No one at the hospital knows yet except a close friend of his and one of the nurses – who caught us kissing in an empty room.' She giggles, and I'm struck again by how *sixteen* she's sounded since this man came into her life. 'That was the first time he said he loved me. When she came in, I tried to pull away, but he held tight, smiled and said, "Marta, have you met the woman I've fallen in love with?" She stared at us a minute and then said, "Well, I knew *something* was going on, doctor. You've been so pleasant for the past few weeks that we figured you were either in love or dying. Glad to know it's the former." We swore her to secrecy.'

I'm laughing and crying at the same time, and strangely, so is Gina, who hands me another tissue while she mops her eyes with her own. 'Wow,' I say, stunned.

'I have a couple of days in a row off in September, so we're planning to make a quick trip home then. I assume you can make it home from Berkeley for an evening?'

'Heck, yes. I wouldn't miss it. When are you telling Mom and Dad?'

'As soon as we hang up, I'm calling them. But first, how are you doing with the Reid Alexander situation? Is the distance helping?' Hearing his name is a jolt.

'Yeah. I'm fine. Haven't thought of him much at all.' I'm crossing my fingers under my leg.

'You haven't heard from him, then.'

'No.' Like he predicted – he's gone back to his life, and I've gone on with mine. 'Out of sight, out of mind.' My voice rings falsely impassive in my ears.

'I can't imagine any boy being stupid enough to put you out of his mind so easily, baby girl. Even him.'

I'm really glad that Gina, who's still eavesdropping shamelessly, can't hear Deb's portion of the conversation. 'Well, thanks. But I think they're all kind of the same.' Deb knows I'm referring to Colin.

'No, they aren't, but guys like Brad are rare. It took me twenty-six years to find him, and look how far from home I had to go. What if I'd done my internship elsewhere? We'd have never met. Brad and I were meant to be.'

I turn on to my side, repressing words I've said to Deb before, words I will not repeat now because I'm determined not to take anything away from her happiness. I know Deb believes that God brought Brad to her. That they were fated to be. But if this is so, then were Colin and I fated? Was what he did to me meant to be? Or perhaps he was a test that I failed, foolishly trusting a boy who exploited some inadequacy that made me blind to reality.

I can't believe either of these. What happened with Colin was simply a failure to heed my own common sense. I made an error of judgement, and I paid for it.

'I'm glad you found each other, Deb,' I tell her, turning on to my back. 'I hope you'll be really happy.'

She sighs blissfully. 'We already are. It's almost too much joy.'

I shake my head and smile. 'No such thing.'

'I hope you're right. You can probably expect a giddy call from Mom soon. I think she thought I was allergic to boys – or they were allergic to me. I love you, baby girl.'

'I love you too, and I'm so happy for you.'

When we hang up, it seems that Gina has forgotten her altitude sickness for the time being. She tells me she's a hopeless romantic who drives her husband crazy buying every romantic movie ever made. 'I think I've watched *The Notebook* about a thousand times,' she confesses, without even a hint of embarrassment. 'I want to hear all about your sister and her new fiancé, but first – who is this boy you left behind? Was it a break-up? Not because of your volunteer efforts here, I hope.'

'No, nothing like that. We only went out once. It was nothing.' I'm crossing my fingers under my leg again, though I've spoken nothing but truth.

'Not meant to be, then,' Gina says, and it takes all the control I can manage not to roll my eyes. Holy cow, you'd think people never made their own decisions about anything, weren't in control of any direction their lives took.

'Yep. Not meant to be.' I force myself to uncross my fingers. Nothing I'm saying is a lie or a fib or even a disputed truth. Whether or not my life is orchestrated by God or some form of fate or nothing but the choices Reid and I make individually or together, we're not meant to be.

32

REID

In three days, I'm leaving for Vancouver, a two-hour flight away. I could jump back to LA often during the next three months if I wanted to, but barring any emergencies, there's no reason to bother. I need a break from everything here. I definitely need a break from my best friend, who's walking the ragged edge of shit-for-brains-annoying at the moment.

'Look, I can't maintain the kind of muscle I've been adding while drinking and getting high every night. I thought you got that.' I've tried to explain this to John multiple times in the past several days, but he's smashed and missing all of my *drop-it* cues. We just got back to his place from a party, the first one we've left together this week.

'I know, I hear you. It's just . . . you're just . . .'

'I'm just *what*?'

'You're not only cutting back on alcohol or whatever. You've been crashing here for the past week, and not only are you almost always stone-cold sober, which is kind of a damned drag, you haven't brought a girl back with you at all. Not once.'

'And?'

He sighs. 'Nothing, man. But you aren't yourself.'

Sometimes my best friend seems perceptive, though I'm never sure how much of his insight is actual comprehension and how much is guesstimated bullshit. We don't have what you'd call a dig-deep sort of relationship. 'Maybe I'm trying to develop some self-control.'

'C'mon, man – *no* alcohol, *no* weed, *no* girls? What the hell is this? It's like you're someone else. I usually work just to keep up with you, and now I'm drinking alone ninety per cent of the time,' he gestures to my Perrier with his beer, 'and I'm stoned by myself, and the only thing you're screwing with is my head.'

I give him half a smile. 'What's the matter, John? You wanna break up with me?'

He laughs and shakes his hair out of his eyes. 'No, man, the bromance is still hot as ever.' He eyes me for a moment. 'Oh, no way. It's that Dori chick, isn't it? You never screwed her, did you?'

My gaze narrows, fingers digging into my leg. 'Don't go there, man.'

He sits up and points at me, grinning. 'That's it! The last time we talked about her, you were just gonna do her and get over it. Don't tell me you grew a conscience because of her little do-gooding act.'

I can't believe we ever had that conversation, that I ever said something like that to John about Dori, but I know I probably did. I'm sure I was drunk and talking shit – a lifetime ago. Before I kissed her. Before I stopped being a complete prick long enough to know her at all. 'I'm serious, John. Shut up.'

He takes a drag from his cigarette and I think he's going to comply. No such luck. 'I'm just saying, dude – you've got a couple more days in LA. Look her up, throw a bag over her head or whatever and screw her respectable brains out so you can get back to normal.'

The combination of John being hammered and me being the furthest thing from it curbs my temper just enough not to beat the ever-loving shit out of him, but it doesn't stop me from yanking him up by his shirtfront and slamming him back into his chair so hard his head snaps back. 'Don't *ever* fucking talk about her like that again. I mean it, John. *Don't*.'

'Okay, man, okay. *Shit*. Chill. I'm s-sorry,' he stutters, eyes wide and startled, hands up in surrender. 'I'm *sorry*. Shit, Reid. I get it.'

I straighten, shaking, run a hand through my hair as I turn away from him. He's right about one thing. I'm not myself.

Dori

My flight was delayed half an hour because of a freakishly torrential but fast-moving rainstorm, but I'm not worried about missing my connection because the layover will still be over two hours. Plenty of time to get through customs in Miami and make the flight to LA – I hope. By 9:00 tonight I'll be home.

The past three weeks have been challenging, but not in the usual way. I finally hit my stride this time, from speaking understandable Spanish to the locals to making concrete changes in the lives of the kids there. We persuaded a few parents to let their children attend school this fall instead of wasting their days soliciting change from tourists for shoe shines that blacken their hands with polish and offer them no hope for a future. And then there are the girls I tutored, who swore they'd email and keep me updated on their progress.

The biggest challenge has been banishing Reid from my thoughts. There were times during that last week when I was so busy and focused that I didn't think of him all day, but that changed the moment I fell into my bunk and burrowed under the blankets at night. There was nothing I could do to keep him out of my head when I shut my eyes. I know I'll get past missing him. His teasing and our tongue-in-cheek debates became a habit, that's all – an exasperating, stimulating and infuriatingly enjoyable habit. I don't know what his motivation was for kissing me, beyond the fact that he seems to do the same with a lot of girls. I don't think he meant to be cruel, though kissing him revived a long-buried hunger in me.

When we land, there's an announcement, and I think I hear my name inside a flurry of instructions, but the words are inaudible because everyone is talking and unbuckling and there's a baby crying in the row ahead of me. She's teething, so she cried most of the trip. I've never been so ready to get off a flight. I'll be home in – ugh – seven hours.

From my place in the next-to-last row, it takes forever to deplane. Before I exit, I stop to ask a flight attendant, 'Excuse me, I think I heard my name during the announcement? I'm not sure. I was near the baby.'

She gives me a rueful smile. '*I understand.*' She asks another flight attendant about the announcement, and he turns to me.

'Ms Cantrell?'

I get a creeping sensation when it occurs to me that having a message delivered at the end of a flight probably isn't a good thing. 'Yes . . .?'

He smiles reassuringly. 'As you exit the jet bridge, there will be an agent waiting for you, wearing a plaid jacket. Please speak with her.'

'Um, okay. Should I be worried?'

The helpful expression on his face never changes. 'I'm afraid we aren't privy to that information – you'll need to ask her.'

I'm the last passenger off the plane. The agent is waiting for me as promised, her expression identical to the flight attendant's. I don't feel reassured. The creeping sensation has become a slow, stomach-churning fear. 'Dorcas Cantrell?' she asks.

'Yes?' My breath's gone shallow.

'Good afternoon, Ms Cantrell, I'm Lucia. Your family

contacted the airline this morning while you were en route. There's been an emergency of some kind, and we need to reroute you to Indianapolis, instead of Los Angeles. I assume this is acceptable to you?'

I nod. The bottom has dropped out of my stomach. 'What emergency?' Indianapolis. *Deb.*

The agent takes the handle of my wheeled bag and motions for me to follow. 'Let's walk while we talk because we need to get you through customs as quickly as possible. First things first – there are no direct flights to Indianapolis from Miami this evening, but we can connect you through Dallas and get you there by 10:30. Is this acceptable, or would you prefer to wait until tomorrow morning, and fly direct?'

My feet are moving, following the agent's clip-clopping steps as she pulls my bag to the line at customs, but I can't feel anything. My whole body has gone numb. What kind of emergency would require me to go to Indianapolis? 'I . . . I can do the connection,' I answer, my mouth dry.

'Very good. Wait here, I'm going to see if I can get you moved up so we can get you through this line sooner. Your flight is boarding in five minutes.' She hurries away, and I stand where she left me, shuffling forward in the line no more than three feet while she's gone. I pull my cell phone out and turn it on. I call Dad's number. It goes straight to voicemail and I hang up. Mom's does as well, and Deb's. My heart is pounding and I'm just concentrating on breathing and standing and not freaking out.

The agent returns, taking my bag, moving me from the back of one line to the front of another. I'm only vaguely aware of the other passengers' stares and speculations. I'm asked if I have anything to declare and I say no. My bags are examined, and I'm through customs in record time. 'The emergency? What is it?' I ask as we board a motorized cart and she gives the gate number to the driver.

'I have very little information, but here's what I was told: your sister has had an accident. She's in the hospital, in critical condition. Your parents are en route to Indianapolis now, and someone will meet you when you land at IND.'

'An accident? Like a car accident? What kind of accident?'

She places her hand on my shoulder and looks in my eyes. 'I'm not sure, honey. I'm afraid that's all the information I got at this end. I wasn't even given the name of the hospital. Your job right now is to stay calm. I'm going to give you your new flight numbers and such, but don't worry, we'll give you a printout with everything on it . . .'

She's telling me gates and flights and times and I can't absorb any of it. Deb will be fine. She's young and strong and healthy. She always wears her seat belt and her car has airbags all over the place and that thing that calls in an accident for you if you're unconscious. Critical condition means she's *alive*, and I'm focusing on that.

The agent and flight attendants essentially put me on the plane to Dallas and all but buckle me in. I have a boarding pass for my flight from Dallas to Indianapolis, with only an hour between flights. I feel like a zombie, and I'm sure I look like one to everyone around me, but it doesn't matter.

My sister is alive, and she's going to be fine. This will be my mantra for the next six hours.

33

REID

Vancouver is exactly the change I need. Given the different atmosphere for this film, the older starring group (I'm the youngest cast member), the physical demands of the stunts I'm doing and the muscle I have to maintain, I've decided to do something I haven't done since I was fourteen. Not that it was a choice then, just the typical restrictions of childhood. While I'm on location, I'm going to abstain. From everything. Alcohol, weed, pills, *sex*.

While Olaf and I were adding that last five pounds, I only got high once, and I cut back on drinking solely to survive his torture sessions. (If he suspected me of drinking the night before a workout, he practically killed me in the weight room.) As for sex, I haven't been with a girl since I kissed Dori. In some twisted way, this fact is like purposefully leaving a sweet taste in my mouth. Instead of my usual hook-ups, which are at best quick and dirty and done just sober enough to recall them, I have a graphically clear memory of her soft lips opening under mine. That thought in mind, I may set a record over this time period for whack-ing off, from which I will *not* be abstaining, for obvious reasons.

The film we're doing is an action thriller plus love story, the script reading like a Guy Ritchie/Nicholas Sparks mash-up. My character's romantic interest is being played by Chelsea Radin, who's drop-dead hot and twenty-seven. Both characters are 'approximately twenty-three', so while I'm playing up, she's playing down. Hollywood, yeah? We're on our third day of filming, and the cast is grabbing lunch from craft services when she turns to me and says, 'You know, you're nothing like what I expected, from all the rumours.'

I'm picking through sandwiches, trying to avoid the tuna because we have our first kissing scene coming up after lunch. Turning to her, holding a turkey on whole-wheat that would make Olaf proud, I say, 'Oh? What were you expecting?'

She shrugs. 'Not that I presumed you'd hit on *me* or anything, but you're portrayed as this sort of evil, virtue-slaying playboy, and I haven't seen any evidence of that. Yet.'

I choke a little on the wedge of sandwich I've just bitten into, and she slams her palm on my back until I can breathe again. I give her a half-grin. 'Chelsea, don't you know you can't trust everything you read on the internet?'

She shakes her head, her short dark hair flipping back and forth. 'Photos, baby. *Lots* of photos. *Lots* of girls. My husband was actually a little concerned when they gave you the role.'

I laugh. 'Um, no offence, but you're safe.' Damn, she's pretty up close.

She frowns. 'I've never been so relieved and so insulted all at one time.' Tilting her head, she peers at me like I'm a map and she's looking for directions. 'So who's the girl?'

'Huh?'

She takes a sip of her diet cola and begins picking through the sandwiches. 'The girl responsible for this transformation from virgin-eradicator to choirboy.'

This train of thought conjures Dori, images of her flashing through my mind rapidly like a slideshow on speed. She should be back in LA tonight, and in a couple of weeks, she'll be at Berkeley, studying to advance from amateur to professional do-gooder.

'I'm no choirboy, and there's no girl.'

'Hmm,' Chelsea smiles. 'If you say so.' She bites into a sandwich – unbelievably, a *tuna* sandwich – and saunters over to another co-star to ask about his new baby.

Virgin-eradicator? Harsh.

The afternoon scenes went well enough, though I've got a hellacious bruise forming on one shoulder from a choreography error. I'm not doing *all* of my own stunts because I'm not suicidal. (In one, my double will be jumping from the roof of a truck to the roof of a BMW, while both are moving at 60 mph.) But the fight scenes, the climbing scenes – those I'm doing. The casualty today happened during a bar fight that should have – and would have – gone off without a hitch, except the guy who was supposed to smash a chair on to the bar top as I rolled to the left screwed up and cracked the chair down right on top of me. The director cut the scene and called a medic, but luckily nothing was broken. Muscle or no muscle, though, that shit *hurts*.

In comparison, the kiss went much better and was decidedly less painful. Chelsea and I have good chemistry, though not, perhaps, what I had with Emma last year. Still, we nailed it in one take. I concentrated the entire time on *not* thinking of Dori. My level of success was questionable, at best. No matter what I'm doing to forget her, she pushes into my consciousness like a walking daydream.

John's Words of Wisdom when I was trying to come to grips with Emma's rejection: 'The best way to get over a girl is to get under another one.' I listened to him then. For the record? That shit doesn't work.

Dori

Not until I see Dad's face does my anaesthetized shield begin to recede, leaving in its place pins and needles of feeling, sharp and stabbing, fear piercing through me at his distressed look. I find myself pleading in my head, *Deb, please don't be dead. Please, please don't be dead.*

Just like that, for the first time I let myself consider the possibility. And then I shove it away violently.

I rush into his arms and he enfolds me tightly. 'Dad, what happened? How is she?' I can't breathe, demanding and fearful of the words I've been waiting hours to hear.

'There was an accident.' His voice is hoarse, tight. He swallows and I want to say, *I know that already!* I want him to skip to the end and assure me that she's alive, but I bite my tongue and let him gather his thoughts and his courage and speak. 'At the hospital, during her rounds. She . . . she slipped. There was a wet spot on the floor, and she slipped. She fell and hit her head.'

Wet spot. Floor. Fell. Hit her head. This is terrible, horrible, but oh so much better than the accident of my imagination – mangled metal, blackened and twisted in the middle of a busy intersection. Infinitely better than the massive loss of blood, the scarring, the internal injuries, the potential paralysis, the possible fatality. I nearly giggle with relief, but it evaporates in my throat because my father hasn't loosened his hold. 'Dad?' My voice is muffled against his chest.

'She's had a closed head injury, Dori. Before your mother and I arrived, she was unconscious, and then lucid and talking for an hour or so, but then her brain started swelling, and they haven't been able to get it to stop. She's been unresponsive since we've been here.'

I pull away and look into his eyes. 'Unresponsive? You mean like a coma? But why –? You said she slipped and hit her head, but I mean, how hard could she have hit it – she's as short as me – we're close to the ground, remember?' My pitch is somewhere between eager and hysterical, my mouth still turning up into a smile because no part of me is accepting that word. *Unresponsive.*

He squeezes me tight and releases me. 'Let's get your

luggage. I need to get back to your mother. We can talk on the way.'

We're silent except for hollow exchanges like, *I can carry this bag, you take that one.* With the push of a button, he releases the locks on an unfamiliar vehicle, a compact SUV in a jaunty red. The rental, more well-appointed than either of our cars, smells faintly of pine and strangers. We stow my luggage in the back, still mute until our seat belts are fastened and the engine has turned over, cool air blowing too briskly from the vents. I reach to the one aimed at my face and point it towards the window as Dad grabs my hand. I open my mouth to say, *Let's go, let's go*, but his head is bowed and the plea hangs in my throat.

'Lord,' he begins, eyes closed, voice breaking, 'we believe in your healing power. We believe in your promises. You watch over the sparrow when he falls. You were watching over my little girl when she –' His voice breaks again and I clasp his hand firmly, tears streaming down my face.

In that moment, I experience a blinding explosion of self-realization: I am two people. The Dori everyone knows is trusting, hopeful and light – like a spark, like a feather. I am full of faith, and nothing is impossible.

The anti-Dori has been hidden away since her formation. She's sceptical and riddled with doubt, doggedly probing dark theories of disbelief. In the wake of my father's fragmented prayer, his gut-wrenching pain that echoes mine, it's her words I hear. *No fate, no destiny, no meant-to-be.*

I want to believe that God is everywhere – in the miracle of life, in the love we have for one another, flying in the face of death. I want to believe there's a reason and a purpose for what happened to Deb.

But there is no reason.

My two selves are old adversaries, forever circling, persistently employing the same inadequate arguments. Each is close-minded, deaf to the other, and I cannot reconcile them.

34

REID

Funny thing about not waking up hung-over on days off – there's more day off to the day. I can't believe I actually dreaded this. I was certain I'd be bored as hell inside forty-eight hours – evenings without the usual entertainment followed by entire days to fill. But what's to miss about headaches, nausea and acute sensitivity to light and sound? My enthusiasm may have as much to do with Vancouver itself as it does the lack of hangovers. I wouldn't know; before this project, I'd had little experience of either.

It's our first Sunday off, and Chelsea and her husband, Chad, invited me along to explore Gastown, an area of the city with cobblestone streets and small shops, galleries and restaurants. A bodyguard trails us, but hasn't been necessary. Vancouver is known as Hollywood North, and the locals are semi-inured to celebrity sightings. No one's bothered us, though cell phones are frequently aimed in our direction and I've heard my name and Chelsea's hissed emphatically a dozen times.

I lace my fingers behind my neck and stretch my sore shoulder carefully. The screenwriter is working the bruise into the storyline for the shirtless scenes because hiding it is impractical. It's huge and ugly, and I wonder at my sanity over the fact that I'm more amused than annoyed by it. I frequently left the Diego house lightly bruised and battered, as did Dori. Once, I pointed out a purple welt on the back of her thigh, and she twisted to look at it. 'Hmm,' she said, shrugging. 'I've had worse.' I wanted to slap myself for how *hot* that was.

'This city is *marvellous*,' Chelsea says now, opening a menu. Chelsea is fond of words like marvellous and fabulous and splendid, lengthening the first syllable as though she's trying to remember the rest of the word. She smiles at her husband. 'I think we should move here.'

We've found a corner bistro across the way from an idyllic green space that's commonplace in Vancouver, mixed in with the modernized buildings and concrete. This one boasts a fountain. As kids are tossing coins and making wishes, one small boy pockets a handful of change and throws his baby sister's shoe into the water instead. Out of nowhere, I'm fighting the urge to call Dori and tell her about it. I want her to tell me I'm mean and try not to laugh as I mimic my co-star's unnatural love for multisyllabic adjectives. I wonder if she'd be more sympathetic or amused that I got slammed with a chair during a simulated bar fight.

'I hope you're suggesting that I become a kept man,' Chad says, 'because I don't think my licence from the California bar extends this far north.'

'Oh, no, no. *You're* the sugar daddy and *I'm* the brilliant artistic type in this marriage.' Chelsea purses her lips endearingly, while I battle a desire to punch one or both of them in the face.

My cell buzzes with a text from Tadd, and I'm elated at the distraction from both the Chelsea and Chad lovefest, and futile thoughts of Dori.

> **Tadd:** Hey dude, are you in vancouver now?
> Rob and i are flying up later this week.
> Would like to meet for dinner if you can. Let
> me know.
> **Me:** I think i can squeeze you in, haha. Text
> me when you get here.

Dori

By the time Dad and I reached the hospital, it was close to midnight. 'Oh, Dori,' Mom said, throwing her arms round me as though I was a life preserver and she would sink and drown without me. She was a wreck – her face blotchy, eyes red, a smudge of mascara dissolved under each eye, giving her delicate skin a grey cast under the greenish fluorescent lighting of the critical care waiting area. We held each other as Dad looked on helplessly.

Deb's medical team gives us periodic updates, much of it too complex to understand. I've tried to take notes, but mostly end up with scraps of paper covered in scribbles like *increased intracranial pressure* and *epidural haematoma* and *Glasgow Coma Scale – 5*. I don't know what any of it means, but the words are menacing and my mother is shaken by them, so I know the prognosis isn't favourable. Deb had a seizure shortly after the accident, one of the many reasons for her sedation.

'The increased pressure inside her skull from the brain swelling is common in this sort of injury,' one of the doctors intoned, but it was clear this wasn't meant as reassurance. If the swelling doesn't stop, my sister could die.

These aren't the circumstances under which any of us wanted to meet Bradford. Deb told me once that he's seldom overcome with emotion because he deals in the realities of death and dying every day. Sitting next to me in the hospital cafeteria, though, he's visibly anguished, hands clasped and rigid on the tabletop, next to his tepid coffee. 'Hardly anyone at the hospital knows about our relationship.' His voice is hoarse, his handsome face pallid and drawn. 'As far as most people know, we were distant acquaintances. I'm not expected to be . . . not expected to feel . . .' I put my hand on his arm as he struggles to stay composed.

When my parents are given Deb's belongings – the clothes and jewellery she was wearing when the accident occurred, a beautiful, unfamiliar solitaire threaded on to a long gold chain is included with her things. Bradford's swift intake of breath and compressed jaw is all the answer we need to confirm that this is Deb's engagement ring – hidden from her co-workers, worn next to her heart.

*

Dad and I travel back and forth between LA and Indianapolis while Mom remains steadfastly by Deb's side. When she can be coaxed to leave the hospital for a few hours, she spends them at Deb's apartment, where she tends my sister's balcony full of plants, but doesn't get enough sleep to remove the circles from under her eyes. My mother and sister have both always been slim. Now they're both more emaciated every time I return from LA. Once I apprise him of the fact, Dad and I begin to press food on Mom – jars of cashews, buttered blueberry muffins, turkey sandwiches topped with avocado.

I postpone my admission to Berkeley for a semester. I don't tell my parents that, at the moment, I can't imagine myself there at all. Thanks to donated air miles, Dad and I get into a rhythm of alternating our visits – hospital, home, hospital, home – so we don't impose further on anyone to watch the house or feed and walk Esther. I hardly see my father, our flights passing each other like that saying about ships in the night. My strongest feelings are reserved for anything relating to a change in Deb's condition.

Her doctors used innovative, controversial approaches to lessen the swelling in her brain, and the terror that we could lose her diminished too. There's been little change since she was successfully removed from life support. The monitors prove a low level of brain activity, and when she's awake, her eyes are open. But if I move directly into her line of vision, it's like I'm made of glass. She just stares right through. She doesn't speak or react to voices unless they're very loud – and then her only responses appear to be irritation or pain.

The doctors yell at her in attempts to provoke a response, and Mom sits stoically, while I can barely stand to watch my sister flinch over and over. They ask me to try, hoping she might respond to my voice.

'Deb, can you hear me?' I say, and they insist *louder, louder*. 'Deb, can you hear me? Can you hear me, Deb?' I'm screaming, but the volume only makes her recoil, and I run from the room, weak and ineffective, gasping for breath and slumping against the hallway wall, sinking lower and swallowing tears. I bury my face against my knees, wishing this was all a nightmare, and I could just wake up.

My mother joins me as I huddle on the floor, opening her arms. 'It's okay, Dori. They won't ask you to do it again.' I let myself cry because I don't want her to let go. This embrace is for me, and I want it desperately even while I berate myself for leaning on Mom for comfort. She doesn't need me to break down and add to her burden.

Bradford remains close by, but I wonder how long that will last. He and Deb weren't married; their relationship wasn't even public knowledge. Excluded from decisions concerning her care except where his opinion is quietly sought by my parents, he has no official place in her life – this woman he wanted to marry, the person with whom he intended to link his future. As Mom and the chaplain prayed over her still form yesterday, requesting miracles on her behalf, my eyes met Bradford's. I saw my grief mirrored there, as well as my recognition of her prognosis. The girl we love is not coming back.

There's no discussing reality with Mom when she

constantly addresses Deb as though she's capable of making a coherent reply at any moment. 'How are you feeling today, sweetie? Looks like your hair is growing back in – time for a trim, don't you think?' Her fingers run lovingly over the sparse spots on Deb's head as my sister stares straight ahead at nothing. Mom chatters on about the weather and I fade from the room because it's almost as unbearable as watching people yell at my sister to get a response.

When I'm home in LA, I see my friends, fellow church members or Nick – who brings me food and stays to sit and talk when he's home from college, though we skirt sensitive subjects like my newly aimless life or Deb's increasingly unlikely recovery. Two months ago, I confided in my sister and counted on my parents. They each encouraged my independence, but they were always *there*. Now there is no hand to steady me and no net beneath me, and I'm more isolated than I thought it was possible to be.

'Dori is such a little rock for Doug and Jocelyn,' I overhear Mrs Perez tell Mrs K one Sunday. 'They don't have to worry about her falling apart.'

Too late, I realize what my show of strength costs me. I've become disconnected, and the people in my life have become mirages. When I reach for them, my fingers go right through.

There is only one exception – Reid.

I can't explain it, but whenever I catch sight of him on television or a magazine cover, I'm connected to my former life, my former self, even if it's just for a moment. I've memorized times and channels for entertainment news programmes that I've never watched, flipping rapidly between channels in the first two minutes. My pulse quickens when he appears in the teasers, like a monkey who's learned to press a lever and get a treat. He's a drug, and I need him. I tell myself that this is a safe obsession because he has no knowledge of it.

Sometimes I wake from dreams of him, shuddering with longing. In these waking moments I come back to reality unwillingly, grounded by Esther, who sleeps pressed to my chest like an extension of me. She is proof that I'm alive – my ear snuggled against her chest, attuned to the faint gurgles of her soft stomach and the steady drum of her heart, my nose breathing in her familiar doggy scent, my face and fingers buried in her fur, stroking her beloved warm body.

'Stay, stay, stay,' I whisper.

She does, and I do.

35

REID

'It's not true, is it?' Chelsea says, plopping down next to me at lunch as I go over the sides for afternoon shooting.

'Of course not.' I have no idea what she's talking about.

She crunches through a salad of mostly raw veggies while I eat as many rolled-up slices of meat as I can stomach. The filming has become more cardiovascular, and my body is burning off muscle as fast as Olaf and I can put it back on. Chelsea doesn't enlighten me about the true or untrue topic of her question, but she's aware I'm curious as hell. She shoves another bite in her mouth and chomps away, grinning like mischief incarnate.

'Okay, fine, is *what* true?'

She finishes the bite and cocks an eyebrow at me. 'Haven't checked the internet lately, huh?'

I steal a couple of carrots from her bowl. 'I *never* check it, where I'm concerned. I'd have been convinced I was the Devil by now if I did.'

She shrugs. 'Or gay.'

'Excuse me?'

'It's the newest rumour in Reid Alexanderland. Ostensibly, since arriving in Vancouver, you've been seen with no one interesting outside of Chad and me – unreservedly in love and married to each other, your friend Tadd, who's gay, and his hot, unknown, probably gay friend. Also one of our bodyguards – who's male and therefore fodder for the gay buzz.'

I almost choke on the swiped carrot and she slams my back with her palm while I fight to breathe. Finally, I manage, 'Well, that's a first.'

'So true or not true? For the record, I don't care either way. Although I do have a brother who would drop everything and bounce up here on a pogo stick to be your love slave –'

'Hold it right there, Cupid. *Not* true.' My phone rings and of course, it's Tadd. I would bet a new Porsche *he* has seen the internet and is laughing his ass off. 'Awesome,' I grumble, heaving a sigh and pressing *talk*. 'Thaddeus.'

'Hello, *lover*,' he says.

'You wish.'

'That's for me to know, and you to never quite be sure of.'

I laugh, covering my face with one hand. 'What does Rob think?'

'Oh, he's for it.'

'*For* what, exactly? Never mind. Don't answer that.' I know better than to word-spar with Tadd.

'Aw, come on,' he says. 'What good is the press if not for

dishing up a serving of innuendo sprinkled with a few unsubstantiated lies?'

I sigh. 'Well, as long as Rob isn't upset about getting roped into the Hollywood rumour mill.'

'Nah, this was something we discussed before taking our relationship public. I'm just not as well-known as you, plus I'm brazenly out of the closet, so it doesn't stir up much interest. *You* on the other hand – if the rumour was true, there'd be suicide watches and black armbands in one camp, and rejoicing in the street in the other.'

'*Stooooop,*' I say.

'So. Have you been practising?' he asks, switching subjects. Tadd plays the guitar, and when I brought up the crazy notion of trying to learn, he insisted I buy the instrument while he was here.

'Yes, Dad.'

Learning to play the guitar is just one of the new things I'm trying out while I search for ways to fill my free time with activities that don't include my usual pursuits. At first, this was both more and less daunting than I'd assumed. I could dream up plenty of things to try, as it turns out. Motivating myself to actually *do* them was another matter. There are hours full of nothing but video games and eating crap Olaf would kill me for eating.

When Tadd and Rob were in town, we spent one night checking out local clubs. I didn't want to impose my no-drinking constraint on anyone else. Having never exactly practised resisting peer pressure (hell, I'm usually conducting the peer pressure), I joined the two of them in a few too many shots of Canadian whiskey and a round of karaoke (Tadd and I *killed* doing a medley of Ke$ha and the Stones).

The entire next day I was renewing my vows of sobriety, especially when Olaf caught sight of my impaired gaze. I knew I was in for it when he narrowed his eyes and all of the sizeable muscles in his upper body seemed to expand with displeasure at once. 'One hundred push-ups,' he barked, pointing to the floor. That was only the beginning.

When it comes to morning-after consequences, spending the evening with the guitar is exponentially less dangerous. I've also tried meditation – an unqualified fail because I can't clear my mind worth shit, and reading – slightly better, same reason. One of the bodyguards hikes, so we've been exploring trails through New Brighton Park. The leaves are turning every possible shade of gold and red, and the weather is cooler but still amazing.

No matter what I do, though, I can't break the habit of talking to Dori in my head. I think about calling her, asking how her classes are going and coaxing satirical observations out of her – the type she's reluctant to voice for fear of sounding ill-mannered. I imagine sitting with her at one of the hole-in-the-wall cafés I've discovered here, telling her about all the on-set insanity.

I remember kissing her. The kiss in the closet that made her run. The kiss in front of her house that didn't. I could have gone on kissing her for much longer that last time because nothing in her response showed wariness. The trouble was *my* response. If our mouths had been joined for another minute, I'd have dragged her right back into that car.

Clearing Dorcas Cantrell from my mind is not proving to be a simple task.

'Reid, I've listened to your voicemail three times. Am I following this correctly – you want to donate money to some *missionary* organization in South America?'

I'm confusing the hell out of my father – an unexpected bonus. 'Yeah, that's correct.'

'Should I be worried about a cult, brainwashing, Hare Krishnas?'

'Yeah, Dad, there are tons of Hare Krishnas in Ecuador.' Before he retorts and we end up in a battle of wits (where the loser is pretty much always me), I add, 'I heard about it from a girl at Habitat. If she's involved, it's legit. I thought it would be a good use of my charity budget.'

'*Oh-kay.*' He draws the word out, derisive as usual. I turn the receiver up and away from my mouth for a moment and force myself to breathe and not react. 'I'm not used to you guiding your charitable contributions, not to mention those recently purchased cars – which, I remind you, are not tax-deductible since they went directly to the recipients and you insisted on anonymity.'

I'm silent for a moment. 'We've already discussed my reasons for that decision, Dad, so I'm waiting for your point.'

'Humph,' he says. 'How much do you want to donate to this . . . mission organization?'

I tell him, and there's no reply. 'Dad?'

The sound of air hissing through his teeth is unmistakable.

'I think I need to meet the girl who's inspired all of this uncharacteristic – *giving*.'

Jesus Christ. I wouldn't introduce Dori to my father if he begged. 'I haven't seen her since she went to Quito, actually. She should be at Berkeley now.'

'She's a student at Berkeley?' He sounds impressed. I tamp down the jealousy. 'What's she studying?'

'Social work.'

'*What?* She's wasting an education at Berkeley to study *social work*?'

I bristle, but recognize that it's more than just my father and his typical disdain for any career path that doesn't make a shit-ton of money. Not that *mine* seems to impress him. 'Dori is exactly the sort of person who should do that kind of thing,' I say. I'm annoyed with myself for having had the same opinion of her chosen career path that *he* does. Honestly, it still shocks me that someone with a voice like she has could purposefully pursue anything but using it.

'Oh?' he says, with an extra helping of disdain. 'And why is that?'

'Because she wholeheartedly gives a shit, Dad.'

Dori

Once the specialists were in agreement that there was nothing further they could do, I knew my parents would accept the truth. Equally inspiring and disconcerting to witness, my parents had maintained their faith in my sister's eventual recovery against all evidence to the contrary. I prepared myself to catch the emotional fallout from my mother, who for all her medical competence and practicality had staunchly refused to concede defeat.

After our final consultation with Deb's medical team, the three of us are silent on the way to her tiny apartment. The damage my sister suffered in her fall appears irrefutably permanent. Damaged areas of her brain aren't expected to recover, though it's possible that at some point she might begin reacting to a stimulus like a familiar voice. 'By *react*,' one of the doctors clarified, 'we mean minute physical responses like a change in breathing pattern, or some small movement of, say, eyelids or digits. We don't foresee her ever regaining the ability to communicate through speech, however.'

Once back at the apartment, my parents slide into adjacent chairs at the tiny kitchen table, shell-shocked. I reheat a pan of lasagne provided by one of the nurses who'd worked with Deb. Finally, Mom clears her throat. 'I'll start calling people tomorrow to get recommendations for a suitable long-term care facility close to home.' I'm relieved to hear the return of her natural pragmatism. She glances round the cosy living room. 'We'll need to rent a truck to move her things, and a storage facility in LA. Hopefully, some day soon, she'll need her things again.'

I pause in slicing the Italian loaf on the cutting board, turning my face away. I want to scream in frustration. Deb will never live independently again. Nothing said by *any* of the doctors could have encouraged this belief, or even a hope of it. Years ago, I might have been willing to join the delusion, but I don't believe in miracles – not for Deb, not for anyone. Maybe I haven't in a long time, and I'm just now aware of it.

Deb's apartment has to be sublet, utilities turned off, creditors notified. These details fall to Dad while I distribute her patio full of plants to neighbours and hospital staff after convincing Mom that they would bring comfort to the people Deb cared for, that it would be impractical to take them with us. As I deliver containers of geraniums and fuchsias and hanging baskets of bougainvillea, I'm greeted with hugs and tears. I meet with Bradford last, in his small private office. I bring him an English ivy, the least demanding plant of Deb's collection, and a box of belongings he left in her apartment. I'd discovered his razor and toothbrush in her medicine cabinet, and a drawer containing a pair of his jeans along with socks, boxers and t-shirts.

'I packed up these things our first night at Deb's,' I say, placing the box on his desk. He stares at it, unmoving. 'I'd hoped that when we went back home to LA, I'd just be whispering to my sister where she could find your toothbrush and extra boxers.' My voice breaks, but I keep talking. 'If there's anything missing, let me know and I'll find it and send it to you. Mom plans to put her stuff in storage . . .'

'Thank you, Dori.' He lays his hands atop the box lid, but makes no move to open it. 'I always wanted a little sister, did she tell you that?' His eyes are full of tears. 'I don't have any siblings, so I was jealous when she'd talk about you.' He takes a shuddering breath as tears stream down my face. 'Your sister changed my life. She changed how I look at the world, how I practise medicine. She changed who I *am*. And I know I can't . . . can't begin to compare how I feel, losing her like this, with how you feel –'

I walk round the desk and put my arms round the man who would have been my brother. 'Yes, you can. She loved you, and you loved her. That's no different than how she felt about me, or how I felt about her.'

A tremor goes through his chest. 'I'm so sorry. I'm sorry we couldn't bring her back to herself, heal her.' His grief and anger can't be separated. 'This happened in a *hospital*. We're *doctors*. This is why I went into medicine – to cure and rebuild people, to make them better. And I can't even fix the woman I . . .' He stops, unable to speak, and I hold him tighter.

'I don't blame you, and Deb wouldn't blame you. If you knew her, then you *know* she wouldn't. She'd want you to go be that brilliant doctor she knew you were, to help people and live your life and be happy –'

'*How?*'

I swallow, glad he can't see my face. 'I don't know.'

The tabloid shows and websites have been going insane trying to figure out who Reid's latest hook-up is. Whoever it is, he's being more undercover about it than he's ever been. Which is probably the reason for one of the theories that was floating around – that he's gay.

I may not know much, but I know enough to know *that's* not true.

There's also a day of speculation that he's reuniting with the girl from his last movie, Emma Pierce, when a photo surfaces of the two of them at the Vancouver Film Festival. The photo is dark, but clear enough that they're both identifiable. She leans towards him with a smile as he speaks into her ear. Media speculation goes crazy, and dozens of photos from a year ago resurface – the two of them holding hands, kissing, stills from the movie where the two of them look all kinds of beautiful together.

The next day, an opposing tabloid publishes the same film festival photo – except this one isn't *cropped*. In the new photo, Graham Douglas, Emma's boyfriend, is sitting on the opposite side of her, his left arm across the back of her chair, his right hand holding her right hand on his thigh. He's listening to whatever Reid is saying as well, and *smiling*. So obviously, the Emma theory is out.

The guy who sold the cropped photo is blacklisted, the tabloid site that originally ran the cropped photo is discredited and I just spent twenty-four hours hating Emma Pierce for no reason.

Throughout all of this, Aimee and Kayla are calling and texting, trying to find out if I have the scoop on Reid:

> **Kayla:** Is reid gay???!?
> **Me:** Not that I know of. Are they back to that again?
> **Kayla:** Photos posted of him with that guy

tadd who played charlie in school pride and
some other hot guy singing karaoke in
vancouver . . .

Me: Old news i think. Not something i am
worried about right now.

Kayla: Aww. :(I know everything is crappy
right now with what happened to your sister.
Aimee and me are going out saturday, wanna
come?

Me: Yes

Kayla: REALLY?!??!?! OMG, stay over in our
dorm??

Me: Okay. Sure.

I'm willing to do anything to become someone else for a few
hours. Someone who isn't invisible to everyone who used
to love her. Someone who isn't the girl who's misplaced her
faith.

They pick me up Saturday, chattering like they're one
person, per usual.

'Did you bring the ID?' Kayla asks before taking off.

'Yeah,' I say. 'I don't think I look anything like her,
though . . .'

Aimee inspects Deb's Indiana driver's licence. 'Oh, this is
doable. We can totally do this. I already have some stuff
picked out for you to wear. We wear the same shoe size,
right? When we get done with you, you will look *so* much
like her. Just wait.'

'Okay.' I stuff the ID in my bag and lean my head back,

trying to subdue the butterflies that are mosh-pitting in my stomach. I'm so tired of feeling everything. Since we all came back to LA, I've been overwhelmed. I'm furious with my parents who continue to act as though my sister will wake up. Their own Sleeping Beauty, with the canned fairy-tale ending.

I've become so good at repressing the desire to scream that I can't even cry. When I think about Deb, I'm dry-eyed and staring, just like her. I am the opposite of thick-skinned. I am no-skinned. I am raw, as though there is nothing between me and everything insisting that I *feel*. I don't want to feel any more. I want to be numb.

Deb was so careful, always. When I began high school, she took me aside and made me promise to never drink and drive, and never get in the car with a friend who'd been drinking. She told me about alcohol poisoning and dehydration, already the doctor-to-be. 'Mom and Dad aren't always realistic about this kind of stuff. I know you're a good kid, but good kids are exactly the ones who end up making the dumbest decisions because they don't *plan*. If you're going to drink – or have sex, you have to *plan*. Capiche?'

I promised to come back for a recap if I ever needed it. Here I was, needing it, but now, Aimee and Kayla are the closest thing I have to advisors, but they're more like highly-strung tour guides.

My sister slipped on an invisible spot on a slick hospital floor. The doctors explained that she'd hit her head in the exact location with the exact amount of force that could cause the sort of damage she'd sustained. Caution and risk aversion had done nothing for Deb. No such thing as fate. No such thing as miracles, either, or my sister would have earned one and fallen on her butt – embarrassed, but still herself.

Tonight I want to stand on the side of a cliff and look down, dare the wind to gust and knock me off. Everyone thinks that falling to your death is the worst thing that can happen. But that's a lie. The worst thing is to be alive for no reason.

36

REID

Earlier this week, the film wrapped up and I said goodbye to Vancouver and goodbye to Olaf for at least a week because John began insisting that I say goodbye to my moral high ground.

'I get the whole abstinence makes the heart grow fonder thing,' he said last night, and I thought, *What?* 'But come on – you're home now.'

I wondered if John was attempting a play on words, but maybe he was right. Maybe abstinence *does* make the heart grow fonder. Other than leaping from the wagon that one night with Tadd and Rob, I'd been clean the whole time I was in Vancouver, and I still couldn't forget her.

'There's this party –' he began.

'Really? A party? I'm not familiar . . .'

'*Shut up*. Jorge and Daniel are coming too. We'll hit a couple of the clubs near UCLA, grab a few college girls who will be swayed by my buttload of charm and your passable looks and illustrious celebrity status.'

'Ah, buttload of charm,' I laughed. God, I'd missed John. He's such a jackass. 'That'll have them lining up.'

When four guys in a Hummer limo pull up in front of a nightclub – three trust fund babies and one celebrity – there is no standing in line. John, Daniel and Jorge fall in behind me, and it's as though I never left this life. Once we're inside, I lean over to John. 'You guys gather whoever you want to bring with us. I'm getting a few shots in before I decide to ditch this whole night.'

He narrows his eyes. 'No ditching allowed. It's like riding a bike, Reid. Jump on and pedal like hell, man.'

I shrug. 'Whatever. I'll be at the bar. And, uh, don't mention my name to any of them, okay? I'm not in the mood.'

'Not in the mood for *sex*?' He looks appalled.

'Not in the mood for some chick who just wants to have sex with Reid Alexander. Find me a cute girl who has no idea who I am, and I'll consider it.'

He shakes his head, dark hair falling into his eyes. 'You, son, are ill, and we're going to get you the cure tonight if it kills me. Or *you*.'

I sigh. 'Give me enough time to get a little numb first, will ya?'

Dori

I've avoided the LA club scene for years, while most of my friends were doing anything to get in. The music is so loud that I almost can't hear it. I feel it, though. Kayla did my make-up and styled my hair in long waves, and Aimee dressed me in a black miniskirt and fuchsia tank top so tight that I feel claustrophobic. I'm teetering on heels that could give me a nosebleed.

Holding Deb's driver's licence, I try to appear like a confident twenty-six-year-old. Kayla and Aimee swear that despite the age difference, Deb and I look (looked) similar enough – same colouring, height, bone structure – and that using her ID is better than trying to sneak a fake past a bouncer. I hope the intimidating guy at the door doesn't examine it too closely. Any direct interrogation and I'll collapse into a heap and start confessing.

He inspects the licence itself more closely than he examines me. Three cover charges later, we're through the door, Aimee with her cousin's licence and Kayla with a fake from Arizona that cost a fortune.

Step One – get in – was easier than I thought it would be. Step Two: drink until I stop thinking about Deb. Stop thinking about Reid. Stop thinking about the future I can no longer clearly see, and the faith I no longer feel.

'I haven't seen you here before, beautiful girl.' I've danced with at least a dozen guys, and here's lucky number thirteen.

I'm not used to strangers standing so close. Or calling me beautiful. Leaning one elbow on the table in interested nonchalance, I sip the drink in my hand, which looks like a Coke and tastes like a Coke with a side of ingestible flames. I think it's my third, maybe fourth. Over the rim of the glass

I see blondish hair and bluish eyes. The eyes regard me in the lazy manner of a predator sizing up dinner, and all of my instincts say *run*. Which is exactly why I do the opposite. Because my instincts are overly protective and useless.

A tilt of my head and a little smile back, and he's moved even closer.

'Let's dance,' he says. Here we go again.

I put the drink down, glance at Kayla (who gives me an eyebrow waggle and a thumbs-up) and Aimee (whose eyes are wandering over tonight's selection of hot guys), and slip from the barstool into this stranger's arms. He slides an arm round my waist as I balance myself. As we move towards the dance floor, I could swear I hear Aimee say, 'Oh my *God*. Kayla, look – have I had too many shots of tequila or is that Reid –'

I don't catch the end of her sentence before I'm out of earshot. She can't mean who I think she means, even if she did say his name, which is debatable, as difficult as it is to hear anything over the music. I glance around, but everything is a whirl of colour and noise and then this guy's hands are on my hips, and we're grinding into each other, following the beat. Closing my eyes, I hook my arms round his neck.

'What's your name?' he asks, leaning in close.

My eyes open and his face is close enough to see his eyes. Ice blue, not like Reid's stormy blue at all. *I don't want to think about Reid.* 'Dori,' I answer.

'Dori. Cute, just like you. I'm Reece.'

Rats. Too close to *Reid*. I don't want to think about him.

I dance with Reece-who-is-not-Reid until I'm hot and thirsty, breaking off mid-song and heading for the table. I resist the urge to look back and see if he's following. I don't really care. If he doesn't, someone else will.

I'm downing the rest of the rum and Coke and Reece settles a hip on Aimee's barstool as she leads another guy to the dance floor. Always another guy. Did I notice this before, how many there are? I was carrying the weight of the world on my shoulders, trying to make a difference, never doing anything reckless or pleasurable, not since Colin. Well. That's not quite true. Reid was reckless and pleasurable. But I'm not thinking about him.

In the end I just wasted my time trying to better the world, and so did Deb.

I force my thoughts away from my sister too, who sits in her chair and stares at nothing, with everything she'd learned, everything she'd become, everything she wanted to be – doctor, girlfriend, wife – *gone*. Reece signals a waitress for two more drinks when I begin to spin the ice in my otherwise empty glass. His fingers trail along my arm, back and forth, like a magician with a hypnotic watch. 'Tell me more about you, Dori with the big innocent eyes.'

I arch a brow at this. 'So I look innocent, do I?'

'Are you?' Another lazy smile. His repertoire of facial expressions appears to be limited.

'Maybe. Is that a problem?'

His nostrils flare slightly, and his lazy smile has turned into the other one. The hungry one. Truth is, I'm a little afraid of him, but it doesn't matter. Nothing matters.

'Depends.' The drinks arrive, and he throws his back, finishing half of it in one long swallow.

'On?' I ask, slamming half of mine as well, shuddering after. It's amazing how easy it is to drink fire once you get accustomed to it.

He leans closer, and I feel his warm breath on my cheek. 'On whether you want to stay that way.' He doesn't pull back, and neither do I, even as he begins to nuzzle my ear, his tongue swirling over the tip of it.

Too fast too fast my brain says, but my new powers of repression shut it up quick. I turn my face towards his and he's kissing me, and within seconds, his hands are wandering, caressing too roughly. It doesn't matter. It doesn't matter. The music deafens me and his arm encircles me, pressing me to his side though I'm still sitting on the high stool and he's standing. He's wearing too much cologne, and it's not the right smell. Too sweet, almost. Not earthy.

'Let's get out of here – the place a couple of doors down is way better.'

I don't recall another club on this block, but it feels like days ago that we came in. I glance across the dance floor, spotting Aimee, and gesture that I'm leaving. She goes to mime *call me* with the wrong hand and almost spills her drink in her ear.

Reece finishes his drink and points to my glass. 'You've still got half of yours.' I gulp the rest, tipping it back until the ice cubes bounce off my upper lip. 'Nice,' he says, leaning closer. 'Time for innocent little Dori to learn some of the sweet facts of life.' My body is moving off the barstool, and

I look down and his hands are at my waist, large hands, holding me, keeping me from falling. Or from running away.

'Wait.' Gripping the table, I close my eyes and wish the room would quit spinning. Closing my eyes helps, but I worry that won't be the case once this last drink finds its way into my bloodstream. I want to be numb, but all I am is dizzy and everything is loud and flashing and this isn't how I thought it would be and I just want to sit back down and cry.

'You'll feel better when we're outside,' he says, supporting my weight and guiding me towards the exit.

37

REID

I've been sitting at the bar, sipping shots of Armadale vodka while the guys round up girls to take to the party. The mirror across the back wall is angled slightly, reflecting the whole place, so I can face away from the crowd and contemplate the accumulated line of empty shot glasses, but still watch everything going on. While deciding whether I want to go for all-out hammered or just buzzed enough to note everything going on but not give a crap about any of it, I caught sight of a girl on the dance floor.

Last summer, I conducted an unsuccessful search for a Dorcas Cantrell lookalike. The closest I came were a few girls with similar colouring. This girl resembles her in some obscure mannerisms I must have become aware of during the weeks we worked together, in addition to a striking physical similarity. But Dori would never dress or behave to be so blatantly seductive, though I imagined her that way more than once. By the end of my stint with Habitat, I found her appealing no matter what she was wearing – even her unreasonably shapeless t-shirts.

For the past hour, my attention has been riveted by this club girl. I lost interest in vodka shots, watching as she glided from her table to the dance floor and back with different guys. Finally, one of them decided to hang around more permanently, leaning on the table as she finished the drink she foolishly left there while they were dancing, which could have easily been roofied by one of his friends. It hadn't – I would have noticed, but still. He leaned in and kissed her, and when they started making out, I went from eighty per cent sure this girl wasn't Dori to one hundred per cent sure. Even so, I couldn't look away.

When she turned to signal to another girl on the dance floor, I got a better view of her face. The resemblance to Dori was so strong, I felt like someone had just punched me in the gut. She downed the rest of her drink before the two of them headed for the door, his arm round her as she staggered in those stripper heels.

That stagger decides it. I slap a C-note on the bar and push it towards the bartender, pulling out my phone and texting John to meet me up front. My eyes never leave the girl as I trail them towards the door. 'Hey, Reid Alexander?' someone says, and I shake my head. I don't have time for that shit now.

We all reach the exit at the same time and I grab the guy's shoulder in the way you'd stop a friend to say hi. 'Excuse me.'

He turns, annoyed, holding the girl upright. She's

crashing fast, her head propped against his chest, her hair obscuring her face. 'Yeah?'

I focus on him. 'Yeah, man, you're gonna have to find someone else.'

His eyes narrow. 'What are you talking about? Do I know you?'

'No, but I know *her*.' I nod towards the girl. I have no idea what I plan to do with her. Bring her to the party? Take her back to her girlfriends and ask them what the hell they're thinking, letting someone this plastered leave a nightclub with a stranger?

'And?'

What a douche.

'And she won't be leaving here with you.'

He sizes me up and isn't impressed. Mistake. 'Who the hell are you? Never mind, I don't give a shit. Just back off before I kick your ass.'

'Yeah, I don't think you'll be doing that, and I don't think you'll be leaving here with her, either.'

I spot the left hook before it's fully thrown, dodge it, grab his wrist and twist his arm behind his back like a pretzel while catching the girl round her waist and pulling her to my opposite side. The big guys never see it coming. They're too conditioned to their size and muscle obliterating any offensive launched.

In the same instant, John shows up with the bouncer, and suddenly we're getting all kinds of attention. For all of his invariable stupor, my best friend is an expert in some things – like inducing authority figures to see things his way. He's already slipped a couple of fifties into the bouncer's hand and they disappear into a pocket as I explain that this girl is obviously in no state to leave the club with a stranger. I'm only guessing they don't know each other, of course, based purely on observation. But no one gives the douche a chance to refute it before he's passed off to another huge tattooed guy and escorted out. His missed punch was enough to get him ejected.

'How do I know she knows *you*?' The bouncer peers at me, smarter than most guys who stand around at the front door flexing muscle, gathering phone numbers for closing-time booty calls.

I look down at the girl, hoping she'll play along, and in that moment I realize that the girl in that hot outfit and under all that make-up *is* Dori.

She frowns and blinks slowly, leaning into me. 'Reid?'

'Hi, Dori.'

'Hi, Reid. You aren't really here, are you?' Her eyes tear up. 'I don't feel so good.'

That's enough for bouncer man. 'All right, off you go. Be safe.'

Too late.

Dori

My eyes are so dry that cracking them open is agonizing. I'm in an unfamiliar bed, in an unfamiliar grey-blue room. The furniture is smooth and dark-grained. The scent of the pillow under my head, though – the scent is vaguely familiar. Not floral or citrus, but something heavier – clean and concentrated. Male. Dark blinds are pulled shut, but light filters in through the crevices between the slats. It's morning . . . or later.

Someone is tapping on a keyboard behind me. I roll over warily and Reid Alexander's gaze shifts from the laptop to me at the sound. Pulling his hands from the keyboard, he leans back in the desk chair and stares at me. A satisfied smile works its way across his face. I must be dreaming. Should I feel this horrible if I'm dreaming?

'Good morning.' His voice is low, and somehow I feel the reverberations of it beneath my sternum. My fingers flutter there, as though I can brush the panic away. I'm not dreaming. I'm in Reid's bed. Not some random stranger's. *Reid's*.

'I thought I dreamed you.' The words whisper from my parched throat.

His head tilts to one side, his mouth shifting to something less sarcastic, more amused. 'That may be the most enchanting thing I've ever been told after spending the night with a girl.'

I swallow the little saliva I can generate. My mouth is as dry as cotton, my lips chapped. 'What. Happened?' My voice cracks, barely above a whisper.

'You don't remember?'

I close my eyes, trying to recall anything past the last guy I followed to the dance floor – the one with the too-sweet smell. 'I . . . don't remember anything.'

I force my eyes to open when he stands, moving to look

down at me. Mouth set in a grim line, he peels the cool grey sheet back and I pull taut, expecting air on bare skin, but I'm still clothed in the tank top and skirt I wore last night. We did it dressed? Or . . . he redressed me?

Taking my elbow, he gently pulls me from the bed, but my head is heavy and throbbing, and my equilibrium is shot. When I sway, he scoops me into his arms and the room tilts crazily. I hold on, groaning. The smell of his bed was just an echo of the spicy maleness of him, stronger now, my face against his chest. I want to curl up into him and sleep, but he's walking away from the bed. I briefly assume that he means to take me outside and deposit me on his doorstep, where I can be picked up for transport like a FedEx package.

He carries me through a doorway leading to a large bath-room, rather than the hallway I'd expected. There's a cushioned bench along one wall, and he deposits me there, his hands gripping my shoulders lightly until he's certain I can hold myself upright. My eyelids slit open just enough to track his movements and position in the room. Dressed in jeans and a faded black t-shirt, he pads across the carpet and marble floor, barefoot. He leans into the shower and a spray of water sounds, and then he's walking back to me as steam billows above the frosted glass.

I never thought I'd see Reid again. Not in the flesh. My face grows hot at that thought and I close my eyes, reopen-ing them when he says, 'Hmm.' He's standing in front of me, fists on his hips, staring down. I'm listing starboard, but otherwise still sitting up. And then he's pulling the fuchsia tank top up and off, and taking my hands to stand me up.

'Nooooo,' I say, and it sounds more like a whine and less like a refusal. He begins to unzip the skirt and I grab his hands. He can't mean to undress me *now*.

He picks up a huge bath towel from a fluffy stack on the opposite end of the bench, flaps it open and holds it up, a makeshift partition between us. 'Everything off,' he orders. 'And then get in the shower.'

I try to glare at him over the towel, but even drawing down my brows hurts my head. I settle for a blank look. He looks back, one eyebrow raised like a challenge. 'You have to go home at some point,' he says, gesturing to the mirrored wall. 'Is this how you want to look when you get there?'

I glance at my reflection, noting the smeared make-up, the sleep-creased skirt and the tangled hair, stiff with the half a bottle of whatever Kayla used to style it last night. With all of the community service work I've done, I know this veneer all too well. I look like a cheap prostitute. I can't show up at Aimee and Kayla's dorm like this.

'Dori. Shower.' It's not a command or a plea, just a statement of common sense. I pull the top edge of the towel towards my chin with both hands and nod once. He returns the nod and leaves the room, pulling the door shut behind him.

I hang the towel on a hook and unzip the skirt, dropping it to the floor. The lacy pink thong and bra that seemed so sexy last night feel incredibly silly now. I strip off the lingerie and step into the warm cascade of water raining from a shower nozzle the size of a frisbee.

As pulsing rivulets course over my face and body, I'm as relaxed as a person standing in a strange shower with almost no memory of the previous night could be. In the warmth and close quarters, every breath I take as I wash and shampoo catalogues the trace of almonds and exotic fruit and answers *Reid*. I had no idea I could recall his scent so acutely. Feeling as though I'm drowning in him, I don't turn the water off until my skin is flushed and wrinkly.

My clothes reek of sweat, cigarettes and alcohol, and the last thing I want to do is put them back on. On the bench next to my tiny purse sits a bundle of folded clothing. Black linen shorts, soft white tank top and a blue top with tiny snaps down the front. I'm reluctant to check the labels, but I do and then wish I hadn't. The cost of this outfit would make a mortgage payment for most people.

After a soft knock, Reid gives me three seconds and opens the door. His eyes drift over me, wrapped in the towel, my hair hanging wet down my back. 'I think those should fit.' He nods at the clothes, walking into the bathroom. 'You and my mom are about the same size.'

'These are your mother's clothes?' I shake my head and immediately regret doing so. 'I can't . . . take your mother's clothes?'

'Sure you can. Or else you'll be wearing that towel home.' His eyes run quickly down my frame and more slowly back up. 'You can give them back later, if you want.' His indifference concerning the return of his mom's things is obvious, but he shrugs, placating me.

'I'll have them cleaned first,' I say. 'Thank you.' Self-conscious, I run my fingers through my hair, trying to remove the bigger tangles and avoid his eyes.

He steps closer and hands me a bottle of water, which I gulp appreciatively. 'There's a blow-dryer, hair products, all kinds of crap in this cabinet.' He leans down, rummaging, and pulls out a bottle of something, pours a little into his hands. 'Detangler,' he says, running it through my hair, his fingers carefully separating strands while I recall him picking bits of fruit from my hair, in a different bathroom, a million years ago.

Eyes closed, I drink as he detangles. As he moves around front, I force myself to look at him. 'Reid . . . did we . . .?'

His fingers continue their careful paths through my hair, his expression all angel-faced innocence. 'Did we . . . what?'

I want to shut my eyes again, but I need to see if he's telling me the truth. I have to look in his eyes when he answers. 'Did we . . . s-s-sleep together?'

He regards me with that bemused expression I know so well. 'You woke up in my bed, Dori. And yeah, I was in it with you last night.'

'Oh.' My gaze falls to the floor. I slept with Reid . . . and I have no memory of it.

'Dori.' He waits until I look up at him. 'Don't look so mortified. We *slept*. I don't do passed-out virgins.'

I swallow. Of course, he's made the same assumption everyone who knows me makes: Dori Cantrell is nothing if not pure and innocent.

38

REID

What I don't tell her: she did just about everything imaginable to break that personal policy. Not that I've instituted much of a code of conduct for hook-ups; I've been with virgins, and I've been with girls who were so stoned or hammered they could hardly recall their own names. I've just made it a policy to draw the line at combining the two, if possible.

Which brings me to the other thing I don't tell her. If I didn't know Dori, her actions in the club would have persuaded me to believe that she might not be as innocent as I assumed. What happened between the club and my bed left little doubt.

There was no way I could deliver her home falling-down-drunk to her pastor father, and I had no idea where to take her besides home with me. In the car, she revived somewhat, her head nestled against my shoulder. Her hands began wandering over my chest, grazing over and under my shirt, caressing lazy orbits around every susceptible part of me she could reach. I thought she would drive me insane by the time we arrived home.

As I carried her up the back staircase to my room, she never stopped torturing me. When I set her down, she looped her arms round my neck and started kissing me, open-mouthed and unrestrained, arching her body into mine. I couldn't help responding, pulling her up hard against me, exploring her mouth with my tongue, rediscovering the feel of her with palms and fingertips. We fell on to the bed, kicking off shoes, and I roughly dragged her on top of me. Her skirt was bunched round her hips and my hands gripped her thighs, and she was practically spilling out of her deep V-neck top as she hovered over me, kissing me.

When her hand found the button fly of my jeans and tugged it open, I grabbed her wrists and choked out her name. '*Dori.*' She froze and looked at me, her dark, dark eyes glazed over and her lips swollen and wet. I'm getting hard now just thinking about how she looked in that moment. How I did what I did next, I have no idea. 'Dori, *sleep.*'

She looked bewildered. 'You don't want me?' Her voice broke mid-sentence.

I groaned. 'Yes, I absolutely do. But you don't want this.'

She blinked. 'I don't?'

'No.'

A small frown creased her brow. 'Oh.'

Without another word, she lay down, curved against me and fell sleep. Her acquiescence was so quick I was almost insulted. I don't know how long I lay there, wondering what kind of strung-out loser I'd turned into to refuse what she'd offered, even if she was unquestionably under the influence. It felt irrational to let her sleep – to *order* her to sleep – rather than turn her on to her back and run my hands and mouth over her until she was so hot for me she was begging me to finish what we'd started.

Once I'd suppressed the desire to coax her awake and to hell with my moral dilemma, I draped an arm over her abdomen and thought about what she'd done to me before she dozed off. Nothing we'd done was new for her . . . and I sensed that we hadn't reached the limit of her experience.

I don't know this Dori. Something happened between last night and the night I kissed her for what I thought was the last time and left her – sweet, respectable and tough as nails – standing in the middle of her parents' sidewalk. I don't know why she was at that club, dressed like a girl hunting for a hook-up and drinking like her goal was oblivion, and I sure as shit don't know what she was doing leaving with that guy.

All I know is – I have to find out.

I left her alone in the bathroom, wearing a towel and an unintelligible expression. She isn't angry and she isn't happy. Beyond that, I can't say. I hear her moving around, the faucet turning on and off. I think of that silky pink bra, imagine how she would have looked five minutes ago in my shower, hear the blow-dryer switch on, think of her in that towel. Imagine it falling to the ground.

Shit.

My agent sent a new batch of partial scripts a couple of

days ago. Sitting on the unmade bed reminds me of last night, so I move to the club chair by the corner window and read through the scripts until I realize I'm not actually absorbing anything I'm reading. Closing the laptop, I set it on the floor, hook my legs over one cushioned chair arm and lean back against the other. Arms folded behind my head, eyes on the bathroom door, I wait for her to emerge.

Dori

I feel strange dressing without any underwear, but at least I'm clean, and the clothes are soft and loose enough to be comfortable going without.

The cabinet Reid indicated is like a luxury beauty supply store, crammed with salon hair products, lotions, packaged toothbrushes and razors. Reid's careful detangling left my hair in damp waves, so I blow-dry it a bit and then leave it to air-dry. I fasten and unfasten the tiny snaps on the blue overshirt, finally settling on leaving a little of the soft white tank exposed at the top. One last look in the mirror, and then another, and then I'm doing little more than stalling.

When I emerge from the bathroom, he speaks from across the room, calm and low, like he's trying not to startle me. 'My mom basically has toddler feet, so her shoes won't fit you. I sent Maya out to get you something. She'll be back soon.' He unfolds himself from the chair and moves towards me so sensually a runway model would be jealous.

I frown. 'Get me – shoes, you mean? As in *buy* me shoes?'

He shrugs. 'Do you feel hungry? I think you should eat something, even if you can't stomach much yet.' He takes my hand as he reaches me, as though I'm a blind girl in an unknown place, and I need to be conducted through rooms, doorways and halls. 'Let's see if anything in the kitchen tempts you.'

As we move through the main part of the house, I'm in awe of the luxury he can't help but take for granted. Everything is refined and lovely, from the art on the walls to the lighting to the cool marble floors between islands of plush rugs. There are no cracks in these walls to camouflage with paint or plants, no worn flooring, no yard-sale furniture. The electronics are big and intimidating, speakers and components set into walls. He keeps my hand in his, which is good because otherwise I would probably walk into a wall or a post while gawking.

I do not belong here.

'Immaculada, just the woman I wanted to see.' We've entered the kitchen through panelled doors with bevelled glass inserts. Stainless steel, granite and dark wood combine to make this room as stunning as the rest of the house. I snap my mouth closed and turn when I realize Reid has introduced me to someone.

'*Señorita*,' the woman says, her accent familiar from my side of LA. 'Nice to meet you.' She's got that middle-aged heaviness around the midsection and her hair is pulled into a coiled braid. She's wearing a *uniform*. Though she's polite, there's something unreceptive in her manner, and my ears grow hot because of course she must know I was here overnight.

'Yes, ma'am, it's nice to meet you too.' I've never felt so out of place. Well, no – I felt equally out of place at the nightclub. I didn't just *step* out of my comfort zone, I've catapulted myself from it. I want nothing more in this moment than to find it and scramble safely back in.

Immaculada leaves the room, and Reid tugs my hand and seats me at a small table near a window. At the high back wall of the property, a man trims a flowering shrub to picture-perfect roundness – not one blossom, stem or leaf outside the visual sphere. Another man whisks the pruned bits from the lawn and into bags, which are loaded on to a motorized cart. This is what people mean when they speak in terms of 'grounds' rather than a 'backyard'. Holy cow.

Toast and a small, plain omelette are arranged on the embossed white plate in front of me, and orange juice in a heavy tumbler sits just behind the folded napkin and silverware. As Reid seats himself next to me, I swallow nervously, unsure I can get anything down. But the juice tastes fresh-squeezed from actual oranges, the toast has been lightly buttered and I even manage a bit of the omelette. We eat in silence, except for the sounds of silverware on china and chewing, and I feel a little better after. Reid is clearly not the slightest bit hung-over – he's ingested three times the amount of food I had on my barely-touched plate, plus coffee, the thought of which makes my stomach turn.

The moment I wipe the soft napkin across my mouth, he pushes his plate away and folds his arms in front of it.

'Are you going to tell me what happened?' he asks without preamble.

I look at him directly for the first time since I left his bathroom, and in the sunlit cheeriness of this room, his face still takes my breath away. There are so many ways to answer his question that I don't know where to begin. 'What do you mean?'

'I worked my ass off next to a girl for a month, almost daily, and though that girl *looked* like the spitting image of you, she and the girl I rescued last night are poles apart. I can't help but wonder – what occurred to cause that sort of change?'

I start to speak and have to clear my throat. 'Rescued?'

His expression doesn't change, except for an almost unnoticeable tic in his jaw. 'You were sloppy drunk and about to go home with some douchebag – and I'm pretty sure he was a complete stranger. I can't say for sure what would have happened, but I have an idea none of it would have been in your best interest.'

'Oh.' My heart is hammering. I'm not a girl who wants to be saved by a boy. I have never been that girl. Even when I fell for Colin, I fell for the myth of thinking we were in love. That we were on equal terms within that relationship. Yes, I was oh-so-aware that he was older and popular, and I was dazzled by these facts at the outset, but that wasn't what mattered to me. The loss of that status when we ended didn't faze me. The loss of what I thought was love, the realization that it was all a lie, was what ground my heart to a slow stop.

If what Reid says is true . . . but I have no reason to believe it isn't, from the snatches of last night that I remember. I know it's the truth. And I know that he did rescue me, simply because I'd neglected, or refused, to save myself. I feel like a child who carelessly ran across a busy street without looking – a child who's been shaken and asked, *What were you thinking?* I have no good answer. I *wasn't* thinking last night, beyond the desire to numb myself.

'So.' His gaze is steady on mine, his voice still low but firm. 'What's going on?'

I force myself to think about the thing from which I spent last night trying to escape, and tears well up for the first time in a while. He seems to stop breathing, fingers curling into his palm, but he doesn't make a move or look away. I take a deep breath. 'My sister, Deb?' He nods once, encouraging me to continue. I stare down at the cold egg and toast crumbs on my plate. 'She had an accident – she fell and hit her head, and is mostly unresponsive now. She can't walk, can't feed herself, blinks and makes some facial gestures, but never looks anyone in the eye, never speaks. Her doctors say that any vocalizations are all involuntary, not reactive.'

A tear blinks out of my eye and lands in a splat on the plate, gets soaked up by an adjacent scrap of toast. I press the napkin to my eyes, glad the make-up from last night is gone.

'Were you – very close? I've never had a sibling,' he stumbles over the last word, 'so I wouldn't know what a normal degree of intimacy would be. She's several years older, right?'

'Eight years. But we're very close.' The effort of keeping the tears dammed inside is excruciating – my throat feels bruised, my entire neck hurts as though someone has pummelled my windpipe just under my jaw. 'She's my best friend.'

He places a hand on top of one of mine, runs the other through his hair. 'Man. That sucks.' He looks at me, exhales heavily. 'I'm sorry, I'm not very good at this.'

My mouth turns up on one side because somehow Reid has said the one weird, true thing no one else would think to say. 'No. I think that sums it up pretty well. Thanks.'

Another uniformed housekeeper zooms into the room then, this one short and thin, so energetic that my head aches just trying to follow her with my eyes. 'I have the sneakers and the thongs,' she says, and my face goes hot.

Reid clears his throat and leans closer to whisper, 'Um, she means flip-flops. That's, uh, what she calls them. Can't get her to stop.'

'I buy two or three sizes of each, just in case.' Oblivious to my red eyes, and without making me feel the slightest bit mortified wearing borrowed clothes, she pulls shoeboxes from two bags. Opening the lids, she reveals shoes well out of my price range. For Pete's sake, there are Coach flip-flops in two of the boxes. I didn't even know they *made* Coach flip-flops, but here they are. There are also running shoes, and these brands are even scarier.

'Thanks, Maya,' Reid says, and she smiles and zips out of the kitchen.

I lean closer to him even though we're alone, thinking I could hyperventilate any moment, and wondering if he knows CPR. 'I can't accept these.'

Ignoring me, he pulls a pair of flip-flops from their box. 'Try these.' When I don't take them, he leans over and puts them on my feet, his hand on my calf. Oh, fudge. Fudge, fudge, fudge as his hand slides down my leg.

They fit perfectly. I am Cinderella with no evil stepmother, no fairy godmother, and no royal destiny. Just a beautiful prince who places impractical footwear on my feet. 'Okay, but I'm returning them with the clothes –'

'Why? They aren't my size. And they're *so* not my style.' He grins. 'Please. Keep them.'

'But –'

'Nope.'

'But –'

'*No.*'

'Hello, Luis.' I'm blushing as I greet Reid's driver, recognizing him from the only other time I was in this car, the night Reid and I went to dinner. Some people endure a walk of shame; I get a whole day of it. Luis smiles warmly and tips his chauffeur's hat.

Reid slides in next to me, his eyes invisible behind his mirrored sunglasses. Our fingers are inches apart on the seat, but he doesn't close the distance. Other than carrying me to the shower, holding my hand while walking to the kitchen and comforting me when I talked about Deb, he's not touched me today.

On the way to UCLA, bits and pieces of last night come back. I don't remember the guy Reid said I was about to leave with last night, but I remember Reid's arm round me as he said, 'John – you guys can take the Hummer.'

That same guy – John? – supported me to a taxi and placed me into it. 'So you're Dori, huh?' he asked, scooting in, but leaving the door ajar. Turning to the taxi driver, he said, 'Hey, dude, the guy leaving with her will be here in a sec. We're keeping her out of paparazzi pics, yeah?'

I closed my eyes as the last drink I'd had hit me full force, adding to the previous four. Or five. My hands gripped the seat. I was on a tilt-a-whirl and there was nothing I could do to ground myself. Flashes shone through my eyelids, like lightning in the distance, and then I heard Reid say, 'Thanks, man.' The seat shifted and sloped as he took his friend's place in the back seat of the cab and pulled the door shut. He reached for me as he gave the cabbie an address. I curled against his solid chest and held on, my eyes shut tight, the world still twirling.

That's all I remember until I woke up this morning.

I text Kayla to let her know I need to be let into her dorm. She and Aimee left a dozen texts and voicemail messages on my phone between last night and this morning, horrified that something had happened to me because I'd disappeared. It turns out that when I gestured to Aimee that I was leaving, she thought I was complimenting her dancing. I guess we need to establish better drunk hand signals, not that I want a repeat of last night ever again.

They're sitting on the steps of their building when the car pulls up. They can't see the interior of the car and obviously don't suspect that I'm the passenger because they continue talking while casting surreptitious looks our way, waiting to see who's being dropped off. 'Thank you,' I say as Reid removes his sunglasses. 'Where should I send the clothes?'

'I can't talk you into keeping them?'

I shake my head.

One corner of his mouth turns up. 'I put my number in your phone. Call or text me and we'll work something out.'

Before Luis opens my door, Reid takes my hand, his thumb caressing the sensitive skin between my thumb and forefinger. 'Be more careful?' he says, sliding his sunglasses back on, and I nod, feeling like a naïve idiot. And then, still a bit hung-over, I slip out of the car and walk up to my stunned friends, wearing a designer outfit and no underwear and carrying my clothes in a shoe store bag.

'Did you just get dropped off by a *celebrity*?' Kayla asks, ogling the car as it pulls away.

'Are those *Coach* flip-flops?' Aimee gasps, and then, pulling the back of the shirt out and looking for the label, '*Ohmigod*, is this top *Versace*?'

39

REID

The ball's in her court; I'm better when it's in mine. I'm used to being in complete control of any relationship with a girl – whether it's for an hour or a few weeks. Keeping control is effortless when the outcome is clear or inconsequential. Neither of these applies to Dori.

It's been four days. Under normal circumstances, I'd be pissed that I'm counting, more pissed that I care. Where Dori is concerned, there's no such thing as normal circumstances.

Returning the clothes was her idea, so I should wait for her to contact me. I *could* contact her first . . . I have her phone number. And I know where she lives.

I sound like a damned stalker.

'You're up early.' Through careful voice inflection, Dad manages to take statements that should be positive and twist the words to sound accusatory and suspicious. It's a gift.

It's also bait, and I'm not rising to it. Without turning, I continue peeling the orange in my hand, separating the smooth rind from the fruit below by tearing pieces away and dropping them into the sink. 'I'm meeting with George in an hour, discussing new project proposals.' I detach a wedge and pop it into my mouth, resisting the impulse to lick the juice from my fingers. I fight the urge to enjoy anything too much in front of him, actually, and now that I'm aware of that fact, my brain gets hung up on why that is.

'Mmm,' he says, as unconcerned as possible. In my peripheral vision, his brows are almost knitted at the centre as he stares at the empty mug in his left hand and the coffee pot in his right, as though he's forgotten how to pour. He doesn't look at me, and I debate whether to turn and head back to my room or wait until he says actual words. I elect to silently count to five first. I'm up to three when he adds, 'Anything of note?'

Sweeping the bits of orange peel into the waste disposal and flipping it on, I savour the tangy whiff of citrus almost as much as the motorized droning that purposefully stalls my reply.

'Yeah, a couple. One has possible critical appeal – maybe even Oscar-worthiness. The other's an action flick. More money, probably.'

'Mmm,' he says again. Strange. Seldom without a blunt opinion of my career, particularly when it comes to finance, this man seems like someone else's father. A minute later, he's snatched a sheaf of papers from his attaché case. My upcoming film choices forgotten, he removes a giant clip and thumbs through the one-inch stack, flagging something in the centre of a page.

Dad is a contracts expert. No fraudulent detail can be buried deeply enough that his expertise can't root it out, for which his clients pay a buttload, as John would say. Too bad the emotional details of life flow by without him noticing, which is why everything Mom and I do strikes him as out of the blue. Suddenly that question I typically dodge pops up: how much am I my father's son? I've become proficient at avoiding emotional entanglement. Funny how my earliest self-protective behaviour turned me into the very thing I was protecting myself from.

I leave him to his standard obsession – work – and head to my room, deciding halfway there that if I don't hear from Dori by the end of the day, I'm calling her.

Her text arrives in the middle of the scheduled meeting with George.

> **Dori:** The clothes are back from the dry cleaner. Where should i send them?
> **Me:** I can get them when i pick you up for lunch tomorrow.
> **Dori:** Visiting my sister tomorrow.
> **Me:** All day?
> **Me:** Never mind. Tonight, then.

Several minutes go by during which my long-suffering manager repeats the name of the director of one of the proposed films two, three times, and I still don't hear him. 'Reid. Let me know when you're actually *listening* rather than setting up booty calls.' His dry tone belies his annoyance with me, only because I know him so well.

Dori: Lunch tonight?
Me: Haha, yeah. Lunch tonight.

'I'm listening,' I tell George, seconds ticking by while I wait for her to reply, clicking the phone to make sure it's still powered up. Finally, she answers.

Dori: Okay
Me: Pick you up at 7

'Colour me unconvinced,' George says, his tone dry as toast, and I give him my almost undivided attention. I'm already planning tonight.

Dori

Here I am, staring into my closet again, chewing my thumbnail and wondering what one wears to return a borrowed outfit to a celebrity.

I arrive downstairs in jeans and a white button-up shirt with three-quarter-length sleeves. The last time I wore this shirt to school, Aimee said, 'Jeez, Dori, you look like my mom.' Her pity smirk said this wasn't a compliment. But what she hates about it is what I like. This shirt says *I'm not trying to be enticing* – not eighteen-year-old girl enticing, anyway.

Mom's on second shift at the hospital and Dad's been in his study most of the afternoon. I dread looking in on him.

Too often, he's staring out the window, or worse, at some invisible thing in his mind's eye, and when I interrupt his reverie, he looks – for a beat or two – as though he's never seen me before in his life.

I stop in the doorway. 'Hey, Dad.'

I'm relieved when he peers over the top of his glasses at me, his hands never leaving the keyboard. This is good. He's *working*. Writing sermons has been gruelling for him the past few weeks. He's always grumbled good-naturedly about striving to hear God speak; when I was little, he'd step into the hallway and tell me semi-sternly that he couldn't hear God while I practised cartwheels in the living room, or when Esther and I rough-housed on my bed, her playful barks mingling with my laughter. Now I suspect that the impediment to hearing God comes from a different source.

'I'm going out. I won't be late.'

He nods, looks back to the screen. 'Tell Kayla and Aimee hello.'

For a moment, I don't correct him, and then I shake myself internally. There's no reason to omit the truth of what I'm doing. 'Actually, I'm seeing Reid.'

His eyes snap up and he frowns – not angry, but baffled. 'Reid Alexander?'

I rarely mention Reid to anyone, but when I do, his surname is always tacked on in return, as though he can't ever just be *Reid*. He's something bigger and more sensational than that, not to be described on a first-name basis like some guy from school. 'He's the only Reid I know, Dad.'

His head tilts to the side. 'Why are you seeing *him*?'

He doesn't know I saw Reid last weekend, of course. (I let Kayla and Aimee believe I left the club with a stranger, for which they lectured me severely . . . and then pumped me for details due to the Versace top, Coach flip-flops and opaque-windowed, chauffeur-driven Mercedes.) I scramble for a sensible answer. 'I think he's, uh, investigating charity organizations for possible contributions and wanted my input.' This could be true. 'You know how people with money are.'

'Not really,' he says.

The doorbell rings and Esther takes up her post at the door, barking. 'Me neither, I guess.' I laugh nervously as I turn to go, my guilt-ridden brain summoning the stunning house and the uniformed maids and the overpriced flip-flops in my closet and the neatly folded designer clothes stowed away in my Mary Poppins bag.

The last time I saw Reid on my front porch, I hadn't yet made my third trip to Quito. Deb was about to get engaged. I was on the cusp of starting college. And I thought I'd never see him again after that night.

He's wearing jeans and a button-down shirt the colour of dark plums, the kind I eat with salt – a habit Deb instilled in me when I was young and mirrored anything she did. His sleeves are rolled to his elbows, the shirt is pressed but untucked. His dark blue eyes sweep over me once, quickly, moving to Esther, who growls. '*Esther*,' I admonish her, but not harshly, and not without stroking a hand over the back of her head. We've been too close for too long for me to reprimand her protective behaviour.

Reid squats down eye to eye with Esther and offers the back of his hand. She looks to me for reassurance that he's not dangerous and I place a hand on his shoulder to prove it. 'It's okay, Esther. He won't hurt me.' She sniffs his hand lightly and then raises her nose with a sort of haughty air, eyeing him with lingering suspicion as a hazy memory emerges from my subconscious – Reid carrying me up the staircase in his house, whispering something my brain refuses to translate now.

When he glances up, I'm staring at him. I'm sure my puzzled expression is odd; he's accustomed to wistful expressions directed his way from most women, and irked expressions from me. I turn and grab the Mary Poppins from the coat rack, severing the connection.

'That is one ginormous bag,' he says. 'Are we shoplifting? Heading to the Hamptons? Hiding a body?'

I elbow him lightly in the side (holy Moses, I forgot he's solid *everywhere*) and precede him out the front door after scratching Esther behind the ears and telling her I'll be back.

Our lunch-dinner consists of sandwiches from a tiny hole-in-the-wall place where they slice the roast beef thick, toast the hard roll, add whatever you'd like, wrap it in brown paper and send you on your way because there's no space for tables or standing around. Across the street, we find a semi-secluded park bench and talk about filming in Vancouver and my college deferral until we finish eating, and then we stroll round an upscale row of shops where a pair of socks would be at the upper limit of my budget.

'Uh-oh,' Reid murmurs. I follow his line of sight to a guy hiding not-so-discreetly behind a mailbox, an unmistakable camera lens trained on the two of us. 'Just ignore him. They usually don't approach if they're alone.' Taking my elbow, he turns to pretend interest in a store window, pulling out his phone and calling Luis, who picks us up on the next corner two minutes later.

It's Sunday before the photos are posted and speculations begin. There'd been no PDA, nothing that could be misconstrued by a sane person. But I'm learning how tabloids work. Scandal sells. The hand on my elbow is taken out of context, along with the way I seem to lean close while laughing at something he said while we were eating. That photographer had been watching us long before we saw him.

It didn't take long for someone to match the girl spending a Thursday evening with Reid Alexander to the girl from Habitat who fell on top of him in the backyard last summer. I suppose it was a simple task to get my name at that point and even easier to begin the conjecture about the length and intensity of our hidden romance and/or friends-with-benefits relationship, because of *course* it must be one of these.

I get calls and texts from Kayla and Aimee, as well as various other people I barely know or don't know at all. Reporters and photographers are camping out in front of our house and following me anywhere I go.

Reid calls to apologize, but I wave it off. 'I'll live. At least there aren't any photos of me tackling you this time.'

He laughs. 'In that case, what about doing something this

weekend? We could see what's playing at the revival theatre, if you're interested. I think they're showing *The Dead*. Have you seen it?'

'John Huston? I love it.' I don't tell him that this film adaptation of an amazing James Joyce story is one of Nick's and my favourites.

'Yeah? Me too.' He sounds like he's smiling.

'We don't want you spending any more time with him.'

I stare at my parents, Mom across from me, Dad adjacent at our small kitchen table. They sit watching my reaction, each of us exhausted from propelling ourselves into work and volunteer efforts until there are no moments to spare in which we might have to think about Deb or ponder why God left her alive, but allowed her identity, her personality, to be stripped from her.

'I don't understand,' I say finally. 'Nothing happened. Nothing will. We just hung out and talked. We're friends, I guess.'

Dad stares at his hands, clenched on the table like he's praying. Or begging. 'We're only saying we don't trust him. This is not an appropriate connection for you, Dori. You must know it can't go anywhere that's . . . suitable. And as long as you're living *here* –'

I gasp. 'Dad, *really*? "As long as you're under my roof"? Mom?'

'Dori, there's no reason to be difficult over this if he's as unimportant to you as you say.' Her voice is logical, which I'm used to, and clipped, which is wholly unfamiliar and sounds wrong coming from the woman who's loved and cared for me my whole life.

My face runs hot and I feel and hear the blood pounding in my ears. My parents have been unreasonable so few times in my life that I can almost recall them all. Making me floss nightly seemed unreasonable when I was nine. SPF 45 sunscreen seemed unreasonable at eleven. Not allowing me to see movies with even hypothetical sex or cursing seemed unreasonable at thirteen. I wonder if there will be some future point when I'll look back at this discussion and realize that what they were asking was sensible. That it was me who was being irrational.

'I don't recall saying he was unimportant,' I say quietly.

'Dori,' Dad begins, and I open my mouth to argue my point, but Mom cuts both of us off.

'We're not discussing this further.' She scoots her chair back and stands, the decisive scrape across the floor jarring. 'You will stop seeing him, Dori. He's not part of our world.'

I look up at her, incredulous. 'What world is that?'

She turns and leaves the room without answering, motioning for Dad to follow. Just when I didn't think my life could get any more bizarre, I'm wrong again.

40

REID

I'm at John's when I get a text from Dori: We need to talk.

I don't like the sound of that. I text her back that I'll call her in a few, grab a beer from the fridge and head on to the balcony. The lights of downtown look like a celebration in progress from this height. I wish Dori was standing next to me because this view is amazing, and people are easier to read face to face, and I'm way more persuasive in person.

I'm constantly off balance when it comes to this girl. 'What's up?'

Her initial reply is a soft sigh, and I think, *Shit*. And then I wonder if I'm going to surrender that easily.

'This is embarrassing,' she says, and sighs again, shoring up for whatever she's about to say. I'm confused, but I wait like I'm patient, which I definitely am not. Even so, I didn't push her when we went out. I didn't even kiss her when I dropped her off. Maybe the paparazzi stuff freaked her out.

'My parents have forbidden me to see you.'

'What, like, tomorrow?' We'd planned to see *The Dead*

at the historically renovated theatre Mom and I frequented before she started drinking. The classic movies we watched there during my childhood were responsible for lighting the acting fire in me.

'No. More like *ever*.'

I've been doing what I damn well please since I was fourteen. I ignore any barrier that doesn't make personal sense, and shove past anyone who stands in my way. I understand the notion of lines I shouldn't cross, etcetera, but I'm nineteen and holding a beer right now for chrissake. The idea that my parents would have told me who I could be friends with five or even ten years ago is unfathomable. A year ago? No way.

'Aren't you eighteen?'

'Yes.' She sighs again and I don't know if she's exasperated with me, or the situation, or what.

'This doesn't make sense.' I sound like a petulant kid.

'I know. And I'm sorry.' Her voice breaks just the slightest bit at the end, and my hand clenches the railing.

We're both silent, but my brain is going full throttle, determined to find a way through this maze. 'So. Question. How do you feel about telling them you're out with someone else?' This is a no-brainer to me, but I know how she feels about lying. 'I can't tell you how many teen movie plots revolve around just this scenario.'

She's quiet for a moment. Considering, I hope. 'Don't some of those end disastrously?'

'Yeah. But I've been in a dozen of them. I know *all* the common pitfalls.'

She laughs and my whole body hums. 'I . . . I don't know. What about the photographers?'

Damned paparazzi. 'They're still following you around?'

'I think they're starting to lose interest. Especially after five hours of trailing me all over Los Angeles a couple of days ago during my Meals-on-Wheels deliveries, with nary a celebrity in sight.' I laugh again at the mental picture that generates. 'But even if they stop following *me*,' she says, 'they'll still keep tabs on *you*.'

An idea pops into my head. I throw it out there, and imagine her chewing her lower lip while she deliberates. Just when I'm sure she's bound to say no, Dori Cantrell surprises the hell out of me again.

I answer on the first ring and she says, 'I'm here,' her earlier conviction all but gone.

I don't give her the chance to slip from doubt to regret. 'Cool. I just hit the gate remote.'

'Okay. It's opening now.' She's definitely panicking. 'Reid, maybe I –'

Oh, no you don't. 'Pull in and park all the way to the right, I'll be right out.'

My bright idea: if we don't actually go *out*, the paparazzi will have no way to photograph us together. Sadly, that's as far as I got with the devious plotting, and this will only last as long as we can occupy ourselves inside my house. I'm trying not to think about the activities with which I'd most like to occupy her time.

'Hey,' I say. Her Honda is at least ten years old. The door

squeaks when she opens it, and her mouth twists almost imperceptibly. Glancing behind me at the multi-bay garage that could possibly contain her entire house, she's speechless. Her eyes range over the rest of the place and I imagine it from her perspective. I want to impress her, sure, but there's a difference between impressing and intimidating. I take her hand and push the car door closed. 'Stick shift, huh? Sick.' I've never met a girl who can drive a stick. That is unbelievably hot. *Down, boy*.

Pulling her hand from mine, she swings her bag on to her shoulder and tucks her hair behind her ear on one side. 'Yeah, my dad loves manual transmissions for some reason, and we share the car, so I kind of had no choice.' She's still staring at the back of my parents' house.

Hands in my pockets, I ask her to follow and turn to walk inside. It's like a reverse of our very first interaction, right after I convinced her of what a complete dick I was by scanning her from top to bottom. I wonder if she walked into the Diego house that day wishing I'd just go away, or worried that I might not follow, like I'm worrying now that she'll abandon the whole idea of spending the evening here, get back in her car and peel down the long driveway.

Immaculada left dinner in the warmer as I requested, and I admit that no, I didn't cook any of it, though I'm surprisingly skilled at table-setting. We eat in the kitchen, and I tell her about the two projects I'm comparing, both filming next fall. I can't do both, but I can't decide which one to reject.

'Ignore the critical regard thing for a minute,' she says. 'Because honestly, I'm not convinced you care so much about that.' We've pushed our empty plates to the centre of the table, and her legs are folded into her chair, one knee poking up. She fixes me with an earnest, direct look, one elbow on the table as she leans forward. 'When you talk about the first one, your eyes light up. Like they could almost *not* pay you to do it, and you'd still want to.'

God, she reads me easily sometimes. 'They *will* pay me, though. A *lot*.' I get up to make coffee.

'Does that make you feel guilty about wanting to do it? Not tortured artist enough for you?' Her voice is teasing, and right next to me. She's brought the dishes to the sink. If I don't stop her, I bet she'll wash them too.

I take the plates from her, set them on the counter. 'People in my business crave recognition. It's in our natures – it's why we step on stage, get in front of cameras. We want admiration, approval. We want to be the *best* at what we do. And Oscars say "You're the best" like nothing else in the film industry does.'

I push the button and the coffee maker grinds the beans, empties them into the coned filter and starts to brew. I lean against the counter and she leans next to me. 'Okay,' she says. 'Imagine you have one of those golden guys. He's sitting on your mantel. Your talents have been recognized by your peers, and all manner of critical acclaim is yours. From now on, you'll be solicited to do more of the same type of work, all the time. How do you feel about that?'

'Bored,' I answer, surprising myself. She smiles at me like my dad did the first time I tied my shoes by myself. Mom tried, but Dad had the bunny-running-round-the-hole trick in his arsenal. He taught me to use chopsticks and floss and do long division too. Somewhere after that, we lost each other. The first time Mom failed out of rehab, maybe.

'Reid?' Dori's head is cocked to one side, a small crease in her forehead.

'Sorry.' I blink the memories away, turn to pour the coffee. 'Let's go watch a movie. I'll let you pick.'

'What about something of yours?'

'*God*, no. I hate to watch myself onscreen.' I own copies of everything I've ever done, but I only watch them alone, the way an athlete might use game footage as a training tool. Like an athlete, I think some of the footage is genius . . . and some is so atrocious that if I could destroy every known copy, I would.

'Really? I always thought that was something you actors just say. That secretly you watch yourselves and think, *Oh, man, look at me. I'm so brilliant.*'

'You caught me.' I chuckle at how close she comes to the sometimes-truth. Narrowing my gaze, I smirk and lift one eyebrow like a classic villain. 'Although, I *am* so bloody brilliant,' I say in my best pseudo-English aristocrat voice, and am rewarded with a laugh and the ear I can see darkening to an unanticipated shade of rose. Hmm.

Dori

Gosh almighty, when he uses that English Boy accent and skewers me with that look simultaneously, he's sin-on-a-stick, as Aimee would say.

The 'media room' is across from his bedroom, and these are the only two rooms in this section of the house. Unable to stop myself, my mouth drops open. 'Holy cow, you have your own *theatre*.' The room features four rows of theatre seating and an angled floor. He steps down to the front row – which is actually a long sofa – and picks up a remote. At the push of a button a screen descends from the ceiling against the far wall. I'm still gaping when he glances back.

'You know, making movies is what I do for a living. Watching them is sort of like homework.' He plops on to the sofa and I snap my mouth closed and join him. From the digital menu, we choose a recent Oscar-nominated film that neither of us has seen.

'Well, this is depressing,' Reid says an hour later, during a lull between stretches of dialogue.

'Critics say it's gritty, realistic and ultimately uplifting.' He's right, though, it *is* depressing. I should have pushed for the chick flick or the animated film.

'I'm just saying, something *uplifting* better happen soon or this glass will be flying at the screen,' he mumbles.

'Bit of an overreaction, don't you think?' Just after I utter this, the cancer-ridden child of the main character dies.

Reid turns his head and points at the screen, brows raised. 'Mmmm?'

'Well, yeah,' I concede, rolling my eyes. 'There's only so far you can uplift from killing off a seven-year-old.'

Our faces are inches apart, both of us slouched into the comfortable sofa, feet propped on a huge leather ottoman. 'I have a proposition,' he says, and my breath goes thin. I wait for him to continue, relishing the excuse to stare at him unguardedly from such a close range, wary but mesmerized. 'I think you went to that club because you were in the mood to be a little . . . reckless. And when I took you away from that douchebag, you didn't have the chance to meet your, ah, objective.'

Whatever I might have expected, this isn't it. *My objective?* The people onscreen erupt into a full-scale screaming match, but neither of us is paying attention now. I stare at my hand, resting an inch or two from his, and murmur, 'I hope you don't think I'm upset with you for that.'

His fingers stroke over the top of my hand, and my breath hitches tight like my lungs are frozen. 'The thing is . . . if you're determined to be reckless, you might as well be reckless with someone relatively safe.' He turns back to the movie, his hand resting over mine. During the next hour, he makes a few more remarks on the film and invites me to join in, but he makes no further move beyond the pressure of his hand on mine.

When I get into my car, he stands with his hands shoved into the front pockets of his jeans, hunching his shoulders in his white t-shirt. The air is crisp and smells like rain, too chilly out for his short sleeves and bare feet. He raises a hand as I put the Civic in reverse and do a three-point turn my dad would admire. In the rear-view mirror, I watch Reid jog back to the house. He didn't ask for a kiss or try for one, and now kissing him is all I can think about.

I'm back to the impression I had months ago: Reid Alexander is the Devil. Except now it's easier to understand the angels who chose to fall from heaven with him.

'Hello, sweetheart!' Mom says to Deb, and I bite my lip, turning to swap the faded, drooping roses on Deb's dresser for the fresh tulips in my arms. I don't think I'll ever get used to Mom's fake-cheerful voice. Maybe it's always been in her repertoire – something she uses on patients at the hospital, perhaps – and I just never noticed it.

I could visit Deb alone, but then no one would be talking.

I take my time folding the dying flowers into the trash and rinsing the vase. In my bag are Deb's floral shears, which cannot be left in a place like this – where people of various abnormal mental states are housed together. I trim an inch from each stem, carefully removing the limp lower leaves. Placing them in the vase one at a time, I arrange and rearrange until they fan out evenly, sunny and happy. By the time I'm satisfied with how they look, Mom is almost finished feeding my sister strawberry yoghurt, spooning it between her lips in minuscule bites like she did in old videos of Deb as an infant, long before I was born.

This undertaking brings me to my knees to watch, so I don't.

We wash Deb's hair, grown in where it was shaved for surgery. It's been kept short all over for ease of care, and falls in wisps and curls around her still-pretty face. I dig my lip balm from my bag and run it over her chapped lips just as her room-mate shuffles in and eyes us, wearing the bath-robe Mom bought for Deb last month, the one we've been unable to find since we left it here in her closet. Also missing are every pair of socks with a pink Nike swoosh and her smooth wood-based hairbrush. Mom's jaw clenches, and she complains to the front desk when we leave. We're told they'll 'look into it'. Neither of us believes they will.

We've driven almost all the way home in silence when Mom says, 'I wish she had her own room.' Her voice startles me even though she speaks softly. She's taken on extra shifts to afford Deb's shared room; we can't afford an upgrade to private. There's no need to remind her of this fact. She knows it as well as I do. I find her hand and squeeze it once between shifting from fourth to fifth. At least this is something on which we can agree.

41

REID

It's Thanksgiving, and I'm sitting in the formal dining room with my parents and our catered meal, counting the minutes until Dad and I can pretend fixation on a football game that neither of us cares about. China, crystal, white linens and we're barely speaking. Mom is drinking wine, abstaining from the hard stuff at the table, but the hand attached to the stem of her wine glass is trembling faintly. I suppress the urge to mix her something stronger, and myself too.

There was a time when Mom cooked. Not every meal, but whenever the staff had a day off. Before my grandmother died, the two of them would get up before dawn on Thanksgiving Day to start everything. By the time I'd wake up, the whole house was suffused with the aroma of roasted turkey and a conglomeration of spices from the stuffing and pies – rosemary, thyme, nutmeg, cinnamon. Mom would wrap me in an apron that fell past my knees and I'd mash the boiled cranberries and sugar through a mesh strainer until only the pulp remained, and later I would tell Dad I'd made the cranberry sauce by myself.

Dad's foot is tapping; he's already anticipating the horror of an entire day with no escape to work, wondering how long he has to perform this farce of family togetherness. There couldn't be a more uncomfortable silence over a holiday meal.

Dori and her parents are dishing out donated portions of turkey and dressing to LA's homeless population now, but she's coming over later tonight. She'll be tired after being on her feet all day, but I don't want to let her go early. A pang of guilt hits me with that thought, and I think about what might make her want to stay longer.

When she arrives, she confesses that she had very little to eat today. I offer to reheat some of our leftovers and she nods gratefully, which tells me she must be ravenous. 'Be right back. Make yourself at home.' I press her down to sit on the end of my bed. From the half-lidded look on her face, I wouldn't be surprised to come back and find her curled up asleep in the centre of it.

Instead, she's nestled into the pillows at the head of the bed, reading. I wonder which book of mine she found interesting and then I get closer. Oh, hell. She smiles up at me, bookmarking her spot with a finger and turning the cover towards me. Her smile is more of a smirk. 'I didn't realize you were a fan,' she says, revelling in her discovery. Nearly every girl in our age group owns this recently popular novel while younger girls snatch up dolls and graphic novel adaptations with stylized manga artwork. What the book *doesn't* have are many male fans.

I shrug, setting the plate on my desk and turning towards the bed. 'My agent sent me the screenplay, and I thought I should check out the novel before I decide if I want to represent it.'

Her smirk disappears. 'They're making this into a movie? And you're being considered for –'

I nod, climbing on to the bed. 'What do you think? Am I a viable contender for the role? Could I bring him to life on the big screen?'

'Um,' she says, her wide eyes on mine.

I shake my head slowly and chuckle. 'I *knew* it. You were one of those brainy girls who only got in trouble when caught after bedtime with a flashlight and a *book* under the covers.' I push her hair behind her ear on one side and can't help the widening of my evil grin; as usual, her ears cannot be trusted to keep her secrets. 'I'm right, aren't I?'

She pins her lips together and doesn't answer. She has no idea what she does to me. I'm used to calculating girls – aware of their sexual power and not afraid to use it. I'd swear on the hood of a new Porsche that Dori is aware of every other power she possesses, but when it comes to this sway over me, she's oblivious.

'Do you remember a few nights ago, when I offered you a proposition?'

Her lips fall open and she blinks. 'You said something about objectives. And recklessness. But you didn't propose anything . . . specific.' She swallows, staring down at the book in her hands.

'Hmm. Then I'll clarify.' I take the book, turn it face down on my bedside table. When I turn back, she's wary. I remain on the edge of the bed, facing her. 'If you want to *experiment* . . . use *me*, rather than some stranger at a bar who could chop you into manageable portions and bury you in a shallow grave.'

Her eyebrows elevate. Finally, she says, 'Manageable portions?'

Our laughter mixes together, dying away when I take her hand. 'Okay, though?'

She nods, her eyes sliding away. 'Okay.'

'Good. Now let's get you fed while I kill demons.' I slide off the bed, handing her the book and picking up the plate on the way to the media room.

I'm going to kiss her before she leaves tonight, that's a goddamned certainty. Enough of this playing around crap. I'll send her home with visions of me as a widely lusted-after literary character, but instead of remaining safely ensconced in the pages of a book, I'll be solid and real and right *here*.

Dori

The plate Reid hands me is loaded with odd gourmet versions of typical Thanksgiving fare, but it smells good and I'm starving. Telling myself this is no time to be finicky, I sample a bite of something that looks vaguely potato-y. '*Mmmm.*'

I realize I've said this out loud when Reid grins and says, 'I'm glad *someone* can enjoy that meal.'

I finish that bite and decide to try the green beans and – whatever that is – on top of them. 'You didn't enjoy it?' I ask, followed by another, *Mmmm*.

Shaking his head, he perches on the edge of the sofa, elbows balanced on his knees as he points the controller and pushes buttons, *click-click*, *click-click*. Eyes never leaving the screen, he smiles again. 'I'm enjoying listening to you eat more than I enjoyed eating.'

Uncertain how to take that, I attempt to muffle the appreciative sounds.

The gore level on his game is high, but thankfully the volume is down low. Without the soggy-sounding death blows, the carnage is somehow less revolting. Or maybe, considering that I'm watching him play while I *eat*, I'm becoming inured to the violence. Weird. Even weirder, I sort of want to play too, though I'm sure I'd be inept. Maybe I'll ask him to teach me next time.

Having been here half a dozen times over the last couple of weeks, I assume there'll be a next time. I refuse to think about the point where that will no longer be true.

When I finish eating, I lean back into the sofa cushions and thumb through the novel. I read it multiple times just before I started high school. Like many of my friends, I had a crush on the male lead – sensitive and strong and yes, a bit brooding. I remember lunchroom disputes over which current star would be perfect for the role if it was a movie, laughing with fellow bibliomaniacs when we ultimately concluded that any of them would put the boys in our school to shame. Now I'm friends with a guy who may star in the movie adaptation. Friends with Reid Alexander. Surreal.

He pauses the game and tosses the controller aside. 'I think there's pie. Want some?'

I nod and start to get up, but he tells me to stay. Soon after he leaves the room, I hear a noise at the doorway. 'Forget something?' I ask, turning to look over the back of the sofa, and standing in the doorway is a woman who must be Reid's mother. She's petite and beautiful and holding a drink in her hand. 'Oh, I'm sorry.' I stand up and smile, hesitant. 'Mrs Alexander? I'm Dori.'

She doesn't move from the doorway, so I walk towards her. Her blue silk blouse swishes as she straightens. She's wearing black dress pants and heels. 'Pleased to meet you,' she says, and her words are slurred. 'Where did you say Reid is?'

I'd hoped he was exaggerating about the alcoholic mother. As I get closer, I see that her eyes – the same dark blue as Reid's – are bloodshot, so disguised by intoxication I almost can't see the resemblance. Her skin appears sallow, even with the indirect lighting. I'm too familiar with the indicators of chronic drinking to discount the symptoms. He wasn't overstating.

'He's getting pie.'

She frowns. 'Oh.'

'Do you want to join us? I think we're deciding between *Breakfast at Tiffany's* and, um, *Goldfinger*.'

'Ah, Sean Connery. One of Reid's favourites. Favourite Bond, anyway.'

'Really?'

'Mmm-hmm. I'll just leave you two alone.' She tilts her head and a trace of a smile hovers around her mouth. 'You're a friend of Reid's, you said? A girlfriend?'

'I – I'm a *friend*.'

She nods, lays a hand on my arm. Her breath is sour – whiskey, I'd bet – and again, I'm more familiar than I'd like to be. 'You seem very sweet.' She leans closer, and I concentrate on breathing through my mouth as she says, 'Don't let him fool you. He's very sweet too.' She turns and walks a meandering path down the hallway just as Reid tops the stairs with a plate of pie smothered in whipped cream, and two forks.

He scowls. 'Was that my mom?'

'She stopped in to say hello. I invited her to stay, but I think she was afraid of intruding. Either that or Sean Connery is not her favourite Bond guy. *My* mother prefers Roger Moore.'

He looks at me a long moment, then hands me the forks and uses his free hand to tug me close. 'Feeling reckless yet?'

I nod once and he doesn't wait for further affirmation, lowering his lips to mine. I forget the pie in his hand and the forks in mine as he opens my mouth with his. He kisses me once, twice, three times, pulling back a hair's breadth each time while reeling me closer and closer until I'm completely off balance and curving into him. 'I really have to know,' he says, holding me securely, our mouths an inch apart, breath mingling, 'how delicious you'll taste after you have a few bites of this pie.'

I giggle and he smirks, taking my hand and pulling me down to the front where we sink on to the sofa. He feeds me a bite of pie before setting the plate and utensils aside on the ottoman. 'I think you stabbed me,' he breathes against my neck before brushing my hair aside and kissing the base of my throat. The feel of his mouth on my skin triggers waves of need in my belly that coil and spring like stretchy filaments of connection to every nerve ending I have.

'I'm – sorry?' I gasp because his fingers are stroking the skin under my shirt, fanning out over my sides. He pulls me on to his lap as his lips move up my jawline, lighting an explosive pathway to my ear.

'Didn't hurt. I barely noticed.' His voice is soft and near, a murmured caress. 'My brain was occupied with more important things than minor flesh wounds.' And then his mouth is on mine, his tongue sweeping through my mouth. 'Mmmm,' he growls softly. 'My God, Dori.' He doesn't speak again, does nothing but kiss me – with occasional pie breaks, like marathoners downing cups of Gatorade for endurance – until it's time for me to leave. I've never been so kiss-drunk; if he hadn't pointed out the time, I wouldn't have noticed it.

He pulls on a hooded jacket and a pair of Vans before walking me to my car. My lips are swollen and my skin is flushed head to toe. Like gravitational attraction, I can't resist his pull when he's within my reach. My teeth chatter as he presses me against my car, unzipping his jacket and folding it round us both, the hood up and shading the edges of our faces from the unobstructed moonlight overhead. 'Cold?' he asks, and I shake my head. The shudders racing along my core have nothing to do with temperature. If anything, I'm burning. His mouth returns to mine and it's no longer strange, no longer new. The feel of his heartbeat and the sinewy muscle layered over it is familiar under my hands, as is the manner in which he coaxes my responses forward, every nuanced turn and dip anticipated.

I drive home thinking, *This is me in manageable portions*.

42

REID

'Man, you suck.' This is John's professed assessment of me when I sink the last solid ball on our second round of pool. Translation: I don't suck and he wishes I did because I've already beaten him once and am about to make it twice.

'So since there's a pool table between us,' he says, 'and I'm sorta sober – enough to dodge if I have to – I have a question.' Considering that the only time I've ever been physically violent with John was over Dori, I assume he's letting me know that she's the subject of this proposed interrogation. He's either a lot braver or a lot stupider than I thought.

'Right corner pocket.' As I lean to take the shot, he clears his throat and I scratch. At my glare, he throws both hands up as if he had nothing to do with it. Standing the butt of the cue stick on the floor and holding it like a staff, I say, 'So talk.'

After taking all day to line up, he pockets his last two balls with one shot, and then sinks the eight ball. Bastard.

I rack the balls for another round as he gulps down the last of his beer, which makes me more curious about what he's got to say. 'Your turn to break,' he says.

'Not until you start talking. And please tell me this has nothing to do with my love life.'

He sighs, chalking his stick, not looking particularly guarded, but not getting any closer, either. 'Well, I don't know, you tell me – *is* it about your love life?' He air-quotes *love life*.

John really is oblivious to how many times during our relationship I've wanted to punch him. This is one of them. 'Cryptic, John. What is this, a very special episode of 90210?' I slam the cue ball into the rest and scatter them across the table.

'Fine. Just . . . don't get all hands-on. It's about that Dori chick.' He's directly opposite me still, the wide expanse of table between us. Smart.

'What about her?'

Palms up, he says, 'See, you're doing it already, man.'

'What?'

'Looking like you're gonna beat the shit out of me, that's what. How am I supposed to be a bro and ask the hard shit if I'm afraid you're gonna kill me for it?' He takes his shot and sinks the thirteen.

While he's lining up another shot – remaining, conspicuously, on the other side of the table – I say, 'Keep from talking about what I should *do* to her and you can ask whatever.' He sinks another stripe and cocks an eyebrow. 'Within *reason*,' I add.

'Okay. You've skipped out on a few parties lately. For, like, the last few weeks. You get a text, you leave.'

One shoulder lifts and falls. 'And?'

He eyes me. 'Okay. The texts are from her?' I nod, leery of where he's going with this, and he rolls his eyes. 'Reid, I've known you since we were sixteen. You're the best friend I've ever had. I think I'm pretty qualified to say – *what the hell*, man? You've never – I mean, *never* – gotten remotely pissed over anything I've said about a girl you've hooked up with. Not to mention going all caveman apeshit.' He misses his third shot and I line mine up.

I wonder if John's jealous in some way. Not that I can ask him that – I'd never hear the end of it. 'What's your point?' I sink my shot, move round the table to sink another. He's fixated on a couple of girls playing one table over, one of whom angles indecently over her table in the shortest shorts possible. Glancing over her shoulder, she's making certain we're watching.

I've pocketed another two balls by the time he answers. 'Uh, my point is, are you *seeing that*?' He tips his head at the two girls, who are openly appraising us and by the looks of things, about to come over.

I stand straight. 'Yeah, John, I am a *guy*. I noticed. I just don't care.' Every guy in the place noticed them the moment they walked in. Heads swivelled, bodies turned, mouths hung open. Your standard male reaction to females in tight, short, cleavage-baring clothes.

'See, that right there – what *is* that? You don't *care*? What does that even mean?'

'Hey.' Both girls saunter up right behind him.

'Hey, yourselves, ladies.' John's standard hunter smile is in place. 'What can we do for you?'

Short Shorts has an expression that matches John's, but she's aiming it at me. 'You guys are pretty good. Thought we could get some pointers. We're willing to buy the next round for your trouble.' They know who I am. Girls don't buy the drinks, guys do. And in a pool hall full of guys more than willing to do just that, they come to our table and offer to buy? I couldn't be less interested.

'Sounds like a deal to me,' John says, giving me the please-don't-screw-this-up-for-me face. Shit. He's going to be *pissed* by the end of this night.

Dori

'So you're dropping out of college? Before you even start?'

The shocked look on Nick's face elicits a new heaviness in the pit of my stomach. 'I haven't decided yet. But I get spacey sometimes lately. I just . . . zone out. I can't go to school at *Berkeley* and do that. I'd fail.'

Nick reaches out before I know what he's doing and places his hand over mine where it rests on the small bistro table. 'Dori, Deb wouldn't want you giving up on your dreams because of what happened to her.' His hand is warm, covering mine completely. I stare at his square fingertips, the flat, short nails clipped evenly. So different from Reid's tapered fingers – long, like a pianist's, his hand still big enough to dwarf mine.

'I know that.' I withdraw my hand to pick at non-existent fuzz on my sweatshirt, hoping the rebuff isn't too conspicuous. As selfish as it is, I don't want to lose Nick's friendship – even if I no longer want anything other than that from him. He knows this, though it took him a little while to accept it. Staring at his hand, still on the table between us, I try to explain. 'I feel lost without her, and detached from those dreams. Maybe they weren't ever really mine.'

He frowns, pulls his hand back to the steaming mug of green tea in front of him. 'What do you dream of doing now, then?'

Reid's image flashes across my mind like one of those ads with a subliminal message inserted – a single frame of a face inside a strip of film. What I dream of now is Reid; everything else is filler. This realization should scare me to death, but it doesn't. 'Nothing,' I say. Before he can form another question, I ask him how he likes Madison, where he goes to school.

'Well,' he gives me a stern look, 'everyone isn't quite as fond of cheese as we've been led to believe.' One side of his mouth sneaks up.

'False advertising?' I ask, smiling back.

When he settled on Wisconsin as one of his top university choices last fall, he bewildered his parents – who are innately incapable of detecting sarcasm – by insisting that 'an abundance of cheese' was one of his motives for wanting to attend. Nick's parents don't get his sense of humour. 'Definitely.'

I sip my latte and smile. 'Cheese aside, how's college life?'

He considers for a moment. 'Challenging.'

'Ah, you must love it there,' I tease.

'Pretty much.' Dunking the tea bag like he's operating a marionette, he adds, 'So what can I do to convince you to go to school, Dori?'

I heave a sigh. 'Everything just feels pointless right now.'

His serious brown eyes regard me closely. 'Because of Deb.'

I nod. 'I guess so. But it doesn't feel like it's *her*, or what happened to her, exactly. I feel more like . . . like I'm finally seeing everything for what it is, and nothing is what I thought.'

'Hmm,' he says.

We sit in our typical companionable silence for a few minutes, watching bag-laden Christmas shoppers scurry in and out of nearby stores. A few nights ago, Reid pulled me into his house, telling me we were going Christmas shopping. 'But –?' I said, following him upstairs and into the media room.

He'd hooked his laptop to the screen, and while we ate dinner, I watched him give new meaning to the notion of online shopping. Armed with a list of people and addresses from his manager, he spent more money in a couple of hours than I could keep track of. When I wouldn't let him buy me anything, he peered at me for a moment before pulling me into his arms and asking, 'So you only want me for my body?'

I bit my lip and nodded, and he growled and kissed me senseless. Once it got dark, Immaculada handed us thermoses of hot chocolate and Luis drove us around to look at Christmas lights.

As though the thoughts in my head are transparent, Nick says, 'If you don't mind my asking – what's the deal between you and Reid Alexander? I don't follow Hollywood gossip even when I'm in LA, but the whole country was speculating over the date – or whatever it was – you two had a couple of weeks ago. The one preserved for posterity on every website from TMZ to People. So I hear.'

Before I left his house last night, Reid asked me to sing something, threatening to tickle me if I refused. When I told him I couldn't sing without accompaniment – which he knows is a lie – he produced a guitar from his closet.

'Do you play?' I asked, sitting on the edge of his bed.

His mouth pulled up on one side. 'Not well.'

'I could teach you.' I tuned the instrument, which was top-of-the-line, expensive. 'I mean, you've taught me to massacre Nazi zombies. It's the least I could do.'

'I'd like that,' he said, watching me.

He sat next to me while I strummed simple chords, singing 'Fallen' by Sarah McLachlan. After, we lay on our sides, staring at each other. He ran a finger over my lips, down my throat. 'You do have a beautiful voice, Dori.' I knew he was withholding something more, but I didn't ask him to say it.

I pull out of the Reid reverie, shrugging at Nick. 'We're friends.' How can I explain to him, or to anyone, that without Deb, Reid is the only person in my life who sees me for who I am?

When it's clear I'm not going to offer any more, Nick

inclines his head and shifts his eyes to his mug. 'Just, you know, proceed with caution. He's not exactly in our league.' He bobs the tea bag restlessly. 'I don't want you to get hurt. You're vulnerable right now.'

I know he's right, and I'm sliding headlong into something that can't end well. Avoiding his gaze, I promise, 'I'll be careful,' and just like that, I'm officially lying to everyone I know. Everyone except Reid.

43

REID

'If you close your eyes, you won't know if he's dead yet,' I say.

Dori's hammering away on the controller, *click-click-clack-clack-clack*, hacking the thing on the life-sized screen until it's a bloody pulp. 'But it's *disgusting*.' We're in the media room where I sit on the sofa with her cross-legged on the floor between my knees. My guy is already dead, so I'm just watching her. For a former non-gamer girl, she's a remarkably quick learner. '*Eww, eww, eww*,' she says. Squeamish, but quick.

'I'm pretty sure you've killed him.' She flashes me a sideways look and I grin, one palm up – *what?* – and then she chops the thing one more time.

'I just want to make sure.'

'And *I* want to make sure you're on my team if demonic predators ever attack Earth.'

My phone buzzes with a text from Dad: Come to my study when you have a minute.

He never puts in an appearance on my side of the house to speak with me – I always get a text summons to his office. Once, I was away on location and he sent one requesting tax receipts. I took great satisfaction in replying that I wasn't in the house, or LA, or *California* for that matter. He prides himself on being a detail guy, but he didn't notice his only kid was out of town? Pretty sure he lost out on Father of the Year for that.

'I've gotta go talk to Dad about something. Back in a sec.' Dori nods without looking at me, alternating between staring at the action onscreen and squeezing her eyes shut – every single time she's killing something. It's so cute that I can't resist leaning forward, pulling her hair away from her neck and running the tip of my tongue along the bumpy vertebrae, nibbling the smooth skin.

'Mmm.' Her arms go a little slack and her eyes drift closed. Her avatar is going to get slaughtered thanks to me. 'You're distracting me, Reid. You're going to get me killed.' I chuckle and she shrieks, hunching her shoulders. 'No tickling!'

'I didn't mean to.' I lean round, turn her face towards me and kiss her, and she forgets to hit *pause* before dropping the controller into her lap – such a *girl*. Judging by the sounds roaring from the speakers, she's dying a quick, bloody death, but she doesn't seem to care.

'You didn't mean to tickle me, or you didn't mean to kill me?' Her voice is a breathy whisper into my mouth.

I kiss her again before saying, 'Neither. I *was* trying to distract you, though. To see if I could break through your bloodlust.'

Something flashes through her eyes, so quickly I almost miss it. 'Mission accomplished,' she murmurs.

'Hmm. What was that look for?' She shakes her head, her ears pink. My arms surround her and I fold over her like a tent. 'Was it because I said –' I lower my voice '– *lust*?' Her skin darkens under the dusting of freckles across her cheeks. 'Is that what you're feeling for me?' I hold her face steady, kissing the corner of her mouth, preventing her from turning her head and fusing our lips together – not yet. 'I feel so used.' I run my tongue along her lower lip and she gasps. 'Good thing I'm totally okay with that, huh?'

When I kiss her this time, her head falls back against my thigh, her torso twisted as her hands reach for me. Winning her desire is like nothing I've ever accomplished. The pathway to it was proving that I'm worthy of her trust, and somehow, I've done that. She was indifferent to everything that usually matters to people in my experience. A bolt of panic shoots through me when I realize I don't even know what it was that earned her confidence.

My phone rings, startling us both. While my jaw clenches, she jumps and pulls away as though someone has walked into the room and caught us kissing. As though we don't have every right to do so, the rest of the world be damned.

It's Dad. 'Yeah?'

'Are you home? I thought I saw your friend's car outside . . .'

I am *not* discussing Dori with him.

'I'm on my way down. It's a big house.'

'I just need a signature on a court doc.'

'Sure. Be right there.' I hang up, and Dori is saving and signing off her failed demon-exterminating mission – the one I wrecked. I can't be sorry for wrecking it. 'You can restart the level, you know.'

She smiles. 'Maybe next time. I've sort of lost interest in, um, bloodlust.'

I'm biting back the licentious replies pouring through my brain because I've already exceeded my daily quota for inciting mad flushes to scurry across her skin. 'We have time to watch a movie. I won't be long – he just needs me to sign something.' I hate giving up even ten minutes with her, a fact that should alarm me, but doesn't.

When I get to Dad's office, he presents a pen and a document with an X at the bottom, my full name typed under the line that needs my signature. 'Once this is recorded, you'll have completed the initial probationary requirements of your sentence.' I scrawl my name as his words sink in.

'My licence suspension?' I feel like it's been years since I drove a car, as opposed to six months.

He sighs, taking the pen, pushing the signed document into an envelope. 'The suspension terminates on the twentieth, though this is a permanent strike against you that *will* be counted if you repeat the offence. Assuming you don't just get yourself killed next time.' He eyes me. 'I'm sure you know – but I'll say it regardless – that I'd prefer you not to drive at all.'

I hear the implication that there will be a next time, and that I, like my mother, should be safeguarded against the combination of alcohol and vehicles. I subdue the resentment threatening to strangle me. 'If I choose to drink, I won't drive. I've learned my lesson.'

His expression is rigid, discontented with my admission that I don't intend to give up drinking, thankful that at least I'm agreeing to sidestep driving if I do. Puffing out a sigh, he says, 'I guess if that's all the reassurance I'll get, I have to accept it.' He stares for a moment, and just when I'm about to turn and leave, he asks, 'So who's the girl?'

Answers skip unspoken across my tongue. The girl upstairs now? The girl I was just kissing like a boy who hasn't screwed so many hot girls in the past five years that there's no hope of remembering the vast majority of them? 'What girl?'

His sardonic expression is a replica of mine, or vice versa. 'The girl who drives the ten-year-old Honda parked in the driveway several nights a week for the past *month* or so.' Dad has never been good at playing along.

'Dori.'

His eyebrows jump. 'The Habitat girl? The Berkeley girl?'

How the *hell* does he remember these details? It's as remarkable as it is grating. 'Yes, but she didn't – hasn't started at Berkeley yet.'

'Oh?'

There's that predictable disdain in his tone, and I can't resist quashing it. He assumes everyone associated with me is dissolute and aimless, his prime (and favourite) example being John. 'Her sister had an accident right before she was supposed to start. Closed head injury. Dori postponed college to be around for her family.'

'That's . . . accommodating of her,' he says. I'm too familiar with his condescension to pretend I don't hear it. His assumption of her possible motives for the deferral is infuriating.

'No, Dad, that's selfless and devoted. Traits the Alexander gene apparently lacks.'

He looks like I've just gut-punched him, which is less gratifying than I'd thought it would be. Shuffling papers on his desk, he switches gears. 'I assume you'll be purchasing another car shortly. If you'll let me know an approximate price range, I'll pull funds from your investments so they'll be available.'

'Sure. We done?'

Straightening and stacking, he says, 'Yes. I suppose so.'

Running a hand through my hair, I wish I could reel back the implication that he's unsupportive. John is studying finance against his will. Dori is being forced to lie to her parents just to see me. Celebs with exploitive parents are a dime a dozen. He could be so much worse. Maybe that isn't the best parental commendation, but maybe it is. Shit. *Shit.*

'So thanks for handling everything.'

Visibly stunned, his hands still as he looks at me. 'You're welcome.'

I nod, he nods and I leave before I examine this new consciousness any more closely.

Dori

Reid's mother just left the room after a conversation that awakened, for a moment, my aspiration to study social work. I've spent the past few months emotionally detached from the volunteer work I continue to do, as though an impenetrable wall stands between me and the joy I once felt when I believed that what I did mattered.

'Am I intruding?' she said from the doorway.

I stood, conscious of the banter regarding *lust* and the suspended make-out session I'd just had with her son. 'No.' I felt myself blushing. 'This is your home, after all.'

She smiled. 'I try not to encroach on Reid's part of it. In all honesty, though, I noticed him leaving and I wanted to talk to you, if that's all right.'

'Of course,' I said, annoyed with my monosyllabic vocabulary, apprehensive about what Reid's mother could possibly want with me.

When she perched on the sofa where Reid had been minutes prior, I sat back down, mulling over my parents' judgement of him and wondering if I was about to be measured by his mother in the same prejudicial way.

'I don't mean to make you uncomfortable – Dori, wasn't it?' I nodded, holding my breath. 'Reid hasn't brought anyone home in so long.' This couldn't be true, based on his well-known exploits, but mentioning that would do neither of us any good, aside from the fact that I'd rather not contemplate it at all. 'You said you and he are – friends?'

I nodded again, my gaze darting away and then back. I tried to keep the eye contact steady, knowing that avoiding her eyes would just make me look guiltier. 'Yes.' We'd not declared ourselves to be anything else or anything more. *Reckless*, my conscience muttered, *that's what we are together*. The blush returned with a vengeance.

'Reid needs a friend who cares about him. When he had that accident last summer, it just seemed as though –' her hands twisted in her lap – 'he didn't care about his own welfare. He's drinking less, going out less since you started coming around, and I just . . . wanted you to know you're welcome here. I'd do anything to make sure he doesn't repeat my mistakes.' Her voice fell to a whisper. 'There's no hope for me, I know . . . but I can't bear the thought that there'd come a point where there's no hope for him.'

'There's always hope.' I heard myself say this, pushing aside thoughts of Deb and my parents and prayer and hope – and my loss of it.

She shook her head. 'I've tried rehab three times, and failed every time. I can't endure another three months away from home.' Her eyes brimmed, so like Reid's eyes that I felt my stomach clench.

'Have you . . . have you tried AA?' Do women like her go to AA? Society women, who can afford to check themselves into luxury clinics for several-month stints? I felt out of my element.

She shook her head. 'Oh, no. It would be horrible if someone found out. I won't embarrass my husband or Reid more than I've already done.'

She was trapped, not only by her addiction, but by her privileged place in society and her son's very public career. She called herself hopeless, but hope was still alive in her because she's examined all the locked doors of her cage – and people don't examine locked doors unless they're looking for an escape.

'There's a confidentiality clause with AA. While it's true that the press often reports on celebrities who check into rehab, I can't remember ever seeing them report on people attending AA meetings.' I leaned closer. 'Mrs Alexander, Reid wouldn't want you to feel unable to help yourself. One of the reasons AA works is that the *individual* makes the decision not to drink, one day at a time. One hour. One minute even. You can do that, right? One minute?'

Her eyes never left mine. Even with the consequences of years of alcoholism, I could see that she's where Reid got his beautiful face. I imagined what they must have looked like together when he was very young, walking through a shop or in the park, his hand in hers, her beauty reflected in the little boy at her side. We sat quietly, and into the silence of those sixty seconds came the staggering ache of missing Deb. I wanted to cry for her and myself and my parents and Brad. I wanted to cry for Reid's mother, and also for Reid. There are a million ways to lose someone you love.

'There's one minute,' I said. 'You're stronger than you know, Mrs Alexander.'

Her eyes flicked to the clock on the wall and back to me. 'Please, call me Lucy. I'll think about AA. But . . . don't tell him yet.' I nodded, and she left the room.

'This may sound odd, given what I do for a living, but I'm not the slightest bit interested in seeing any of these movies.' The screen goes blank as Reid tosses the remote aside. 'And,' he draws my legs over his lap, 'I can think of a *lot* of other things I'd rather do.'

'As in a lot of kissing?' My words light a fire in his eyes and he stretches out on the wide sofa, pulling me alongside him. Our bodies touch from knees to chest, and I'm feeling more daring than I've ever been with him. Trailing fingertips across the planes of his face, I brush his hair out of his eyes, touch the lips I want to touch me.

'Among other things,' he says huskily.

'What other things?' I'm making myself blush, but my usually reticent mouth isn't cooperating. He closes his eyes and leans his face into my hand, kisses my palm, wraps his arms round me.

'That, as always, is up to you.' His lashes feather up. The lighting, perfect for a home theatre, is too dim to see the blue of his eyes.

'As always, huh? So it was *me* who attacked *you* in that pink closet?'

He smiles wickedly. 'I was just reading your mind that day.'

I stare at him, wanting to be audacious and brash; my shaky whisper is anything but. 'Can you read it now?'

One eyebrow quirks up. 'Feeling reckless tonight, are you?' I nod. 'Mmm,' he hums. 'Let's see what I can do about that.' His devilish grin appears in the same moment his fingers stroke the skin of my lower back, and then he kisses me, moving from gentle pressure to hot and deep and back to gentle. He pulls away to sit up and it's all I can do to silence the protest that proves unnecessary when he hauls me up to straddle his hips, facing him.

I lean in to kiss him as his hands wander under my thin,

loose sweater, unhooking my bra with a slip of fingertips that graze bare skin and leave a trail of goosebumps in their wake. He's unbuttoned buttons and loosened clothing for better access, but he's never removed anything. I don't have the guts to pull the sweater over my head. Instead, I reach under the sweater and pull the bra straps down my arms, one at a time, pushing each arm back into the sleeves that hang over my hands, before dropping the bra on the otto-man behind me.

He smiles, probably having seen that trick a thousand times. Before I lose my nerve, I scoot forward until I'm pressed to him, wind my fingers into his hair and kiss him like he kisses me when I haven't seen him in three or four days – hard and hungry, sweeping my tongue across his lower lip. He grips me tighter and moans into my mouth, spurring me to move my attention to his neck, just behind his ear, one hand moving painstakingly down his chest, lower across his firm stomach, lower still until he grabs my wrist. This movement feels familiar, though I could swear he's never held me like this before.

'Dori.' His breath is hot in my ear as he holds my wrist securely, and then he rests his forehead against mine, pant-ing. 'I . . . need to take a break.'

'What?' I pull back, confused. This is not a moment in which guys request a break.

'I need a minute or two.' Something in my expression must disclose my worry because his hands come up to surround my face. He closes his eyes and takes a deep, slow breath and then he looks at me more earnestly than he's ever done. 'I want you too badly. I need time to cool down because I want to be *inside* you.'

Relief floods through me, filling me with the courage I lacked moments ago – short-lived, existing just long enough to force out four small words, barely audible, that could change everything between us.

'I want you to.'

44

REID

'What?' I lean back, cup her chin in my hand. 'What did you say?'

She closes her eyes because I won't let her hang her head, won't let her turn her face away. 'I said I want you to,' she murmurs.

Everything goes silent then. The echo of our breathing, so thunderous just a moment ago, fades. 'Dori. I didn't mean to imply that I can't control myself. We don't have to have sex.'

I brush her hair back on one side, checking her mood-displaying ears. Her rosy, telltale ears. Her voice is just above a whisper, her eyes still closed. 'I'm not – I'm not a virgin, Reid. So . . . it doesn't matter.'

Yeaaaah . . . probably best if I don't tell her I figured that one out a while back. But – *it doesn't matter*? What the hell does that mean? 'It matters to me.'

Her eyes pop open and her mouth works for a moment, and finally, she says, 'Oh. I understand.'

I'm trying to read this, attempting to avoid a misstep with her, and for a moment I think she's shifting – her foot's gone to sleep or her knees are locking. Then I realize she's pulling away, and she's almost fully standing before I grab her wrists. 'You do *not* understand.'

Pausing in her effort to escape, she inhales a shaky breath. 'I've misrepresented what I am to you, to my parents, to everyone.' Her eyes brim with tears. 'I'm a total fraud.'

'What, because you're not a *virgin*?' I sputter. 'Dori, I of all people would never hold *that* against you. How hypocritical do you think I am?'

Her brow puckers, a wave of tears cascading down her cheeks, and I don't want to talk any more. I want to pull her back down on to my lap and kiss her until she can't think of anything but me, and us, and what she wants right now.

'But you said it matters –' She sucks in a small sob.

'Yes, it matters, goddammit.' I stand and take her face in my hands. 'It matters that you never throw yourself away on someone you don't really want just because of some archaic black and white concept of morality. I don't care if you've slept with one guy, or dozens.' She winces and I hold her steady. 'You're a good person, Dori.'

She tries to move her head side to side in my hands and I won't let her so she closes her eyes. 'I'm not.'

'Oh, yes you are.'

She sucks in a shaky breath. 'You aren't . . . disappointed?'

I shake my head. 'What? *No.* At times like this, I'm confused. And sometimes, when you leave, I'm frustrated as hell. But disappointed? Never.'

'I don't understand.' She blinks up at me with her big Bambi eyes.

'Like I said.'

Pushing my hands through her hair, I pull her closer, and she leans into me. My thumbs sweep the remaining wetness from her cheeks. 'Do you want me, Dori – or do you think having sex with me seems like the only honest decision to be made?' My thumb grazes across her mouth as the tip of her tongue snakes out to wet her lips – running over the sensitive pad of my thumb. It takes every scrap of self-restraint I've got not to crush her to me and forget this entire conversation.

She stares at her hands, curled against my chest. 'Is it . . . horrible . . . if it's both?'

I exhale. 'Not horrible.' *But not okay, either.* 'Come here.' I sit back down, and she sits next to me, turned towards me, knees under her chin, feet hooked under my thigh. My fingers run lazy patterns over her hands, down her shins through her jeans, swirl round her bare ankles. She shivers once and waits, looking at me.

'Look, we don't have to talk about –' *Other guys? Your sexual history?* '– the, uh, specifics of anyone who came before. I could tell you that everyone makes mistakes . . . but I can't say that guy, or those guys, were mistakes for you.' Brows creased, she doesn't reply. 'Driving drunk and slamming into someone's house – *that* was a mistake. You were exploring your body. Learning about yourself.'

'It was one guy,' she says, her voice breaking, and I feel like a total shit that this disclosure makes me euphoric. 'And then one day . . . it was just *over*. And I don't know why, or wh-what I did wrong. I was s-so *stupid*.'

God, guys are dicks. 'Dori, you trusted him and he hurt you. He didn't stick around, he lied, he made you feel used because you cared more than he did . . . and that misplaced trust felt like one huge mistake. But believe me, it was *his* mistake. Not yours.'

'Reid . . .' She buries her head beneath my chin, her body folded up like she's trying to crawl inside me. 'He . . . he . . . I . . .' Her breathing is quick and shallow and I'm scared to death of what she's going to say because, so help me God, if she tells me that guy forced himself on her, I'll have no choice but to find him and kill him.

My arms surround her and I fight to keep my voice level, unwavering. 'Tell me.'

'I *can't*.'

I stroke her hair. 'Yes, you can. Trust me, Dori. You can trust me.'

Her face is pressed to my shirt and she's shaking. 'I got pregnant.' Reverberations hum through my chest, like it's me who's crying. 'Except for Deb, no one ever knew. Not my parents, not Colin, not my friends. Only Deb.'

Oh, hell. 'You never told him?'

Words muffled by her knees and my chest, she shakes her head. 'He was already . . . with someone else. He wouldn't have cared.'

Five-second epiphany: I did this to Brooke, who *did* come to me, who *did* tell me. Even if she had been with another guy – or guys – the relationship was her and me, as failed as it was. I left her with a wretched choice to make and no way out of making it. I checked out because I could. Damn, damn, damn. I shove this realization aside for now because what I owe Brooke, some guy owes Dori – but I'm the only one here to pay it.

'If no one knew, that means you decided not to . . .' I stop. 'Not to have it.'

Her sobs are the only answer I get. So this Colin guy dumps her, then she finds out she's pregnant and her sister helps her take care of it. She's probably been raised on abstinence, and pro-life to boot. And to top it off, her sister – the only person in the world who helped shoulder this burden – is now one step up from a coma, with no interaction, no emotional connection to be had.

Christ, no wonder she went off the deep end.

Speaking of which, I am in *way* over my head.

Dori

I can't believe I've just dumped all of this on him. Minutes ago, we were making out, and he said what he said, and I told him about Colin, and there it was, this secret, beating on the walls inside where I thought I'd locked it away forever.

Deb and I didn't discuss it again, after the decision was made and carried out. She tried, once, but I promised her that I was fine and swore I'd rather forget it and get on with my life because that was the reason for the decision in the first place. To get on with my barely fifteen-year-old life.

I faked the flu for a couple of days before going back to school. And then I survived the remaining weeks of my freshman year – seeing Colin in the halls with his entourage, or his new girl, always smiling, not a care in the world. I learned to cry soundlessly, locked in a bathroom stall, doubled over, the heartache so bad it made me physically ill. I skipped class when I could get away with it, had trouble concentrating when I was there.

Maybe he had no idea what he'd done to me. Maybe he was just a careless boy, with no idea that I would be emotionally crippled by his offhand dismissal. At the time, it felt orchestrated to crush me.

Submerging myself in an endless loop of depressing music and isolation, I was hollow and faded, a ghost haunting her own life. When summer began, I started spending most of the day in bed with the blinds closed. I contemplated suicide briefly, but couldn't wrap my head round carrying it out.

Deb had just finished her first year of medical school, and her plans hadn't included coming home for summer. Suddenly, though, she was there in her old bedroom across the hall – her tidy shower caddy stored under the sink, her off-key serenade of pop songs in the shower echoing down the hallway every morning. She also resumed volunteering for community service projects – something I'd always been too young to do.

On her third day home, she plopped on to my bed with her cup of coffee, brushing the hair from my face. 'C'mon, lazy butt. Get up. I need your help. These benevolent deeds aren't gonna do themselves.' I moaned into my pillow, but didn't budge. I remember the feel of her fingers pulling gently through my hair. Maybe not from that morning, exactly, but because I couldn't remember a time when that wasn't part of her wake-up-Dori protocol. 'Dori, honey. Listen . . . maybe you can't keep this to yourself any longer. Maybe you need to talk to Mom and Dad.'

I turned over. 'You'd be in trouble if they knew.'

She shook her head. 'I'm a grown woman of twenty-three, and I can take care of myself with our parents. I'm worried about *you*. Staying in bed all day, not seeing your friends, barely eating anything. You sleep non-stop and still look exhausted.'

Mom and Dad must have called her. I was the reason she'd come home. They knew about the break-up because there was no hiding the fact that Colin stopped coming to pick me up on the weekends. When asking me what happened only resulted in tears, they stopped asking. They must have got worried when the depression got worse instead of tapering off.

'I'm fine. I don't want to talk about it. I just want to go on with my life like he never happened.'

She bit her lip. 'Okay. If you get up. If you keep getting up every day, eat normal meals, sleep normal hours.' She sniffed lightly. 'And if you shower daily because Lord knows you smell like a puppy rolled in poop right now.'

I couldn't help smiling. It had been so long since I'd smiled that the movement felt unnatural. She leaned her forehead to mine, whispering our declaration of devotion, spoken countless times over many years: 'I love you, baby sister of mine.'

'How much?' I played along, whispering back as she swam, blurry through my tears.

'As many grains of sand as there are on all the beaches in all the world.' She recited the words like a tender incantation.

'For how long?'

With the edge of her soft pink robe, she wiped away the tear that escaped at the corner of my eye and murmured, 'Forever and forever and forever.'

Reid is dressed like a doctor – lab coat and stethoscope – and he's talking to God. Or someone wearing a shimmering white robe and looking an awful lot like God. 'Yes, sir, I understand. She will. Bye.'

At the snap of my cheap flip phone shutting, I open my eyes. I'm lying on the sofa in Reid's media room. Everything comes into focus slowly. 'Who were you talking to?'

He slips my phone back into my bag. 'Your dad.'

I frown. 'My dad? Why?'

He crouches down next to me so we're at eye level. 'I guess we fell asleep. It's really late. I heard your phone ringing, so I answered it – I figured it was best for them to know you're safe. I told him you'd be home in the morning.'

'What did he say?'

'A lot of dad stuff. Don't worry about it now. C'mon.' He takes my hand and leads me across the hall and into his room while I'm thinking about everything I told him earlier. At the edge of the bed he stops and his eyes travel the length of me. 'I think you'd be more comfortable in something of mine.' From his dresser, he chooses Oxford-stripe boxers and a blue t-shirt, frayed at the neckline and sleeves, soft and faded from hundreds of washes. Putting the clothes into my hands, he stops me, one hand on my arm. 'Dori. Are you all right?'

I nod, certain I'm lying. I am so, so far from all right. I should feel weird that I'm about to sleep in Reid Alexander's bed. For the second time. But I forget, sometimes, who he is to the rest of the world.

'I'll, um, change in the bathroom.'

When I come back into his room minutes later, the lights are very low – just bright enough to see my way to the bed. The clock reads 3:11 a.m. I climb in and hesitate before moving into his arms. His hands stroke up and down my back, his lips at my hairline. I feel exactly what I felt earlier – I need him to hold me so badly that I don't care what comes with it. Maybe that sounds weak-willed, but it isn't because I *want* all of it. I just know that at some point, my wanting will exceed his ability to give, and that will be that. Until then, I don't want to think or analyse any more. I just want to feel. I tip my face up and nuzzle the underside of his jaw, and he shifts slightly and kisses me. So careful, deliberate.

My eyes are adjusting to the dim light when I move to brace above him, my hair streaming down like a screen around my face. His hands are at my waist, on top of my shirt – his shirt – fingers drifting back and forth across the small of my back, as though they're stuck in a loop, waiting for me to release them to wander with some magic word.

I don't know, exactly, what he wants from me. But I know what I want from him, and I lean down to claim it, my mouth slanting over his. Not until my tongue reaches out to lick the soft, full part of his lower lip – once, twice – does he trace the interior of my mouth, gently, with his own. I run my fingers through his hair, marvelling at the baby softness of it at the nape, and he follows suit, winding strands of my hair round his fingers, tugging me closer. When my hands slip below his shirt, tracing the planes of his chest with my fingertips, he strokes the curves of my breasts, mimicking every move I make.

'I can't see your ears clearly enough,' he murmurs, hooking my hair behind my ears. Heavy and uncooperative, it falls right back into its previous position, bordering my face.

'My ears?'

'Yeah. They're very perceptive. They blush when the rest of you won't.'

'I don't feel much like blushing.'

'Oh?' he says, bemused. I sit up and back, straddling him, trembling and anxious. My apprehension isn't going to stop me. The sheet falls away behind me. 'Dori?' He rises to his elbows as my hands find the hem of my borrowed t-shirt, trace the edge back and forth.

'Reid,' I whisper, 'do you have condoms?'

He stares at my face for just a moment. 'Yes,' he answers, low and sexy. 'But –'

Before he finishes, before the fear sinks in, before I change my mind, I grasp the bottom of the t-shirt, duck my chin and pull it off in one fluid movement, dropping it over the edge of the bed. Fighting the urge to cover myself, I force my arms to still at my sides, my hands braced on my thighs.

I can't breathe.

45

REID

I can't breathe.

I won't say I haven't imagined sex with Dori because I have and I do imagine it, but I didn't expect it to go this far tonight. That night at the club, I'd have given odds of thirty to one that she wasn't a virgin. But I didn't see the heartbreak connected to that fact, or how it would play out. Even still, her restraint has always seemed like a part of her genetic make-up. I assumed if I let her set the pace, it wouldn't happen for a while.

We've been hanging out here two or three times a week for the past five weeks – watching movies, playing video games, talking . . . We're not *reckless* every time she's over, though it's happened more often the more she trusts me. Now I'm propped on my elbows, eye level with naked breasts, when I've been celibate for a longer spell – by *far* – than any other time since I became sexually active. I want her so badly that I'm dizzy with it, buzzing with the desire to roll her under me and take what she's offering.

No cold shower could rid me of this hunger. I'd need a tub full of ice.

I sit up and she rocks back a bit, her chest grazing mine, only the thin fabric of my t-shirt between us. Her breathing is shallow, warm little puffs of air, cinnamon-tinted from the toothpaste. Licking her lips, she stares at mine. I pull her close and kiss her, deeply – an echo of a promise my body intends to keep.

She slides her hands under my shirt, and I break from her long enough to let her pull it off. And then we're skin to skin and I'm losing my mind from the craving pushing every other thought and feeling aside. We kiss for long, torturous minutes, until finally I trail slow kisses down her neck, over her breasts, and in one movement I turn her on to her back, my tongue swirling round her navel, grazing the tiny belly ring I discovered there a couple of weeks ago, during one of our reckless episodes.

'That . . . is *so* unexpected and hot,' I told her then, and watched her ears go scarlet.

Her hands clench fistfuls of bedding, and when my fingers dip into the waistband of her shorts, she lifts her hips. I want her more than I've ever wanted anything, and she sure as hell wants me.

Through the haze of longing, my brain switches back on, reminding me that for years, sex has been nothing more to me than a temporary remedy for isolation. I felt no actual connection, not once, since Brooke. There have been times when the solitude would return only moments after, pulling me under. I don't trust myself now because this wanting is familiar, and Dori deserves to be more than another momentary high.

'Please,' she breathes, her hands kneading my shoulders insistently. My untimely scruples aside, there's no way I'm not satisfying her. The boxers are loose and low on her hips, no barrier to my palm slipping beneath to stroke her soft skin as I return to kissing her until we're both breathless, before sliding open-mouthed to return my attention to her breasts and belly, travelling progressively lower to the places my fingers have already explored. Her shocked response tells me that there were some things *Colin* left out of her sexual education, the self-centred bastard.

I'm grateful for the remoteness of my room from the rest of the house because she can't keep her lower lip clamped between her teeth, can't contain what I make her feel. I'm transfixed by the sound of her crying my name, her fingers twisting in my hair, her body trembling against me. She's soon satiated and drowsy, while I anticipate hours of struggle before I find oblivion.

'Reid?' she says, so softly that I'm not sure, at first, that she's awake.

'I'm here.' I gather her closer, stroking her hair over her shoulders, splaying it out over the pillow. 'Go to sleep, Dori.'

She inhales slowly and breathes out a sigh, her eyes still closed as she cuddles against my chest, and then she mumbles faintly, 'No. Your turn.' Without further warning, her fingers move over me, cautious but unerring, and she strokes her tongue over my nipple.

It doesn't take very much. Or very long, I'm embarrassed to say.

Despite the crushing weight of the expectations placed on her, from the theological to the self-inflicted, what I needed was the last, selfless thought in her sleepy head.

Sated and awed, I fall asleep with her locked in my arms.

Dori

This waking is only similar to the last night I spent in Reid's bed in one respect – the hangover sensations: headache, dry eyes, exhaustion. The cause is far different, though; a thick outpouring of grief will do that.

Unlike the last time, though, I'm wearing his boxers and the t-shirt I wore to bed . . . and took off. Blurred memories surface of him reaching for me, pulling it over my head, caressing me to sleep like Deb used to do when I had nightmares. He lies next to me, breathing metrically, his lashes feathered closed, his lips barely parted. We're curled in on each other, all arms and legs intertwined. One of his hands holds one of mine, loosely, while the other rests on my hip. It takes several minutes to carefully untangle my limbs from his.

I can't think, and I need to get home. Last night, when Reid told me he'd talked to Dad, I was too fuzzy to think about consequences, but this morning, the cost of this night is staring me in the face. I may be eighteen, but I'm still the daughter of concerned parents, still financially dependent on them, still eager for their admiration. Even if I'm unworthy of it.

I always knew my secrets were safe with Deb. That she'd never tell, never judge. And while she was there for me to lean on – somewhere in the world, loving me – I could stand it. Perhaps I created a ticking time bomb, ignoring it all this time, and this pointless remorse would have come bubbling up even without the loss of my sister as a confidante. But I *have* lost her. She's not gone, but she's not here. My parents still plead with God for a miracle, believing that Deb can be restored to her life, to her future, to us. I'd give anything to walk into her room and have her eyes meet mine instead of staring through me as though I'm invisible.

I know that's never going to happen.

Maybe my lack of faith prevents the miracle from occurring. This is what my conscience, if that's the name of the voice in my head, tells me. I don't know if a conscience can be wrong, or misguided, simply ignorant of all the facts. Whatever the voice is, wherever it comes from, it's subjective and unrelenting. Just not convincing.

Deb was the only person who knew who I really was. All of me. Now Reid knows.

I'm not sorry for what we did. I didn't think I was capable of ever trusting like that again. Letting go. Touching and being touched without a trace of self-consciousness. Instead of leaving me feeling dirty, I feel clean. I unloaded my soul. I burdened him with my ugly little secret. He doesn't have to carry it forever. Once I'm gone, he can lay it down. Leave it there. Forget. I'll never be able to do that, and I couldn't deal, alone. Not for a single day more.

I pull on my jeans, brush my hair back and fasten it at my nape with an elastic I dig out of my bag, wash my face, brush my teeth. I have a travel-sized Crest in the Mary Poppins bag, but I use Reid's organic whitening toothpaste instead. It tastes like him.

When I come out of the bathroom, he's still sound asleep. He's rolled on to his stomach into the warm place I left behind, sculpted arms around the pillow, bare shoulders above the sheet. I swallow the lump in my throat as I walk to his side and pull the covers higher. He sighs and burrows further under, and I can't stop my fingers from sweeping the hair from his forehead. I don't know what we've been playing at – hiding from the paparazzi, from my parents, from everyone. I don't know what this is, or was.

And then I think: I could fight for it. For him.

Turning the thought over in my mind, I stare down at the shell curve of his ear, poking out between wisps of tousled dark blond hair. He's overdue for a haircut because I'd whispered that I like it a little too long. My gaze moves to the relaxed lines of his mouth – lips both yielding and demanding. I think of what he did to me last night with that mouth, and I can barely breathe.

I could go home and inform my parents that I love and respect them, but I'm eighteen and I have my own life to live, my own choices to make. Adrenalin spikes through me as I imagine their possible reactions in light of Dad's statement: *As long as you're living here.* Would they yell? Lay down the law? Kick me out? I'm terrified of their anger and disappointment, but the thought of severing my connection with Reid before I even know what it could be seems far more dismal.

I kiss Reid's forehead. He's such a sound sleeper that he barely stirs beyond another sigh. I pull on my jacket and leave a note under his phone: *Going home to face the music. I'll call you later.* I chew my lip, take a deep breath. My optimism is trying to push through. At least I won't have to lie about seeing him any more – that cover is blown. Mom and Dad won't actually throw me out, will they? I've never defied my parents before, not like this, not even close. I have no idea what they'll do. But I feel strong. I can do this. I can do this.

Don't worry, I add to the note, and then sign *D*.

After I let myself in, I find them both in the kitchen, parked in their usual places at the table. I take a deep breath and try to assess where we stand. Mom is in her hospital scrubs, the baby blue ones with the tiny darker blue stork print. Dad is dressed, shoes and all, despite the early hour. Coffee mugs are clenched in their hands. Both of them glance in my direction and then at each other, silently communicating, a skill they've perfected.

I pour myself a cup of coffee even though I'm far too on edge to add caffeine to my system. I pull a chair out and lower myself into it, hoping they've already told each other that it's time to let go, let me make my own decisions, come to my own moral conclusions. Heat floods my face as I realize that they believe Reid and I had sex. Of course, there was intense intimacy in what Reid and I did. The fact that we did *sleep* together, for the second time, was also intimate. All of it, however, is not their business, and I prepare to say this to them for the first time ever while I wait for one of them to speak. My heart is pounding.

Dad clears his throat. 'Dori, your mother and I have some things we'd like to say before you . . . tell us your thoughts.'

Gripping the warm mug in my hands, I am perfectly still, listening.

'First, we want to apologize. We've neglected you, ignored you even, since your sister's accident. Please understand, we never intended for you to think you weren't important to us too. That you weren't as . . . as loved as Deborah.' He falters and I feel tears burning. 'We know you're not a child any more, but you don't have the life experiences we do. We can't stop wanting to keep you safe just because you're a legal adult.' This approach is unanticipated and I can't shift gears fast enough to catch up.

Their earnest expressions mirror each other. 'Dori.' Mom's voice is hoarse – she must have cried all night. She takes my hand. 'Honey, what you're doing is dangerous and self-destructive. I understand why you'd react this way, after what's happened to Deb. But please, don't do this. This boy isn't safe. This relationship can't last – you must know that. I remember how you were after your break-up with that Colin . . . we couldn't shake you out of your depression. Your dad and I were terrified at how you reacted to that loss. If not for Deb coming home . . .' She breaks with a sob, tightening her grip. Deb will never come home again. 'I can't lose another daughter now. Please, Dori.'

Tears stream down my face and my brain races back over the past several weeks. I *have* behaved dangerously and acted in a self-destructive manner. I went to a club, got falling-down drunk and almost left with a stranger. I could have been raped or beaten up. I could have been killed.

My relationship with Reid is unspecified and tenuous. I've known, and even last night I knew, that it won't last. Basking in him, I closed my eyes to the inevitable conclusion and how it will affect me. For the first time, I compare my feelings for Reid to what I felt for Colin, and I realize I'm in deep. I'm in so deep. I'm falling for him, and if I allow it to grow any stronger, the end will devastate me in a way that would make Colin's desertion seem trivial.

'I'm sorry.' I start to sob, my face in my hands. Their chairs scrape like Mom's did the last time we discussed Reid, but they aren't storming out. They're putting their arms round me, telling me they're sorry too. And I know I'm going to call Reid and thank him for everything he's done because he's been better to me than I ever could have expected him to be. And then I'm going to tell him goodbye.

Half an hour later, alone in my room, that's exactly what I do. He doesn't speak for a full minute, but I hear him breathing so I stay on the line and let him absorb what I've said, and I close my eyes and hug Esther and pray I can take whatever he says because he's bound to be angry, and he has every right to be.

'I understand,' he says, controlled and quiet. 'Goodbye, Dori.'

The line goes dead and I cry until I fall asleep, curled into a tight ball in the middle of my bed and holding on to my dog, clinging to any comfort I can find.

46

REID

'I haven't seen your friend's car out back in a while.' Mom is perched on my bed, skimming through the pages of that novel with the hot-but-sullen fictional boy who reminds me of my Will Darcy role from *School Pride* – if Will Darcy had been created in the pages of a dystopian novel. (What the hell is it about brooding guys that's attractive to women, anyway? I've become one since Dori's call three weeks ago, and it's made me *more* of a chick magnet. I shouldn't be surprised – being a dick never hurt my appeal before.)

'That's because she hasn't been here.' I would wonder that Mom noted her absence, but she has a way of noticing everything, even when she seems to be in too much of a stupor to notice anything but her own feet, shuffling through the house. Her eyes seem clearer now, however, staring at me like a reflection.

'Did you two have an argument?' She asked this same question when Brooke stopped coming over, after we broke up.

I shrug. 'There was no fight at all, actually. Her parents didn't want her seeing me, so she just gave up.' I don't know if this is true, but it feels true. I should have known she'd submit to their wishes eventually. Did they make her feel ashamed of spending the night with me, or just spending time with me at all? Did they threaten to kick her out? I've never understood the ultimatum-delivering parent. Part of me rises to that – I could have rented her a place if they'd followed through. Or hell, I could have got *us* a place.

Wow, shit. Got *us* a place? I am *gone*. Over Dorcas Cantrell, a girl who convinced me in a one-minute phone call that I meant nothing to her: *I'm grateful for everything you've done for me – you probably saved my life. But I can't see you any more. I've got too much going on right now, and I don't know what we're doing anyway, you and I. It's just . . . my parents need me, and it's time I get back to my life and let you go back to yours. I'm sorry.*

She'd choked back a sob then as I lay in my bed with my phone to my ear, trying to wake up and waiting for her to say something else. To take it back. She hadn't.

After I hung up, I threw my phone across the room where it struck the wall with enough force to leave a dent in the sheetrock and crack the screen irreparably. And then I found her note next to the bed. The one with *Don't worry* preceding her scripted *D*. An hour later, after I calmed down enough to form coherent thoughts, I dug the crumpled note out of the trash, smoothed it out on the desk and read it through fifty times, trying to make sense of the combination of her spoken and written words – absolute antitheses of each other.

'Hmm,' Mom says, going back to reading.

'What?'

She angles one eyebrow, but doesn't lift her eyes from the book. 'Maybe *you* gave up too easily.'

I laugh. *Right*. If only it was that simple.

She checks her watch, slides off the bed and walks over – steadily – to ruffle my hair. 'I have a meeting to get to. We can talk later, if you want?' Newly manicured fingers under my chin, she tilts my face up, and I notice her eyes *are* clearer. She's trying to stop drinking again. I don't want to ask. Don't want to jinx it.

I stomp down the burst of hope in my chest, nod into her hand. 'Sure, Mom.'

'Will there be anything else, Mr Alexander?' The rep delivering my new Ferrari FF is smokin' hot and practically purrs this question. She's taken every opportunity to brush against me or lean in such a way that I can see right down her silky top, the top three pearled buttons unfastened. We've gone over every spec and completed a thorough inspection to ensure that not a single surface scratch mars the metallic pewter-grey paint or the pale grey leather interior. No further reason to keep her here unless I want to do her on the hood (totally possible – this girl is *not* in the running for a subtlety award).

In my head is John's voice – *Why the hell not?*

My newly enlightened thought processes, that's why not. Such as wondering what she sees in me, aside from a young, rich celebrity. None of that counted worth a shit to Dori. I don't know what *did* count to Dori. I don't know what changed between the day I met her – when she couldn't wait to be rid of me – to the kiss in the closet, to the night out before Vancouver and Quito, to the moment she agreed to defy her parents and hang out with me several nights a week. What happened to make that last night together possible?

'Thanks, I'm good,' I tell her, and she huffs a disappointed sigh. No doubt she'll report to everyone she knows that I'm definitely gay. I don't give a shit.

'I'll just, uh, call for a car to pick me up, then.' She gives me a pouty glare while I'm wondering why she didn't just ride back with the delivery truck.

'No problem, I'll drop you off. We can test the zero to sixty in what was it – 3.7 seconds? This baby needs a little breaking in before I park it in the garage.' She perks up for a moment, until she figures out I'm actually interested in the car, and only the car.

My sunglasses are almost unnecessary with the darkest legal tint possible on the windows. Though I hit sixty before the end of my street, I'll have to wait for a deserted highway to test the highest recorded speed of 200 plus. Within minutes, we're on Santa Monica and turning on to Wilshire.

'If you're sure there's nothing else you need –' she begins, leaning towards me all surplus cleavage and lacy bra when I pull up in front of the showroom window. I'm ready to shove her out the door because yeah, sure, I can't help wanting some of *that* when it's tossed on to a platter and served hot. *Why. The. Hell. Not?* the John voice says.

'Nope, nothing.' When you finally figure out what you

really want, everything else pales in comparison. I never got that before. I get it now. 'Thanks, uh . . .'

'Victoria.' She bestows a tight smile and hands me her card.

'Yeah. Thanks.' As I shove the card into my wallet, it sticks on a scrap of paper among the receipts and cash – Frank's cell number, scrawled on the back of an In-N-Out burger receipt. I haven't talked to Frank since August – my last day at the Diego house. Maybe I should check in.

Dori

Three days until Christmas. Four weeks until school begins. Talking to Nick helped me realize that part of my absent-mindedness can be attributed to the fact that I have nothing mental on which to focus. I began regarding school as something to ground me, rather than something too challenging to handle. I saw an advisor, registered for classes and got very lucky on a vacated dorm room, all within the past two weeks.

I'm dumping pasta into the colander when Mom comes home from visiting Deb. 'Dinner on the table in ten minutes,' I tell her, turning to stir the sauce.

When she doesn't reply, I glance back and she's dropped into a chair at the table with a bewildered look. My stomach drops at her expression. I should have gone with her this afternoon instead of evading her let's-pretend-Deb-responds display by spending hours in the kitchen making a from-scratch sauce that could have just as easily come from a jar.

'Mom? Is something wrong?'

'No.' She's still frowning, but she looks perplexed, not distraught. 'They needed my approval to move Deb to a different room.'

'What? Why?'

She shakes her head slowly. 'Someone set up a trust to pay for a private room.'

'That's – that's great. Who?'

Her head is still moving placidly side to side. 'They have no idea beyond the law firm that administers the trust. I could call them tomorrow . . . but wouldn't that be looking a gift horse in the mouth? This is a miracle . . .' And just like that, Mom's crying, Esther is resting her head on Mom's knee and whining and Dad is bulleting out of his study in a panic.

'Maybe it's someone from church?' I offer, while my brain suggests, *Reid?*

'What's someone from church?' Dad says, moving to Mom's side.

They discuss the likelihood of anyone putting that kind of money out for Deb while I turn back to the bubbling sauce, reducing the heat and stirring. If Reid had anything to do with it, his attorney father would set it up, right? Easy enough to check. 'What's the name of the law firm?'

Mom shrugs. 'I don't know. I was so shocked, I forgot to ask.'

I'm ashamed to admit that this is the first time I've visited Deb without Mom or Dad. At the same time, I was relieved when Nick agreed to come with me. He says hello to my sister, sticks around long enough to make sure I'm not going to freak out and then tells me he'll be in the lobby chatting up the receptionist if I need him.

I grin at his shy smile. 'Her name is Sophie, and she likes cats and historical memoirs.'

He taps his lip with one finger. 'Cats, huh? I think I could work with that.' Squeezing my hand, he says, 'Text if you need me.'

I glance at Deb, telling Nick, 'Go talk to Sophie. We're good.'

I haven't been alone with my sister since we moved her to LA. Before we came in, the nurse told me, 'She's just finished lunch followed by a couple hours in the sun room, so you two can just spend time talking in her room if you'd like.'

Talking. Right.

I stroll round the room, straightening things, until there's nothing left to rearrange, and then I perch on the upholstered chair in the corner. Deb's new room is located on the second floor, and has a window shaded by tall oaks, overlooking the landscaped common area – home to a native flower garden, slate pathways and smooth, worn wooden benches. Several residents sit with guests or wander the trails admiring the winter blossoms, flanked by aides. Deb sits in her chair, staring out the window, her eyes following nothing.

In my pocket is a slip of paper the office manager just gave me citing the law firm administering the trust paying for Deb's new room. It's incredibly upgraded – not just in privacy, but in understated touches like the chair and the south-facing window, the better-quality bedding and furniture, the patterned rug underfoot. When I get home, I'll explore the law firm's website and look for clues to the anonymous benefactor. For now, I'm here with Deb, alone in the mute space between us, missing her laughter and her listening ear.

'Hey, Deb,' I say, my voice just above a whisper, but crashing like waves into the silence. She doesn't stir, of course. 'I like your new room.' Out her window, clouds move in streams across the leaden sky, lazy and slow. It never gets frigid in LA, but winter is still chilly. 'Next time I come, I'll bring a heavier sweater and we'll check out the garden.' Staring at her, I wonder if it's possible that she can hear me, even if she can't respond.

I clear my throat. 'I'm going to find out who your secret admirer is too.' I remember giving Bradford the box of clothes and the ivy plant, and I can't speak around what feels like a fist in my throat. I've discarded the notion that the room is from him. He's too immersed in medical school debt to do anything so extravagant. He checks in with Mom now and then, but the frequency is falling off. Bradford is moving on with his life because he can.

'I decided to go ahead and start at Berkeley next month.' I glance at my watch. 'But I'll be around for a few more weeks, and I'll visit on long weekends and breaks.'

I've only been here *eleven minutes*. How does my mother stay here, chattering to *herself*, basically, for an hour or more at a time?

'I'm starting a new Habitat project in a couple of weeks. Roberta's the crew leader on this one. I'm calling her tonight, to get details. I'll tell you about it next time.' I adjust her chair so she can see out the window without catching any glare should the sun emerge. I don't know what she sees, or if she can perceive or mentally process what she sees. Kissing her forehead, I squeeze her limp hand. 'I'll be back soon. I love you.'

Using the call button, I let the nursing staff know I'm leaving and walk down the hallway. Not until I reach the stairwell do my eyes well up with tears. I breathe in and out, concentrating on keeping control, and I congratulate myself for visiting my sister, alone, for twelve whole minutes.

47

REID

'Okay, I'm returning your call – or should I say *calls* – since apparently, blatantly ignoring you doesn't work like it does on normal people. What d'you *want*, Reid?'

I knew this wasn't going to be painless, but good God, Brooke can still wind me up as much as she did at fifteen. When she's pissed off, her Texas drawl shows up. As much as she'd like me to believe she's just annoyed, the accent tells me she's still angry.

My therapist would say this is a good time to utilize those anger-management tricks I've been practising when dealing with my father. One deep breath, in and out, and then another. Counting to three or ten or fifty before replying. 'I don't want anything, Brooke. I just need to say something, and I'd like you to let me say it. Please.'

Silence. Shock? Considering the things we said to each other during our last few conversations, shock would be about right. 'So talk,' she says, not as tough as she'd like to sound.

'I want to apologize –'

'Are you *kidding* me? Is this some kind of twelve-step bullshit? We haven't spoken in months. What you thought of me came through loud and clear. This, Reid, is what's known as *too damned late*.'

I run a hand through my hair and over my face and I admit, my first instinct is to abandon this whole plan. After all, Brooke hating my guts matters *nada* in the general scheme of things. I'm a bigger Hollywood entity than she is, so I don't need to worry about her vetoing my ability to obtain roles. But this isn't about *me*.

Sucking in another deep breath and pushing it out, slowly, I'm determined to get this apology out or die trying. 'Brooke, I was wrong to abandon you when you found out you were pregnant, no matter what had happened between us. You were my girlfriend, and I should have been there to support whatever decision you made.' She's not butting in, so I plunge ahead. 'The only excuse I have is that I was a *child* then. Still, I screwed up, and I'm sorry.'

There's no answer, and I count seconds, wondering if she hung up somewhere during that speech. Almost two minutes tick by. And then, 'I was thinking about . . . trying to find him,' she says. 'Not to interfere or anything. Just to make sure he's okay. Would you . . . would you want me to let you know what I find out?'

My jaw clenches while I fight the deep-rooted soreness of her betrayal, like a toothache that's never been dealt with. Not for the first time, I wonder why she acts like she *knows* it was mine. I'm not saying that to her, though. Not again.

With time comes perspective. It doesn't matter if it – if *he* – was or wasn't mine. 'Sure. That'd be fine.'

She sighs. 'I know what you're thinking. At the risk of trashing this little interlude, I'll repeat what I've said before. He's *yours*. He can't possibly be anyone else's because when I turned that stick blue, I'd never slept with anyone but *you*. So unless it was an immaculate conception, he's *yours*.'

Okay, wait. 'Brooke, the story, the photos, that guy –'

'Complete tabloid lies. I *never* cheated on you. Yes, after we had that fight I dirty danced with that guy at that club. I wanted to make you crazy jealous. I wanted you to come running back to me and say I was yours and no one else could have me. I did not, would not, have cheated on you. Not with him, not with anyone.'

I've been pacing my room, and now I sit heavily on the edge of my bed, suddenly *really* glad I didn't call her when I was out driving around because the surge of adrenalin is making my whole body quake.

'Brooke, why did you let me think –'

'Because I thought you loved me and I didn't think I should have to *convince* you that I hadn't done something *I hadn't done*! And then I found out I was pregnant . . . and you didn't –' She stifles a cry. 'I can't talk about this any more. What's done is done. If I find him, I'll send you the info. If you want.'

My thoughts are spinning too quickly to take shape. 'I do. I do want.'

She sniffs, her voice smoothing out. 'Okay. I'll let you know. Goodbye, Reid.'

She hangs up before I reply.

I don't know why I believe her now, but I do. I have a son. Correction: I *had* a son, for a few minutes. Now he belongs to someone else – and that's definitely just as well. We were children. We would have had no business trying to raise one. That kid is, what, four? And this is the first time I've ever really thought about him. That's fucked up.

Dori

The wall above my desk is covered in cork squares. Tacked to these are photos of those important to me – my parents and Deb, Kayla and Aimee, Nick and, of course, Esther. In one corner are two group shots of my VBS kids from last summer – one taken the night of their Parents' Night performance, everyone standing straight and tall around me, all toothy smiles and Sunday-best clothes, and the second with Mrs K at the pool – the kids clustered all round her like bees on a honeycomb, Jonathan clinging to one hip and Keisha to the other, grinning at each other. There are snapshots of people from Habitat, from church, from Quito, and people from school I may never see again. Everyone who matters to me is represented on this board.

Except Reid.

I checked the law firm administering Deb's trust. It isn't his father's firm, and I didn't recognize any of the attorneys on the site by name. I couldn't find a connection.

I'll be helping out on a new Habitat project for the next

couple of weeks, until I leave for Berkeley. When I talked to Roberta last night, she told me that an anonymous someone donated three new cars to the Diegos the day they got the keys to their house. I was in Quito then, and hadn't talked to her about anything but Deb since I got back.

'You have no idea who did it?' I pressed.

'None at all. I confess, I thought perhaps Mr Alexander . . . but he'd have wanted the publicity, wouldn't he?' I heard the other question in her voice. Like everyone else, she'd seen the reports of the two of us together and she suspected I knew more than I was letting on.

'I don't know.' It's been a month since that last phone call. I'm fine when I'm busy, when I purposefully throw myself into anything that will block out the thought of him. Like when I was in Quito, though, the nights are the worst – staring into the darkness and recalling everything I'd begun to love about him, from the way he challenged me to the way he touched me.

'We have a celebrity group helping out this time,' Roberta said, switching gears. 'I thought you'd be ideal for this project, with your celebrity experience.' I wanted to interrupt her to ask exactly what experience she was referring to, but decided against it. 'There may be paparazzi issues again.' She actually sounded a bit enthused by this idea, and I fought not to snicker. Roberta, star-struck. 'People filming from rooftops and leering over fences – insanity!'

I shook my head, glad she told me this over the phone so she couldn't see me fighting back laughter. 'Who are the celebrities?'

'They're from some movie that's coming out soon,' she said vaguely. 'These publicity things are so helpful. Remember when we had those people from that soap opera? Donations and volunteers were up for months afterwards.'

'Which movie?'

'Hmm, I can't quite recall . . .' Too weird. Roberta is never unfamiliar with the people showing up on her worksite. She launched into project talk, and I forgot to ask again.

Now I'm staring at an email from Ana Diaz, the mission director in Quito. We've been emailing about what had happened to Deb, and how I plan to start at Berkeley a semester late, and whether or not she can use my help this coming summer.

> Dori,
> I can't believe I forgot to tell you – several months ago,
> we received a large donation from an anonymous
> source. It was enough to balance our books for the first
> time in a decade. Then, just before Christmas, a law
> firm in Los Angeles contacted us about a trust someone
> set up. The disbursements are enough to run the entire
> project, leaving other donations to rebuild schools and
> fund medical projects. I only wish I knew who to thank!
> Ana

I hit reply to ask the name of the law firm, and minutes later, I get her answer. It's the same firm administering Deb's trust. Ana included the name of the contact attorney – Chad Roberts. I have no idea who he is, but I'm determined to find out.

'Popsicles,' I mutter, staring at the search engine results. There are a *lot* of guys named Chad Roberts in the world, and none of them are directly connected to Reid Alexander. I don't have time to do a more thorough search now. I have to be at the new Habitat project in twenty minutes – we're restoring two foreclosed homes in the same neighbourhood this time, with the help of an entire group of celebrities, apparently.

Oh, joy.

48

REID

Dori is facing away, standing in the centre of a room so similar to that first room we painted together that we could have been transported back in time. She's humming while examining the spec sheet and wearing the same familiar shorts and construction boots with her faded M.A.D.D. t-shirt. Ponytailed, her hair hangs down the centre of her back. Buckets of paint and painting implements are spread across the tarp in the centre of the room.

Everything would be déjà vu except for this – I know how soft her hair feels when I push my fingers through it, and how it looks loose around her shoulders or flowing over my pillow while she sleeps. I know her scent, like something sweet and edible, an observation I whispered months ago when I wanted nothing more than to make her shiver from wanting me. I know her muscular shoulders and arms, her soft breasts. I know the feel of the tiny silver ring in her navel, its single heart-shaped charm brushing against the tip of my tongue. I know the firm curve of her waist, the smooth flare of her hip, the taste of her mouth. I know the feel of her losing control against me and trusting me to catch her when she comes apart.

Even so, there's more to this complex girl, and the physical craving I feel for her is merely an index of that. I know her patience, her kindness, her inherent desire to leave the world a better place than she found it. I've felt her forgiveness, her strength and her ability to see something good in anyone. The whole of her is overwhelming, and the fact that I may have found her only to lose her scares the hell out of me.

Having sensed my presence in the room behind her, she raises her head from the paperwork in her hands. Turning slowly, her eyes connect with mine and widen, and she blinks in disbelief. My heart slams against my ribs, daring me to close the distance between us.

'Hey, boss,' I say. We're standing ten feet apart and I want to know if she's experiencing the same gravitational pull towards me that I'm feeling towards her. Her eyes are black from this distance, and I stare at her lips, her ears, her hands that still hold the specs – they're shaking. That tremor is for me, though I know better than to feel infallible because of it.

'Reid?' Her voice almost undoes me, speaking my name. I have this injudicious urge to do whatever the present-day equivalent is of grabbing her up, tossing her over my shoulder and finding a cave to make her mine. My hands clench and she notices.

'I heard you need an experienced painter in here.' I lower my chin and stare into her eyes. 'And I think I'm your man.'

Her breath catches as I move closer. 'Just so you know – I don't believe in going halfway. I won't quit until the job's been performed to your complete satisfaction.'

Her lower lip trembles and she sucks it into her mouth just enough to catch it with her teeth. 'What then?' she asks. 'When everything is done?'

Carefully, I touch my fingers under her chin and her lips open, her breath hitching again as she looks up at me. 'Then I start over, yeah? No such thing as "done".'

Her eyes slide down and she steps back, and I drop my hand. 'Y-you can paint this room, and I'll do the other.'

'Whatever you want,' I say, and she nods and leaves the room at an almost-run. When she's gone, I release a pent-up breath.

Round one, tied? This is going to kill me.

Two photographers and a reporter from *People* have been assigned to this goodwill story. The public loves to see celebs acting like regular, generous people (who remain naturally beautiful while performing charitable acts, of course). Fans don't see the schedule interruptions we impose on said charitable project due to our lighting prep and rearrangement, or the make-up crew, or the video camera getting a few short takes for the online mag. The positive side is less paparazzi outside, since sanctioned photographers allowed up close – with an authorized story – trump any photo someone could nab from a distance, even with the finest in telephoto lenses at their disposal.

Just before lunch break, I'm alone and wondering if Dori

will be the one to retrieve me when my co-star appears in the doorway. 'Hey, sexy,' Chelsea says, slinking across the room in her white shorts and cherry-red tank top, her hair in a messy updo, cascading perfectly round her flawless face. 'Ooh, look at you!' She turns a little pirouette mid-room, admiring my work. 'You're harbouring some wicked DIY skills behind that pretty face and those buff biceps. Who'd have thought?'

'Who indeed,' I say, automatically posing for the cameraman who followed her in – full awareness of which side I'm presenting, all wide smiles and exaggerated laughter. I'm looking at Chelsea and not the camera, like we're alone in the room. We do a few shots with me re-creating rolling mint-green paint on a wall, though I've already finished the first coat, including the patching, priming and cutting in top and bottom. There's not so much as a swipe of green on the ceiling or the floorboards, either.

As though I invoked her, Dori stands in the doorway the next time I glance up, taking in the room, the cameraman, the fact that Chelsea is hamming it up, holding a brush tipped in green paint and pretending to dab it on my nose. I take Chelsea's wrist and move the paintbrush away as Dori whirls and disappears. I call her name, but she's gone.

Chelsea takes all of this in with wide green eyes and I roll mine when she says, 'Is that *the* Dori?'

And then I squint at her. 'Wait. How do you know – *Chad*. Dammit, Chelsea. What the hell happened to attorney-client privilege?'

'He didn't say a thing to me, I swear!' She holds up one hand and pantomimes placing the other on a bible. 'I just, you know, see things on his desk occasionally . . .' Her fingers wrap round my arm and she whispers frantically, 'Reid, please don't tell him. Oh, God, I would be in *so* much trouble. I swear I haven't told anyone anything and he's not discussed a *thing* with me.'

I sigh and examine her face. Chelsea is a girl who absorbs gossip. She loves it, but doesn't spread it unless it's common knowledge. '*Fine.* But leave it alone.'

She locks her lips and tosses an invisible key behind her, nodding.

'Come on, gossip girl, let's go find your husband and get something to eat.'

Dori

Every time I convince myself I'll never see Reid again, he turns up. Roberta straightens every item on her desk and avoids my gaze while pretending she'd forgotten that Reid was one of the celeb volunteers. The two red spots on her cheeks beg to differ. 'And anyway,' her brows crinkle, 'I was under the impression you two were friendly.'

Now it's my turn to be visibly flustered, and with my darned ears fully exposed too. What can I say? *My parents don't want me dating a Hollywood heart-throb who'll just use and discard me*, or how about, *I told him I couldn't see him any more and he couldn't comply fast enough, and now*

I haven't seen him in a month and I didn't think I'd ever have to be this near him again.

When I continue to stand there, silent and disconcerted, she misinterprets my uneasiness as repulsion. 'We'll find you a different project to work on. They'll only be here this week. You can come back next week. I'll just call –'

'No, I'll be fine.' She thinks I dislike Reid, when nothing could be further from the truth.

When I saw him this morning, I wanted to run across the room and throw my arms round him and not let go. I wanted to tell him I would take whatever he could give me, however long it lasts. That's when I recalled the Janis Joplin quote Deb taped to her bedroom mirror years ago: *Don't compromise yourself. You are all you've got.*

And then he said, 'Hey, boss.' So glib and casual and over whatever had been there between us. Whatever I'd imagined was there. The other stuff, the flirting, that was just classic Reid – sexy and effortlessly seductive. And replicated with his stunning co-star ten minutes ago.

Maybe I *should* switch projects. Be smart and bolt while I can.

'He's got enough experience to be given specific tasks, so you won't have to supervise him or even be near him,' Roberta says.

Fighting the urge to tell her she's got it all backwards, I nod and slip out back to get something to eat. I don't look round the yard for him, and don't intend to remain outside any longer than it takes to gather lunch and go back inside.

As luck would have it, what I grab is a bowl of fruit and

an iced tea, and my ears go hot remembering the first time Reid tried to kiss me, when I shoved him away. I'm conscious of someone speaking nearby, hearing the name before I'm fully paying attention. '. . . Chad Roberts, and despite my good looks, I'm not an actor. I'm just Chelsea's husband.'

Frank laughs in response. 'That is not a position to be taken lightly, young man. That girl is a firecracker.'

'Oh, don't I know it!' They both laugh.

My head is spinning.

Chad Roberts.

Chelsea Radin's husband.

The same name of the attorney in charge of Deb's trust.

'Mr Roberts? Could I speak with you a moment, please?'

'Certainly.' He seems genial, and he *is* good-looking. I've had a hard time catching him separated from Chelsea's side. He and his actress wife are obviously friends with Reid, and I've concluded that what I thought was flirting between Reid and Chelsea earlier was just the two of them play-acting for the photo shoot *People* is doing that will benefit both Habitat and the opening weekend of their movie.

Jealousy is an unpleasant, alien sensation.

We walk a few feet from the demolition site – Chad has been helping Frank take down a dilapidated shed in the backyard. 'This may be an odd question, but by any chance . . . are you an attorney?'

'Yes, I am.' He gives me a perplexed look. 'Do you need legal assistance?'

This is too bizarre to be coincidence. 'No. Maybe. Um. Do you work for Barnes, Bancroft and Cole?'

He pulls the work gloves from his hands and takes the water bottle I hand him. 'Yes, I do.'

I take a deep breath as all the dots connect. This has to link to Reid. There's no other explanation.

After a long drink, he peers at me. 'What is this in relation –'

'There's a trust that you administer, I think. It's for Deborah Cantrell?'

His eyes flick towards the house, where Reid is, then right back to me, like he realizes he's giving something away. 'Um, yes, that's true.'

'I want to know who's funding it.'

Swallowing, he frowns. 'Look, Ms . . .?'

'Cantrell. Dori Cantrell.'

His eyes widen and understanding dawns. '*Oh.* You're her sister, I assume?'

I nod and he purses his lips, laying a hand on my arm. 'While I can certainly appreciate your wanting to know that information, I'm afraid I'm not at liberty to say.'

I glance towards the house. Reid is inside, assisting with the kitchen demolition. Has he told his attorney not to tell me anything? And if so, why? 'How can that be? I'm her *family*. I have a right to know.'

His look is placating, which makes me want to scream. 'I understand your feelings, Ms Cantrell, I assure you. And there are copious details of the trust that I *can* divulge, if you'd like. In fact, I'd encourage you to come by my office sometime next week perhaps so we can discuss those details – but the identity of the donor is restricted information.'

'How is that possible?' I know I'm not going to get anything from him, and my frustration mounts higher with every composed rebuff he offers.

'Our client wishes to remain anonymous.'

'But . . . *why*?'

'I'm afraid I can't answer that.'

Reid exits the back door, glances around and catches sight of us speaking. 'Can't, or *won't*?' I ask while staring at Reid, who hasn't moved. Chad follows my gaze and sighs, compressing his lips again – a perfect analogy for the fact that I won't get anything further out of him.

I don't know what game this is, including the questionable twist of fate that put Reid on my Habitat project *again*. His eyes shift from his attorney to me and he remains frozen at the door. Did he think I wouldn't research that trust, wonder where it came from and who was behind it? I'm torn between intense gratitude for what he's done for Deb and crushing terror of how easily it could end. And then I do the only thing I can do with this jumble of information.

I turn and leave.

49

REID

Wearing the same bewildered expression she wore this morning when she turned and I was there, and with the same tone of voice, she says, 'Reid?' from the opposite side of the still-closed screen door, making no move to open it. Her dog stands next to her, staring at me with – I swear – its eyebrows knitted in aggravation. 'What are you doing here?'

I want to be exasperated with her, angry even, but I can't. What comes out is the thing that built and ran through my head all day, but without the fire. Like all that's left of me are these smoky whispered words before I dissipate and blow away. 'I've come to ask how you do it. How you feel what I know you're feeling and then walk away like that.'

'How do you know what I feel?' she returns, but she can't be angry, either. There's surrender in her tone, and I focus on nothing but the hum of it, threading through her armoured words to find me.

'Open the door, Dori.'

She shakes her head slightly.

'Are you alone?' I ask and she nods, and I tell her again, 'Open the door.'

She reaches towards the inner handle and pauses. 'Did you do it? The private room for Deb?' I nod once. 'Why?'

My hands bracket the door frame and it's all I can do not to fall to my knees, standing here looking at her and knowing that this is it, this is my one shot and there may not be another. She's strong and she's stubborn, and if I can't get her to admit how she feels, she'll be lost to me. 'Dori, open the door. Please. And I'll explain whatever you want me to.'

Her fingers brush over the lock and it clicks, but she doesn't move to push the screen door open, so I do. I step inside and let it close behind me, and our eyes link as I reach back and blindly shut the solid door, too, and turn the bolt. 'Come here,' I say, reaching for her, and she sways towards me, bracing her small hands on my chest. Keeping me at arm's length, in the most literal sense.

'Why? Why?' she asks, and I'm struggling to comprehend how this could threaten her.

'Why did I do it? Because I love you. There's no other motive – I really am that simple.'

Holy shit. I just told her I love her. There's no going back. Nothing to do but own it. But there's the crux of the matter – I want to own it.

Her eyes are full and her mouth trembles. 'What do you mean, you *love* me? And what about when you stop? What then? What happens to my sister then?'

My hands are at her shoulders, tracing her arms and cupping her elbows as they bend to my need for her. 'I think *love* is a fairly self-explanatory emotion. And I don't plan to stop. But there's no stipulation. The trust Chad set up for your sister is life-long and has nothing to do with what I feel, or what you do – or don't do. It can't be annulled, if that's what worries you.'

She starts to cry, tears running slowly down her face. 'Everything worries me. How can you love me? I'm – I'm nobody.'

'How could I *not* love you?' I insist. 'No one has ever affected me like you do. When you told me goodbye last month, I tried to let you go. I told myself it was the best thing for you because you wanted it. But you're wrong, Dori. I'm good for you even if you don't know it yet. I know because I've never *been* good for anyone before.' I fight to keep the pressure of my hands on her relaxed and controlled. 'You all but lost your sister, and fought through a loss of faith that would destroy most people, and you didn't fall to pieces. You manned up when your parents needed you. But just because you're strong and resilient doesn't mean you never need someone to be there for you, to take care of you.' I grip her elbows. 'You needed me that night at the club.'

She swallows. 'I did. I did need you. But I can't be that helpless somebody-save-me type of girl –'

'You're *not* helpless. In fact, you're the most maddeningly self-reliant girl I've ever known –'

'How is that maddening?' she cries, pulling her elbows from my grip and wrapping her arms round herself.

'Because you won't let yourself need me,' I say, the words echoing in my ears like the battle cry of the co-dependent.

377

'Both of us are so good at resisting being controlled, or having any control over someone else, that we don't know how to need and be needed. Last summer, I let myself believe I could get past what I felt for you, not because what I felt was insignificant, but because *I always have*. I don't linger over relationships. Hell, I don't *have* relationships. I didn't realize until I saw you in that club that I was no closer to getting over you than I'd been the last time I'd seen you, three months before.'

I lower my voice and step closer, narrowing the gap between us. 'I've changed since I've known you. Not because you made me into someone else – but because you showed me a path I'd never paid attention to, and I chose to follow it. And yes, I've asked myself over and over, *can it be that easy to just choose to be a better man? Can it be that fucking easy?*'

She flinches and I take her hands from where they have her opposite elbows in a death grip, prise them loose gently until our fingers intertwine. 'I'll be more careful with that word. I'm not trivializing this.' She raises her eyes, wide and dark and wet. 'I know exactly what I'm saying. I'll wait, if I have to wait. I'll do whatever it takes. But I want you, and will continue to want you, and I should warn you – I don't see it ending. I'm all in, Dori. And I won't be holding back this time.'

I've laid my heart in front of her like an offering. I've made my case and rested it. There's nothing more to say. We stare at each other, both so silent that I hear her dog's nails tap arthritically across the floor to a large oval cushion where it flops down and regards us both with a sigh. Our hands are locked between us, and hope is there between us too, because she isn't pulling away.

Pushing up on to her toes, she presses her lips to my chin and along my jaw. I release her hands to grab her up, wrapping my arms round her while her arms twist round my neck and her fingers shove into my hair. 'Reid,' she gasps, her dark eyes on mine. 'I do . . . want you.' My hands slide over her hips and when I lift her, she wraps her legs round my waist and fuses her lips to mine. I moan into her mouth and she responds in kind.

I stride to the stairs and go up, releasing the bottled-up need in one long, breathless kiss. I can't get enough of her. 'Where?' I say when we get to the top. She points down the hall, and I obey, no sounds but the greedy hum from her throat and mine, our mouths working in perfect unison, and the thump of my decisive steps on the ancient floor.

I lurch into her room – watery blue walls and fish swimming in a school across the ceiling and *nothing* out of place. Kicking the door shut behind me, I move to her bed and press her down on it. There's no contemplation or circumspection because she's pulling at my shirt and kissing me harder than she ever has and we're frantic, like it's been years since we touched each other. Yanking buttons through buttonholes and stretching fabrics and unzipping zippers is all done in the few seconds in between kisses when we come up for air because all I want to do in this moment is worship her with my eyes, hands and mouth.

Trailing her nails down my back, she arches into me,

stilling the breath in my lungs. She protests when I pull back, but grows mesmerized as my fingers slip over and around and under and through, and I follow the path with my lips and tongue. I kiss her stomach, flick the belly ring with the nail of my index finger and she gasps.

'Please,' she whispers, and because of what has just occurred to me I'm thinking *godfuckingdammit*, but have enough sense not to say this aloud.

'Dori . . . as much as I seemed like a man on a mission when I showed up here, I didn't plan for . . . I didn't think . . .' I rest my forehead against her ribcage. 'I don't have a condom,' I confess.

'There are some in my bag,' she says, so quietly that I barely hear her. I glance up in surprise and her ears go pink. She's lying alongside me wearing nothing but her cotton panties and she's mortified that she has condoms in her purse?

'Oh?' I say, reaching to unloop the strap of her huge, familiar bag from the headboard where it's hooked over the smooth post cap.

'Aimee and Kayla – the quack shack on campus was handing them out last week. They grabbed like a year's supply and insisted I take some.'

I thrust my hand into her bag and root around among all manner of odds and ends, hearing the crinkle of square cellophane packets when my fingers brush them. I grin, arching a brow. 'There've got to be at least a dozen in here.' I drop a handful on to her bedside table, watching as the blush spreads to her face and descends down her neck. Her heart hammering beneath my palm, I kiss her. 'They'll be put to good use, I promise.' My voice is heavy and predatory, and she shivers under my hand.

I remove the last bits of clothing from us both, stroking and kissing her slowly and deeply until I can't hold back any longer. Rolling on to my back, I lift her on top and tell her that she's in charge – this time.

Dori

'I should probably ask when your parents are returning,' he murmurs into my ear. I can't believe he can still make me bury my face in his neck after what we've done, but apparently, my sense of propriety survived intact. 'Because I *will* win them over, eventually, and I assume I'd be starting at less than zero if the moment they realize I'm back is the same moment they walk in on me satisfying the hell out of their daughter. For the third or fourth time.'

He's lying on his side, propped on one elbow and tracing patterns across my skin. The sunlight flooding my room when we began has filtered to the ruddy, muted light of sunset.

My fingernails rasp across the light stubble on his chin and his eyes close. 'Have I satisfied *you*?' I whisper, and he growls and kisses me.

'*No*. I think I'll need consistent access to you for some interminable amount of time to even begin to get full of you.' His touch feathers across my belly and climbs upwards.

'My parents are on a couples' retreat. They won't be back until Sunday.'

His fingers halt at the lower point of my sternum and he crooks an eyebrow. 'Please say you aren't teasing me.' I turn my head back and forth against the pillow and he kisses me hard and deep. 'Can I stay the night? Is that allowed?'

I trace the line of his nose and one eyebrow and he leans into my hand and closes his eyes. 'I don't know. They wouldn't approve, and it's their house. Of course, they wouldn't approve of this, either.'

He nods, opens his eyes. 'I'm willing to do this however you need, with one exception.' I frown, my mind a riot of possibilities until he rolls his eyes. 'The *exception* is I'm not going away. Don't ask me to do that ever again.'

'Are you sure?' I say, ever doubting him. It isn't fair, how I doubt him, and I wonder if he'll gather that my loss of faith extends further than I'd ever known it would, severing lines of trust and levelling my confidence like a city-flattening tornado. I'll be rebuilding a belief system from scratch over the next few months, maybe years, and it won't be easy. Or pleasant.

'I've never been this sure of anything.' His serious demeanour is broken when my stomach rumbles as though I've forgotten to eat for days. His smile turns up on one side. 'Except possibly that I'd better feed you. Let's go out.'

'Out, where people can see us?'

'You might as well get used to being Reid Alexander's girlfriend.' He laughs at the look on my face. 'Oh, come on. It can't be *that* bad.' He pulls the sheet over our heads, straddling me in the darkness. 'Fine, we'll order in. One more day's reprieve to keep me a secret. Any longer and I'll think you're ashamed of me.'

Some rough, vulnerable edge to his voice tells me this statement isn't as offhand as it sounds.

'I don't want to be *Reid Alexander's* girlfriend,' I say, and his smile fades. I reach up and frame his face with my hands, the heartbreaking need there so exposed that my eyes sting with tears. 'I want to be *your* girlfriend. As long as you're who you are right now, with me, I will *never* be ashamed of you.'

'Are you sure?' He echoes my earlier question, his dark blue eyes locked on mine.

'I've never been this sure of anything,' I say.

ACKNOWLEDGEMENTS

Thanks to my wonderful critique partners Elizabeth Reyes, Carrie Sullivan and Jody Sparks. Each of you challenges me to continue honing my craft by being as liberal with the criticism as you are with the praise. Thank you for both. Through every step of the process, and while slaving over your own projects, you've been encouraging and inspiring. I couldn't have done this without you.

To my beta-readers – Ami Keller, Robin Deeslie, Hannah Webber, Zachary Webber, Alyssa Crenshaw, Lori Norris and Joy Graham – thank you for being willing to trudge through the manuscript in rough draft form. Your comments and suggestions were fantastic, and the feedback was crucial.

To my BFF Kim Nguyen-Hart, you're the reason I stepped out on to the indie-publishing wire at all. If you hadn't given me a love-filled shove, I might never have done it. Hugs forever.

To Sarah Moreau for your knowledge and experience with mission trips to Quito. Bless you, baby girl.

To my copy-editor, Stephanie Lott (aka Bibliophile): you're the best safety net *ever*. Thank you for the time spent on multiple read-throughs, for your determination to make what I write appear as close to perfect as is possible and for the discussions of what, exactly, constitutes irony.

Thanks to Zachary, Hannah and Keith, for never telling me to shut up when my characters take over my every waking thought, and I can't stop talking about them. Ditto Mom, who excels at confidence-building, and Dad, whose patience is endless.

Thank you, Paul, for everything. I adore you, and I hope you never, ever doubt it.

Finally, as always, thank you to every reader who reads the stories I'm compelled to tell. I love and appreciate your enthusiasm and support.

ABOUT THE AUTHOR

Tammara Webber is the author of *New York Times* and Amazon bestseller *Easy*, and three novels in the Between the Lines series. Before becoming a full-time writer, she was an academic advisor at the University of Texas. Tammara lives in Texas with her husband and too many cats. She loves baby carrots and happily-ever-after endings.

Read on for a preview of

Easy

tammara webber

1

I had never noticed Lucas before that night. It was as though he didn't exist, and then suddenly, he was everywhere.

I'd just bailed on the Halloween party still in full swing behind me. Weaving between the cars crammed into the parking lot behind my ex's frat house, I tapped out a text to my roommate. The night was beautiful and warm – a typical Southern-style Indian summer. From the wide-open windows of the house, music blared across the pavement, punctuated with occasional bursts of laughter, drunken challenges and calls for more shots.

As tonight's designated driver, it was my responsibility to get Erin back to our dorm across campus in one non-mangled piece, whether or not I could stand another minute of the party. My message told her to call or text when she was ready to go. The way she and her boyfriend, Chaz, had been tequila-soaked dirty dancing before they linked hands and tripped up the stairs to his room, she might not be calling me until tomorrow. I chuckled over the thought of the short walk of shame she'd endure from the front porch to my truck, if so.

I hit send as I dug in my bag for my keys. The moon was too cloud-obscured and the fully lit windows of the house were too far away to provide any light at the far end of the lot. I had to go by feel. Swearing when a mechanical pencil jabbed a fingertip, I stomped one stiletto-clad foot, almost certain I'd drawn blood. Once the keys were in my hand I sucked on the finger; the slight metallic taste told me I'd punctured the skin.

'Figures,' I muttered, unlocking the truck door.

In the initial seconds that followed, I was too disoriented to comprehend what was happening. One moment I was pulling the truck door open, and the next I was lying flat on my face across the seat, breathless and immobile. I struggled to rise but couldn't, because the weight on top of me was too heavy.

'The little devil costume suits you, Jackie.' The voice was slurred, but familiar.

My first thought was *Don't call me that*, but that objection was quickly dismissed in favour of terror as I felt a hand pushing my already short skirt higher. My right arm was useless, trapped between my body and the seat. I clawed my left hand into the seat next to my face, trying again to push myself upright, and the hand on the bare skin of my thigh whipped up and grabbed my wrist. I cried out when he wrenched my arm behind my back, clamping it firmly in his other hand. His forearm pressed into my upper back. I couldn't move.

'Buck, get off me. Let go.' My voice quavered, but I tried to deliver the command with as much authority as possible.

I could smell the beer on his breath and something stronger in his sweat, and a wave of nausea rose and fell in my stomach.

His free hand was back on my left thigh, his weight settled on to my right side, covering me. My feet dangled outside the truck, the door still open. I tried to pull my knee up to get it under me, and he laughed at my pathetic efforts. When he shoved his hand between my open legs, I cried out, snapping my leg back down too late. I heaved and squirmed, first thinking to dislodge him and then, realizing I was no match for his size, I started to beg.

'Buck, *stop*. Please – you're just drunk and you'll regret this tomorrow. Oh, my God –'

He wedged his knee between my legs and air hit my bare hip. I heard the unmistakable sound of a zipper and he laughed in my ear when I went from rationally imploring to crying. 'No-no-no-no . . .' Under his weight, I couldn't get enough breath together to scream, and my mouth was mashed against the seat, muffling any protest I made. Struggling uselessly, I couldn't believe that this guy I'd known for over a year, who'd not once treated me with disrespect the entire time I'd dated Kennedy, was attacking me in my own truck at the back of the frat house parking lot.

He ripped my underwear down to my knees, and between his efforts to push them down and my renewed effort to escape, I heard the fragile fabric tear. 'Jesus, Jackie, I always knew you had a great ass, but, *Christ*, girl.' His hand thrust between my legs again and the weight lifted for a split second

– just long enough for me to suck in a lungful of air and scream. Releasing my wrist, he slapped his hand over the back of my head and turned my face into the leather seat until I was silent, almost unable to breathe.

Even freed, my left arm was useless. I leveraged my hand against the floor of the cab and pushed, but my wrenched and aching muscles wouldn't obey. I sobbed into the cushion, tears and saliva mixing under my cheek. 'Please don't, please don't, oh, God stop-stop-stop . . .' I hated the weedy sound of my powerless voice.

His weight lifted from me for a split second – he'd changed his mind, or he was repositioning – I didn't wait to find out which. Twisting and pulling my legs up, I felt the spiky heels of my shoes tear into the pliant leather as I propelled myself to the far side of the bench seat and scrambled for the handle. Blood rushed in my ears as my body rallied for all-out fight or flight. And then I stopped, because Buck was no longer in the truck at all.

At first, I couldn't figure out why he was standing there, just past the door, facing away from me. And then his head snapped back. Twice. He swung wildly at something but his fists hit nothing. Not until he stumbled back against my truck did I see what – or who – he was fighting.

The guy never took his eyes off Buck as he delivered two more sharp jabs to his face, bobbing to the side as they circled and Buck threw futile punches of his own, blood streaming from his nose. Finally, Buck ducked his head and rushed forward with bull-like intent, but that effort was his undoing as the stranger swung an easy uppercut to his jaw.

When Buck's head snapped up, an elbow cracked into his temple with a sickening thud. He collided with the side of the truck again, pushing off and rushing the stranger a second time. As though the entire fight was choreographed, he grabbed Buck's shoulders and pulled him forward, hard, kneeing him under the chin. Buck crumpled to the ground, moaning and cringing.

The stranger stared down, fists balled, elbows slightly bent, poised to deliver another blow if necessary. There was no need. Buck was almost unconscious. I cowered against the far door, panting and curling into a ball as shock replaced the panic. I must have whimpered, because his eyes snapped up to mine. He rolled Buck aside with one booted foot and stepped up to the door, peering in.

'You okay?' His tone was low, careful. I wanted to say yes. I wanted to nod. But I couldn't. I was so not okay. 'I'm gonna call 911. Do you need medical assistance, or just the police?'

I envisioned the campus police arriving at the scene, the partygoers who would spill from the house when the sirens came. Erin and Chaz were only two of the many friends I had in there, more than half of them under-aged and drinking. It would be my fault if the party became the focus of the police. I would be a pariah.

I shook my head. 'Don't call.' My voice was gravelly.

'Don't call an ambulance?'

I cleared my throat and shook my head. 'Don't call anyone. Don't call the police.'

His jaw hung ajar and he stared across the expanse of

seat. 'Am I wrong, or did this guy just try to *rape* you –' I flinched at the ugly word – 'and you're telling me not to call the police?' He snapped his mouth closed, shook his head once and peered at me again. 'Or did I interrupt something I shouldn't have?'

I gasped, my eyes welling up. 'N-no. But I just want to go home.'

Buck groaned and rolled on to his back. 'Fuuuuuck,' he said, not opening his eyes, one of which was probably swollen shut anyway.

My saviour stared down at him, his jaw working. He rocked his neck to one side and then back, rolled his shoulders. 'Fine. I'll drive you.'

I shook my head. I wasn't about to escape one attack just to do something as stupid as get into a stranger's car. 'I can drive myself,' I rasped. My eyes flicked to my bag, wedged against the console, its contents spilled across the floor of the driver's side. He glanced down, leaned to pick out my keys from the bits and pieces of my personal effects.

'I believe you were looking for these, before.' He dangled them from his fingers as I realized that I still hadn't moved any closer to him.

I licked my lip and tasted blood for the second time that night. Scooting forward into the faint illumination shed by the tiny overhead light, I was careful to keep my skirt pulled down. A wave of dizziness crashed over me as I became fully conscious of what had almost happened, and my hand trembled when I reached out for my keys.